THE WITCH WITHOUT MEMORY

Also by Maithree Wijesekara

Obsidian Throne Trilogy
The Prince Without Sorrow

THE WITCH WITHOUT MEMORY

MAITHREE WIJESEKARA

HARPER
Voyager

Harper*Voyager*
An imprint of
HarperCollins*Publishers* Ltd
1 London Bridge Street
London SE1 9GF

www.harpercollins.co.uk

HarperCollins*Publishers*
Macken House,
39/40 Mayor Street Upper,
Dublin 1, D01 C9W8
Ireland

First published by HarperCollins*Publishers* Ltd 2026
1

Copyright © Maithree Wijesekara 2026

Map and interior illustrations copyright © Julian De Narvaez/Folio Art

Maithree Wijesekara asserts the moral right to
be identified as the author of this work.

A catalogue record for this book is available from the British Library.

ISBN: 978-0-00-867209-6 (HB)
ISBN: 978-0-00-867210-2 (TPB)

This novel is entirely a work of fiction.
The names, characters and incidents portrayed in it are
the work of the author's imagination. Any resemblance to
actual persons, living or dead, events or localities is
entirely coincidental.

Typeset in Adobe Jenson Pro by Palimpsest Book Production Ltd, Falkirk, Stirlingshire

Printed and bound in the UK using 100% renewable electricity by CPI Group (UK) Ltd

All rights reserved. No part of this publication may be reproduced, stored in a
retrieval system, or transmitted, in any form or by any means, electronic, mechanical,
photocopying, recording or otherwise, without the prior written
permission of the publishers.

Without limiting the exclusive rights of any author, contributor or the publisher of this
publication, any unauthorized use of this publication to train generative artificial intelligence
(AI) technologies is expressly prohibited. HarperCollins also exercise their rights under
Article 4(3) of the Digital Single Market Directive 2019/790 and expressly reserve this
publication from the text and data mining exception.

For my family.

Simha

Golden City

Odhi Ocean

STATE OF
DEVRAM

Trikalinga

Luth

KINGDOM OF
KALINGA   The Sea
Dragon's Wall

Kolakola

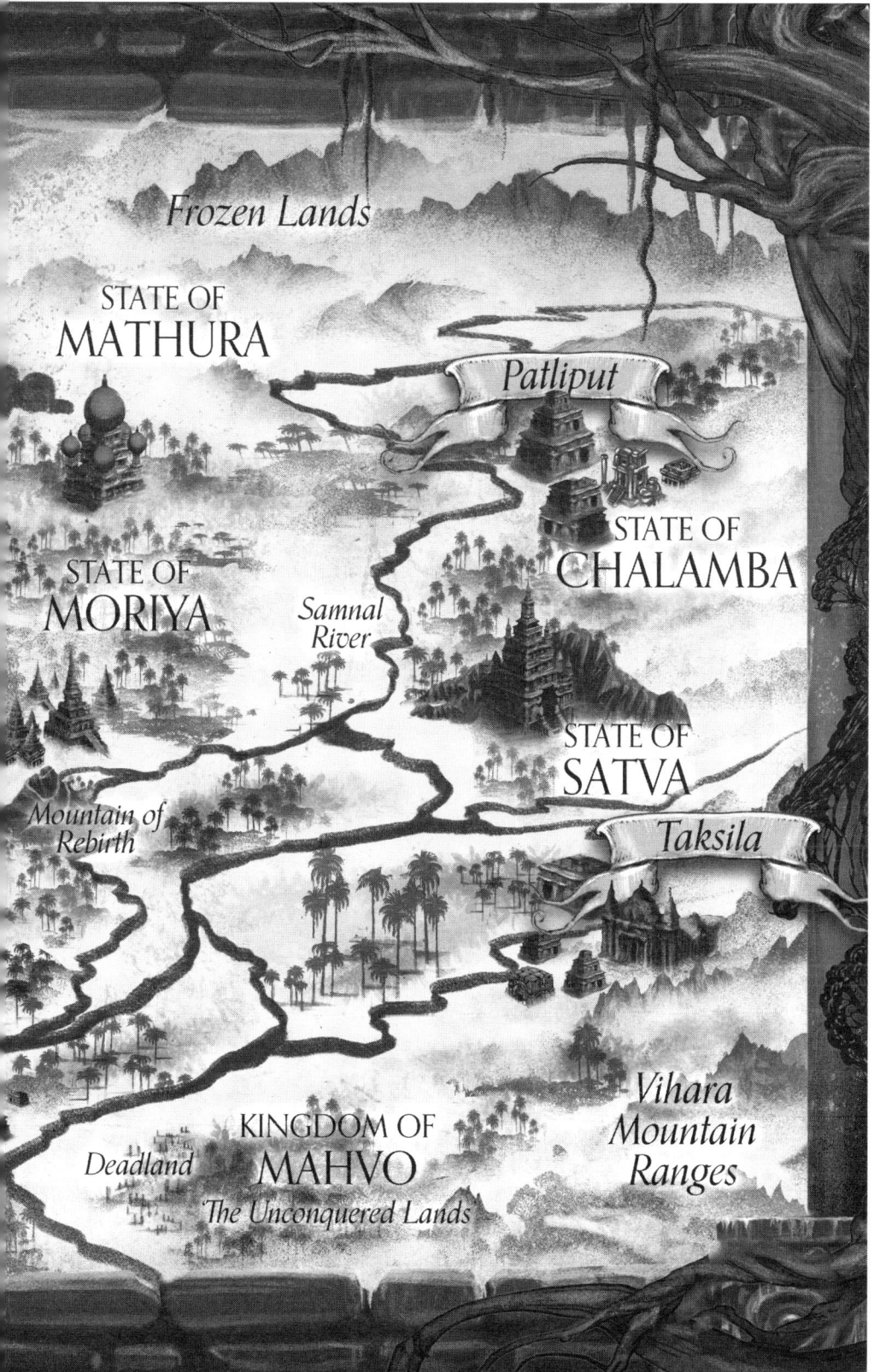

CHAPTER ONE
Shakti

Little bird.

She groaned.

Little bird, I love you.

Jaya – it was Jaya's voice. But Jaya was dead. She saw the charred remains. Blue fire. She couldn't be alive.

One eye cracked open. It was difficult, like the lids were congealed with glue. The ground was cold, her arms wet. A metallic smell permeated the air. Thudding. Vague shapes of boots on the ground. She moved. Tried to move.

Shouting.

'—her hands, tie them—'

'—give her the—'

What's happening?

She couldn't tell if she'd asked the question out loud. No one answered.

Where am I?

Her body felt heavy. A weight was on her chest – a boulder, a foot, a curse. Pain lanced up her arms. She turned her head. Shadows moved around her. People.

Soldiers?

The world wasn't sharp but blurred; a line drawing smudged by an incensed painter. That pulling sensation – there it was again. *A boulder. A foot. A curse.* Suddenly, she couldn't move her arms.

'—keep her pacified—'

Her legs were held still. Chains rattled around her, and she opened her mouth to scream—

'—now!'

Shadows hovered over her. Fingers were on her skin, hot, hot, hot, and unwanted. She tried to close her mouth. The blurry figures halted the movement. Then, liquid ran down her throat. The taste was nutty and wretched.

This isn't water. She coughed it out.

'Stop!' she cried, thrashing wildly. 'Stop, I—'

Her stomach heaved, gullet responding in kind as she tried to spit. Droplets of white liquid and clear spittle flew out.

You cannot die, Shakti. You must not.

Jaya? No, not Jaya. This was him.

Wretched witch. You may as well die.

Do not lose the Collective. Do not.

Dead tyrant. Golden Emperor. Their voices came in quick succession, echoing and disjointed.

'Mayakari.'

Her heartbeat was slowing. That voice was so *familiar*. Familiar, yet she couldn't place it, not when her mind was struggling to flit from one coherent thought to the next.

Where am I?

I don't want to be here.

A harsh prick rushed down the pit of her stomach. Her muscles seized and cramped. Was she bleeding?

'Mayakari – obey me—'

The shadows retreated from her line of sight until only one remained. It sharpened into a human figure, one with a gold circlet atop a glossy head of hair. A smile as wicked as the dead tyrant. The hard, flinty eyes that resembled his, right down to the shade. She was here.

The princess. *Aarya.*

A collection of memories resurfaced in quick succession. For a moment, she remembered.

Aarya. The one who had carved into her back with a dagger.

The one whom she'd pleaded with to save her own life before she was taken away. *Aarya*. Locked in this dark cell with no sunlight.

Keep me alive and I can help you conquer the world.

'Curse for me.'

She couldn't think. Words escaped her. Fatigue wrapped its arms around her chest and squeezed tight enough to crack her ribs. She opened her mouth to scream. Or to whisper. Did she need to whisper? All she wanted was an answer. Didn't she want to scream?

I don't know. I don't remember.

'Can't . . .' she burbled, '. . . won't. Shouldn't.'

'Mayakari, *curse*.'

Her bones were tired. She just wanted the voices and the hurt to go away. She just wanted to rest.

'I want . . . sleep . . .' she said. The buzzing in her ears returned. The noises grew louder. Hordes of bees descending upon her, stinging skin, leaving sharp, angry red welts.

'—give her more?'

'—no can't risk her heart—'

There was pressure around her throat now. Pain on her thighs. Pain on her back, where the princess had taken a dagger to her skin and carved into it in the manner of an angry butcher. The agony of it.

She heard her voice again:

'—my father's life, witch. *Curse*—'

Wetness. There was wetness on her cheeks. Tears.

I don't want to cry. I want to sleep.

'—keep him alive, I know you can—'

Lids heavy, she struggled to respond. She didn't understand what she said next. Her words were gibberish. Unintelligible. Somewhere in between the buzzing in her ears and the pain in her chest, she rolled over. Cold stone pressed against her back. For a moment, she imagined taking off the shackles around her legs and looping them around her neck. Squeezing tight enough that the brown skin compressed and turned blue, and she could no longer breathe. She would be gone from this world, free to join

Jaya in the next one, if she was lucky. Dying held a promise of comfort that living didn't.

You can't die, little bird. Not like this.

Useless, wretched girl.

What would death feel like?

In the crowd of voices fighting for dominance, she knew the last one without question.

That voice was entirely hers.

CHAPTER TWO
Ashoka

'My decree was clear – do not kill the mayakari. Do not harm the mayakari. Flouting the law will have you punished.'

Prince Ashoka Maurya stood before a large crowd in Taksila's city centre. Silent as death, they watched a man be frogmarched across a podium by two Ridi soldiers. His face was bitter. Fearful.

A month since his reinstatement of the ban on mayakari killings, and some people still refused to listen. He had ordered for this punishment to be made public the day before, inviting all those interested to observe. Historically, such notices had been reserved for mayakari burnings. This time, the intention was wildly different.

'Using counterfeit Ghost Queen teas to accuse a neighbour who rebuffed your romantic intentions of being a mayakari,' he continued, raising his voice, 'only for the innocent woman to suffer severe pains from spirits-knows-what was mixed into the powder. She was no witch, but she vomited blood for hours on end.'

The rare, iridescent Ghost Queen flowers were purported to reveal a mayakari's existence without the need for burn testing. Ever since Aarya's open quest to locate and source the rare plant in deadlands, merchants and swindlers alike had been creating their own false concoctions claiming to be infused with the flower. Often, the false compounds were a mixture of green tea and stomach or throat irritants that acted equally on mayakari and human alike, leading to wrongful confirmations of witch blood. In the case of the woman who had been falsely accused, the man standing trial before him had seen – and waited – for the side effects to occur before assigning blame.

People were foolish. They judged and acted without thinking. Three days ago, when Ashoka was first informed of the commotion in the small village just outside Taksila, he'd sent Naila, one of the resistance's members, to investigate. The smaller townships and villages were more resistant to his decree of nonviolence against the mayakari. Their defiance was living legacy of his father's hatred.

All it had taken was for Naila to attempt conversation in spirit-speak for the accused woman's face to crumple in confusion. The language that could be understood by all mayakari was unable to be deciphered or spoken by non-witches. The woman hadn't understood a word that Naila said.

The shocked expressions amongst the crowd were satisfying. 'It was a mayakari who treated and saved her. Created a healing tonic to counteract the effects.'

He turned to the offender, a surly young man with a clean-shaven face and close-cropped hair, and leaned in. 'Did you want her to burn?' he asked. 'See the blue flames? Because you won't get to see them, and neither will they.'

The young man scowled but kept his chin up in defiance.

'Mayakari sympathizer,' he spat. 'Not all of us have fallen victim to your lies.'

All this young man saw in front of him was a dead emperor's foolish son. Ashoka knew this well, but it irritated him all the same. Truths were lies in their minds. His skin crawled, upper lip curling in disgust.

He stepped away from the young man and turned back towards the crowd of onlookers. 'This will be the last time I tell you all – violate the laws I have set, and you will be punished. This offender wanted to see a body be burned. Then, I will show him what it is like to experience it.'

Whispers of 'experience it?' and 'what does the prince mean?' were heard in the din. Ashoka paid the crowd no mind – his focus was on the young man, who had gone still. Rigid, like a body some hours after death.

'Experience it?' he echoed, brows furrowing.

You fool, thought Ashoka. *Marched up here like a mayakari and you still don't understand?*

In response, he stared at the offender in silence. Cocked his head and tracked his gaze to the crowd and back to him. When the ghost of a smirk flitted across his lips, the young man blanched.

'Wait!' he called out, voice taking on a note of desperation. 'Prince Ashoka, I beg of you – *please*. I don't want to burn. I don't want to die! Not like that. Please!'

Good. Let him drown in the fear.

He knew all too well how this would appear to the crowd. How it would be spun a myriad different, unsavoury ways till it reached his sister, now the acting regent.

The youngest Maurya prince conducting a public punishment against one of the empire's good citizens. Except, these good citizens often failed to remember that the mayakari were included in it, too.

Ashoka was keenly aware that he made for a controversial governor. Though stopping the spirit rampages had earned him praise, killing Governor Kosala and ordering a ban on mayakari burnings had ruffled some feathers. But no one in the city could deny that there was now a tentative – if still uneasy – sense of peace.

'Not death,' he proclaimed. 'I am not so cruel. This is an eye for an eye. You've caused harm, and now harm will befall you.'

Motioning towards Sachith, who had been watching them on the sidelines with a haggard expression, Ashoka let his guard wander closer with two pitchers that he held in his hands: one oil, one water. At his presence, the young man began to thrash about and try to flee, but to no avail.

He waited as Sachith poured oil over the man's ring and little finger, feeling a stab of discomfort while he watched. However, as it always seemed to do these days, the newly crowned voice in his head offered a familiar rebuttal.

This is necessary. This is nothing.

To avoid further abuse and violence against mayakari in the future, he had to conduct his own in the present. Show the non-witch population the costs of not bowing to his orders.

Just like it was necessary to kill the governor . . .

As it often did, Governor Kosala's pale face and severed veins flashed across his mind's eye. The man's dead body had invaded Ashoka's dreams for several nights after he'd killed him, and in visceral detail. In his dreams, Ashoka slew him again and again – there had been no alternative. And, again and again, he woke up with his heart beating erratically, sweat soaking his brow, and the phantom sensation of a sword in his hand.

Necessary violence.

Sachith handed him a lit matchstick. Ashoka took it, feeling the warmth of the flame above his fingers. He stepped closer, drowning out the young man's pleas.

Necessary. Necessary. Necessary.

With gentle movements, Ashoka let the flame kiss the man's two oil-soaked fingers. Orange-yellow heat burst forth like lightning.

The young man screamed. Gasps erupted from the crowd.

Brown skin blistered. He could see the vesicles forming, waiting to pop. Then came the scent of roasting meat, and he tried not to retch, harkened back to the days where he attended a mayakari burning with his father. Back then, that blue flame had been a horrible sight. Here, now, the pale yellow-orange flames were a warning.

Disobey me and face the consequences.

Another figure caught his attention. Rahil, standing off to the side like a Great Spirit observing its domain with detached curiosity. Except, Ashoka could glean his guard's feelings through the silent front he'd put up. Rahil was perturbed by him. Concerned by the actions he'd taken.

Was he wrong? Were his actions wrong reflected in Rahil's eyes? Guilt was hard to summon when his actions were justified.

Ashoka waited till he saw the hint of blackened fingertips and ordered Sachith to make use of the second pitcher. Dutifully, Sachith emptied the jug of water, dousing the young man's burning skin until the fire vanished with a hiss, leaving behind angry red fluctuant boils and the beginnings of charred skin. Would they be damaged permanently like his own ear? It was a possibility, but Ashoka found it hard to scrounge up any empathy for him.

'Thank the spirits you still leave with your life,' he said. 'Mayakari have been murdered for less. And for anyone who still dares to flout my orders – *this* is a taste of your punishment.'

Following the public punishment, they returned to the royal estate. The journey back was unbearably quiet.

Riding atop Rāga, Ashoka tightened her reins absentmindedly, causing the giant leopard to let out a warning huff. Next to them on Māra, was Rahil. Sachith and the Ridi soldiers followed behind on their own leopards.

The silence between him and Rahil continued to unsettle. Ever since Ashoka had raged at him after arguing over Governor Kosala's death a month ago, Rahil had made not one attempt to remedy the situation. Then again, it wasn't his situation to rectify.

Ashoka glanced at his hands; the thick black leather bands wrapped around them. They were the hands of a prince who'd once forsaken violence.

I did what had to be done. Violence to prevent more violence. He's lucky I didn't burn more than his fingertips.

The mayakari of the Ran Empire didn't have the same privilege. A couple of burned fingertips was nothing compared to what they faced.

Had there been another way to force the few in Taksila and its surrounds into not harming the witches, he would've done so. Politics and calming words only went so far. Unfortunately, these people seemed to respond more to threats. It was one of humanity's glaring flaws. That show of force had been necessary.

'I did the right thing,' Ashoka found himself telling Rahil to break the silence between them. He didn't want reassurance, not when he knew his statement to be true. Seeking reassurance was a weakness that did not befit a royal. The children of the late Adil Maurya didn't doubt. They certainly wouldn't seek reassurance from someone who was considered below their station. What Ashoka really wanted was conversation; for any sign that Rahil was thawing to him.

You're not my moral compass, so don't pretend to be.

'If you think so,' Rahil responded flatly, dashing any hope Ashoka had. He'd answered in the manner of a schoolchild being forced to recite the founding of the empire word for word with dispassionate precision.

Ashoka frowned. He would've got a better response out of Sau, his advisor, but she was still in the Ridi Empire's capital, an ocean away.

Despite wanting to accuse Rahil of being childish, Ashoka kept quiet. There was no sense in aggravating him further. 'I burned his fingers to show others the consequences of their actions. To make sure that mayakari aren't hurt in the future,' he continued instead. 'I taught that man a lesson; did what was best.'

The words hung in the air between them for so long that Ashoka thought Rahil hadn't heard him, or if he did, had chosen to ignore him. Finally, Rahil said, 'Whatever you feel is the best course of action, Prince Ashoka.'

He flinched. *Prince* Ashoka. After their argument, Rahil had resorted to addressing him only by his formal title. One word he never thought would cause so much distress was wounding his heart. It was a small trick but an effective one. Rahil continued to keep his distance; the wound failed to heal.

It was torture.

These days, Rahil was always beside him but never *there*. Whenever Ashoka needed a soldier, he was ready with his broadswords strapped to his back. However, when Ashoka attempted conversation, Rahil reverted to a detached manner that called to mind an uninterested teacher.

At first, Ashoka had let him stew and allowed him to hate his existence, because Rahil veered towards pettiness when driven to anger – a rather grievous flaw of his. He spoke less and responded with more acerbity until he was apologized to. But despite Ashoka's repeated attempts at apology, Rahil was yet to break.

Ashoka didn't know what else to do or say. He could only walk forward pathetically while Rahil followed close behind, ready to defend him with his life. His father would laugh at his pitiful condition. He would force Ashoka to forgo any emotional weakness.

Right on cue, Emperor Adil's voice came like the high tide:

Simpering over your guard like a miserable rat. You continue to be weak. You continue to disappoint me, son.

Silence resumed and Ashoka forced himself to pay attention to the road. The last part of the road to the royal estate was marked by a tunnel of trees, the green canopy a welcome shade from the hot sun. As they passed by, Ashoka thought he heard a sunbird and tilted his face up towards the twisting branches above. To his surprise, he was greeted instead by a single, minuscule ghostly blue head poking out of one of the thick branches: a minor spirit. The rest of its body was obscured. Its eyes were oddly shaped and reminded him of a mangosteen stem. Opening its little mouth, the spirit let out the same sound he'd heard before.

He smiled bitterly. Not being able to understand or speak to spirits like the mayakari did was one of the world's crueller tricks.

When they eventually arrived at the royal estate, Ashoka spotted a lone figure dawdling at the front steps. Naila – one of the mayakari he had befriended during his stay. She stood and walked down to meet them when they dismounted, and the leopards were taken away by a stable hand.

'Is something wrong?' he heard Rahil ask.

The young mayakari shook her head. She wore a deep green blouse and trousers. Her hair was tamed with coconut oil and a single jasmine blossom nestled in her hair. 'I've just returned from the village. I wanted to see how the young woman who ingested the tea was doing since I treated her,' she said. 'Thought you'd want to know. Thankfully, she's recovered well. I told her to avoid taking anything with spices for a few more days to avoid irritating her stomach.'

'Good,' Ashoka replied, relieved. 'Her accuser left the city square not long ago with two burned fingers and a bruised self-esteem.'

'Good,' Naila echoed, but she appeared troubled. 'You won't be able to stop people from buying these counterfeit concoctions, Prince Ashoka. It's a difficult endeavour.'

He knew that. Placing a ban on the sale of Ghost Queens in Taksila had done little to curb people's curiosity. After all, what could be more fascinating than a flower that could supposedly reveal a mayakari without the need for burn testing? The easiest method for traders to get them through the city walls was to label them as standard green teas. Unless they were being openly marketed as Ghost Queen teas, they were difficult to catch. Still, it was worth the effort, though Aarya would be none too pleased by his actions. She never was.

After temporarily assuming rule following Arush's fall into a coma, it seemed that his sister was intent on reversing everything he'd done in Taksila.

Lift the ban on mayakari killings. Obey my command.

His sister's words followed him around like a pungent odour. Failing to submit to her orders was arguably treason now that she was the acting regent, but there were witches under his protection. Achieving his goal of peace only to give it up was a special kind of betrayal. When Aarya's messenger had asked for a response, he had the inciting words ready to fire:

I refuse her commands. If she wants war, she'll get one. You will not sit upon the Obsidian Throne for long, sister.

He'd caught himself after the first sentence. The natural sibling rejoinder was to goad and exacerbate, but he couldn't be like Arush, who would've been all too happy to start a conflict. Aggravating Aarya now was unwise. Instead, he had hedged.

He'd sent the messenger back with a letter to inform Aarya that he would temporarily refuse under the guise of continuing to restore the razed lands to their original glory with the help of the mayakari before submitting to her orders. He'd guessed that adding in the promise of excavating newfound natural resources should have lulled Aarya for a short while, and it had. However, it was Ashoka's mistake in forgetting that his sister was the most distrustful out of the three of them. A week ago, she sent him another letter, this time with a new order. She would be sending a consul to Taksila to 'observe his rebuilding efforts' for a week. A not-so-subtle way of saying that he'd best be telling her the truth, and to make sure any underhanded efforts on his part would be stopped immediately. The consul, Daman, was due to arrive in Taksila in around two days' time.

The consul's arrival was truly an unfortunate turn of events, given that he was also anticipating a response from the queen of Kalinga. Planning to take the Obsidian Throne for himself was still a laughable dream with his measly numbers. What he needed was an army, an ally, and an inciting incident that he needed to manufacture.

The answer lay to the south, in the Kingdom of Mahvo. His father had planned to annex the far southern kingdom until his death. While Arush had temporarily redirected soldiers to the north, Aarya wanted to carry out their father's original plan. Since assuming the throne, his sister had already recalled troops from the Frozen Lands, ready to travel to the Satvan border once more. With its lack of advanced artillery and weapons, Mahvo was weaker than their empire. Easier to annex. Unless they had a stronger ally to help defend their land.

The ally would come in the form of the Kingdom of Kalinga. The island continent was known for its superior navy, but refrained from dealing with troops like the Ridi Empire to the far west did. If he were to convince the Kalingan queen, Kalyani, to arrange a deal that assured Mahvo's security against the looming threat of the Ridi Empire, Kalingan troops could be sent to Mahvo's border.

However, that would only create a tense stalemate. Neither side would want to risk aggravating the other. Aarya wouldn't want to fruitlessly expend lives for the sake of expansion if the Kalingan soldiers remained at Mahvo's border. Similarly, the Kalingan Kingdom couldn't simply up and declare war against his family's empire. One side needed to trespass into the others, and it had to be his sister.

His plan hinged on the approval of the Kalingan queen. She would need a monumental bargain to agree, and he had a proposition planned. He'd sent a purposefully vague letter to Queen Kalyani close to a fortnight ago now but was still awaiting a response. Impatience was starting to eat away at him. It was hard to temper, especially as Aarya's voice taunted him in the moments where he doubted himself the most, reminding him of his place. Runt of the family and the late emperor's unfavoured son. He was nowhere near the throne and, thanks to his father's will, had no legal right to it, either. Despite Adil naming Arush and Aarya as successors, he'd been left out.

Since their father had failed to include him, he and Arush had come to their own agreement before he left for Taksila. If he was able to rectify the spirit rampages in the capital, Arush would not only allow him to take Aarya's position on the war council but also acknowledge him as a successor to the throne. It would require his brother to supersede their father's original will by writing his own as the ruling monarch.

But now that Arush was comatose, Aarya was the acting regent, and he had no care for a position on the war council, the will seemed redundant. Would an acknowledgement of succession really matter if he were to usurp the throne? It wasn't as if he was a nameless rebel. No matter how much his father had disliked him, they were blood. He was still Adil Maurya's son. The Obsidian Throne was his right, too.

If you fail to comply, rest assured Ashoka – I will bring war to you.

Aarya's words continued to plague him. Threatening war as an *acting* regent was a high call. A bluff, surely. No one knew if or when Arush would reawaken. Yet, it was exactly this uncertainty that Ashoka suspected Aarya was using to her advantage. It was as if she'd already assumed herself to be the permanent ruler. His sister was very much like a cat in that way, sauntering in expecting everybody to bow to her commands.

Poison or mayakari magic. Aarya had been tight-lipped about the true cause of Arush's condition up until the last week, when she'd sent him another letter.

Our dear brother ingested a tea laced with crushed sea mango. A witch has been suspected of carrying out this most grievous attack, and one has been apprehended after attempting to flee the capital.

Ashoka almost thought the letter to be falsified when it was first presented to him. A mayakari being the culprit made little sense. There were only two in the palace. Harini was too meek to ever consider poisoning the emperor, and Shakti . . .

He paused. The second mayakari was still somewhat of an enigma. Her temperament was in complete opposition to Harini's.

Bolder. More impulsive. While he wouldn't put it past her to start a brawl, he couldn't imagine her choosing to murder someone, let alone the emperor. Something else was afoot that Aarya wouldn't tell him. Something missing, or unsaid. This was his older sister, after all. Surely Aarya knew he would doubt her letter.

From what he'd heard through the estate staff and his soldiers, rumours of Arush's condition ranged from the believable to the fantastical. He feared for the poor mayakari who had been apprehended. Worried more for the two working in the palace. Shakti especially, considering she was one of Aarya's newly appointed personal guards. He wanted to return to the Golden City to see Arush and confirm that the two mayakari were alive and well. However, the knowledge that a letter from the Kalingan Kingdom was due any moment kept him tethered to Taksila.

Ashoka was unceremoniously brought back to the present by the sound of Rahil's voice. He was in the middle of asking Naila if there were any new mayakari who had travelled here from neighbouring states. Whispers of his ban must have travelled faster than initially thought, for both Nayani – the leader of Taksila's mayakari resistance – and Naila tended to make offhand statements about a lone or group of mayakari migrating to Taksila from the empire's surrounds. He couldn't bring himself to wonder how many would have been found on their way here and burned.

'I fear you think a great number of mayakari are finding their way here, but it is hardly an army's worth,' Naila was telling Rahil. 'It's only about a dozen so far, and none of the older mayakari are willing to learn to fight. You should see the looks on their faces when they're asked – like we're committing some sort of crime.'

Making the decision to train those within the mayakari resistance in combat had been a dubious move. After all, in what world would the pacifist witches agree to be taught the ways of a sword? But he'd been surprised at just how many consented to be trained. Skill in swordplay was simply an additional asset. Using their magic for a rebellion was their true power. Some were still reluctant, their thoughts bound by the mayakari code. The younger witches like Naila and Nayani, fed up with the cruel hand the world had dealt them, were itching for revenge. They were willing to fight with him to depose the reigning monarch to be freed from persecution.

The witches of the Ran Empire had suffered enough, and Adil's legacy was no longer a solid model to stand on. A reversion was needed, one that harkened back to the relatively stable days of his grandmother, Empress Sarla. To the time before Emperor Adil carried out his ruthless onslaught against the nonviolent mayakari. Out of Adil Maurya's three children, he was the only one who could.

'I'm sure you're all picking up the basics of combat well enough,' he remarked, thinking of Shakti again. If they became as adept with a sword as she was, they would make decent soldiers.

'You're giving us far too much credit, Prince Ashoka,' Naila said. 'It's still difficult for me to use a weapon in such a way.'

'To defend?'

'To kill,' she replied, casting her eyes to the ground with a grimace. 'Some part of me is holding back, I know that. You should see Nayani, though. She swings her sword like she's held it all her life.'

'That doesn't surprise me.' Ashoka had no doubt that the vengeance-driven mayakari picked up swordplay with ease. Trained well enough, she could become a force on the battlefield.

He watched, bemused, as Naila tilted her head like a pup. 'Although, some of us were wondering if Rahil could spare some of his time,' she said. 'The soldiers continue to refer to you as the model to follow, and I must say, their praise has me interested.'

Ashoka heard Rahil shift before he even spoke. 'Unfortunately, I cannot. Prince Ashoka is my priority.'

'Well,' Ashoka attempted lamely, 'perhaps I can spare some of Rahil's time. Have Sachith with me instead.'

Rahil looked not at him but at Naila when he said, 'My apologies, Naila, but Prince Ashoka is mistaken. I am duty-bound to him. Wherever he goes, I follow.'

An uncomfortable silence followed his words. Naila glanced between them with a poorly concealed frown.

Ashoka resisted the urge to scream out of sheer frustration. Before he could respond, they became distracted by the sound of the entrance doors opening. A maidservant dressed in black rushed out, her hands clutching a piece of parchment stamped with a glittering blue seal.

'Prince Ashoka.' She bowed as he approached. 'A letter arrived for you while you were away. It bears the Kalingan seal.'

He perked up at the mention of the name, frustration vanishing. 'Kalingan, you say?' he murmured before thanking the girl and sending her on her way. Indeed, stamped upon the blue seal was the imprint of a sea dragon.

Rahil came closer. 'The queen has responded?'

'I hope so.' Forcing his hands to still, Ashoka tore open the seal. Dread and hope played a dance of death in his head as he read its contents with bated breath:

Prince Ashoka,

It was with great surprise that I read your letter requesting an attendance with me. Even more surprising that you wished your letter to be viewed separately from the Maurya royals. To your credit, it served as enough fodder to keep me interested.

Your words were strong. Convincing, even. But they were ambiguous, and I assume, purposefully so. 'A monumental favour made to reinvent the bloody history of the Ran Empire.' One wonders what this favour would be.

You have piqued my curiosity. I will accept your request for an attendance with myself in a week's time. Bring this letter with you as proof, for my soldiers will not bow to you.

Queen Kalyani

CHAPTER THREE
Shakti

She was awake.

There was pressure on her arms. Legs. *Pressure* – were those . . . hands? There were hands on her.

A nightmare?

Her stomach muscles hurt, breathing slow and laboured. Panic set in. It was hard to breathe properly. *Why was it hard?*

'I – I can't – breathe!' Shakti cried out. 'Let me – why can't I—'

Dizzy. She was so *dizzy*. Her head felt swollen. She vaguely remembered seeing Emperor Ashoka's face. Then Arush's. She didn't know why. A familiar voice whispered in her head.

Let me tell you a story, Shakti . . .

A great wracking cough escaped her lips, spraying spittle all over the floor. Those hazy figures came into her field of vision again. Bodies. With swords. And noises – all those noises—

'—make sure she won't move—'

'—on my count—'

She choked when liquid ran down her throat. It felt horrifyingly familiar. Had they done this before? What was she drinking? It tasted nutty and wretched, wretched, *wretched*.

Familiar, little bird.

You've played this game before.

Jaya was here.

No, she wasn't. She was dead. Shakti's mind was the haunting ground from which she spoke, a ghost disobeying all laws of rebirth.

'—mayakari, do it again. It didn't work—'

Oh, now this voice, she wished she could silence.

The dead tyrant's daughter. The one who poisoned her own brother. She never left. Sometimes, when Shakti thought she was awake, Aarya was there standing across from her. Observing her, as if she were a rare insect discovered in the mountaintops. Sometimes, when she was sure she was dreaming, Aarya rushed towards her with a sword and impaled her with it. She left her to bleed out on the grass as time accelerated and her body decomposed and became one with the earth.

'. . . do what . . . again?' Shakti ground out the words with great difficulty.

Her body seized and she coughed violently. This hurt. She wanted to stop hurting.

If I do what she asks, will she stop?

But it was hard to recall. What did the princess want?

'—sake, *curse*. Your mind can't be that—'

Oh. Curse. *That's what she wants.*

No. I can't. Shouldn't, but . . .

. . . maybe she won't hurt me if I do.

A voice in the back of her head kept screaming at her not to, that this was wrong. But she didn't want to feel any more pain, so she pushed that voice away.

When Shakti next spoke, each word sounded like death. Her bones felt weaker. Her spine prickled, as if she were calling a Great Spirit, only to find that none existed. She was drowning beneath still water. The ashes of those killed in Kolakola revived and reached for her with grey hands. A winged serpent hunted her from above. A stranger awaited her in the dark, holding a knife in their hands. She heard her voice, hoarse and weak:

'. . . *suffering . . . your own heart . . . hate . . .*'

Pressure snaked around her arms and legs again. A strange chorus began to chant dark songs and tragedies.

And then—

*

When she came to, Shakti felt that something was wrong. She just couldn't understand what it was.

'*Ugh*,' she groaned, vaguely sensing cold stone behind her. 'My back . . .'

Slowly, Shakti opened her eyes. She had been slumping against the wall. Her vision was blurred. Slightly hazy. Unfocused. She looked up and saw two people in front of her. A man and Aarya. Aarya and a man. Was this another nightmare? The princess wouldn't leave her alone.

'Alive, are you?' Aarya's voice was tinged with distaste. 'Do you remember doing it?'

Shakti frowned. 'Doing . . . what?' Her words came out slurred. The taste of that horrible, nutty fluid still coated her tongue. Aarya's next words were hard to follow. Shakti didn't have the strength to listen, but she pretended to. Something about curses. Something about helping her.

That didn't sound right. 'Help who?' she asked. '. . . you? Have I helped *you*?'

'Enough. Unfortunately, some of us must stoop to levels that our fathers did not.'

Foolish, foolish Aarya. Fathers' daughters were so blind. This one, especially. Shakti giggled. The giggling soon turned to loud, echoey laughter.

'Is she . . . well?'

'Delirium. Milk of poppy can do that, Your Highness . . . I'll be outside . . .'

A door thudded loudly. There was a strange burble at the bottom of her throat. Confused, Shakti pressed her palms against her chest. The sensation travelled up, and she dissolved into a sudden fit of hiccups.

'Do you . . . hate having to use me . . .' she burbled, head lolling forward. There was wetness on her chin. She wiped it with her palm to have it come away with spit.

'Unsavoury . . .' Aarya's voice came in and out. '. . . associate with a mayakari. Disgusting.'

That was wrong, too. Why was the princess lying? Adil had

known one. He'd burned one here. A memory returned to her with startling clarity.

'You think your family's blood is witch-less?' Shakti said, voice hoarse. 'Because it isn't. Your aunt was a witch. A *witch*. Can you believe it, Princess?'

A long silence followed her words. The footsteps came closer. Aarya came closer. Sudden pain lanced at her fingers, and she squealed. Squinting her eyes, Shakti tried to focus on the princess. She looked horrified. Livid. Very livid. She was stepping on her hands. It hurt.

'Even half-lost to the world, you lie to save yourself,' came Aarya's voice. 'My aunt died of an illness, you pathetic wretch.'

Shakti laughed again. 'No.' She smiled and tapped the side of her temple. 'Your father told me. He's in my head, you know. He won't leave. But he told me. Your . . . mother's sister. A mayakari. Take *that!*'

More silence. Silence made her uncomfortable, especially here. She needed to fill it.

'Do you know . . . what separates us, Princess?' Shakti mumbled. The strength in her upper body was fading. Slowly, she slid down from her place against the wall.

A snort. 'Title.'

Wrong. '*Magic,*' Shakti said in a loud whisper. 'Humans are all the same but . . . mayakari . . . we have magic. You may love your father but if – if you were born into your family as a witch . . . hmm. He would've burned you just the same.'

Where am I?

Letting out a weary groan, Shakti cracked her eyes open. Soft darkness surrounded her, illuminated only by little spots of torchlight. She was on the floor. It was unbearably cold. *Cell.* Prison cell. She was in a prison cell. How did she remember; how did she know?

Little bird.

Jaya.

Little bird, wake up.

Her aunt's voice was a temporary balm. The rounded vowels and comforting lilt vanished like smoke the moment her body registered heat, then a sharp ache all throughout her body.

Bits and pieces of memory rushed at her like ocean waves. Her, fighting Aarya. Her, offering Aarya her abilities in exchange for her life. After that—

Soldiers. Chains. Thrown in a prison cell. Then—

Then what?

Then what?

Shakti's mouth was dry. Rough like sandpaper, and no amount of spit could help it.

I can't remember. Why can't I remember?

Her mind was as dark as her surroundings. Memories failed to piece together. They came half-formed or not at all.

Missing. Missing. *Missing*. Something was missing. What was she missing?

In her panic, her heart began to respond in kind. It beat furiously; a leopard trapped in a metal cage. It cracked its teeth and shattered its claws trying to escape. It was tired, fur matted. Dried along its silky coat—

Blood.

There was blood. On her skin. Her clothes. Shakti's skin crawled. What had they done to her?

Terror crept in. She hoisted herself up from where she had been lying curled up on the floor. Metal rattled and clinked. Shakti glanced down at her bare feet, bloodied like the rest of her body. Red, puckered skin oozed a watery fluid from the centre.

She stared at her legs, covered by black cotton trousers. Parts were worn, slashed. In a panic, she yanked her left arm only to be pulled back unceremoniously. Silver glinted on her wrist – *shackles*.

Reaching out her left arm in gentler motions, Shakti felt the skin of her legs, travelling up, up, up—

No. Thank the spirits, she didn't feel sore there.

But then—

What happened?

Hundreds drowning in stormy waves. A stranger holding a knife in the dark. A vial of poison. A terrified sob escaped her lips.

What did she do to me?

CHAPTER FOUR
Ashoka

'An invitation to visit Trikalinga in the midst of a consul's arrival,' Nayani remarked. 'My, my, Prince Ashoka, you *are* in a bind.'

Lounging like a cat on a plush settee, the mayakari offered him a sympathetic grimace.

So too, did Sachith. Beside him, the captain of the Ridi guard stationed in Taksila, Kanna, tilted her head to the side. All three had been summoned into Ashoka's study the following morning to address the issue regarding Consul Daman, who would be arriving from the Golden City the following day. Ashoka couldn't delay Queen Kalyani's invitation, considering that time was of the essence.

Departing for Kalinga was no issue. It was the threat of Aarya finding out from the consul where he'd gone that was the problem. Meeting with Queen Kalyani without her consent was akin to bringing wood into a burning house. Being absent for the duration of the consul's visit would also give Aarya enough reason to force Ashoka out of his governorship. He needed a plausible reason to turn the consul away.

'The problem is that I can't simply turn one person away from Taksila,' he told the group. 'And to have it be a consul, no less. That's more than enough reason for my sister to act against me. I may have to deny all individuals who are trying to enter Taksila. Possibly those who want to leave, too.'

'There will be opposition from Taksilans, Prince Ashoka,' Nayani argued. 'They'll want to move freely. Stopping them will be difficult.'

'Prince Ashoka,' Kanna remarked. She was a small but domineering woman, mostly amicable unless he were to suggest anything that would put the Ridi soldiers in a bind. 'I agree with Nayani. You will need a practical reason to enforce a travel ban. If I may – a perceived danger to public health is always a safe bet.'

'Ah.' He knew why the captain would suggest it. 'Like the Red Sickness that hit Makon? I remember my father was hesitant to have our merchant ships return from the capital. That's not a bad suggestion, captain.'

'Declaring a city lockdown due to a false illness that no one can see the effects of is a terrible risk,' Rahil spoke up. He stood by the bay window with his arms crossed, appearing more princelike than Ashoka ever had. 'People aren't foolish, Prince Ashoka.'

The comment was laced with an undercurrent of derision. Ashoka scowled at him. To his utter frustration, Rahil fixed him with a blank stare and said nothing more.

Out of the corner of his eye, he saw the two soldiers and Nayani share a look. It made him self-conscious, having others know that there was a problem between him and his personal guard. Almost as if he didn't have control. Gritting his teeth, Ashoka made to argue against his claims, but it seemed that Rahil's remarks had already created damage.

'Unless,' ventured Kanna, 'you wish to declare a lockdown, say, in search of a dangerous witch.' When Nayani shot her a scowl, the woman added, 'but I gather that would go against your interests.'

It certainly would. The idea of a rogue mayakari was one he hadn't even bothered to entertain.

'Not to mention unbelievable,' Nayani replied, scoffing. 'Why would you disrupt an entire city's operations for one witch?'

'A dangerous mayakari is not so unbelievable,' Sachith murmured.

'Ah yes,' Nayani shot back, tone acidic enough to strip skin raw. 'Perhaps we can curse the entire Taksilan population, see how that pans out. Though I can't guarantee if a plague can be created in time.'

'Don't joke about those things.'

'Then don't offer us as a scapegoat.'

He noticed Rahil continue to observe him in the same way he did during combat training. Watching, or in this case, *waiting* for a mistake. As if he would be proven correct. He wouldn't give Rahil the satisfaction.

'The new mines,' Ashoka said, silencing them both. He stood, chair scraping against the floor as he wandered over to the giant map of Taksila that hung on the eastern wall of the study. After they'd freed the Great Spirit trapped in his father's statue, Ashoka had replaced the map his father had put up. That map was an abomination; marking areas where mayakari resided, many pockets crossed out to indicate where burnings had occurred. The new map had changed to reflect the mines with extractable iron ore discovered close to the Vihara Mountains. 'Halt operations there. Have your mayakari ask some minor spirits to cause a ruckus.'

'Halt operations?' Nayani echoed in disbelief. 'But the ore . . .'

The mayakari's displeasure was understandable. Since the angered Great Spirits had been pacified, the northern lands were slowly regrowing. Rebuilding efforts were slow but steady. Following his first letter to Aarya, the resistance had conducted appeasement rites around the mining areas in the north to allow iron ore to be extracted without irritating any nature spirits. The iron ore was then used to create standard Ran military weapons. Swords, crossbows for artillery, khandas – the like – all emblazoned with the empire's seal. They were made and kept within the state or sent to the capital, to keep Aarya placated.

However, Ashoka had ordered some of the Ran weapons – which were delivered from Mathura to Taksila – to be carefully concealed and imported down south past Satva's border. Ran-made weapons were the best in the known world. For any unconquered kingdoms to use their own weapons against them would be a wonderful irony. However, there was only so much that could be secretly traded. He expected the Ran soldiers stationed in parts of the border to take note and ban the entry of their weapons into Mahvo. The hope was that it would reach Aarya's ears soon and sow the seeds of discontent.

During his correspondence with Mahvo's queen, Malika, Ashoka had made his intentions very clear. If he was able to obtain security for Mahvo with the Kalingan Kingdom's assistance, she would help him to take full control of Satva and onward. Queen Malika had agreed to his plan, and awaited word on his dealings with Queen Kalyani. He knew he had placed his game pieces early, but he was willing to take a risk. The Kalingan queen could be convinced. If there was a chance to weaken the Maurya dynasty, she would do it, that much he knew.

'It'll be temporary,' Ashoka said. 'Just over a week at most, while I'm away.' Journeying to Kalinga would take about three days, and he was unsure of how much time he would have to spend in the capital before returning.

Nayani seemed to mull it over. 'A week . . . all right, then,' she said.

'Good,' Ashoka replied. 'This is the story we'll give Taksilans and Consul Daman: Sachith and Kanna, while I'm gone, you and the mayakari resistance will be attempting to contain another errant nature spirit fallen victim to my father's exploits. For safety reasons, a barrier will be set up, and no one is allowed to enter the city. When the consul arrives, apologize and have him return to the capital. They can revisit me later.'

The soldiers bowed. 'Understood, Prince Ashoka,' they replied in unison.

Nayani fixed her gaze on Rahil and asked, 'What do you think?'

If only Ashoka could silently communicate his displeasure at her comment. She seemed intent on causing chaos in this meeting, but he could only settle for a warning glare.

Rahil, however, appeared unruffled. 'Prince Ashoka is the governor,' Rahil said smoothly. 'If he deems this to be the best decision, I agree with him.'

If I didn't love him, I would strangle him.

'We're done here.' Clasping his hands behind his back, Ashoka tipped his chin towards the direction of the door. 'All of you may leave. I shall draft a notice ordering the city gates to be closed to residents and visitors.'

First to depart was Nayani, who shot him a probing uptick

of an eyebrow before she did. Kanna and Sachith were the last to leave, shutting the doors quietly behind them. Once he was sure they were alone and no one was listening, Ashoka stood abruptly and stalked towards Rahil, stopping only a hair's breadth away. Myrrh soap and sandalwood assaulted his senses. Ashoka could see his outline reflected in Rahil's eyes, a vaguely human shadow on its last shred of patience. That overwhelming need to be violent surged up again; to grab Rahil by the shoulders and tackle him to the ground as if that would get him to surrender this futile war.

'You're petty,' were the first words that tumbled out of his mouth.

'What an astute observation,' Rahil countered.

'Trying to oppugn me in front of them was low,' Ashoka said, scowling.

'That wasn't my intention, Prince Ashoka,' Rahil shot back, his expression infuriatingly neutral. 'I apologize if you felt that way.'

Pinching the bridge of his nose, Ashoka closed his eyes. It was as if he were speaking to one of the council members. 'You're irritating me to no end,' he said.

Rahil's mouth set into a hard line. 'I should fucking hope so.'

He cracked one eye open. *A reaction* – interesting. Anger came to Rahil about as frequently as Adil showered praise upon Ashoka. When he *did* succumb to intemperance, Rahil didn't turn violent. Rather, he became silent, as he was now.

'I *apologized*. Multiple times. What else do you want me to say?'

'Nothing.'

Frustration bubbled and boiled over like a cauldron under higher heat.

'Are you going to hit me?' Rahil asked, nodding towards his clenched fists. 'You look like you want to.'

'I do,' Ashoka admitted, 'but I won't.' Besides, Rahil would have him on his knees, in pain, within moments.

'*Nonviolence*. How surprising.' A short, terse response, but Ashoka knew what went unsaid.

'If you don't want me to say anything, then why bother keeping up this charade?' he asked, vexed.

'You think this is a charade?' Rahil retorted, scowling.

'Isn't it?' Ashoka argued. His inner voice begged him to stop, to take a breath and reconsider his words, but he ignored it. 'I've chosen to take the high ground and apologize for something that, in the midst of all this, feels irrelevant.'

Rahil flinched, and Ashoka's chest tightened. It was the wrong thing to say in the heat of the moment. '*Irrelevant,*' he echoed. 'You're not the same, Ashoka. Ever since I came here, you – I—' Rahil seemed to catch himself and pursed his lips together, refusing to speak further.

'What?' Frustrated, Ashoka made to push him back, but Rahil caught his wrist before it ever landed on his chest. 'Do you hate me? Tell me you hate me. At this point, I would rather you say that.'

Rahil's grip on his wrist tightened. Silence clouded the room like a stubborn morning fog as they stared at each other, unwilling to break. It was only when there came a sudden, feeble knock on the door that Ashoka was forced to avert his eyes and wrench his hand back. 'Come in,' he called out.

The door parted to reveal an elderly man with a neatly trimmed white beard and impeccable posture: Varun, one of the royal estate's most senior staff. 'Forgive the intrusion, but there is a visitor for you, Prince Ashoka,' he stated.

Frowning, Ashoka crossed his arms. 'I don't recall planning any further audiences today, Varun,' he said. 'Unless . . . is the visitor a mayakari?'

The older man shook his head. 'She is not,' he said, and pushed the door open wider.

The moment Ashoka spotted the untamed hair and wide smile, he rushed forward. So did Rahil. Spirits, he hadn't seen his advisor's face in months.

'*Sau!*' he exclaimed, stopping short to allow Rahil to get to her first. With a delighted squeal, Sau launched herself into Rahil's open arms like she was seeing family after many years away. Rahil hugged her back, just as fierce.

He still harboured a grudge against Aarya for taking his advisor away from him. To hinder his success in Taksila – and in doing so hinder part of the bet Ashoka had with Arush that would've seen him as head of the war council – Aarya had convinced their older brother to send Sau away to Makon for negotiations with its recently appointed crown prince.

'I'm alive,' Sau said with a laugh. 'Although I haven't missed the heat.' Gently detaching herself from Rahil, she turned her attention to Ashoka. There were dark shadows under her eyes, as if she hadn't slept for days. She was dressed in what appeared to be Ridi clothing; a short black wraparound tunic and grey linen trousers that tapered at the ankles. It was odd to see Sau without her saris.

'Taksila hasn't burned to the ground, so can I assume that you've survived well enough without me, Prince Ashoka?' she asked, quirking an eyebrow. 'Although, I'll need to take a closer look at – *oh*!'

Ashoka didn't let her finish. In what his father would have deemed to be an unsavoury act, he gathered Sau in a relieved, welcoming embrace. He felt her stiffen at the sudden contact before she relaxed. A sea-salt smell lingered in her hair, and from her clothes wafted the scent of wet wood and cardamom, familiar and unfamiliar at the same time.

'I'm happy you're here,' he murmured. After missing her presence throughout his first few weeks in Taksila, to freeing the Great Spirit, to now fighting with Rahil, he needed some sense of comfort.

'My, my,' Sau remarked, patting him gently on the back. He could sense that she was smiling, but her tone carried some perplexity with it. He felt her fingers skim his hair where it now curled at the nape of his neck and fell around his ears. 'You've grown your hair out. It suits you.'

Instinctively, Ashoka's gaze landed on Rahil who was watching him with an unreadable expression. Throat suddenly dry, he gently detached himself from Sau, keeping his hands on her shoulders. 'You were able to help Prince Ryu? There was nothing too difficult?' he asked, knowing he sounded like a concerned father rather than a prince. Despite Rahil having returned from Makon several weeks ago, Sau had stayed behind after having struck up an unspoken deal with the Ridi prince, Ryu, in exchange for his soldiers to be stationed in Taksila. Ashoka hadn't been sure when she was to return, but her face was a welcome sight. 'And how did you *get* here?'

Sau shrugged, her grin vanishing for a split second before it resurfaced. '*Help* is a strong word. I merely provided some advice,' she admitted. *Still tight-lipped about the deal*, Ashoka noted, though he saw no need to press upon it further. 'And what do you mean how did I get here? I boarded a ship headed to the Golden City's port – what an arduous journey that was, mind you – and then I made the journey here by boat. The privateer charged me a *ridiculous* sum, but it wasn't as if I could argue with her.'

A long and tiring journey by any means. If Sau had simply returned to the palace to have a soldier fly her here, that would have been much easier. However, Sau's fear of winged serpents was well known. Besides, he wasn't sure if Aarya would have let Sau leave. 'Have you eaten anything?' Ashoka inquired instead, noticing her unusually hollowed features.

'Today? Water, a piece of roast paan, and that's about it,' Sau replied. 'Can I have something to eat? I'm famished.'

'I'll have the cooks prepare a meal for the advisor, Prince Ashoka,' Varun called out from his position by the door before he departed for the kitchens.

'Lovely man, Varun. Told me his son-in-law is from Anurapura, too,' Sau commented idly before her face turned sombre. 'Now, tell me how exactly Aarya became acting regent. I heard from some portside traders when I landed and thought they were joking.'

It took longer than expected for Ashoka to explain how Arush fell into a coma and Aarya had assumed rulership despite there not being many details to spare since all that he knew came from his sister's letter. Rather, he was more concerned about what he had accomplished in Taksila, and how Sau would respond. After all, killing the governor had not been in their original plan.

Sau appeared dazed once he finished his recount of killing Kosala in the razed lands. 'I . . . that's certainly one way to take control,' she replied. Disbelief was clear across her face as she eyed him with newfound fascination. 'Finally abandoned those romantic ideals of yours, then?'

At least her reaction was better than Rahil's.

Ashoka frowned. 'I didn't *abandon* them,' he said. 'I simply came to understand that I was viewing the world foolishly. Sometimes actionable steps must be taken.'

Behind him, Rahil huffed at the mention of *actionable steps*. He saw Sau's eyes flicker to him before she refocused her attention. 'You can't ban mayakari killings here for long,' she said. 'Pri – Empress Aarya will resume control soon enough. Acting empress – *hah*. I can't quite believe it. Neither can I believe that one of the mayakari would poison Arush.'

'We're in agreement there. Aarya's already impatient, too. I'm trying to ward off Consul Daman—' When Sau shot him a confused look, Ashoka sighed, 'Surveillance. He's set to visit us, but I've made provisions to turn him back at the city gates.'

'Whatever for?'

'We need to travel to Trikalinga to meet with Queen Kalyani without Aarya's knowledge,' he replied. 'She wants me to give up on Taksila, but I won't let her destroy what I have already saved.'

'Kalinga?' A sigh escaped Sau, louder than a beleaguered dog on a hot summer day. 'Please catch me up to speed as fast as you can, Ashoka,' she said. 'If we're to commit treason, I would like to agree to it with a clear conscience.'

CHAPTER FIVE
Shakti

SHAKTI HAD CURSED. SHE WAS SURE OF IT.

Waking up relatively clear-headed in her sunless cell, she felt like a rotting carcass. She was locked in the holding cells within the palace grounds. Stone walls surrounded her on all four sides. To her north was a large wooden door with metal grilles. No bed had been afforded to her, only the cold comfort of the floor.

For a long, horrible moment, she couldn't remember how she'd got here.

Memories and elapsed time continued to elude her. There were so many gaps in her memory. Her body was a canvas of suffering, and yet she couldn't remember how it came to be this way.

What she did remember was the unmistakable, eerie feeling of slipping into the cursed tongue.

Shivers down her spine. Death in all its forms. The guilt of taking a life. That uncanny, unnerving sensation she had felt when she first placed a curse upon Adil. It was the same.

A curse, and one uttered without any memories of it. *Fuck*. Had she done so of her own volition, dazed and spewing nonsense? Or had she been forced?

Dread settled like a dead weight upon her chest at the realization.

'Who did I . . . ?' she mumbled to herself, struggling to sit up. 'What . . . ?'

But nothing came. No recollection, only the feeling.

She was parched, lips dry and cracked. Even stretching out an arm stung as the scabs that formed over her wounds threatened to split again. Her stomach pleaded for food, even a small grain of rice. Her whole body felt hollow.

Suddenly, there came a shuffling outside her door. If she strained her ears, Shakti could catch the conversation between soldiers as they changed guard. One voice bid the other goodnight.

Ah. It was nighttime.

Shakti needed to know what was asked of her during those crucial moments that she couldn't remember. Screaming at the soldiers stationed outside wouldn't help. They only followed orders, keeping her bound. In fact, she would likely be subject to those memory lapses again if she raised her voice.

A sharp pain lanced through her head, and Shakti groaned, clutching the side of her temples to soothe herself. Adil's face surfaced in her mind, cruel and haughty, before it morphed into—

Aarya.

Aarya, Aarya, Aarya.

She had been there, in those hazy scraps of memories Shakti fought to cling on to. The royal circlet that used to rest upon Arush's head. The bittered sugar tones. The order:

'Do it again.'

Do *what* again? Do what—

'Curse.'

The words came rushing back, but the voice wasn't her own. It was Aarya's.

Shakti's heart was beating so furiously that she thought it would soon sputter to a stop, overworked.

Whom did I curse? What was it?

I need to undo it . . .

. . . or is it too late?

The last thought alarmed her the most. Curses were unpredictable. They could enact in a matter of moments to years. What if this one had acted as quickly as the one that she cast on Adil? What if someone was suffering – or dead – because of her? Cursing was acceptable if she was in control. But she hadn't been.

Aarya would know what had transpired here, what she'd forced her to do. She needed to speak to her.

Unable to find the strength to sit cross-legged, Shakti lay down, staring at the ceiling. It was almost impossible to ignore the hunger pangs, the lacerations that pleaded for treatment and the spasms in her stomach. *Almost.* But she needed to know who – or what – she had cursed. Perhaps it was too late, but perhaps not. If she was lucky, the curse could be undone. She just had to *remember*, and there was only one way to do it.

At first, pain was all she could feel. On her chest, her head, her back. Vaguely, she recalled Aarya carving a bloody mark between her shoulder blades when they fought. Alas, there were no mirrors in this cell for her to see what it was. Whenever she twisted her arms to feel her back, it hurt. The telltale bumpiness of scabs was there, but so too was the moist and raw sensation of tissue that covered a still-healing wound. It probably looked horrendous.

Focus. Shakti allowed herself to concentrate on the breath. Weak, sputtering exhales came first, until they became longer and drawn out. Bodily pains faded into the background. At some point, her thoughts petered out into nothingness, and her mind turned silent. Deep in the pit of her stomach, she sensed a familiar tug. In her mind's eye, it presented itself as a faint blue thread glowing in the dark, begging to be pulled. Shakti tugged.

Whatever air she held in her lungs released with a sharp exhale. The thread pulled her haphazardly, forcing her to tumble into a deep, dark cavern. Oh, how she'd missed this feeling.

Shakti thought of Emperor Ashoka and entered the Collective.

'Shakti. You have returned.'

Emperor Ashoka, the first of his name, the first Maurya to be named emperor, greeted her. She'd entered, thinking of him, which was a relief from the last few times she'd arrived with the sole purpose of speaking to Adil. The emperor's ethereal features were marked with concern as she materialized. The two of them had appeared on what seemed to be the peak of the Mountain of Rebirth where nature died and flourished in equal measure. The grass beneath her feet was a swirl of green and yellow, looking both dewy and dry, but she couldn't feel it. A terrible shame – she longed to feel the grass beneath her feet.

To her right, the view of the valley where the Golden City lay was surrounded by a thin mist, but it wasn't how she remembered it. It was smaller, with larger swatches of unfelled forests, and houses on the outskirts still under construction. She quickly realized that this was likely how Emperor Ashoka remembered the Golden City when he had been alive; an army of ants expanding their colony above ground.

'Emperor,' she huffed as she approached him. Entering the Collective had tired her.

The ruby-studded circlet upon Emperor Ashoka's head lustred like blood when freshly let. His deep brown skin gleamed in the false sunlight. He sat a few paces away, cross-legged on the ground. 'Have you come to hear a story again?'

Shakti halted in her tracks, flummoxed. 'Excuse me?'

'A story,' he repeated. 'You asked for one before.'

Before? That didn't make any sense. *I never entered the Collective after I fought Aarya. Unless I don't—*

'—remember,' Shakti whispered, her breath hitching. 'I don't remember *anything*.'

At some point during her proclamation, Shakti had dropped to her knees on the ground, head bowed into herself. She didn't realize until she saw a pair of sandaled feet and glanced up. The emperor stood before her, his dark brown eyes assessing her with unease.

Slowly, he knelt until they were face to face. She couldn't imagine any of the current Maurya brood kneeling the way he did in front of a commoner. A mayakari. Except perhaps for Prince Ashoka.

'You came here before,' the emperor told her gently, 'in a fit of terror. I don't think you arrived here on purpose, Shakti. It seemed like you'd appeared out of instinct. Fear. You were panicked. Restless. You called me. You asked me to tell you a story.'

'What kind of story?' she whispered.

'One with many iterations,' Emperor Ashoka replied. 'It was of how the Mountain of Rebirth came to be, and I told you the one

I knew. One of a warrior, a mayakari and a Great Spirit. But I gather you aren't here for another tale.'

Shaking her head, Shakti glanced over his shoulder. White pinwheel flowers rotated, drooped, and died. At the same time, an infected branch of the na tree beyond them revived and sprouted leaves.

'I've been thrown into the palace prisons,' she said. 'I can't remember anything after I fought Princess Aarya, and I think I've been drugged countless times. There's this bitter taste in my mouth I can't shed. And – and—'

'Yes?'

Unable to look him in the eyes, Shakti hung her head. Embarrassment, guilt, shame, and fear made for a nasty blend. 'I've cast a curse,' she admitted to the ground. 'I know I have. I think . . . I think Aarya made me.'

'How can you know for certain?' he asked. 'You could simply be recalling a nightmare.'

'I know that I have,' she insisted. 'There's . . . there's a similar feeling to when I cast that curse on Adil. Speaking in the cursed tongue brings with it scenes of suffering. I can't explain it with logic, only intuition. It's unnatural. Like you're being followed. Marked for death. Scraps of my memories come back. They bring images of deaths I've never witnessed. Drownings at sea. Being buried alive. Being afflicted with illnesses that can't be cured. These images are the aftereffects of casting a curse.'

'Then undo it.'

Articulated like it was something obvious. A problem so simple that a child could solve it. Shakti laughed bitterly. 'I can only undo a curse if I remember the exact words I used, and I don't,' she said. 'I don't even know whom I've cursed.'

This'll hurt someone. Unless it already has.

It bothered her to think that she might've been the cause of someone else's suffering, especially if the harm was unintentional. That part Shakti kept unsaid. Instead, she picked herself back up, the emperor following her motions. She might not remember the target of her curse, but Aarya would.

'There's one person I can force it out of,' she said. Aarya would likely be asleep now; it was the opportune time to invade her dreams.

Understanding dawned in Emperor Ashoka's eyes. He made no move to counter, instead gestured in a way that said, *go on, then*. If it had been Adil here, he would've put up more of a fuss, but Aarya was his child. Such condemnation on his part was expected. Emperor Ashoka, however, was far removed from his successors. Shakti liked to think that was why he didn't care as much.

Closing her eyes once more, she thought of Aarya. Of dead peacocks and a sunless room. The back of her eyes descended into vivid streaks of bright colours against the dark. When she opened her eyes, the emperor and the mountain vanished, and she was left standing outside a hazy dome of fog, while behind her was a vast stretch of complete darkness. Beyond the foggy wall, she found herself staring at a strangely picturesque scene. Aarya was in some sort of study, dark head bent in concentration over a set of maps sprawled over the desk. Standing next to her, looking unnervingly gentle, was Adil. She was dreaming of her father.

Shakti wanted to kill them both where they stood.

Pushing all murderous intent aside, Shakti stretched her hand out and pushed through the wall of fog to enter Aarya's dream. There was more resistance than she remembered as she entered. Aarya's mind was still reinforced, will still strong. Or perhaps it was Shakti's own lack of strength. She knew that she wouldn't be able to stay in Aarya's dreams for long. Time was of the essence.

Shakti willed herself to appear as Emperor Adil. In addition to her powers of dream invasion, the trick of altering her form within them was a useful one. There was no sensation when she transformed; the only clues were what she saw. When she glanced down at her arms, they were Adil's thick, burly ones and not her own.

Materializing in front of the desk, she was almost bemused to find that Aarya hadn't noticed. Tapping the wood, she finally got the princess' attention.

Aarya's head snapped up as they locked eyes. 'Father?' she asked, confused. 'You were just—' she looked to her left. The other dream-Adil had vanished. 'Oh. My apologies.'

Behind Aarya were shelves upon shelves of books. The spines

glimmered an unnatural gold. The wood fractured into spiderwebs, and from the cracks appeared trails of ivy. Shakti half-expected a minor spirit to emerge from between the books.

'Daughter,' Shakti said, her voice coming out in Adil's usual baritone. 'The royal circlet – it suits you well.'

It hadn't been there before. Princess Aarya shifted, the deep blue of her sari shimmering like sunrays hitting a body of water. She wore a proud smile on her face, befitting a daughter receiving praise from her favoured parent. 'Thank you, Father,' she replied.

There was a sudden visceral, painful spasm in her belly. Shakti winced and tried to ignore it. Her head felt too full, swollen with water.

'Father, are you all right?' Princess Aarya rushed towards her. Waving her hands, Shakti kept her away, grimacing at the fresh flash of pain. With her body weak, her mind suffered, too. It was taking far more energy than she expected to dream invade. She needed an answer from Aarya, and quick.

'I'm fine, daughter,' she said, before glancing at the princess in curiosity. 'Are you?'

'What—?' The princess looked down at her chest. A dark black stain was spreading across it, a mirror image to the one Shakti had seen blossom on Adil before he died. The dreamworlds were such a strange place. 'What is this?'

'I don't know,' Shakti replied hastily. 'The mayakari you're keeping down in the cells, daughter. What did you do to her?'

Princess Aarya appeared distressed by the cobwebbing stain on her chest. The dreamscape began to darken at the frays. 'I – I fed her milk of poppy. The physician added some other ingredients to the concoction. She had to be kept pacified.'

Shakti's vision turned double for a moment before it reverted. *Milk of poppy*. That must've been the bitter, almost nutlike taste that she vaguely recalled. No wonder she couldn't remember anything. How much had they forced down her throat? How much had it made her forget?

Pools of viscous red liquid began to seep through the cracks on the floor. Before Shakti could think better of it, she rushed towards Aarya and grabbed her by the shoulders, shaking her like a doll.

'What did you make her do, Aarya?' she urged. 'The mayakari has done something. *What did she do?*'

'Father, please, calm down!' Aarya gasped.

Shakti didn't listen. Neither did she care. She continued to shake the princess viciously even as that horrifying ache sunk its claws into the last dredges of her strength. 'Tell me!' In Adil's voice, the command was terrifying. It seemed to unnerve the princess, too, for her lower lip trembled, and she shook her head.

Agitated, Shakti-as-Adil let out a thunderous, deafening, '*Tell me!*'

Aarya yelped. 'I made her curse!' she exclaimed. 'While she was drugged. I made her curse.'

Wretched woman. You made me curse.

You made me hurt someone, and now I can't remember.

Shakti couldn't help but wish that wasn't the truth. Aarya's admission only made her guilt worse. Cursing Adil was an active choice that she had made despite knowing the karmic consequences. This wasn't. This was a violation. Unconscious harm against someone or something.

The ugly sensation of being used clawed its way up her throat. Never had Shakti felt so dirty. Using her own powers against her. How unbelievably cruel. Fresh anger swelled anew.

'Whom did you have her curse?' Shakti yelled. The throbbing pain became too much. It paralysed her, seized her, like a cobra having sunk its venomous fangs into soft flesh. 'Who did you – argh!'

Her hands left Aarya's shoulders and came to clutch at her own head. It was as if her head was splitting open. Spirits, she needed to leave. But not yet. *Not yet.*

Who did I curse? I need to know. There was no chance she would vanish before getting her answer.

Dimly, she heard Aarya shriek her father's name. Moments later, she glanced up at Princess Aarya's frightened eyes. It made her look so small. Childlike.

'Tell me, daughter,' Shakti ground out in torturous breaths. Her control was slipping. '*Who was it?*'

'I asked her to curse . . .' Aarya began, teary-eyed, before her expression stilled. Whatever concern there had been on her features vanished, only to be replaced by that of an angry viper. '*You.*'

'Me?' Shakti asked, confused.

But Princess Aarya had now scrambled away from her, fresh horror and disgust painted across her features. 'Witch. *Witch*. Get out of my head!'

Startled, Shakti glanced down at her arms. They weren't Adil's brawny gold-banded ones any more. Thinner and marked with cuts and bruises – they were hers.

If they had indeed been facing each other, the princess would have killed her, such was the venom in her eyes. In fact, she launched herself at Shakti, hands visibly aimed at her neck.

But just before Princess Aarya could reach her throat, the last of Shakti's strength gave out. The dreamscape fractured, cracking in half like split wood, and she was unceremoniously snatched out.

CHAPTER SIX
Shakti

When Shakti startled awake, her entire body felt broken.

Sweat drenched her skin, mixing with the grime and blood. For once in her life, a dream invasion had been far too taxing for her to bear.

And I was so close, too.

Clenching her right hand into a fist, she slammed it onto the ground with a frustrated scream. The resulting pain barely registered; only irritation lingered. Aarya had been on the cusp of telling her who she had ordered to curse, and her mind had collapsed at the worst possible moment.

Spirits, she was tired. So unfathomably tired.

Curling into herself to ignore the ever-persistent rumblings of her stomach, Shakti let out a sob. Tears came thick and fast, stinging her dry skin as she fought to muffle her cries. She didn't want to give the soldiers outside the pleasure of hearing her weep.

I want my memories back.

She hadn't eaten. She hadn't bled. She hadn't succeeded. Karma truly wanted her to suffer after cursing Adil. But it wasn't fair. *It wasn't fair.*

All she wanted was justice. To avenge Jaya. And yet here she was, potentially waiting to suffer the same fate.

In the dark, her vision was obscured by tears. Phantom voices called to her. Shakti saw herself tied to a stake, waiting like Jaya would have as Aarya carried a flaming torch. The image flickered, the torchbearer sometimes Emperor Adil, sometimes a strange ghostly elephant, sometimes the princess. And then, in a turn more terrifying than she could imagine, the hand that held the flame morphed into her aunt.

This isn't your fault, little bird.

'I . . .' Her voice cracked. She couldn't think. With each passing moment, Jaya's hand lifted higher and higher until she sobbed. Pleaded for her life to be spared. Her breath caught the way it did when she first saw Jaya's blackened corpse.

Her aunt turned back into Aarya before she tossed the flame at her feet.

Blue flame erupted around her as the world fell into darkness.

Sometime later, a soldier arrived and kicked her awake. Taking one look at her bedraggled figure, the man wrinkled his nose in distaste and set down a pitcher and a plate.

'Here. Eat.'

Shakti glanced at her food, a sad-looking heap of rice and curried okra. How did it look so unappetizing when she was this hungry?

Better than nothing at all, she eventually decided, and began to shovel it down her throat like a starved tiger chancing upon fresh meat. Grains of rice fell on the floor as she washed her hands with the pitcher and drank ravenously.

'Enjoying your meal, mayakari?'

Shakti stilled. In her hunger, she hadn't noticed a second figure slip into the cell.

Aarya.

The ruby circlet suited her better than her brother. It glinted viciously along with the layers of solid gold necklaces and garnet-studded rings. The deep, lustrous red of her sari brought to Shakti's mind the eyes of an angered Great Spirit, the sharp, thin line of kohl and the scabbard at her side an understated threat as she approached.

Despite herself, Shakti flinched. Aarya knew what she had done last night. Some kind of punishment awaited her. She had half a mind to remain silent but realized that would bring her more abuse than she could already bear. 'Yes, Princess,' she replied by accident. Not even a quarter of an hour in and she'd started off on the wrong foot.

Aarya's left eye twitched. '*Empress*,' she corrected her, expression frosty as she took a step forward. Just behind, the guard copied her movement, hands ready by his sword — what, did they think she could turn into a nature spirit? — eyes trained intently on her. 'Leave us.'

She spoke to the guard, who appeared just as baffled as Shakti was. 'But, Your Highness,' he began, 'the witch is—'

'She is no threat to me in chains, soldier,' Aarya remarked stiffly. 'Return on my command.'

Bowing, the man left, shutting the door behind him. The space became deathly silent as Aarya padded closer. Shakti stayed still, not wanting to give the new empress the satisfaction of seeing her cower or squirm. *Empress — hah*. She must be delighted at having given herself power after poisoning Arush.

For a moment, Aarya watched her with a kind of detached curiosity. Each passing moment sent Shakti's heart beating faster in terrified anticipation. *What was she waiting for?*

'You're an audacious one,' Aarya finally remarked as she produced a slim dagger and crouched in front of her. 'You tell me secrets. Invade my dreams again. But you were too weak, weren't you? You slipped.'

Would she pierce her with that dagger? Shakti wouldn't be surprised if Aarya did. Her pulse quickened as the empress brought it closer to her, and in response, she edged further and further back until she hit the wall with nowhere else to go. 'I needed . . .' Shakti began, breath hitching as Aarya placed the dagger right beneath her jaw, '. . . answers.'

'Answers?' Aarya hissed. The blade's tip was cold. 'You illusioned yourself to be my father *again*. You keep—' She paused, as if trying to collect herself. 'I will carve into your back like I did the last time if you reattempt it. Make sure the scar remains permanent. You will not violate me any more; I'll make sure of it.'

Violate. As if *she* was the victim. As if she hadn't forced Shakti to cast a curse. Shooting Aarya the most murderous glare she could muster, Shakti made to edge to the side, but the dagger followed her every move. 'You made me curse,' she spat.

There came a sharp prick beneath her jaw as Aarya retracted her dagger. The tip came away with a single splatter of red. 'So, you remember?' she asked, incredulous. But when Shakti didn't respond, Aarya shot her a smug, knowing grin. 'Ah, but you don't *really* remember, do you? Who the curse was for. How utterly terrible. Does the guilt eat away at you, mayakari? Because I hope it does. I hope you spend your days wondering when the curse enacts, or if it already has.'

'Tell me what you asked!'

The cruel upturn of Aarya's lips made Shakti want to curl into herself again. 'I wonder what else you don't remember,' she said, before snapping her fingers. 'Oh, yes. Causing me more turmoil. Telling me my aunt was a witch. Do you remember that? What a conversation that turned out to be with my mother. Dreading the possibility that I had witch blood. Even in a state of delirium, you were trying to play mind games with me.'

Momentarily caught off-guard, Shakti fell silent. She'd said that? That was a vague conversation she recalled having with Adil in the Collective. Empress Manali's adopted sister, Subhadrangi, was a mayakari. Adil had her burned. The empress had told her children she'd died from an illness – both an act of cruelty and self-preservation.

'I was hoping to spare my mother the knowledge that her husband's consciousness rests inside a witch, but alas. Between Arush's health and this new information, she's quite overwhelmed,' Aarya continued. There must've been confusion on Shakti's face, for she laughed. 'I see. You don't remember telling me that, either, do you?'

'How can I? You drugged me and made me forget,' Shakti gritted out, 'and I hate you for it.'

Aarya clucked in mock-sympathy. 'It tortures you, doesn't it? Not knowing.'

Her fury boiled over. 'Of course, it does!' Shakti screamed. 'At this point, I would rather die but you won't kill me! Why won't you kill me?'

The empress' expression stilled and turned inscrutable. She had been watching Shakti scream as if it were nothing more than a child's dramatization. 'Do you want to die?' she asked.

What would death feel like?

No, Shakti. Death is not meant for you yet.

'Yes,' she spat out. 'Do it. End my life.'

A statement uttered out of anger, aimed to goad, but a small part of Shakti wished for it all the same. She wouldn't get a rebirth, but at least she could be free of this nightmare.

'Liar,' Aarya replied softly. 'Death is not what you want. I told you before, witch – you seem like the type to fight death just to steal back the chance to live, and I'm going to give you a reason to live. And behave. An offer. You have yourself to thank for it.'

Offer? Shakti's head snapped up. At her inquisitive expression, Aarya smiled, delighted. 'I thought that might interest you. A conditional offer.'

Though she was loathe to accept any offer from Aarya, Shakti couldn't help her curiosity. 'What's in it for me?' she asked.

'To have your wounds attended to,' Aarya replied, 'To have no more milk of poppy forced down your throat.'

Glancing down at the lacerations on her arms and legs, and feeling the uncomfortable twinge on her back, Shakti was inclined to agree to whatever it was. Some wounds were badly infected. If she declined and left them untreated, her body would start to decay further. She could get blood poisoning, go into shock, or have her organs fail. It would be a slow, painful, unwanted death.

'What are your conditions?' Shakti asked curiously.

Aarya let out a slow, satisfied catlike grin. 'You will not invade my dreams again. Instead, you will use your . . . abilities on my behalf,' she said. 'You will follow through with my orders. Execute them without question.'

A wager not even a seasoned gambler would make. The orders called for her to be a soldier with no voice. 'If you despise my kind so much, Empress, then why would you ever employ our abilities?'

'I am not employing other mayakari,' Aarya replied, wrinkling her nose as if the very thought was nauseating. 'I am using you alone because you have someone they don't. Count yourself lucky — it is the only reason you haven't been burned alive.'

Adil. His consciousness was both a blessing and a curse. 'Using your father to justify using my abilities is no excuse.'

'Hah. It's not just my father, witch,' Aarya scoffed, twisting one of the diamonds hanging around her throat. 'Count yourself, too. Or have you already forgotten what you promised me back then?'

You want to conquer the world? I can help you, princess.

Shakti remembered the moment, but it had been a last-ditch attempt at saving her own hide. Part of her almost knew that Aarya would never accept a mayakari's help, and yet here they were. Witches used to be employed as mediators between humans and the land. Whatever Aarya needed her abilities for, Shakti hazarded that it was nothing good.

'No,' she spat out. If Aarya wouldn't kill her, there was no reason to help her, either. 'I will never help *you.*'

'Oh,' Aarya sounded far too calm about this. 'You think my father's consciousness is leverage.'

'Isn't it?'

'No,' Aarya remarked. 'A prideful creature, aren't you? If the promise of tending to those disgusting wounds of yours isn't enough, there is more incentive.'

Before Shakti could inquire what exactly Aarya had in mind, the empress glanced over her shoulder and yelled out, 'Bring her in.'

The hairs on the back of her neck prickled. Moments later, the door of the cell flew open. Scuffling was heard outside the door for a moment, before an additional guard arrived, bringing with her a woman shackled in iron chains and bound with a cloth gag. Shakti's heart rate rose instantly, body stiffening, paralysing her like lionfish venom.

'*Harini,*' she choked out.

I thought I told you to leave, Shakti wanted to scream out. Her friend's eyes were blood red, hair matted. How had they found her?

'One of Ashoka's. You can't fault me for being suspicious of the staff my brother chose to assign for himself over the years,' Aarya said, her smile unsettling. 'Imagine my surprise when I ordered for his female staff to be accounted for, only to find out that one had mysteriously left the palace before I could have them drink the Ghost Queen tea. Rest assured that in my city, you can't hide for long. You will be found. Unfortunately, by the time we located her, I had no more of the Ghost Queens left, but her little finger burned blue.'

'Don't hurt her,' Shakti said desperately. '*Please.*'

From the upturn in Aarya's lips, Shakti knew she was trapped. 'Her safety depends on your cooperation,' the empress replied. 'Obey my commands, and she will remain alive.'

'I can curse you.'

'Curse me and she'll burn for your transgression. Besides, there's always the chance I'll live longer than her if you do.'

So unfazed by the thought of being cursed. Or was she? Silently, Shakti searched the empress' face, only to come up short. Nothing in Aarya's expression gave her away.

Harini stared with a pleading expression, almost as if to say *please, let me live.* Hunching her shoulders, Shakti looked away, gritting her teeth.

Shame washed over her, but cold, harsh reality followed soon after. Harini couldn't suffer. She had to live, and for her to live, Shakti had to obey. Wracking her brains, Shakti considered her options. The ideal scenario was to escape Aarya and this hellish prison, but to do so was near impossible.

I have no choice.

'Fine,' she said. 'I'll agree to your demands, but you must not harm Harini.'

Twisting her lips like she had just received some rather unpleasant news, Aarya nodded. 'It is settled,' she said. 'I will have a physician bring you a healing tonic and tend to your wounds. Rest today, and you will be up early tomorrow.'

Out of the cell. Shakti frowned. 'For what?'

Aarya smiled, but it was unsettling. It recalled the eerie stillness of a cobra before it attacked. 'I command. You obey without question,' she said, clearly sidestepping the question. Shakti had the feeling it was done on purpose to heighten her unease. 'I shall see you in the morning, witch. Don't forget whose life hangs in the balance.'

CHAPTER SEVEN
Ashoka

THE SAMNAL RIVER GLITTERED UNDER THE FADING BLUISH moonlight as Ashoka saw the outline of buildings in the city of Luth come into view from the bow of his boat. Above him, the moon was slowly descending. Sunrise wasn't far away. He let himself enjoy the quiet sounds of water lapping against the hull, the hooting of owls, the chirping of crickets and the soft gush of wind.

He, Rahil, Sau and Naila had left Taksila on a boat in the midnight hour after the citywide lockdown was enacted. The capital city of the state of Devram to the west, Luth was the closest port city to Trikalinga, as the Samnal River eventually emptied out into the Odhi Ocean.

The journey to Luth from Taksila took roughly the same time as it took to the capital city: a day and half, give or take a few hours depending on how many rest stops a traveller took. Along the way, they'd moored once to sleep and docked by local townships twice to replenish their food and water supplies.

From Luth, they would leave the boat at a holding dock and charter a large passenger ship towards Trikalinga.

It was just the four of them, with Rahil navigating the vessel. Sau and Naila were asleep in the cramped cockpit. The boat was too small. Stifling. He wanted to be up in the skies, the cold vicious and unforgiving against his skin.

Ashoka had wanted to take Sahry since she was able to fly long distances without tiring but it was too risky. Word that an opalescent winged serpent was seen flying towards Trikalinga would spread quickly and reach Aarya's ears. Neither would it take long for his sister to determine whose beast it was, since Sahry was the only opal-coloured serpent in the empire. Instead, he'd left her in Nayani's care. Despite Sahry being well-known for being a general menace and shirking away from anyone other than him, she was calm around witches. All animals tended to be.

Out of instinct, Ashoka reached under his cloak, fingers dipping into the satchel slung across his chest to feel for Queen Kalyani's letter. He'd often found himself repeating the same action since leaving Taksila. This was paranoia working. Wanting to make sure it hadn't got lost somewhere along the way. Without it, his entry would be denied.

Old memories of Queen Kalyani were all he had. He'd never spoken to her, only seen her present during rare dignitary visits as a young child. Though the Ran Empire and Kingdom of Kalinga maintained stiff pleasantries and mutual trade agreements, the queen disagreed vehemently with his father's relentless persecution of the mayakari. It was one of the rare times he knew of anyone opposing his father.

But it didn't serve her well to meddle with the affairs of another state, especially one with a large military. How unfortunate then, that it was exactly what Ashoka wanted her to do.

A sudden, loud chorus of flutes and wind chimes startled Ashoka out of his reverie. Minor spirits. Their voices came from the pockets of forests on both sides of the river. Ashoka stood and listened until eventually they faded as the forests slowly shifted into flat land the closer the boat approached the city.

Sleep escaped him. Nervousness and trepidation continued to keep him awake. At best, he could force himself into sleep on the passenger ship bound for Trikalinga. For the time being, Ashoka continued to observe the river in tense silence.

By the time they arrived at Luth's riverport two hours later, the world was beginning to stir awake. Soft purple streaks dotted the sky. After Rahil secured the boat and paid the keeper, they made their way into the city centre. Getting to the main seaport required them to cut through it.

Pastel-washed buildings were clustered together like sardines. The roads were damp and slippery. The soft shuffling of stragglers and the odd, sharp clicks of canes against the footpath were audible. By accident, he bumped shoulders with a pair of inebriated women stalking out of a tavern who swore at his clumsiness. He saw Rahil's hands reach for his weapons before they relaxed as the women walked away.

Despite the hour and their situation, Ashoka found himself relaxing. There was something endearingly peaceful about the temperate silence. Other than Rahil, there was no one watching him, no one who bowed at every appearance. For now, there was freedom in no one knowing him or his name.

A crisp chill surrounded them as the group wandered down to the port where flames from oil lamps were dotted between every berth. Small boats lined the docks closest to them, the smell of salt and fish pungent. Larger ships were stationed towards the end. By the sea, there was far more activity. Workers loaded crates onto ships, fishermen hauled their nets to their boats, and merchants dragged their wares down planks. Ashoka would have kept walking had Rahil not grabbed his shoulder in a firm press. He had stopped in front of a moderately-sized passenger ship that was allowing several people on board.

'Wait here, Prince Ashoka,' he said. 'Let me speak to the privateer.'

'I'll come with you,' Naila offered.

Prince Ashoka, Prince Ashoka, Prince Ashoka.

Even now? he thought. Rahil was already walking away with Naila beside him, so he couldn't see his disappointed expression. Although Ashoka had a strong inkling that Sau had. Determined to avoid her eyes, he focused on Rahil and Naila as they stopped in front of a tall, plainly dressed woman and began to speak to her.

While they talked, Ashoka wandered away to observe the sea. The heavy thump of footsteps behind him told that Sau had followed. Stopping in his tracks, he turned to face her. 'Are you all right, Sau?' he asked. He anticipated her response would be a simple 'yes' or 'no'.

'Care to tell me about your lovers' quarrel?' Sau asked instead, tone light as she wrapped her cloak tighter around herself.

Ashoka stiffened. 'Excuse me?' he ground out. 'Lovers' quarrel? That's not—'

Sau's forceful, knowing gaze stripped him bare, every fragile little emotion laid out for careful inspection. Though satisfying to see her intensity directed at others, it was uncomfortable when turned on him. He wanted to look away but that would only provoke her further. 'Did you think I wouldn't notice the monstrous unease between you two?' she replied. 'Or are you going to treat me like I'm an idiot?'

His shoulders drooped. 'No,' he admitted. When she continued to stare expectantly, he winced. 'I . . . it's childish. After I killed Governor Kosala, Rahil . . . he judged me for it. We had an argument. I told him to stop pretending to be my moral compass. It's insulted him to an unfathomable degree.'

'Oh.' A note of relief passed through Sau's voice. 'And here I was thinking that something far worse had transpired. Respectfully, Ashoka, you're both idiots.'

'*Far worse?*' he echoed, flummoxed, ignoring her jab. 'Rahil won't speak to me!'

'Because you insulted him,' Sau replied with the temperament of a resigned schoolteacher. 'Did you—'

'Apologize? On multiple occasions.' It was a relief to purge his bottled-up thoughts. After all, Rahil hadn't been there to listen to him. 'He hates me.'

'Did he tell you that?'

Tell me you hate me. 'No.' Admitting it made him feel more childish.

To his utter confusion, Sau shot him an amused smile. 'He doesn't hate you,' she said. 'He could never, but we both know Rahil can be petty. Don't you remember when I called his singing "an ear-splitting nightmare"?'

Despite himself, Ashoka let out a chuckle. He remembered it vividly. When they were younger, Rahil had a habit of singing an old lullaby of his mother's on a whim. His singing could have made baby birds cry, but Ashoka had been too polite to tell him that he could neither carry nor hold a tune. Sau, meanwhile, did not waste her words on niceties. As a result, Rahil had petulantly refused to speak to her for several days.

'I should shake some sense into him,' Ashoka remarked.

'Yes, you should,' Sau agreed. 'Although, I can understand why he's like this.'

'You do?'

'You've shattered an illusion,' Sau replied, shrugging. 'For so long, you've been adamant on who you are. Even when others have suggested violence in the past, you refused it, and it has become an expected response. Suddenly, you kill a governor in his absence. I think, to Rahil, who you are now doesn't correlate with who you have always been.'

Ashoka frowned. 'You think I should apologize to him for that?'

'Not necessarily,' she replied. 'But maybe you can understand why he's hurt.'

'There's no reason for him to be hurt over that. Besides, he was the one who advised that I learn the middle path,' Ashoka said, exasperation worming into his veins. 'But now *I'm* the wrongdoer?'

Sau arched her brows. 'I know, but you killed a man, Ashoka,' she said, enunciating each word with painstaking slowness. '*You.*'

He scowled. 'Yes. So what?' he shot back, voice hard. The image of Kosala's blood, pooling thick and fast from his neck, ran through his mind anew. The old governor now lay buried, rotting in the grounds of his home, noncremated as the bastard deserved. When a baffled expression flashed across Sau's face, he retreated. 'I'm sorry.'

'You apologize for no reason,' she said. 'Can I ask you a question?'

'Anything.'

'Would you do it again?' she asked. 'Kill?'

Part of him wanted to avenge the remnants of his past self and say no, but there was only one right answer. 'Yes,' he said, noting the way Sau's eyes widened at the speed of his response. 'There can be righteous violence. I've learned that the hard way.'

For a long time, Sau said nothing. Then, 'It would be hypocritical of me to disagree,' she replied, 'but for spirits' sake, make peace with Rahil or I will throw you both overboard. You're both adults – there should be no need for a mediator.'

'I told you I've tried,' he muttered.

'Try harder. He just needs some pretty words. *Honest* words,' she remarked. 'You love him, don't you? Why continue being angry when you can be the bigger person and – what?'

At that moment, Ashoka couldn't tell what he looked like. His throat went dry. Sau's voice descended to the dull buzz of a honeybee. It was as if someone had sliced open his chest, torn apart his ribcage, reached in to pull out his heart and placed it inside a glass box for display. How he wished his heart was made of something stronger, like a diamond. Harder to shatter, harder to hurt. But alas, it was nothing but flimsy red muscle.

'Ah.' Sau's voice held a note of sympathy. 'Forgive me, but you are quite obvious. As is he.'

As is he.

'As is . . . he?' Ashoka echoed. 'What do you mean?'

Sau shrugged. 'I don't know,' she replied in a tone that signalled she very much did. 'In Makon, I found that once I got Rahil inebriated with enough bitter plum spirits, he'll mention your name in every second sentence. Make of that what you will.'

Ashoka's heart jolted. 'I'm not sure how to,' he said.

Sau appeared as if she were about to affectionately berate him more, but they were interrupted by the sound of Naila's voice. 'We can board the ship,' she called out, waving her arms excitedly. 'Come.'

'Ah, right on time,' Sau commented before grabbing his arm with one hand and pulling the hood of his cloak further over his head with the other. Ashoka grabbed her hand, pressing it tightly.

'What did you mean?' he asked. 'When you—'

'Like I said,' Sau replied, looking maddeningly smug, 'make peace with each other. You can't afford to be distracted.'

Ashoka paused. 'So, love is . . . a distraction.'

He'd meant it as a straightforward remark, but Sau seemed to interpret his words as a question. 'It becomes a distraction only if you let it,' she said, frowning. Such practical sentiment wasn't unusual for her. 'Don't twist my words. I only meant that you're both being childish.'

Sau's previous remarks of an inebriated Rahil lingered. He

couldn't move past it. 'Does he love me, too?' Ashoka asked her quietly.

'That's a question you should ask Rahil,' Sau replied. 'Settle this silly argument. In your case, love can make you a passionate leader. Just make sure it doesn't become your worst attachment.'

CHAPTER EIGHT
Shakti

Shakti had been given several healing tonics.

Part of her wanted to refuse when she saw one of the vials coloured a milky white. Memories flashed of her jaw being forced open, swallowing a cream-coloured concoction, spitting the foul-tasting liquid out.

The physician, a gruff, balding man, snapped at her initial refusal, asked if she would rather suffer instead, and finally assured her the tonic didn't contain milk of poppy.

What if she lied to me, Shakti wondered as she held the vial up. *What if this makes me worse?*

'Hurry up, mayakari,' the physician ordered.

Without a better option, Shakti threw her head back and swallowed the tonic in one go.

Despite the tonic not containing milk of poppy, there must've been a different sedative mixed into it, for when Shakti awoke, she couldn't remember how she fell asleep.

I can't keep forgetting. This is—

She winced. Dizzying, ghastly afterimages flooded her mind like a torrential downpour. Skin being stripped down to bone. Bone being taken to with a chisel and mallet, bleeding fresh and red. Soft murmurs of a killer in the dark, weapon raised and ready to strike. Then came the whisper – eerie and gentle:

Want you to hurt . . . pride.

That was new. The fragments sounded like Aarya's voice, but what was it – a memory lived, or a memory made?

Shakti coughed irritably, unable to come to a solid conclusion. Rheum had collected at the corner of her eyes, making it uncomfortable to blink. Picking it away, she focused her attention on her surroundings to ground herself: four walls, door, stone floor. Her muscles felt oddly lethargic and stiff, as if she had not used them for months. Jaya's pendant against her neck was cool on her skin.

Spirits. How long had she slept?

It took her some time to reorient herself before noticing two changes. The first was her body. Bandages were wrapped around her arms, back and legs; some areas already stained a yellowish red. The second was a roughly hewn mattress upon which she had been sleeping. The material chafed any exposed skin, but it wasn't as unpleasant as sleeping on stone. She wondered if Harini had been afforded the same grace.

As she moved, her shackles rattled. The noise must have alerted the guard outside, for the door to her cell opened and a clean-shaven man peered in. His stance was cautious, one hand not visible, likely gripping onto his sword. When his gaze drifted down to the floor where she lay slumped against the wall, his eyes narrowed.

'You're awake,' the guard stated. He sounded disappointed.

'How long was I asleep?' she asked, the shackles around her wrists clanging dully against stone. No doubt the Ran soldiers would rejoice if she was found dead in her cell.

The guard ignored her. 'I shall have the empress notified,' he remarked, more to himself than her.

'*How long was I asleep?*' she asked again, this time with more force. Her tone must have infuriated the man, for he shot her a venomous glare.

'Watch your tongue, witch,' he snapped, 'the empress has been quite generous in ordering a physician to attend to you. If it were up to me, you would be long dead.'

'If I had the strength, I would curse you into your next rebirth,' she retorted.

Abject fear ran across his face as the guard stepped back and slammed the cell door shut. Drained, Shakti let out a half-hearted chuckle before resting the back of her head against the wall. These people were so consumed by false stories that they really thought a mayakari starved of nature, strength and will would curse them without a second thought.

Thankfully, her body didn't feel like it was about to burn from the inside. Sweat didn't coat her like a second skin as it had before. Though Shakti was tired, she didn't feel weak.

Death is not meant for you yet.

She frowned. That sounded like Emperor Ashoka's voice.

Let me tell you a story. One of a warrior, a mayakari and a Great Spirit.

It *was* his voice. Or at least, a memory of it. He did tell her that she'd asked him for a story, though now it came in bits and pieces, not quite whole.

... the mayakari taught the warrior ... the Great Spirit, angered by the warrior, destroyed its own domain ... sapped the warrior of strength ... slept while life and death flourished ...

She couldn't recall the rest. She stared numbly at the floor, thinking of Harini. Time must've passed quicker than she thought. Though Shakti assumed only a few minutes had passed since her brief conversation with the guard, her cell door opened.

Aarya sauntered into the cell, as smug as the patchwork cat that used to steal into her and Jaya's home in search of food. She was dressed in midnight blue training gear, stripped of all kohl, rouge and jewellery save for a thin, gold necklace from which a small moonstone dangled. 'Finally awake, are you?' she asked.

'How long was I asleep?' Shakti couldn't stand to repeat herself any further.

'Careful, mayakari,' Aarya crooned, 'don't forget my title – empress, now. You slept for two days.'

'*Two days?*' she echoed. Her body must have been spent. A sudden panic coursed through her. 'Harini – where is she? Is she—'

'The mayakari is alive for now,' Aarya replied in a dismissive tone. 'Do you feel better? You don't look as close to death.'

Shakti huffed. 'Not well enough to fight you yet,' she replied.

It was with pure condescension that Aarya watched her. 'You know, Master Kudha was surprised to learn you were a mayakari. She wondered how a witch, of all people, had learned to fight so well.'

'Upset that I can best you?'

'Don't flatter yourself. I get irritated by anyone who bests me,' Aarya replied in a rare moment of candour, 'but you're a witch who has picked up a sword and fights . . . decently. There is an added humiliation to it.' She couldn't seem to bring herself to say that Shakti was superior in swordplay. It bothered and delighted her at once.

'Are you really so surprised when the oppressed start to fight back, Empress?' Shakti asked. The question prompted a fleeting frown to cross Aarya's face before she stood and motioned for the soldiers behind her to approach.

'Unshackle her,' she ordered.

Shakti stilled. A shiver ran down her spine. 'You're releasing me?'

Aarya let out a bark of laughter. 'Release?' she chuckled. 'Stupid witch. You're a leopard with a muzzle. You are not free.' She smiled, but it was unsettling. It recalled the rumble before a thunderclap.

'Then what?'

'Is your memory so addled that you've already forgotten our agreement?' Aarya asked her. 'I command. You obey. Now, get up.'

CHAPTER NINE
Ashoka

Defensive stone walls loomed like giants as their charter ship sailed into the Port of Trikalinga, capital of the Kalingan Kingdom. Atop the thick walls were turrets where Ashoka could spot soldiers stationed next to cannons. The carved bronze image of a giant sea dragon formed the archway of the entry gate.

Shielding his eyes from the glare of the sun, Ashoka took a sharp intake of breath as the city came into view. Trikalinga was a masterpiece of architecture blending seamlessly with its landscape. Upon enormous hilly terrain, thousands upon thousands of dwellings large and small were built, crowds of people travelling up and down roads like ants in a cave. Kalingan buildings were not as colourful as the ones in the Golden City; simple brick and stone houses were painted ironwood brown or an unusual greyish white. Only the more ostentatious buildings had domes coloured sky blue or aquatic green.

A singular lighthouse was built right in the middle of the ocean, it too fortified by small vessels. There was markedly less artillery here than in the ports of the Ran Empire, but the number of naval vessels far eclipsed theirs.

Their charter ship docked in the bustling port. Amongst the many trading and passenger ships, myriad Kalingan battleships dotted the area in an excessive display of naval aggression. He also noted several vessels marked with the silver crest of the Ridi Empire.

While Rahil and Sau stayed behind to pay the captain, Ashoka and Naila disembarked, pushed forward by the moving current of the crowd. Queen Kalyani's letter was still tucked safely inside his satchel. He'd continued to check its presence consistently since boarding the ship.

'Remarkable,' Naila murmured, her voice filled with joy. Ashoka smiled. She had never been outside the confines of Taksila, so seeing an entirely new kingdom would be novel for her. 'Oh – Prince Ashoka, look up!'

He followed her upward gaze to see multiple aerial bodies darting in and out of the clouds. 'Winged serpents,' he remarked. Dwarfing the gulls and crows, the serpents were present in droves. Save for those whom he assumed also to be visitors, no one else spared them a second glance. They were native to Kalinga, after all, and therefore not an unusual sight to its citizens. How unfortunate that he'd had to leave Sahry behind.

'The fee is settled,' came Rahil's voice behind him. 'Let's go – it'll be a long walk to the palace.'

Situated on the highest peak, the royal palace was hard to miss. A giant stone and marble structure the colour of the sea on a perfect summer day, it had a dozen interconnecting turrets with the Kalingan flag fluttering in the breeze. Roofs of many of the domed main buildings, he guessed, were built using glass, given it reflected light the same way the ocean did, sparkling like shattered diamonds. Though not as large as the Golden Palace, it stood out like a lone blue lotus growing amongst a sea of unbudded stems.

At the mention of the palace, Ashoka saw Naila clutch the ends of her cloak tighter.

'You aren't in Taksila, Naila,' he reminded her. 'There are no flames to fear.'

Sau squeezed her shoulder, a gesture that seemed to relax the young mayakari. 'The mayakari aren't persecuted here,' she said. 'Is that not good?'

'No,' Naila replied, her face pinched. 'That's infuriating.'

Ashoka reminisced back to when they first met; him holding the decapitated body of her friend, and she the lopped head. He hadn't quite known how to comfort her then, except to promise, 'I'll make certain it will never happen again.'

'Be careful with promises, Prince Ashoka,' Naila had replied sombrely. 'Some tend to be curses in disguise.'

Clucking his tongue, Rahil motioned them forward. 'We should get going,' he told them. He sounded tired. Ashoka wanted to comfort him but kept quiet. 'Dally and we waste valuable time.'

Despite Rahil's insistence on no delays, he was the only one in their party who succumbed to distraction. Drawn to a striking merchant's shop, they had to haul him away from attempting to barter for a curved mixed-metal blade with an emerald inlaid on its hilt. Ashoka made an offhand remark about how Rahil would have paid too much for it and the jewel would likely have been a counterfeit. It had been entirely extemporary, but perhaps his tone suggested otherwise, for Rahil had shot him a look so withering that his skin felt suddenly desiccated. He didn't miss Sau's exasperated expression either — a very pointed *have you not made amends yet?*

He hadn't. Of course he hadn't. Despite coaxing himself into making conversation with Rahil multiple times on the ship, Ashoka always lost his courage at the last moment. Fear and pride held him back. The punishment was self-imposed.

Waiting with the queues to pass through the palace gates felt even more punishing. They were all restless from their journey, impatiently awaiting entry to see the queen. Amongst the Kalingan soldiers, Ashoka spotted the telltale all-black uniform of Ridi soldiers as well. Briefly, he wondered if there was a Ridi dignitary visiting the palace before concluding that there were far too many troops for one person alone.

'Halt,' the guard closest to him ordered, spears blocking their entrance. 'What business have you here?'

Behind him, Rahil tensed. Ashoka put his right hand up, both to halt Rahil and to show peace. 'I come bearing a letter from Queen Kalyani,' he replied. 'She has requested an audience.'

The soldier opposite them let out a disbelieving huff. 'A letter?' she scoffed. 'Personal letters are rarely sent to commoners.'

'Would you like to read it yourself?' Ashoka said, keeping his tone pleasant as he produced the letter. Impatience was already stretching its claws, ready to cause damage. 'It would be a shame to keep a guest waiting.'

Narrowing her eyes, the female soldier plucked the letter from his hands. The seal was already broken, but recognition flashed across the soldier's face as she opened the letter and began to read its contents. When she finally glanced up, she pointed to the hood of his cloak which he removed. The circlet around his head was the only symbol he needed.

'*Prince* Ashoka Maurya?' she asked, appearing somewhat bewildered. The soldier opposite her blinked in rapid succession, as if he couldn't believe what he was seeing. 'The queen did indeed mention your arrival, but . . . are you not here with a formal party?'

'An informal one,' he replied. 'I'm here with my guard and . . . two advisors.'

'A rather unusual entry, you must understand,' the soldier remarked. 'Royals typically arrive with much more . . . fanfare.'

'I understand, soldier,' Ashoka said. 'Next time, I shall bring a ship filled with giant leopards and gold carriages. Now, may I be taken to see your queen?'

His sarcasm swept them into action. 'Of course, Prince Ashoka,' the female soldier said with a bow.

They were shepherded through the gates, where a new group of guards accompanied them past the courtyard and up the seemingly endless flight of stairs. Gargantuan wooden doors opened with an ancient groan to reveal an expansive passageway tiled with intricate mosaics depicting images of the sea. Towering white pillars were engraved in Kalingan script. Ashoka understood enough to know its meaning: *conquer not for the sake of conquering.*

He felt Sau sidle up next to him. 'Did you notice the Ridi soldiers?' she murmured, tipping her chin up to whisper in his ear.

'Along with their ships,' Ashoka replied, nodding. 'But is that a cause for concern? They're longstanding trading partners.'

Sau shook her head, clearly perturbed. 'Yes, but . . . the number of soldiers we passed in the city was abnormal.'

Just as Ashoka was about to placate Sau's worries, he was

interrupted by one of their accompanying guards as they halted in front of yet another door, this one created from iron.

'The throne room lies just beyond, Prince Ashoka,' she informed him, and pushed open the door.

The scent of wild orange, sea salt, and sandalwood wafted over him the moment he stepped inside. He was immediately struck by the sight. Where the throne room of the Ran Empire was a vision painted by night itself, the Kalingan throne room was befitted in warm, aureate colours. Two inbuilt pools lay on either side, the centre path tiled with lustrous white mosaic that led up to a series of stairs to where, backed by crested flags, an elaborately carved wooden throne stood alone.

Seated upon the throne was a woman around his mother's age. The closer he approached the base of the steps, the more her profile came into view. Tall, with tightly curled hair that hung loose at her waist, and a distinct white butterfly-shaped lesion across her cheeks. An ornate gold crown interwoven with precious coral and pearls sat atop her head. She wore something of a modified sari coloured a deep, deep green. The drape and blouse were similar to the fashions of the Ran Empire, but instead of the usual skirt, the queen wore loose, tapered trousers which the drape was pinned into. Ashoka couldn't help but think it was more suitable for a fight.

'Prince Ashoka Maurya and his party from the Ran Empire, Queen Kalyani,' a booming voice behind them announced.

Queen Kalyani watched him advance with inscrutable eyes. *Yes, the hazy memories of her remained the same from dignitary dinners long past.* She held the same aura of inscrutability; an entity unknown to him, beholden to nothing but her people and the seas.

Suddenly, Ashoka felt like an ant surrounded by a dozen human feet ready to crush his body without remorse. The gravity of the situation sunk in. He was in Trikalinga, speaking to their queen about furthering his own agenda. Garnering support to take a throne he couldn't claim, because he was left out of his father's will.

This was a mistake.

No, he reeled his anxiety in. *Don't second guess yourself now.*

His anxiety, albeit disgruntled, crawled back into the deep dark cave to which it was habituated.

'Prince Ashoka Maurya,' Queen Kalyani greeted him, a curious but hospitable smile on her lips. Her voice was deep like Sau's. Pleasant. She spoke in the Ran language, but the accent was softer. 'Welcome to Trikalinga.'

He bowed, as did his friends. 'Queen Kalyani,' he replied, 'thank you for accepting my request for an audience.'

The queen stood, and he spotted the same white patches across her face in irregular, haphazard marks on her arms. 'How could I not?' she asked. 'Asking to be viewed separately from your empire, and in the same sentence, asking for a favour. You are an enigma, Prince Ashoka.'

Ignoring Sau's furtive whisper of *what in spirits' name did you write to her?* he shot her what he hoped to be a self-assured smile. 'On the contrary, I have long been told that I'm anything but, Queen Kalyani.'

'Disloyal, then,' the queen replied.

He frowned. 'Disloyal?'

'You are actively committing treason against your own blood by seeing me without royal consent. Is that not disloyal?'

'Is it?' he asked. 'Considering that it is necessary for the greater good?'

Queen Kalyani snapped a finger at him. 'There it is: *the greater good*,' she said. 'That is why you interest me. What is it that forced you to come here seeking my help? What is it that turned you from your brother – or rather, sister – at this time? My sincerest condolences for your brother, I must add.'

'Arush isn't dead,' Ashoka replied.

'But a poison-induced sleep? He may as well be.' Queen Kalyani stepped closer. As she did, she wrinkled her nose. 'I would like to speak with you further. You shall join me for dinner, Prince Ashoka, but first I shall have you and your party escorted to the guest quarters.'

His audience would be delayed. 'But—' he began, and was swiftly silenced.

'I insist,' she stressed. 'Although Kalingans pride themselves on being children of the sea, we do not care to smell heated leather and day-old mackerel.'

CHAPTER TEN
Shakti

Hands shackled, Shakti was led out of the palace prisons and into an oddly familiar study room.

Aarya led the way, leaving Shakti to glare at the back of her neck while two soldiers walked on either side of her. Resting atop the empress' head, the royal circlet taunted her. Briefly, she entertained the fantasy of catching Aarya unawares, pressing a dagger between her shoulder blades and cutting a straight line down her back. Separating skin and inner muscle to reveal the sharp bones of her spine.

Little bird, stop.

Too violent. Too distanced from how a proper mayakari should think and act. Shakti knew it but couldn't help herself. Harini's life was on the line, and here she was being made to act like a military dog to keep her friend safe. It made the thought of casual violence easier to digest. The empress had been largely quiet about what she wanted Shakti to do, but it didn't take a fool to assume the task to be entirely unpleasant.

To her surprise, Aarya ordered the soldiers to remain outside the study room once the door was opened. While she was barking out an order, Shakti observed the oddly familiar space. *Where had she seen it before?*

In the centre was a large desk made of na wood. Neat stacks of parchment and quills sat atop it, along with an empty lanternlight.

On the left wall was a large, coloured map of the Golden City. On the right wall hung portraits, beautifully drawn, of past monarchs including Adil. Behind the desk stood a row of bookshelves, some texts with their spines coloured gold, and it was then that Shakti realized why the room looked so familiar. She'd seen it when she invaded Aarya's dreams.

Before Shakti could confirm her theory, she heard a soft click and turned around, startled. Aarya had locked the door and was now watching her with an eerie expression. Shakti returned the look, not wanting to break.

What is it? she wondered. *More cursing? Dream invasion? What do you want?*

The thought of cursing made her stomach twist into knots. The unknown recipient of her mystery curse lingered in the back of her mind like a stain that was unable to be removed. An empty space in her mind that she should remember.

Despite herself, Shakti broke their eye contact by flicking her gaze towards the door. 'Don't want any observers, Empress?' she asked.

Aarya smiled, as if pleased by the fact that she'd won a petty staring competition. 'I'm not going to harm you,' she said, though Shakti heard the unspoken words as if they were being said aloud. *Not you. Not yet. The other witch, however, won't have the same privilege.*

'What is that you want me to do?' she asked.

Aarya laughed. 'Sounding more like a soldier,' she replied. 'Good. I assume you know what this room is, considering you invaded my dreams last night.'

'Adil's study,' Shakti answered, watching the empress' lips twitch downward at the mention of the late emperor's name without his title. Strangely enough, she didn't make any move to correct her. Perhaps the constant correction was fast becoming bothersome. Shakti took that as a minor victory.

'Yes. This was his private study. It was Arush's as well, but now it's mine. As you can see, he kept an extensive number of books here. Some texts were written by his own hand,' Aarya said. 'Some time ago, I was perusing his notes for any more information on Ghost Queens when I came across a few bound journals with notes scribbled in handwriting that wasn't his. The owner's name was so faded that I couldn't make head or tail of it. An "S" and perhaps a "u". Then, you so kindly told me in your delirium that my aunt was a witch. After confronting my mother, I realized these journals were hers: *Subhadrangi's*.

'I couldn't understand why Father kept these, but as I continued to read, I understood. There's a lot of useful information in them. Theories on the deadlands, for one. She postulated that magic affects magic, hence why the Ghost Queens it produces cause a reaction in the mayakari but not others.'

Shakti felt a nauseous reminder of the flower-infused tea she'd drunk and subsequently coughed up. At first she kept quiet, until she noticed Aarya's expectant expression. The empress was waiting for an answer.

'That's the main theory,' she replied, wondering where Aarya was going with this. 'Ghost Queens grow in deadlands, which themselves are formed when a Great Spirit dies an unnatural death. Since the mayakari and spirits are connected by magic in a way humans aren't, there's an argument to be made about why it affects us and not you. Like affects like, after all.'

Aarya listened with interest, but Shakti knew that it wasn't the same way Ashoka listened about the mayakari and the nature spirits. The prince did so out of academic interest. The empress did so that she could weaponize the knowledge for her own gain. Telling her felt wrong.

'And deadlands regrow,' she remarked. It wasn't uttered as a question.

'Yes, as nature always does,' Shakti said, 'but as I said, for us the land supposedly feels tainted. We can sense that something is inherently wrong.'

'Does it affect what you can do there?'

'What do you mean?'

'Speaking to spirits, summoning them,' Aarya responded.

'I—' Shakti paused. In truth, she didn't know. 'I'm not sure. Fortunately, I've never come across a deadland.'

The little hum Aarya let out sounded frustrated as she crossed the floor to stand in front of the city map. Shakti's eyes were drawn towards the illustration of the mountain east of the city. The artist had even painted the perpetual fog at its peak. 'The Mountain of Rebirth,' the empress began, 'is it considered a deadland?'

Shakti startled. It was a good question. She could understand why Aarya had posited it. Unfortunately for the empress, she was no scholar. All she had were stories and guesswork. 'Hard to say,' she admitted. 'One can make the argument that it is, but the mountain has been half alive, half dead since the first emperor's reign. Personally, I don't think it can be categorized as one.'

'Why?'

'Because its Great Spirit isn't dead,' Shakti responded. 'At least, I don't think it is. There's something wrong with the mountain and magic is involved, that much is clear. But the area has never withered completely. It flourishes and dies in equal measure. That isn't a deadland.'

'You're completely sure there's a Great Spirit?' Aarya questioned. What was her intention? Shakti couldn't see it. 'Some stories say it hasn't been seen—'

'Stories contain fiction,' Shakti interrupted. 'Fiction isn't truth. Perhaps you would have a better answer if Adil hadn't burned the Great Library and its mayakari along with it. My answer is based on intuition. You're not a mayakari; you'll never understand it.'

Pursing her lips, the empress crossed her arms and stalked towards the middle bookshelf in the back of the room. Warily, Shakti followed her, chains rattling with each step, an unwilling pet. All the while, possibilities were running amok in her head.

'If you're looking for Ghost Queens on the Mountain of Rebirth, I'd hazard you won't find any,' she told Aarya, who whirled around and gave her a cold glare.

'This isn't about Ghost Queens,' she snapped. 'I'm looking for something else.'

'The Great Spirit?'

'No. A group of youths found a strange mineral at the base of the mountain recently,' Aarya began. 'One dropped it, and it caused a small explosion. Scarred his entire right arm. They had the good sense to leave the area alone and report it.'

Shakti frowned. *An explosive mineral?* That was certainly new.

'I sent my soldiers out to investigate. They reported back saying that they found an abandoned tunnel with pieces of that same mineral visible,' Aarya continued. 'It was why I went through my father's old logbooks. He had information on every mining venture around the capital. In one such logbook, I found descriptions that matched the mineral the young boys and my soldiers had described, but nothing further. No record of tunnelling permits. Nothing. It's strange; my father was meticulous. This journal of my aunt's detailed much more than his. It describes the mineral as my father did, but also suggestions on how they tried to extract it.'

'May I see it?' Shakti asked. To her surprise, the empress turned back towards the shelves and pulled out an old, worn, inconspicuous leather journal before handing it to her. Interest piqued, Shakti flipped through the pages quickly, catching the faded name on the first page. Just as Aarya had told her, she could only make out a 'Su . . .'. The rest had faded away.

There were a lot of sketches of minor spirits and plants. Notes on the Mountain of Rebirth and its peculiarities. Observations on the length of time it took for a millipede walking along the ground to die and revive. The density of the mist. The general temperament of the minor spirits. A coloured drawing of a greenish rock, with the note beneath it saying 'cursed?'. That must be what Aarya was talking about.

Shakti kept flipping. On another page, she came across a perfect sketch of a man that she realized was a young Adil. Had the two once been friends? As she perused the book, Shakti became aware of Aarya keenly observing her. 'This is a far reach, mayakari,' she said, 'but would you happen to know what this mineral is?'

There was an odd glimmer of hope in the empress' eyes, barely visible behind the flint and fire that was usually sent her way. Shakti shook her head. She too, was intrigued. Her mind was racing through the possibilities. Was it difficult to handle in one's hands? What was its relative strength? How easy was it to mould? For a moment, she found herself back in Kolakola. Standing in Master Hasith's forge and observing him smelt a weapon. His explanations that she'd once found tedious returned with a sharp clarity.

'I thought as much,' she heard Aarya mutter. 'No matter. Time to put you to good use.'

'How? By sending me to an abandoned mine?'

The empress' jaw ticked. 'All in due time,' she said. 'Use your ability to speak to . . . my father. Find out what he knows. If he kept it hidden, there must have been a reason.'

Shakti's entire body stiffened. It was the first time that Aarya had acknowledged her abilities in a long while.

'I can speak to him tonight,' she began, 'it'll—'

'Not tonight,' Aarya interrupted. 'I want you to speak to my father here. *Now*. You should be healed enough.'

A sharp refusal was on the tip of her tongue, but Shakti held herself back. *Leopard with a muzzle.* That's what she was. A wild animal forced to bow under Aarya's command. How shameful. If there was no other threat looming over her shoulder, she would've declined out of sheer spite. Accepted the consequences, the punishment that awaited her. Perhaps then she could die without regret.

The empress seemed to mistake her prolonged silence for defiance. 'Decline, and I will burn your friend's fingers one by one. Then her toes. After that, her tongue.'

'I understood the first time you threatened Harini's life,' Shakti snapped. Wretched woman. 'All right. You have your wish, *Empress*.'

'Good. The study should provide you with enough privacy,' Aarya replied, gesturing dismissively around the room. 'No tricks.'

I'll kill your friend, otherwise.

At least the study was cleaner than the prison cell. Huffing, Shakti wandered to the wall where the portraits were hung. She sat on the floor, legs crossed and shifted into a meditative pose. The shackles made it difficult to lay her palms flat on top of each other, but she made do. Aarya watched her with lethal intensity the entire time.

'Well?' she asked impatiently as Shakti closed her eyes and let out a long exhale. 'What does this process entail? Are you going to start floating?'

'Your silence is preferable,' Shakti replied, eyes still closed. 'Otherwise, this won't work, and we'll be here all day.'

Thankfully, Aarya spoke no more after that, though Shakti hazarded that the young empress had some curt remarks ready for later. For the moment, she focused on the darkness. The uneven breathing. The shaky inhales and exhales, and the way her chest expanded and constricted with each one. Shakti didn't know how long she sat there, examining her breath as if she were a voyeur. Eventually, it evened out. Became regular. The healing tonics helped. There was little chance of her entering the Collective if her body was too exhausted.

Suddenly, there was a familiar tug at the pit of her stomach. Focusing on it, Shakti noted the appearance of a pale blue thread appearing in her mind's eye, waiting to be tugged. Imagining her own ghostly hands plucking the string, Shakti held a breath as the darkness turned into a bright array of colours. It was as if she were being pulled down rapids at a breakneck pace. Belatedly, she thought of Emperor Adil as the colours around her paled, turning into a startling white light.

Bright, bright, bright, until—

Shakti opened her eyes. The bleak, dark throne room greeted her. She'd appeared at the base of the steps to the Obsidian Throne. When she glanced up, a brief spark of fury coursed through her.

Sitting upon the throne was Emperor Adil.

It felt like aeons since she'd last seen him. The man who murdered her aunt. Her swords master. Her village. Dressed in battle armour, with a deep russet cape pinned to his back, and the royal circlet resting gracefully atop his head, Emperor Adil appeared every bit the walking terror that two of his children aimed to be. Sharp brown eyes pinned her in place. He made no move to stand. She made no move to bow.

'Adil,' Shakti remarked.

'Mayakari.' The word was uttered with an air of exhausted distaste. 'It has been some time since you called on me alone.'

She didn't bother with a curt rejoinder. 'I need your help,' she said. 'Or rather, your memories.'

'Of course. You're never here for no reason,' Adil replied.

'The reason is your daughter,' Shakti said, watching his eyebrows tick upwards in surprise. She needed to establish the rules quickly. Bringing Aarya in would make Adil more compliant. One of the late emperor's few weaknesses was his only daughter. 'She's commanded me to speak to you.'

'Aarya . . . knows?' Adil asked her, shock evident on his face. 'She knows I'm alive?'

'You're not alive,' Shakti retorted. 'Not really.'

'My physical body is gone, but I as an individual with thoughts continue to exist. Does that not make me a living being?'

Shakti groaned. He was pulling from old mayakari philosophies about the self. 'I'm not here to debate,' she said, and took a single step upward. Adil's expression remained impassive. 'This isn't what I want to be doing, either.'

'Ah, an unwilling messenger,' Adil laughed. 'My daughter has held something – or someone – against you, hasn't she?'

When Shakti glared, Adil clapped his hands together in glee. 'My golden daughter,' he preened. 'For her, I will give everything. What is it that she wants to know?'

Quickly Shakti reiterated Aarya's findings. The explosive mineral. The abandoned mine. The lack of tunnelling permits in his logbooks. Her aunt's journal. When she finished, Adil looked perturbed.

'You tell Aarya to leave that mineral alone,' he snapped, expression thunderous. 'Mining around the mountain will have disastrous consequences.'

Shakti had thought the same. Plundering the Mountain of Rebirth was a risky gamble. The place was no Deadland, but neither was it normal. 'But you've tried?' she pressed.

'I know a failed venture when I see one,' the late emperor responded.

'That's not a very good answer.'

'What do you want to hear, you wretched girl? That I did have the mountain mined? That it caused a disastrous mudslide? A flood? It did, which is why Aarya shouldn't. Leave the Mountain of Rebirth alone.'

His insistence was unusual. Here was an emperor that didn't

care one bit for cutting down forestland for natural resources telling her to avoid mining at any cost. 'What happened?' she asked. 'Did mining trigger the mudslide or . . . was it the spirit?'

Each question that she threw at him seemed to make Adil more tense. 'That mountain is not to be disturbed,' he reiterated. 'If there had been a way to safely extricate the mineral, don't you think I'd have tried?'

'How did you come to find it in the first place?' Shakti asked. When he didn't answer, she let out an aggrieved sigh. 'This is for your precious daughter, not me. At least show me that memory. I'll let her know of your concerns.'

The late emperor closed his eyes. A muscle ticked in his jaw. His hands clenched the throne's armrests. 'You ask for a memory, and I'm compelled to give you one,' he said, opening his eyes. He sounded like he'd rather discuss anything else. 'Fine. Let me show you, mayakari.'

Without another word, he swept his hand out. The throne room faded, and Adil along with it, leaving Shakti in complete darkness. A sudden buzz rang in her ears and only got louder. Disoriented, Shakti closed her eyes, and when she reopened them, found herself standing in front of a large ironwood door that was partially ajar.

She glanced around quickly. Or rather, *Adil* glanced around. The glass windows to her right reflected his face back at him. A more youthful, less harsh face. In this memory, he looked to be in his late twenties.

A lengthy corridor was behind her, a plush red rug covering the wooden floor. The walls were temple flower white. Impressive glass windows to her right streamed midday light on her skin. Between two windows hung an oil portrait of a middle-aged woman wearing a ruby circlet. Her features were sharp – like Adil's. His mother, Empress Sarla. It took Shakti some time to realize that she was in one of the royal wings. Was it his? She'd only ever set foot in Prince Ashoka's or Empress Aarya's chambers. The buzzing in her ears vanished, and slowly, Shakti heard voices coming from behind the door. It sounded like two women talking:

'. . . the library is beautiful. So many books on deadlands alone . . .'

'... glad you've found it interesting ...'

Because Shakti was viewing the memory through Adil's eyes, she couldn't simply push open the door to place the voices. She had to watch it play out. Though she didn't recognize the first voice, the second was familiar. Soft and lilting – it sounded like Empress Manali's. Was Adil eavesdropping on them?

'... the Mountain of Rebirth ... I think there's something buried there, Manali ...'

She-as-Adil had leaned in even closer to the door. In doing so, she became imbalanced, and her right arm knocked against the door with a soft *thud*. At the sound, the voices inside quietened. Moments later, she heard the shuffling of footsteps before the door was thrown open, and she came face to face with Empress Manali.

'Adil?' she asked, brows pinching.

Long, unlined black eyelashes. Plum-coloured rouge on her lips. A small, delicate nose. The empress had the same regal features, but they were a little softer. She looked about Aarya's age. She wore a plain black sari. A lone red saraca flower was nestled behind her left ear. On her right ring finger, a gold band winked in the light. Adil had one, too.

Adil cleared his throat. 'I was ... I came to get you, Manali,' he said gruffly. 'If you could join me for a walk.'

'Oh.' Manali sounded surprised, but it dissolved into a small smile. 'Of course. I was just talking to Subha.'

She opened the door wider and allowed Adil to step inside. The room was nothing like the usual sterile walls of the palace. Instead, it was almost obnoxiously colourful. Blue walls with dark curlicue patterns. A wooden desk and adjacent shelf stuffed to the brim with books. A balcony that looked out onto the front courtyards. Multicoloured sitting cushions on the floor. A large bed covered with linen that was the same colour as red sand. White gossamer netting hung from the bedpost.

Sitting on one of the cushions was another woman. Subhadrangi – Manali's adopted sister. The mayakari. The owner of the journals that were kept in Adil's study. She stood as he entered and bowed politely.

'Emperor Adil,' she greeted him.

'Subhadrangi,' he replied, sounding wary. Though, Shakti noted with mild surprise, he didn't outright denounce her or declare her scum of the earth.

Was this before he hated us?

The two women looked nothing alike, but that was to be expected since they shared no blood. Where Manali was short, Subhadrangi was tall. Slim, with fuller breasts, accentuated by the tight blue blouse she wore. She had large, wide-set doe eyes, and dark brown skin. There was a single mole above her right brow. She too had the same flower in her hair. A lone gold bangle encircled her right wrist. She was beautiful like Manali, but where the empress' beauty was regal, the mayakari's was ethereal. There was an otherworldliness to her, much like a Great Spirit materializing in a dense, misty forest.

'Subha was just talking about the Mountain of Rebirth,' Manali remarked. The sisters shared a brief, indecipherable look. 'We've never seen such a strange place, truly. She's been studying it.'

'Have you?' Adil's focus went back to Subha. 'What have you found?'

The mayakari sighed. 'Asking as if you didn't overhear us, Emperor,' she replied. Shakti was impressed by her bluntness, even more so that Adil seemed to ignore instead of reacting to it. 'I went to try and summon the Great Spirit.'

'You *what*?' Adil gaped. 'That's – are you mad? No mayakari has been successful. Few have dared to try. The stories about that mountain—'

'There are far too many stories, that's what,' Subha interrupted, shrugging. She didn't seem to share Adil's concern. 'Most of them are likely false. Especially the ones that claim the spirit to be dead. You'll be happy to know I never got the time to summon the Great Spirit. A strange-looking minor one distracted me, and I followed it, only to end up at the foothills. There's a cave entrance down there, did you know that?'

'No,' Adil said. 'I didn't. Did you enter it?'

Their conversation was strangely polite. He'd tolerated witches at some point, then. Where had it gone horribly wrong?

'I went in,' Subha admitted, 'and found these odd, green, glowing rocks embedded further into the cave. Never seen them before, but I got a very eerie feeling and left.'

Adil snorted in derision. 'You left because of a *feeling?*' Now this sounded more like the man she knew.

Subha glowered. 'Intuition is a mayakari's best weapon,' she said. 'I can't explain it to you. It felt unnatural. Almost like a deadland, but not quite.'

'Hm.' Adil ran a hand through his hair. It fell just below his shoulders. 'You might have to tamp down that wariness, then. I'd like to see this cave.'

His last words echoed in a crescendo, and the memory began to fade. Manali, Subha, and the room completely leached of colour until all that Shakti could see was white. That dizzying sensation came rushing up her spine again, and new colours appeared like brushstrokes, congealing together until she found herself back in the Obsidian Throne room. Adil was upon the throne once more.

'You spoke to a mayakari and didn't run to burn her,' was the first thing she said.

The scowl Adil sent her way was ferocious. '*That* was what you learned, foolish girl?'

'Yes,' she replied dryly. 'What Subha found was the mineral you eventually mined, wasn't it? And it's the same mineral Aarya has rediscovered?'

'Correct on both accounts.'

'And it caused a landslide,' Shakti remarked. 'Which means that there *is* a Great Spirit, and it was angered? If you were speaking to a mayakari without rushing to burn her, why didn't you have them perform an appeasement? This is the Mountain of Rebirth. Surely all precautions would've been taken.'

When Adil didn't respond, an answer dawned on her. 'You didn't, did you? What didn't you do?'

'It's not what *I* didn't do, it's what the mayakari failed to tell me,' Adil retorted. 'This is what happens when you trust a witch. She told me that she tried to summon the Great Spirit to appease it, and it didn't respond. Not just once, either. Twice on her own, and then had others try to no success. From what I was initially told, there was no Great Spirit. I assumed I could proceed with mining the mineral.'

Shakti could understand the conclusion Adil had drawn. No Great Spirit appearing suggested that there was no need for an appeasement. 'But when you began mining, the Great Spirit appeared.'

'No, it didn't,' Adil replied, much to her confusion. 'The spirit never appeared, but the mayakari heard its cry. It caused the mudslide. I couldn't get those witches to help me the second time. They refused. And I saw fit to pay their defiance back in kind.'

'You killed them?'

'I should have,' Adil mused, running his fingers absentmindedly through his hair. 'Though, I was more generous back then. I took away money that my mother allocated for the mayakari to further their studies at the Great Library. What use was it when they refused to find out a better way to mine the mountain.'

Unlike humans, mayakari knew when to stop. Shakti knew without a doubt that if she were ever approached to desecrate a Great Spirit's domain without appeasement, she would decline. The land wasn't hers to take as she saw fit.

Adil, meanwhile, seemed lost in his own memories. 'My move angered the mayakari, but I held firm. She was furious, too, but I lost no sleep over it. Not when they refused to help me – their *emperor*.'

'*She*,' Shakti recalled his comment. 'You mean Subha?'

An unreadable expression crossed Adil's face. 'She was intent on becoming the first witch to summon the Great Spirit where none had before,' he said. 'Even after the other mayakari stopped trying to summon it after the landslide, she continued her quest.'

'Why?'

'I don't know,' Adil said, lifting a shoulder in a lazy, one-armed shrug. Shakti couldn't tell if he was being deceitful or not. 'For notoriety? Academic interest? Hard to say.'

'Did she manage to summon the Great Spirit, at least?' Shakti asked.

Adil's nodded. 'Three times, she tried to summon it with me present, but it didn't fully work,' he said. 'She just heard its voice each time. It never materialized. Only once did she succeed in making the Great Spirit appear in its true, unangered form. She was the only one who could.'

'*You* saw it?' When Adil nodded, Shakti fell silent, stunned. Adil Maurya had seen the Great Spirit of the Mountain of Rebirth when no one else had. How many more secrets did he keep buried? 'What was the Great Spirit's true form?'

'An elephant,' Adil replied.

Shakti tucked this piece of information away for later use. 'Then, knowing it existed,' she said, 'did you not try to convince the mayakari to appease it again and then reattempt mining? I'd be surprised if you didn't.'

'That mineral has great potential to be moulded into weapons,' Adil agreed, but he didn't meet her eyes. Strange, coming from him. 'But I made the decision not to mine any further. Doing so would put the Golden City's populace at risk. That Great Spirit is an . . . odd creature, witch. So is its domain. It should not be disturbed. Tell Aarya to leave it alone. She might repeat history if she does otherwise. I won't tell you again.'

In a rare instance, she agreed with Adil. 'Thank you,' she replied. 'I'll relay this to your daughter. Don't mine the mountain.'

'I wouldn't,' Adil agreed, 'but I know my daughter. She will find any way to help me complete what I left unfinished. She is a good, devoted child.'

Instinct drove Shakti to spit out a hasty reply. 'I won't help her.'

Emperor Adil eyed her like a worm beneath his feet. 'When it comes to Aarya, you might not have a choice,' he said.

Raising her eyes skyward, Shakti made a shooing motion with her hands. 'Begone, Adil,' she said.

The emperor faded away slowly. The throne room followed suit, paling and blinding her eyes. The tug in her stomach returned, and Shakti focused on it. Felt warmth hitting her skin. With a deep exhale, she pushed herself out of the Collective.

When she opened her eyes, Aarya sat directly across from her, kohl-lined eyes like a predator. Shakti yelped, startled by her presence. Last she remembered, the empress had been on the other side of the study.

'How long was I gone?' she asked.

'A good half hour,' Aarya replied. 'You didn't float. Just seemed lost to the world.'

Perturbed, Shakti stood up hastily. The empress followed her movement. 'Did you speak to my father?' she asked. A note of apprehension had crept into her voice.

'I did,' Shakti said, and with a great degree of reluctance, recounted Adil's memory and his advice.

Aarya listened in disbelief; lips pursed tight. Shakti knew that look well. Pure scepticism.

'How do I know you're not lying?' she asked at the end of Shakti's summary.

'Why would I lie? It certainly doesn't help Harini,' Shakti replied. 'Your father was against it. Take his advice. Leave the Great Spirit and its domain alone.'

'But Father didn't try mining without performing an appeasement rite,' Aarya retorted. 'He decided not to pursue it any further. I can still try this way.'

The contesting told Shakti that the empress was unwilling to abandon her plans so easily. 'Why are you so invested in this?' she asked. 'Even your father disagrees. I thought you followed him without question.'

For a moment, Aarya didn't answer her. 'I agree with my father on almost everything,' she snapped, 'but this mineral can be weaponized to our advantage. Keep this empire stronger, more of a threat. I could even consider exporting it, for a price. My father didn't pursue every avenue to obtain this mineral, so I will succeed where he didn't.'

Arrogance drove her, then. The need to continue a legacy and create her own. Aarya and Arush weren't so dissimilar, they simply had different visions of achieving it.

'Listen to Adil,' Shakti advised. The words were bitter and foreign on her tongue. 'Don't take such a risk.'

She feared that she was speaking to a wall, for Aarya's expression was hard and determined. 'I'm willing to take it, mayakari,' she remarked.

Shakti snorted. 'A risk was poisoning Emperor Arush and hoping it didn't kill him,' she replied. 'This will end in a disaster, I know it.'

Moments after she uttered the words 'Arush' and 'poison', Aarya's eyes darted towards the closed door. When her gaze returned to land on Shakti, there was nothing but murder in her eyes.

'Be *quiet*,' Aarya whispered, stepping closer. 'Continue to test my patience, mayakari. I dare you.'

With that, she grabbed Shakti's shackles and hauled her towards the door. Pulled like a puppet, Shakti was forced to follow.

'What now?' she grunted.

'For now, I'll have you sent back to your cell,' Aarya replied. 'Tomorrow, you and I will pay a short visit to the Mountain of Rebirth.'

Shakti expected it. Pride would kill this family, that much she knew. 'This isn't a good idea,' she warned the empress again, even though she knew it was futile. 'Trying to appease this Great Spirit might not work. Listen to me. Listen to your *father*.'

'It's not your place to question me,' Aarya retorted. 'You told me that my aunt summoned it, but no one proceeded to appease it. That means there is still a possibility we can, and you will do it.'

Shakti didn't respond at first, only watched the empress in silence. She spoke about her aunt so dismissively. How was she so unmoved?

Aarya frowned. 'What?'

'You don't seem to be affected,' Shakti said. 'I thought the knowledge that your aunt was a mayakari would be more . . . overwhelming.'

'Was that your hope?' Aarya's smile was mocking. 'To your credit, it was an unwelcome surprise, but my aunt is long dead. She's not a blood relative, either. She might have been a witch, but Mother wasn't. And what's another dead witch against the possibility of new weapons?'

Schooling her face into a pleasant smile before opening the door, she added, 'Sleep well, mayakari. Tomorrow, you have a Great Spirit to appease.'

CHAPTER ELEVEN
Ashoka

Freshly bathed and lathered in coconut and sage-scented oils, Ashoka watched the sun set on the balcony of his guest quarters.

Before him, Trikalinga with its white domed houses gave way to the purple-red sea. Boats dotted the waves even now, though they consisted of more warships than passenger ships, patrolling the area. Despite the relative calmness of the scenery before him, Ashoka's hands had adopted a slight tremor in anticipation of—

'I'm ready, Prince Ashoka.'

He turned, breath hitching, and he fervently hoped the sound went unheard. Rahil stood behind him, dressed in black trousers and a dark blue tunic. His skin gleamed like he had bathed in moonlight, thick hair tied in a half-knot, drawing attention to the sharp planes of his jaw. With his dual broadswords at their usual place strapped behind his back, Rahil looked like a handsome, lonely warrior holding the weight of the world on his shoulders, doomed by birth. He doubted Rahil had noted his obvious staring, for his gaze was kept firmly over his shoulder, towards the horizon.

Ashoka cleared his throat. 'Right. Yes,' he said, but when Rahil stonily gestured for him to walk ahead, Ashoka found that he was rooted to the spot, unable to move. Sau's imperative repeated like a parakeet who had learned a new phrase from a recalcitrant master.

'*Right. Yes,*' Rahil repeated. 'Are you not going to move, Prince Ashoka? There's a dinner to attend.'

Anxiety and worry were forming a tidal wave, and he needed to gather his courage before it drowned him. 'In a moment,' Ashoka blurted out, a little too quickly for his liking. 'Do you . . . want to join me here? On the balcony?'

He didn't miss the way Rahil stiffened, as if he too didn't know what to make of this sudden request. 'If you need a moment to yourself, I will give you time,' he began, 'and I will wait.'

'I don't want a moment to myself, I want one with you,' Ashoka said without thinking. His face heated immediately. There came an instinctual need to hide, to encase himself within a tomb and die quietly. Neither of his siblings would act like this. Thankfully, his request seemed to neutralize Rahil, who came and stood next to him an arm's width apart, keeping his forearms folded on the balcony railing, still avoiding his gaze. The response was better than nothing.

Ashoka let out a soft breath. 'Did you know that the night brings blue light to the shores here?' he asked. 'Apparently, the ocean glitters.'

'It's not the ocean,' Rahil corrected him. 'Some living creatures can produce a natural light in their bodies. Even seaweed. That's the reason the sea glows.'

When Ashoka shot him a bemused look, Rahil sighed. It sounded less aggravated and more like the soft exasperation that used to be reserved for him. A welcome change. 'My mother told me about it. It was one of her favourite things about Trikalinga,' he explained. 'What's your real question?'

'Did you hate Sau when she dismissed your singing?'

Unpredictability was the first step in disarming Rahil. Sure enough, his expression turned into one of confusion. His rigid posture loosened. 'I don't recall that.'

'She said that you sounded like a dying bird.'

Rahil glared at him. 'Yes, thank you for the helpful reminder.'

Back to his usual tone. Ashoka panicked, mind scrambling to salvage what he'd just re-fractured. 'I was just repeating—'

'What's your point,' Rahil interrupted him, 'in bringing up some vague memory?'

There was mild irritation, but he hadn't ended his question with that infuriating, newfound polite title. Good.

'Would you have hated me if I told you the same?' Ashoka asked, keeping his gaze anywhere but on Rahil. He needed to execute his wayward plan, not be led astray.

'No, and considering I can't recall this memory, I can only hazard that I didn't hate Sau's existence, either,' said Rahil. Then, 'I assume you agreed with her.'

Clamping down the smile that threatened to break loose, Ashoka nodded. 'Yes, but I also found it amusing,' he admitted. 'Endearing, even. I didn't have the heart to tell you otherwise.'

A beat of silence passed between them before Rahil let out a long exhale and fully turned towards him. 'What are you trying to get at, Ashoka?'

No point in delaying the question. 'Do you hate me now?'

'*This* is an entirely different set of circumstances compared to your irrelevant hypothetical.'

Deflection. 'Do you hate me now?' Ashoka repeated. Part of him didn't want to turn. Part of him was so sure that locking eyes with Rahil would only lead to disappointment, but Ashoka soldiered through layers of doubt. Inscrutable smoky quartz eyes stared back, unflinching, as Rahil said, 'Hating you is difficult.'

Relief flooded his body like a warm bath. 'Good.'

Before Ashoka could talk himself out of it, he reached up and cupped Rahil's face, taking care to keep only the pads of his fingers against his skin. Rahil's eyes widened at the contact. There was no time to consider if he was being reckless, not when his mind failed to string three coherent words together. Explosions ricocheted inside his head, the weight of unsaid words causing an unwelcome build-up of pressure. He would need a chisel and mallet struck hard against his skull to relieve it.

His balance and thought were further disturbed when Rahil grabbed his arms and tugged him closer. A strangely delayed reaction from him.

'Your hands are cold,' Rahil murmured. Up close, Ashoka could count each individual eyelash, see the odd, permanent scars against his temple from fights long past, and observe the single mole on his throat. If he had been a better artist, he'd have been able to draw Rahil perfectly from memory alone.

You don't hate me, but do you love me?

'If you don't hate me, then perhaps you can forgive me,' Ashoka said quietly. 'I'm sorry for what I said, but I stand by it.'

A huff. 'Some apology.'

'I meant' – his fingers pressed against Rahil's face harder, scrambling for words that usually arrived in a heartbeat – 'we aren't each other's moral compass. I can't expect someone else to be that for me – not even you. That burden rests on me alone. You are, however, someone whose opinion I regard highly. That won't change.'

Rahil appeared sceptical. 'Didn't you tell me to keep my opinions to myself?'

Ashoka cringed. 'I was angry at being judged,' he replied, 'and I reacted poorly. What you think does matter to me, more so than anyone else. I . . . I felt as though I'd undergone a necessary change while you were gone, and when you arrived you didn't like what you saw. But wasn't it you who told me to let go of my idealism a little and learn the middle path?'

The grip that Rahil had on his arms tightened. He looked conflicted. 'Yes,' he admitted. 'Although, once I saw the change, I couldn't think of why I had suggested it in the first place.'

'I broke your illusion,' Ashoka said, repeating Sau's words. 'People don't like having their preconceptions broken.'

Rahil's brows furrowed before he let out a grating laugh. 'Maybe I need to do some self-reflection,' he remarked. A note of hesitation crept into his voice as he said, 'I know I can be childish and petty, and . . . I'm sorry for that. I forgive you.'

I forgive you.

For a moment, Ashoka was breathless. If such a thing as a soul existed, his would have lightened like a feather, suspended in mid-air. 'I understand,' he said. 'I'm glad that you forgive me, and I – I missed you.'

His skin prickled when Rahil let out a full-blown smile and leaned forward so that their foreheads touched. 'I missed you, too,' he said.

Closing his eyes, Ashoka revelled in the moment, aware of his trembling hands. Had he crossed an unseen line? Had Rahil crossed it with him unknowingly? He did not know but neither could he summon any more courage to ask. He could have made this moment mean something other than forgiveness, but insecurity and uncertainty kept him rooted to the spot.

Do you love me?

If he remained this way, he would never know.

Dinner was a magnificent affair. The Kalingan people prided themselves on their seafood and it was evident in this arrangement; pearl fish, cuttlefish, crab, prawn and oysters decorated the dining table, curried and infused with delicious-smelling spices. He eyed the dishes, searching for one without meat, and was satisfied to find a few to his liking.

Queen Kalyani met the four of them in the same clothes they had seen her in. She was whispering to another woman who had bent over to hear her. Given the plain clothes underneath light armour, and the longsword strapped to her side, Ashoka hazarded that she was a personal guard.

Beside him, Sau placed a firm hand on his shoulder. Her hair was tamed with oil, and her practised smile never once wavered. 'Don't prattle,' she warned. 'Be direct. I know your Kalingan is rusty but try to sound confident.'

Rahil sighed. 'Don't mother him, Sau,' he said with the seasoned exasperation that was usually reserved for a younger sibling. 'Ashoka will do perfectly fine.'

'I'm not mothering him, you fool,' Sau began in mock irritation before a knowing glint dawned in her eyes. '*Ashoka?* Have you two made amends, then?'

In response, Rahil sent him a crooked, endearing smile. 'We have,' he said. Ashoka tried very hard not to look at him for too long. If he did, he feared his emotions would be as obvious as a blue flame emerging from a burning hand.

'Good,' Sau replied. 'You two were fast becoming pathetic.'

Rahil snorted. 'Coming from the woman who called Prince Ryu a worm in front of his advisors—'

'—that was an *accident*! The words have similar inflections . . .'

As the two descended into hushed bickering, Naila offered him words of reassurance. 'You survived through Taksila, Prince Ashoka,' she said. 'You will most certainly survive a dinner.'

'Esteemed guests, come, come,' came the queen's voice. 'Take a seat, please.'

She sat at the head of the table, so he took the spot to her left, complimenting the aesthetics of the provided dishes. Afterward, they were silent, shovelling food into their mouths with overwhelming awkwardness. He and Naila attacked the vegetable-only dishes while Sau and Rahil had a helping of everything. The queen made an idle remark about his dietary habits, to which Ashoka made a long-winded response about his choice to forsake meat. After catching Sau's warning glance, he caught himself and stopped his prattling.

'Prince Ashoka,' Queen Kalyani began, 'I can't keep my curiosity at bay any longer. What is this "monumental favour" you ask for?'

Swallowing the last of his roasted brinjal, Ashoka set down his spoon. 'I govern the city of Taksila,' he began, 'as instructed by my father, who was under the assumption that I would not live up to the task. Nature spirits rampaged along its northern borders and mayakari were killed like any other part of the empire. With the help of the mayakari resistance in Taksila, I was able to resolve the issue with the nature spirits, depose the governor' – he saw Rahil flinch at the word 'depose' – 'and ban mayakari killings.'

'Ban?' Queen Kalyani repeated. 'Without retaliation from your brother? Or sister?'

Ashoka shook his head, hands fidgeting beneath the table. 'My brother didn't castigate me too much for it,' he said. 'But now that Aarya is the acting regent, she's commanding me to repeal my laws and give up Taksila.'

'As an *interim* regent?'

'According to Ran law, the acting regent has the same power that is afforded to the rightful monarch,' he answered.

'The rule is usually enacted for a short period of time, Your Highness,' Sau added. 'In Emperor Adil's day, if he were to leave for state visits, Empress Manali ruled in his stead with the same rights and responsibilities. But there is an . . . unspoken social convention that an acting regent carry out their duties in the manner befitting their superior until their return. Empress Aarya's situation is a novel one. No one knows when Emperor Arush will wake. It could be days or months. In all fairness, the acting empress doesn't have to follow convention because the situation she finds herself in is unconventional.'

'I see. Thank you, advisor,' said the queen before turning her attention back to him. 'Then, your sister has every right to command you.'

Out of her mouth, the words sounded wrong, but all he could say was, 'Correct.'

The queen's face was impassive. After taking an agonizing, slow bite of her food she asked, 'Then why not give up Taksila? I see no problem, Prince Ashoka. You would only return to the Golden City and live without a care in the world.'

'Because I *will* care,' he replied. 'I won't leave the mayakari to fend for themselves. To do so would be to break my promises, and I'm not coward enough to do so.'

'Hm.' Ashoka could not gauge Kalyani's mood whatsoever. 'But why are you so attached to Taksila? It is but a city within a much larger state, of which your empire has several. I can imagine that you will only govern more in your lifetime.'

She posed a fair question. 'Because I was able to make good, necessary changes there,' he said, but the response rang hollow. There was more to it, but the answer made him sound more like his father and siblings than he cared to admit.

From the queen's resulting frown, she didn't seem to believe his half-hearted reply, either. 'You don't seem convinced of your own answer,' she remarked. 'I am no stranger to the allure of power, Prince Ashoka. You can be honest here.'

Perhaps honesty would get him closer to securing an alliance. 'Deposing the governor didn't give me complete freedom, but it gave me enough,' he said. 'I was able to protect the mayakari as best as I could in Taksila. There's a certain sense of . . . vindication, too. My father's last order was to send me to Taksila to govern. I think he sent me there in part knowing I'd fail to do anything of consequence. I righted his disasters when no one else could or would. I find it hard to believe that my siblings will trust me to govern any city after my time in Taksila, and I might as well act now rather than later. Besides, I can't leave my people to die.'

'Ah, but they are not *your* people,' the queen rebutted. 'They are your sister's.'

The curried vegetables on his plate began to look unappetizing. The words stung more than he thought they would. Made him furious, too. Beside him, Naila grimaced.

Beheadings. Burnings. Torture. Torment. Those were not the actions of a just ruler. 'My sister hates the mayakari just as our father did,' he said. 'She doesn't consider them as people, only a problem.'

'Perhaps your sister sees the mayakari as a threat to *her* people,' said the queen. 'The common citizens.'

His temper flared. 'My father persecuted witches because he saw their power as a threat. Aarya blindly does the same. You know that the mayakari aren't monsters. That's why I wish to fight for the mayakari. *With* them.'

Queen Kalyani laughed, but it didn't sound cruel. 'Spoken like a king,' she said. 'Except you are not one.'

Not yet, he thought. Glory would come when he sat upon the Obsidian Throne, the newly crowned emperor.

He didn't attempt to skirt around the queen's words. 'I agree,' he said. 'I'm not one. Yet. But I plan to be. My brother is in a coma with no signs of waking. My sister commands that I vacate Taksila, but I want to refuse, defend, and remove her from the Obsidian Throne. To depose Aarya, I need numbers. An army. And I need yours.'

A hush descended the table. The hand that the queen reached to grasp her cup stilled. Sau and Naila watched her warily. By accident, Ashoka caught Rahil's eye.

You've openly declared treason, his expression seemed to say. *You can't take back your words.*

I know, he thought.

Faint lines marked grooves on the queen's forehead as she leaned forward and rested her chin atop clasped hands. 'Is this your monumental favour?' she asked, appearing rather unnerved. 'You wish for me to aid an *insurrection*?'

'Yes,' he replied. 'I do.'

Queen Kalyani shook her head. 'No,' she said. 'I won't send my soldiers to war over your family dispute.'

An invisible executioner looped a frayed rope around his neck. His father materialized with a lit match and approached his unburned ear. *Family dispute.* Phrased that way, it sounded so trivial.

'Neither of my siblings will change their ways,' he pressed, undeterred. 'My father's shadow looms over all of us, but I'm the only one who can chart the empire back to its original course. If my siblings continue to rule, more witches will die.'

'While your tenacity is commendable, I can't find it in myself to agree to your demands,' Queen Kalyani replied. 'You want me to expend lives for a problem we didn't create? No, Prince Ashoka, I will not send my people to their deaths again. Enough died trying to protect the Saankru Islands from your ancestors, and it cost us dearly.'

In his mind's eye, the Obsidian Throne began to fade into nothingness. For a moment, Ashoka saw a vision of the world if he gave in to Aarya's demands. Fewer lives lost, yes, but those few would continue to burn. Any chance of the mayakari living a life free from persecution would be gone.

Submitting to his sister was the peaceful thing to do, but it was also the most cowardly. He was no coward.

'I have a sneaking suspicion that my brother will never wake. The more he lies unconscious to the world, the more my sister will act for herself. She is planning to conquer the south as our father hoped to,' Ashoka said, 'Mahvo is in her line of sight, and once she's done, she'll come for you. One of my father's loftiest dreams was to conquer Kalinga. In his name Aarya will do anything.'

His response rendered the queen silent again for a few moments, but she did not appear to be intimidated. 'Kalinga can withstand an assault from the Ran Empire,' she said. 'You forget that our conquest will require your sister to employ naval warfare, and we both know who will win that battle.'

'Will you?' he replied boldly. When the queen shot him an incredulous look, Ashoka kept his tone polite but firm. 'Best navy in the known world, but your predecessor was unable to keep hold of the Saankru Islands. What's to say it won't happen again?'

'That battle was won by pure luck,' the queen replied. 'An angered *ocean* spirit supposedly rose from the waves. Your monarch conducted a surprise attack. Safe to say we've adapted since then.'

After several decades, the Saankru Islands remained a sore point for Kalingans. They lay in the back of his mind, a risky last resort deal if his original offers didn't suffice.

'While I have no doubt of your navy's prowess now, once Aarya takes the south, no army in the known world will defeat ours,' he said.

Sau, as usual, jumped in to assist him. 'Queen Kalyani, I implore you to view this logically. This may not seem like a problem for you now, but it will be in the future. Empress Aarya will have resources from the south, and she will have the people. Despite your excellent navy, she will eclipse you by numbers alone. Of bodies and weapons both.'

'And what if you lose in your grand quest to usurp the throne?' Queen Kalyani replied. 'Death will come for you all while war will wait for me and my kingdom.'

Ashoka grimaced. 'War isn't ideal,' he agreed, 'but it's necessary.'

Queen Kalyani seemed not to have heard him. 'My allegiance and army . . . how do you expect me to help you? By landing on the shores of the Ran Empire unprompted and declaring war?'

'You'll never have to enter our empire's borders,' he replied. 'Instead, you'll be the hunter waiting for its prey to walk into a trap. You will not start a war. My sister will.'

Now *that* caught her attention.

'With Queen Malika's approval, I've arranged for Ran military weapons to be delivered to Taksila and then transported down south,' Ashoka continued eagerly. 'Our soldiers are sent there for defensive purposes, and I'm counting on them to find these weapons and then relay this problem back to my sister. Selling our military weapons is illegal. It'll give Aarya more motivation to invade yet another state. However, if another empire has perhaps stepped in and negotiated protections with Queen Malika against the Ran monarch, and if Aarya breaches such safeguards . . .'

'It gives us the right to declare war regardless,' Queen Kalyani concluded, watching him with newfound interest.

Creating conflict. Placing pieces in the correct position and watching them fall into place. It sounded like something his father would do. But Ashoka was not his father. Their intent was different. Intent was all that mattered.

Though Queen Kalyani appeared intrigued, he knew she wasn't yet fully convinced. 'But you've started the game without telling me,' she continued. 'Quite foolish, don't you think? Moving pieces prematurely when I see no reason to help you. What does my kingdom – what do *I* – get out of it?'

Aid in exchange for power. Nothing new. Quickly, he rattled off his proposals: access to Mathura's iron ore mines, including a cut of the profits. Lowered taxes on agricultural imports, and perhaps his least favoured idea – leasing out the Golden City's port for a defined term. Sau had harangued him over that last point on their way to the capital, but in truth, it wasn't as risky as the deal he had in mind if Kalyani were to refuse.

Queen Kalyani listened quietly. Pondered over it. It was difficult to gauge her expression.

'Unfortunately, I can't accept. Weapons and a lease in exchange for thousands of my people? Their lives? That's not a fair deal,' she said. 'What protection can you offer me? I hazard that it will be next to nothing.'

When Ashoka made to refute this, she held up a hand. 'However, I admire your conviction. What I can do is provide an addition to your resources that your sister won't have: the mayakari. Using their abilities to your advantage. However, if you want my army, I need something more substantial from you.'

'How, Your Highness?' Naila, who had been silent so far, asked. 'By cursing the living? Because that power is unpredictable. I don't think one wants that in a weapon.'

The queen shot them a sympathetic grimace. 'How unfortunate that your mayakari are not given the chance to advance their abilities,' she said. 'You need not think of your powers so narrowly, child. Here, select witches have learned to weaponize their cursing abilities. Quite literally.'

When all four of them remained bewildered and silent, the queen gestured towards the swords that her guards carried. 'Cursing a living being outright leaves too much to chance and time. Here is an advantage I suggest you observe.'

'Weapons?' Ashoka echoed.

The queen's eyes glinted. 'Even better,' she replied. '*Cursed* weapons.'

CHAPTER TWELVE
Shakti

THE NEXT DAY, SHAKTI FOUND HERSELF BEING SHAKEN awake by soldiers.

Her movements were sluggish as she struggled to sit up, mind even more so. Her limbs ached. After being escorted out of Adil's study and back into the cell the day before, she'd been given more healing tonics. Some tasted like grass, others had a pleasant sugary taste. Whatever was in them was quite strong. She barely felt the rough kick the soldier gave to her upper thigh, barely heard the impatient 'Hurry up, witch' as they released the shackles around her legs.

As she was directed outside by a trio of guards, dread strung her intestines into knots. Her orders today were clear. Performing an appeasement rite to placate the Great Spirit of the Mountain of Rebirth.

It felt wrong.

Outside the palace gates, there were three carriages stationed, one behind the other. The last one, Shakti guessed, was for her. Who else in this party would suffer the misfortune of being hauled into a metal cage.

Waiting in front of the middle carriage – this distinctly more elaborate than the rest – was Aarya. Save for the royal circlet, the empress was free of her usual jewellery. Gone, too, were the formal saris, replaced by her combat uniform, dagger strapped to her left thigh. There were likely more concealed weapons on her. Shakti tended to forget that, despite the glamour, Aarya was trained in combat. She could use brute force just as well as she could make threats.

As they approached, Shakti could sense a dark storm cloud hovering over the empress' head. She appeared to be in a foul mood. For a moment, Shakti's curiosity piqued, wondering what had happened, before realizing that there was no point in caring.

'Witch. You're finally here,' Aarya remarked, tone cold.

'Empress.' She greeted her with a formal bow, watching her tense expression slip at the polite address. No need to infuriate the woman more. It seemed wise to be quiet for now, lest Aarya take that dagger to her skin again. Or worse, burn Harini's fingers. Shakti hadn't been able to glean any more information about her friend, how she was, what state she was in. All she knew was that the mayakari was being held in the prison cells as she was.

'Move her into the carriage,' Aarya ordered the guards standing around Shakti. Though, she wouldn't call it a carriage. Not when it was simply an iron cage that was fastened to a wooden undercarriage and pulled by another black leopard. 'We'll be departing soon. Hopefully those tonics have worked their magic, mayakari. You will not leave the mountain until the appeasement rite has been performed.'

Far beyond them, Shakti could spot the mountain. Its perpetual mist. During her limited time in the Golden City, Shakti was ashamed to admit that she had never visited the Mountain of Rebirth. She'd only ever seen it through Emperor Ashoka's eyes in the Collective. Looking at it now, every bone in her body told her that this wasn't a good plan, but she had no choice in the matter.

You're just a muzzled leopard. A witch who cast a curse with no memory. You're a disgrace.

That voice was both Jaya's and her own. Strange. Her aunt's voice was never admonishing. Jaya would never call her a disgrace.

Actively helping those who kill your own kind? What else are you.

Shakti silently followed the soldiers, one of whom unlocked the cage and pushed her inside. Fresh shame bloomed in her chest. What kind of mayakari would help the current royals? It was a betrayal of the highest degree. They would rather accept death, believing that rebirth would grant them a better life. A traitor to her own kind, that was what she was.

Not long after she was put inside, the carriages began to move. They took the steep path down, reserved for wheeled vehicles. Aarya's travelled in the middle, while Shakti's was last. Her cage rattled uncomfortably and threw her off balance. At times she wondered if the soldier manoeuvring the carriage was taking such sharp turns on purpose.

Leaning her head against the metal gratings, Shakti watched as the royal palace shifted further and further away from view. Its blinding white walls never stopped reminding her of funerals. She was thankful to find distraction in the trees and flat grassland that emerged as they descended the hilltop. Passing through a small copse, she spotted the telltale shimmer of a minor spirit floating amongst the leaves. She had to stop herself from calling out to it, shifting into the comforting lullaby of spirit-speak. The soldier directing the carriage would hear her and suspect foul play. Sighing, Shakti tipped her face up to the sun. It was pleasantly warm. However, when the party arrived at the fork in the path where the right led to the capital, and the left to the mountain, she slowly noticed a change. The closer they came towards the Mountain of Rebirth, the crisper and sharper the air became. Inhaling it was invigorating, like entering lands untouched by human feet in centuries. Eerie too; unsettling in the way a beautiful corpse was.

She wondered how Subha had succeeded in summoning the Great Spirit where others had failed. Either it was weakened to an unhealthy degree or was permanently dormant, unable to wake. What had she said, or done, differently?

The carriage came to a sharp halt once the party reached the base, shouts announcing Aarya's arrival. Glancing around her, Shakti observed the small camp that had been created far from the path that was available for the public to climb to the peak. Tents had been constructed, with several men and women milling about. Multiple wooden carts sat off to the side, unused. They were waiting, Shakti realized. Asking for both her and Adil's opinion yesterday on the Mountain of Rebirth had been a kind of courtesy, then. Knowing what she knew of Aarya, the empress would have wanted Adil's approval, but it seemed that she had already made up her mind to proceed with or without it.

Stretching her tense muscles as best as she could, Shakti glanced down at her bandaged arms in surprise. They didn't ache. In fact, she felt as sprightly as a foal. *Strange.*

Once it was unlocked, Shakti was shepherded out of her cage to where Aarya awaited her. Shakti was acutely aware of the looks she was getting from the people around her – more soldiers, and some who appeared to be civilians based on their mundane clothing.

'Stay silent unless you are asked to speak,' was Aarya's order before she turned on her heel and stalked towards a tall young woman who waited in front of a large black tent.

'Empress Aarya.' The young woman bowed. Not a soldier, Shakti realized, but not just a civilian, either. She spared Shakti a cursory glance. There was a question in her eyes that, Shakti suspected, was likely answered the moment in which the woman noted her bandaged arms and shackled hands. She made no move to acknowledge her presence.

'Rasi,' Aarya replied, flicking her fingers up in greeting. 'Any changes since my last visit?'

The woman shook her head. 'No, Your Highness. We're still marking the area. There's a minor spirit around the abandoned mine that won't leave. However, your father's notes were quite helpful. Thank you for providing them. We were able to use the rough sketches to set out a similar working field.'

Shakti bit her lip as the two women continued their conversation. There was a minor spirit involved? That should've told any rational person to leave the mine alone. Yet, these foolish people – rather, their foolish empress – had already ordered for it to be further disturbed.

'Good,' Aarya told Rasi. 'I come bearing a gift.' At this, she pointed to Shakti. The word *gift* was enunciated with a cruel smile.

Rasi finally cut a glance to Shakti. 'Empress?'

'The mayakari here has agreed to perform an appeasement rite for you to safely extract the mineral from the mountain,' Aarya said. *Hah* – 'agreed'. What a sterile word. It left out every threat that got her here.

Rasi shifted uncomfortably. 'And she is . . . willing?'

'Of course. I've made sure that she understands . . .'

The way they stood there, not acknowledging her presence made Shakti feel small when it usually would've made her angry. The need to interject, to push herself into the conversation wasn't there. Perhaps it was the area that was making her like this. Though she'd never stepped foot into a deadland, the Mountain of Rebirth came close to the descriptions. Unnatural. Damaged. She had the oddest sensation that a creature lay hidden. Asleep, or even hunting.

Makes sense, she thought to herself, *what with all the stories about the Great Spirit here.*

'. . . mayakari?'

Startled out of her reverie, Shakti refocused on Aarya and the young woman, both of whom were now staring at her.

'What?' she asked ungraciously.

The empress' left eye twitched. 'Watch yourself,' she snapped. 'I asked you if there were any particular objects needed for an appeasement rite?'

Shakti scoffed. Thanks to Adil, the empress didn't know a single thing about the mayakari. 'Nothing is needed,' she replied, adding, 'Your Highness,' after a brief pause. Aarya didn't seem to appreciate her tone.

'If you think me a fool, you're sorely mistaken,' the empress told Shakti. 'I only ask because the Mountain of Rebirth is an anomaly. Any idiot can tell that caution is required in this place. I'm being prudent.'

'And yet you want to disturb this area,' Shakti replied. 'For a *rock*.'

Shooting her a surprised but reproachful look, Rasi huffed. 'For a mayakari, you don't seem to understand the significance of—' she began but was interrupted by a stone-faced Aarya who held up a single hand.

'Follow me, witch,' she ordered, before turning on her heel and walking away towards the tents set up closer to the craggy face of the mountain. Having no choice but to follow, Shakti ambled forward. She was given a wide berth, but didn't miss the whispers as she passed:

'—that's the mayakari, isn't it? The one who poisoned—'

'—never know. Wonder why she hasn't been burned—'

'—she looks *brutal*—'

Not brutal, Shakti thought. *Brutalized.*

Aarya led them around to a crumbling part of the foothill where it appeared as if a localized landslide had taken place. Debris and boulders scattered the area, some piled atop each other and fractured into jagged pieces. Wild weeds sprung up between cracks, some withered, some flourishing. Judging by the footprints visible on the dusty rocks, people had climbed to the top, where Shakti spotted a small fissure. An opening.

It must be the entrance to the abandoned mine.

'That opening up there,' Aarya remarked, 'was what the group of children discovered. Apparently it collapsed in on itself.'

'Has anyone ventured inside?' Shakti asked. 'Have *you*, Empress?'

'I haven't, but a small group of miners have,' Aarya replied. 'However, it requires a ladder or pulley system to lower a person down to the floor since we're descending from the apex. From what they've told me, there is indeed a large tunnel, with faint speckles of greenish-white light on the cave walls as one wanders further down.'

'The mineral,' Shakti guessed aloud, recalling Subha's notes.

'Yes,' Aarya replied. 'It appears to be woven into the rock. However, we couldn't explore any further. One of the minor spirits is being . . . a nuisance. Fortunately, a dislodged chunk was discovered in the rubble . . .'

Shakti was no longer concentrating on the empress' explanations. 'There's a minor spirit inside?' she interrupted. When non-mayakari complained of the small creatures being a nuisance, their claims were usually unfounded. At times, minor spirits acted like little guardians. Wise elders that were rarely listened to by the young and foolish. If the Great Spirits were to be thought of as kings, the minor spirits were their foot soldiers.

She remembered the small spirit she'd talked to in Kolakola. The creature had fussed over her intent to curse. Looking back, it hadn't been wrong. The curse she'd uttered against Adil had caused consequences beyond her wildest imaginations, and with it suffering. But she'd long since forgiven her past self. There was no guilt when it came to Adil. *Living misfortune.* The curse had been necessary.

Unlike the one you can't remember.

She pushed the stray thought aside. There was no time to worry about that for now. 'What's it doing?' she asked.

'Nothing terrible. It's more of a pest,' Aarya replied, but she seemed visibly irritated by the thought. 'From time to time it appears and disappears. I assume it was trying to stop us, hence why you're here today. If the Great Spirit is appeased, the minor spirits will be too, yes?'

Shakti nodded. It was how appeasement rites worked. Pacify the Great Spirit, and you pacify the minor ones. Allow for the land's natural resources to be used with less retaliation. But this was the Mountain of Rebirth. For all she knew, the appeasement might not work.

Suddenly, Shakti heard a weak chittering. Wrenching her gaze from Aarya, she spotted the location where the sound came from, and her stomach dropped.

Floating through the rubble came a minor spirit.

It was a strange and twisted creature, unlike the ones she'd seen before. Its pale pinkish-brown body appeared to be stretched thin. The colour reminded Shakti of her own skin, puckered and scarred. Two eyes. Two legs. Four arms. Most minor spirits had a healthy glow to them, but not this one. Groove upon groove marked its face. It had the same appearance as an old, weathered tree.

Its gaze landed on Shakti, eyes widening. The spirit must have sensed her.

At the periphery she heard someone say, 'Oh, not this thing again,' and bristled. How dare they speak of a nature spirit like it was a nuisance?

Shakti stepped forward. So did the spirit.

'Mayakari,' Aarya warned behind her.

Shakti shook her head. 'It won't hurt us.'

They met halfway, spirit and witch. It seemed even more fascinated by her than she was with it. Stretching out an arm, it traced the bridge of her nose. She felt nothing.

'*Little spirit,*' she greeted it. '*Are we disturbing your home?*'

Behind her, Shakti heard furious murmurs. The people around her would be hearing nothing but birdsong coming out of her mouth.

The minor spirit floated around her in a circle, continuing its chittering. Its response came in afterimages and sensations. An eerie coldness. Heat. A lotus that blossomed, died, and blossomed again. She couldn't make head nor tail of its answer. Instead, she watched it get up close to her face and blink slowly before inclining its head towards the mountain's peak where the mist lingered.

Images came again, of hands bound by string.

'*Are you . . .*' Shakti struggled to understand the meaning. '*Are you permanently bound here? Is that what you're telling me?*'

The minor spirit shook its head. Shakti watched, astonished, as it drew itself up to its full height, saw its little chest expand.

'*Wheel,*' it told her in a rush. '*Bound.*'

Chest deflating, the creature curled in on itself. Minor spirits didn't like to communicate verbally. Using words seemed to have exhausted it, and the spirit already looked weak. Shakti still couldn't quite understand. It was too ambiguous.

The uneasy prick in her stomach returned harder than ever. Every bone in her body screamed at her to leave the mountain untouched. The air continued making her feel strange, too. Sharper. More aware. Stronger. Not that those were terrible afflictions, but mayakari shouldn't feel this invigorated from being in the wilderness.

'What is it saying?' Aarya asked her.

'I . . . I don't know,' Shakti confessed. Keeping her eyes on the minor spirit, she said, 'but my instinct is telling me not to appease the Great Spirit.'

A lengthy silence followed her admission. 'I beg your pardon?' Aarya eventually asked. Her tone was devoid of emotion.

'The Mountain of Rebirth exists in the state of life and death, does it not?' Shakti replied. 'Anything that's found here will suffer the same predicament — there is a danger in excavating. Don't do it.'

As if in agreement, the minor spirit whirled around in the air furiously.

'We are appeasing the Great Spirit because the ritual wasn't carried out during my father's time,' Aarya said, frustration evident in her voice. 'Frankly, mayakari, I don't always trust your so-called knowledge. You don't know the history of this mountain. All I want you to do is follow my orders. Remember whose life is on the line.'

Shakti bit the inside of her cheek hard enough to bleed. Perhaps this was what the minor spirit meant by 'bound'. That Shakti couldn't refuse.

'No more time-wasting,' Aarya snapped at her mutinous silence. 'Get rid of this creature and appease the Great Spirit.'

Curse, her mind goaded. *Curse. You know you want to.*

The minor spirit seemed to sense her anger, for it moved in front of her again, and the afterimage that flashed in her mind's eye was clearly meant to soothe. A paddy field in rain. Smoke wafting from sticks of incense. A wound healing over time.

Shakti inhaled deeply and let her anger go. 'Thank you, little spirit,' she told it.

The straight black line that was the spirit's mouth curved into a smile. It turned around and wandered back into the mouth of the cave. Shakti watched it go, a cold emptiness in her chest.

She'd given Aarya a warning. What came next would not fall on her conscience.

'Fine,' she said after the minor spirit vanished. 'Give me some space and silence. And these shackles—'

'Oh no,' Aarya interrupted, 'those stay on. You will proceed as you are, mayakari, but I shall give you silence. And space.'

Irritated at having to bow to pressure, Shakti nodded and stalked towards an area away from the tents and people. Aarya and her soldiers followed behind. Shakti sat down on the grass in a kneeling position. As she'd promised, Aarya gave her a wide berth. Shakti pushed her anger away. Instead, she allowed her eyes to close and her breathing to settle. It came easier than it had in a long time. She placed her palm flat on the ground; warm and dry.

'Great Spirit of the mountain,' she began, 'surveyor of this vast domain, I call upon you.'

There was no response. An absolute stifling silence threatened to drown her. Everyone around her had gone quiet. Unlike the Great Spirit of Kolakola, there was no sign to suggest that a creature was even approaching. No change in temperature, no eerie stillness as if the land itself awaited its coming with bated breath. Could it even hear her?

The silence stretched on for so long, that she briefly wondered if Adil had lied to her. Or perhaps had hallucinated seeing it.

'Great Spirit of the mountain,' Shakti repeated, 'surveyor of this vast dominion, answer my call.'

'Well?' Aarya demanded from behind her. She sounded impatient.

So much for silence. Shakti chose to ignore the empress and refocused on the sensation of soil beneath her palms. *Nothing.*

'Mayakari, I asked you a question.'

Irritation came, and with it, a sudden surge of power. 'Be *quiet*,' Shakti snapped without thinking. A furious chorus of mutters followed instantly, the crowd ruffled by her audacity against Aarya. In the din, Shakti heard the declaration of a man threatening to whip her soundly for such a transgression. Hypocrites, the lot of them. Using her abilities and then punishing her for existing. Shakti wanted to burn them all, watch their bodies burn orange-red.

With each passing breath, her body seemed to string tighter and tighter until, suddenly, images of colourless eyes and rough transparent greyish yellow skin flooded her mind. Her chest constricted, as if the air was being sucked out of her lungs. A gaping maw with no bottom, endless, endless rage. Dark, dark, dark, like her memories. The memories she couldn't remember. The curse she cast and couldn't recall.

Suddenly, Shakti's rage became too much. Too big for her body. Too big to comprehend. This was all Aarya's fault—

'*Little witch.*'

Shakti glanced up sharply at the disembodied whisper, anger

simmering to a low pulse. Two words spoken, but they hummed with ancient power.

The Great Spirit was here.

Craning her neck left and right, she tried to spot the telltale glimmer of the spirit appearing in its animal form. Nothing. But it was *alive*. Silent for so long, and suddenly awakened.

'Great Spirit,' she repeated.

Behind her, there came horrified shouts. When Shakti glanced up, she saw a thin mist rolling down from the peak with unnatural speed towards their base camp. Uncomfortable pressure lanced at her right shoulder, and it took Shakti a moment to realize that it was Aarya who had materialized behind her, who had placed her hand there. The empress appeared both alarmed and livid. 'Is it here?' she asked.

'*I have awakened,*' came a deep, guttural voice that she still couldn't locate. '*And the false chakravartin has returned.*'

Shakti's breath sputtered in shock. She'd summoned it. Somewhat.

Its words bewildered her. *Returned?* Was it confused – disoriented after not being summoned for decades? Furrowing her brows, she turned to lock eyes with Aarya. Chakravartin. *Ruler.* Why was it speaking to her?

'Well?' the empress urged.

'It's here,' she bit back, pushing away the empress' hand. 'Please be quiet and let me speak to it.'

To her surprise, Aarya didn't castigate her impudence and instead stepped back, eyes darting in every which direction. Shakti resumed her concentration. *It was here.* Here but nowhere. She could see no ghostly animal.

'*Spirit of the mountain,*' she said loudly, '*I wish to seek permission. I wish to use the land upon which you dwell for resources that will help the humans who live here.*'

A lie, and it seemed as if the Great Spirit knew it. In response came an aggrieved roar so deafening that it caused the workers around her to cover their ears, cringing at the sound. It recalled an eternal inferno, unable to be quelled.

'*Too much. You have taken too much,*' it said. '*Too much. You have already taken too much from me.*'

Shakti felt its rage intensely in her chest. This was an unwilling creature. Weak and resistant was an easier battle than strong and resistant, and the Great Spirit was clearly the latter. This was *wrong*. Going against a Great Spirit foretold severe karmic retribution, and who was she to go against the wild? She was no god.

'Great Spirit.' She hated herself for repeating a request she didn't want to make. '*I seek appeasement if you are willing to bestow it.*'

Shakti could sense its frustration so acutely then, that she was half-inclined to believe those emotions were hers.

'*Tell your precious humans this, little witch: take what is mine, and I will respond in kind.*'

For a moment, time seemed to slow, and Shakti found herself stuck staring at a crossroads. Telling the empress that the Great Spirit refused would only leave her frustrated. Neither would she believe Shakti. Aarya would always suspect her of lying and would likely harm Harini as a result. If she lied, and said that the Great Spirit was appeased . . .

How could they refute her? The empress had no way of knowing. She wasn't a witch, and therefore couldn't speak to spirits to confirm or deny what Shakti told her. And if the Great Spirit retaliated – well, Shakti had given them countless warnings. *This Great Spirit is an anomaly. It's unpredictable. There is danger here. Something will go wrong.* Surely, she couldn't be punished for that.

This lie might cost several lives to save just one.

When none of these people cared about her, Shakti found it hard to find even a shred of compassion.

Doesn't matter, she thought. *I will protect my own.*

The disembodied voice of the Great Spirit was still waiting for her answer. Shakti swallowed audibly. '*I shall tell them*,' she promised. 'Thank you, Great Spirit.'

There was a sound akin to laughter. '*Liar. You and I are the same, little witch. You, me, and the false chakravartin.*'

A sudden, sharp chest pain overcame Shakti as she fell on her backside, clutching the ratty fabric of her tunic. Gasping for breath, she attempted to steady herself. This didn't feel like a weakness of the body, but rather the opposite, as if too much power had built up inside and was trying to seek a release. She was too big for her body. This wasn't her.

Had she insulted it? 'You – *you're no liar, Great Spirit*,' she coughed out.

The fog began to recede back up the mountain. Time appeared to invert as it did so.

'*I did not say that I was a liar, little witch*' – the spirit's voice was turning into a whisper – '*only that we are the same.*'

The same as Aarya? She doubted it, but the final phrase echoed as the chill vanished, and then – silence. Both around the site and in her head. Whatever buildup of power she'd sensed in her body had gone, too. The Great Spirit had retreated.

Left confused, Shakti could only work to regain her breath. *Damn the spirits for their ambiguous language*, she thought. What had it meant?

Vaguely, she heard the beginnings of movement behind her.

'Fucking nuisances,' she heard Aarya mutter, and quelled the urge to wring her neck. 'Did the appeasement work? The Great Spirit conceded?'

Too much.

You have taken too much from me.

Liar. You and I are the same.

They were. She had lost, and it *would* lose, to Aarya. The Great Spirit didn't deserve any more pain. She had warned them, and they continued to disregard her.

Everyone here needed to face the consequences of their actions.

'It *agreed*,' Shakti corrected her. 'Excavate what you need, Empress.'

CHAPTER THIRTEEN
Ashoka

Inside a glass atrium flooded with climbing florals, moss and vines, three mayakari huddled around a large wooden table whispering intently among themselves.

With Queen Kalyani leading, Ashoka, Rahil, Sau, and Naila entered. The latter had a drawn expression on her face ever since the queen mentioned cursed weapons. He could understand her apprehension; curses were unpredictable. But he was interested to see how the Kalingan mayakari had weaponized them.

Ashoka trained his eyes on the glass ceiling above. Cloud-white, the moon nestled in the sky amongst a sea of stars. Its light filtered through and lit his skin in a dark blue glow. Lanterns hung haphazardly about the area, allowing him to spot multiple papers and trinkets scattered on tables. Weapons, too, he realized with a start. Swords, maces, daggers and hammers, but all in various states of disrepair.

'What a shame Emperor Adil removed all traces of nature from the royal grounds,' Rahil murmured beside him. Like Ashoka, he had noted the sheer abundance of plant life around the Kalingan palace.

Ashoka grimaced. It was difficult to imagine the Maurya palace smothered by this much greenery. It had been once, but he only knew towering white walls, sand-coloured floors, and jade pools. The only foliage was the sparse, carefully maintained grass on the courtyards and training grounds. The Maurya palace's beauty came from its many intricate sculptures, carved columns, and paintings.

When Queen Kalyani motioned for them to halt they obeyed, watching silently as she made her way towards the three women. Upon noticing her presence, they bowed. The queen bent her head, speaking in Kalingan.

'I've brought with me some valuable guests,' he heard. 'May I show them what you know?'

How surprising that the queen of Kalinga needed permission. His family would've taken without asking.

Queen Kalyani swept a slim hand towards Ashoka, motioned him forward. 'This is Prince Ashoka Maurya of the Ran Empire,' she declared. 'He and his travelling party are guests of mine for the duration of their stay.'

Ashoka didn't miss the way the mayakari tensed at his family name. A muscle ticked in the jaw of the oldest woman as she bowed stiffly. The other two followed suit. One turned her gaze towards the queen and said something in a furious jumble of words, clearly upset. The oldest one continued to stare, unwavering. He didn't need to read minds to know what she was thinking: *Son of a tyrant. Enemy. Threat.*

The severe urge to distance himself from his father arose once more as Ashoka cleared his throat. 'Pleasure to make your acquaintances,' he greeted in Kalingan, meeting their bows. Looks of bewilderment met him when he rose, from the mayakari as well as the queen and her guards.

'Prince Ashoka, this is Raya,' Queen Kalyani gestured towards the oldest mayakari, 'her daughter Aarvi, and Neeru.'

Raya continued to eye him with suspicion. 'Why is the son of Emperor Adil here?' she asked as if she had just discovered a cobra nestled in a baby's cot.

'I have made young Ashoka aware of the existence of cursed weapons,' Queen Kalyani supplied for him. When the three witches shot her horrified looks, the queen chuckled. 'Fear not. The little prince is . . . unlike his father. In fact, he is rather insistent about it.'

Aarvi let out a sceptical hum. Her disbelief bothered him.

Ashoka let his middling Kalingan take over as he tried to explain the situation in Taksila, grateful to have Sau take control whenever he couldn't articulate the right words or string the correct sentence structure together. She spoke with much more assurance than he did, too, but that was her duty.

'Making the mayakari fight like human soldiers,' Raya tsked. 'You're a man been given the power of a witch.'

Ashoka faltered, unable to understand the phrase. 'I – what?'

'Colloquialism: *a dangerous fool*,' Sau translated, smirking.

Despite himself, he grinned but it soon faltered. 'There was – is – no other option for me,' he replied. 'There aren't enough soldiers to defend Taksila when my sister eventually reclaims it, so I made the decision to involve the mayakari. Many agreed to fight. Some, understandably, chose not to.'

'Be that as it may, they are only as strong as a human soldier with a sword,' Neeru said. 'Despite what the people of your empire believe, we don't have superhuman strength, Prince Ashoka. We need our abilities to propel us.'

Aarvi glanced at Naila. 'You appear repulsed,' she said.

When Naila shot them a confused look, Sau quickly interpreted. In response, Naila schooled her expression into a more ambivalent one. 'The act of cursing is already a heavy burden,' she replied. Not a beat behind, Sau translated her words. 'To somehow *innovate* it—'

'Have you ever cursed a living being?' Aarvi interrupted, tilting her head in curiosity.

Naila glanced at him briefly. 'I haven't had to,' she replied, 'not yet. Others I know have, but it's not done out of . . . carefree abandon.'

'Yes, well, the mayakari of the Ran Empire are more traditionalist that way,' Neeru replied, 'but I can't blame you. When your livelihoods are annihilated, there's no way to move forward. Either you stay rooted or regress. There is no room for change or innovation when survival remains the most pressing concern. Cursed weapons would be the furthest thing from your mind.'

Naila still appeared wary. 'But cursing brings on—'

'—negative karma?' Raya finished. 'You're right.'

'But . . . I don't understand,' Naila said, frowning. 'Cursing is for the living. How do you use it on an inanimate object?'

'Because what matters is the intent,' Raya answered. 'The function of a curse is to harm a living being. The weapon acts like an intermediary. Here, you don't need to curse a specific person, you only speak the curse, imbue magic into a weapon. Whoever the weapon is used on, the curse manifests.'

'What's the point, then?' Naila asked, frowning. 'It's the same principle, isn't it? Infuse a weapon with a curse to use against another, but you have no idea how or when the curse will enact.'

Ashoka hummed in agreement. Although Queen Kalyani had suggested their existence like a monumental discovery, he had been wondering the same thing. *Was* there a difference?

Raya shook her head. 'Yes, cursing as you currently would is unpredictable in that it can express itself in the blink of an eye or in several years' time. What we've found with cursed weapons, however, is the opposite. I must tell you that how the curse enacts still remains up to chance. However, one can be a bit more specific in wording, and there is a . . . consistency in manifestation.'

Naila continued to appear disbelieving. 'How so?'

'Think of usual cursed speech as a low-concentrate energy. When you distil cursed speech into an inanimate object, however, the concentration of energy becomes higher. More potent. A higher build-up of energy results in a quicker release, and when struck results in—'

'—faster acting curses,' Sau murmured.

'How quickly do they work?' Ashoka asked.

Aarvi's eyes gleamed. 'So far, on impact.'

The damage I could do on impact . . .

Shivers of excitement coursed through his body. He heard Naila's sharp intake of breath and Sau's quiet expletive in response to Aarvi's comment. Only Rahil didn't react. He had instead taken to wander around the atrium, under the watchful eye of Queen Kalyani's guards, in silence. From his periphery, Ashoka could see Rahil's figure languidly sauntering around until it stopped.

When he turned, Rahil was running his hand over a table laden with daggers and swords. 'Are these your cursed weapons?' he called out.

'Be careful!' Queen Kalyani warned, her voice panicked. Her guards jumped into action at her tone, beelining for Rahil, who cocked his head, amused, but stepped away from the weapons.

'Must the weapons be specially made?' Sau asked.

'Natural metals are ideal,' Raya replied. 'We've found silver to be the most conducive for curses. Gold is too weak. Alloys don't work at all. Go on – have a look. They're not as explosive as the queen believes them to be.'

'It's wise to be wary of weapons,' the queen replied. 'Especially cursed ones.'

'Point taken, Your Highness,' Raya said.

Ashoka frowned as he joined Rahil by the table and picked up a longsword to assess it. Polished silver with a rudimentary bronze hilt; it looked nothing out of the ordinary. But really, what had he expected – for it to emit sparks?

'Is there no way to tell a cursed weapon from one that isn't?' he asked.

'What're you talking about, Prince Ashoka?' Naila asked. She appeared confused by his question. 'Can't you see the glow?'

'The glow?' This was said in unison by himself, Sau, and Rahil.

Casting uncertain eyes towards the three mayakari, Naila shrugged in response. 'The sword is emitting a faint blue light,' she said. 'It reminds me of the fire that burns when . . .' She swallowed. His stomach lurched uncomfortably.

'Just as a mayakari burns once and dies, so too do cursed weapons,' Neeru remarked. 'Their use is limited to one strike. Whatever curse has been distilled into the weapon, you must hit its target to enact it. A small scrape or a debilitating wound, it doesn't matter so long as you've caused some kind of harm.'

'Can you undo a curse imbued into a cursed weapon?' Naila asked. Ashoka started; he hadn't considered that.

Neeru shook her head. 'No,' she said. 'Considering that they work upon impact and tend to be more violent than spoken curses, there's no way to undo them.'

Neeru spoke about harm so casually that it was almost laughable to know she was a mayakari. It made his father's fear of their power seem more compelling.

'How many have you created, Queen Kalyani?' he asked.

'We can't mass-produce cursed weapons,' Queen Kalyani told him. 'Understandably, very few mayakari wish to undertake this endeavour. Those who do agreed to create them in limited number for my personal guards alone. I have been told that cursing expends a great deal of a mayakari's energy. Hence, their use must be calculated.'

Calculated. Ashoka understood her sentiment. Weapons with such power weren't meant for regular use.

'Humans can wield cursed weapons as well, yes?' he asked, nodding towards one of the queen's soldiers.

'Correct.' The queen's expression was grave despite the admission. 'I'm aware of how hypocritical this will sound, but mayakari magic is not meant for humans. In the wrong hands, you can surely understand what consequences this will bring.'

Ashoka was only half listening. His entire focus was on the weapons.

'Prince Ashoka?'

He glanced up. Queen Kalyani and the three mayakari were watching him curiously. He gestured to the swords.

'The cursed weapons,' he said. 'May I see them in action?'

CHAPTER FOURTEEN
Ashoka

'A demonstration?'

The queen didn't seem unsurprised, but the mayakari did. Ashoka hazarded that they were equating him wanting to see cursed magic with his father's known penchant for violence.

'It's a reasonable request,' Rahil spoke up. 'Combining weapons and magic is . . . novel.'

'You distrust our words, soldier?' Aarvi retorted.

'No,' Rahil replied. 'But it's better to see these weapons used in practice, so we know what we're dealing with. Right, Ashoka?'

'Rahil is correct,' he said. 'If it's no trouble . . .?'

Out of all of them, only Naila looked perturbed. Sau, ever practical, agreed with him instantly.

Raya shot him a blank expression. 'We can show you a cursed weapon in action, most certainly,' she replied. 'But you can choose its target, Prince Ashoka.'

He faltered at her words. 'I – what?'

'The target,' she repeated patiently. 'If you intend to see them in use, I request that you select someone or something. Did you expect us to?'

Like a child caught stealing sweets from the kitchen, Ashoka froze under scrutiny. *Wouldn't it be common courtesy for the demonstrators to choose a suitable target*, he wondered. *Pinning it on me . . .*

Does such a choice make you unsure, pathetic boy? It seems the traits of a ruler evade you still.

Adil's voice felt like a thousand needles against his back.

'No,' he eventually said, still wanting to play the game safely. 'Then . . . a tree, perhaps. It's living, after all.'

Neeru appeared rather repulsed by his proposition. 'You wish to harm a minor spirit to satisfy your curiosity, Prince Ashoka?'

'No,' he said quickly.

'An animal, then?' Sau suggested.

Catching Naila's grimace, Ashoka shook his head. 'No,' he repeated, 'but I'm at a loss in thinking of an appropriate subject. I won't suggest my friends. Or anyone here, really. No matter, then.'

Coming up beside him, Rahil pinched his elbow. 'We can't accept a weapon that we haven't seen in use,' he reminded him.

'He's right, Prince Ashoka,' Naila whispered. 'I . . . I would like to see what these cursed weapons can do, too.'

Stuck at a crossroads, Ashoka was rendered mute. There were no alternative ideas to pick from.

A sudden clap of hands diverted his attention. He glanced up to see Queen Kalyani. 'Not to worry. You wanted a demonstration, Prince Ashoka,' she said, 'and I will give you a choice. Come with me, all of you.'

They were transported to the capital's prison by horse and carriage.

Night had long since fallen. As they travelled past the city outskirts, Ashoka glanced to his left. The sea glittered with speckles of blue light. Beautiful, but he found it hard to appreciate, given the tense silence inside their carriage.

The moment he saw looming grey walls and a heavily guarded entrance in the dark of the night, Ashoka knew exactly what awaited him.

'You're going to ask me to pick a prisoner to injure, aren't you, Your Highness?' he asked the queen once they were escorted inside.

'Correct,' said Queen Kalyani. 'Unless . . . you wish to change your mind?'

He became acutely aware of his friends waiting for his response. If they were waiting for the old Ashoka to resurface, drowning in guilt, he wouldn't appear. This was necessary violence to prevent more violence.

'No,' he replied.

'Curses will work in unpredictable ways, Prince Ashoka,' Raya remarked. Of the three mayakari, only she had come with the queen. The two younger witches were hesitant and had refused flat out. 'You may badly injure, mentally torment, or kill. Can you accept such a choice?'

'You think I can't?'

'You did claim to be so unlike your father,' said Raya dispassionately. He didn't know how to respond to that.

The interior of the prison was grim, fixed torchlights illuminated rows upon rows of cells, each assigned a guard. 'This prison isn't for petty crimes, Prince Ashoka,' the queen remarked. 'If that eases your conscience.'

He couldn't tell if it did.

Queen Kalyani led them to a large cell block where the iron doors were opened. Peering inside, Ashoka saw that it was empty. He waited as the queen gave out an order to her soldiers that he couldn't fully understand.

'She asked them to bring the two inmates that arrived three nights ago,' Sau whispered. She appeared discomfited by her surroundings. Ashoka couldn't blame her.

Moments later, he heard scuffling. Advised to step back, he watched as two figures, bound and shackled, were led into the empty cell, along with two chairs. Two men – one old with peppery white hair, and one young, looking to be around his age. Both were tied to the chairs, leaving Ashoka to assess them in stunned silence.

'Two prisoners. One faces capital punishment,' the queen remarked so emotionlessly that she might as well have been discussing recent agricultural innovations. 'This one,' she pointed to the old man on his left, 'bludgeoned his brother to death in a fit of rage. Soldiers could hardly identify the face.'

Spirits. Glancing at the old man, Ashoka would hardly guess that he possessed the physical strength to beat someone to death. But the scowl on his face, the harsh features – they oddly reminded him of his father.

'This one,' the queen pointed to the young man, 'stole a chest's worth of jewellery from a widower and crashed market stalls in his haste to escape.'

He frowned. 'You want me to guess the one who faces death?' The insinuation was clear – one of these men was ordained for death, so whatever guilt he had at the use of the cursed weapon would be eased.

'Correct. Choose your target, Prince Ashoka,' said the queen. Her demeanour was no longer relaxed, but rather assessing. 'Just one. And I will give you the weapon.'

He felt rather than saw Rahil and Naila stiffen. For different reasons, he gathered.

Ashoka glanced at the old man. He looked past his shoulder, eyes empty.

He's taken a life, he reasoned. *This is Kosala all over again. They've both killed. Justice is punitive. Justice is equal.*

Do I really need to see a cursed weapon in action? Why not wait to use it at the right time?

There is never a right time to use a weapon.

He pointed to his left. 'Him.'

The queen said nothing, but motioned to Raya, who produced a long, silver pin from her satchel. Glinting in the low light, Ashoka could only look at it in confusion. It looked like something a lady would wear on her head to keep their hair fastened. 'A pin, Queen Kalyani?'

'For those who can't carry swords around every waking moment, such as myself,' the queen replied. 'It's not a blunt instrument, Prince Ashoka. One can use this pin to puncture skin. Weapons don't always have to come in the form of swords and arrows. Even an object as inconspicuous as a silver hairpin is sufficient. Here.'

With tentative hands, Ashoka grasped the pin. It looked so innocuous. All he had to do was prick the skin, let a bead of blood drop, and he could watch a curse take effect in front of his eyes.

Chance was at play – perhaps this wouldn't kill. Perhaps this would only injure. Only time would tell.

When he approached the old man, Ashoka was surprised that he didn't appear frightened. Instead, all he saw was weariness. Resignation. *Strange*. If faced with the prospect of death, wouldn't any sane person be pleading for their life? Kosala had been afraid to die; Ashoka had seen it in his eyes. Pleading for his life after allowing for multiple to be taken – there had been a vengeful exhilaration in driving his weapon into the man's neck.

This old man wasn't frightened. Killing someone who wasn't afraid of death seemed senseless.

Queen Kalyani's previous words nagged at him. Why offer two prisoners when one clearly had committed a greater degree of harm than the other and then ask him to choose who he wanted to use the cursed weapon on?

Unless she's testing me.

Lowering the pin to his side, Ashoka turned around to face the monarch and the mayakari.

'Something the matter, Prince Ashoka?' asked Kalyani, hands clasped behind her.

Asked so casually, but he knew that tone all too well. It was the same tone his tutor, Lakshini, used to adopt after she presented him with a complicated philosophical term. She was waiting for something. *Questions*. Common-sense questions.

'The old man,' he began. 'What made him bludgeon his brother to death?'

Queen Kalyani's face was impassive. 'The brother assaulted this man's daughter as she slept,' she replied.

His blood ran cold. 'And what happened in between the young man stealing jewels and being caught?'

'Murdered the lover he stole the jewels from,' came the answer, 'and set her house alight. Care to change your choice?'

Slowly, Ashoka became aware that he'd tightened his grip on the head of the pin. 'Yes.'

Queen Kalyani waved her hand, and the old man was escorted out, returned to whatever cell he had been placed in. Still alive.

The young man, who had been calm and quiet thus far, now

began to shift in his seat, straining against the bonds to no avail. Unlike the old man, there was no sense of fatigue. No exhaustion. This one was fearful and angry.

Violence enacted to prevent more violence.

Ashoka grabbed his hand, turned it up to see the palm, uncalloused and smooth. The prisoner's struggling posed some difficulty in steadying the hand, but Ashoka, without a second thought, brought the pin down and pricked the fingertip. A drop of blood bloomed like a rose under the morning light.

A single heartbeat passed, and he half expected it to not work. That argument inside his head would have been useless.

But then the young man began to scream, the sound muffled by the gag. At first, Ashoka couldn't understand what was happening. There were no outward signs of injury, nothing to suggest that anything more than a prick had been dealt.

Ashoka watched with bated breath as the young man's struggling began to cease. It looked less as if he were going limp, and more as though his entire body was stiffening. Drops of perspiration shone on his skin, and Ashoka wondered if he was overheating, wondered if he would faint.

It seemed not, for the young man let out one last muted groan before he sat unblinking, extremities turning unnatural shades of purple and yellow. He heard soft gasps from behind, saw Sau with her hand over her mouth, Rahil watching without expression, and Naila staring at his hands. The pin.

Ashoka had never seen a curse work so quickly and with such brutal efficiency. Cautiously, Ashoka reached out his free hand in front of the young man's face and snapped his fingers, watching for movement. He found none. The prisoner was dead.

This was unimaginable. Unthinkable. The stuff of fantasies, and yet here he was, having used a weapon blessed with powers only a mayakari could use. Dangerous and inviting – a perilous combination.

Murderer.

A sudden sharp *clink* startled him out of his reverie. When he looked down, he saw that in his distraction he had dropped the pin.

One of the soldiers who had restrained the young man performed a quick assessment. 'Dead, Your Highness,' he called out to the silent queen.

Heart thundering, Ashoka reassessed the dead body. The eyes were wide open, shining as brightly as dewdrops. It was only when he was close enough that he could see that what he had thought was sweat was in fact—

'Frost?' he said aloud, both terrified and awed. 'This is – he's been frozen to death.'

'It appears so,' Raya murmured. 'The effects of a curse are always surprising.'

'What was the curse?' he heard Naila ask Raya quietly. 'That was in the weapon?'

'To waste in the cold,' Raya replied with a heavy sigh. 'That was what we meant earlier by saying one can be more specific in their wording. The resulting curse will relate somehow. Think of curses in weapons to be more like riddles.'

'I see,' Naila remarked. She stared at the dead body intensely. 'There's something else that I've been thinking about. This curse affected only one person, but some curses can affect entire bloodlines. I assume curses in weapons can't act in the same manner?'

'You're right. Some curses can affect lineages,' Raya said. 'I've seen that happen once before. A nasty piece of work. You're also correct in assuming that curses in weapons can't act the same as spoken ones. By virtue of their make, they cannot. That isn't to say multiple victims can't be affected. Depending on the wording, imbued curses can act like . . . a contagious disease, I suppose. The curses can infect those who are in close proximity to the victim. Perhaps through touch. Or taste.'

Ashoka's hands were trembling again, tremors that were present even when he tried to relax them by his side. If either of the two women noticed, they didn't comment. It was only Rahil who seemed to note and respond with firm pressure on his shoulder.

Ashoka turned to the queen. She had been watching him carefully.

'Why didn't you tell me which prisoner faced capital punishment at the start, Queen Kalyani?' he asked.

'You're like a starving lion cub being presented fresh meat, Prince Ashoka,' the queen replied, watching her soldiers take the body away. 'It means you'll pounce and devour without appraisal. Who gave the cub meat? It is infected. Poisoned? Fresh? None of these thoughts matter except satiating your hunger.'

Ashoka found that point hard to argue.

'I have given orders for Raya and Aarvi to teach your mayakari the ways of crafting a cursed weapon,' Kalyani continued. 'But I made you do this so you can understand what sort of power you now have in your hands. The Ran Empire's mayakari are just like you, Prince Ashoka. All are hungry lion cubs.'

'You could've simply told me all this beforehand, Queen Kalyani,' he said. 'Without me having to guess which prisoner deserved death.'

'I disagree,' said the queen. 'I wanted to see you make the choice yourself. Theory is all well and good, but when it comes to warfare, you will never understand the weight of your actions until you take a life yourself. This is my gift to you, but if you want my army and my allegiance, you must give me something your family would not. I do not take the lives of my people lightly, Prince Ashoka. Think on it – there is always something I'm willing to bargain for.'

CHAPTER FIFTEEN
Shakti

Shakti was carted back to the palace from the Mountain of Rebirth in the twilight hours. Calling the Great Spirit had given her a strange rush of power. She couldn't explain it, but the sensation was both overpowering and pleasant. Addictive. It was unlike the time she'd summoned the tiger spirit in Kolakola. Part of her wanted to summon it again.

The moment she left the vicinity of the mountain, however, her energy vanished. Her muscles and bones ached. Upon noticing her tiredness on the way back to the palace cells, Aarya ordered for the physician to prescribe another healing tonic.

The gesture should've been touching, but Shakti could only imagine what else the empress was planning to use her at full strength for.

After she drank the tonic – given by the same gruff, balding physician – Shakti fell fast asleep. She dreamed of the Great Spirit she hadn't appeased, its anger rotting the earth. Killing those who hurt it. Raining down destruction, a torrent of fire and ash that smothered the Golden City and its empress. She dreamed of a greyish yellow elephant with a broken tusk, her reaching out to grasp its trunk. Then came darkness, along with a disjointed echo of a voice, dry and rough:

'... I curse you ...'

Shakti knew that voice. Felt the chill down her spine. It was hers.

Curse with what? she yelled into the dark.

As if in response, the echo became louder. Multiplied tenfold, such that it sounded like a thousand screams. It was the same phrase over and over: *I curse you, I curse you, I curse you.* Deafening and useless.

With what? Shakti screamed. *What was it? Who did I curse?*

Deep down, she knew it was a useless endeavour. All she was doing was yelling at herself. Stomach lurching, Shakti felt a sudden chill along her arms and legs and recognized what was happening immediately. She was being pulled out of the dream.

When she opened her eyes, Shakti found that she had slipped off her bedding and onto the prison floor. Disgruntled, she let out a soft expletive as she rolled her stiff muscles, blinking away the grogginess.

Logic told her that she might eventually remember, or she never would. There had only been one option left to find out, and she'd attempted it already, with little success. She wasn't stupid enough to enter Aarya's dreams again. Not when Aarya could torture Harini as punishment. Besides, she had a feeling that the empress expected her presence.

Shakti twisted her neck. The bones cracked pleasantly. Through the small grating above the cell door, she could spot the familiar flicker of lanternlight. Nighttime. She must've slept for hours.

Sighing, she moved to lean against the stone wall. Now that she was awake, it was hard to go back to sleep. How long before the Great Spirit retaliated against the mining? How long could she keep Aarya's suspicions at bay? How long could she keep her friend alive? There was only one answer to all three: *not long.*

She needed to speak to Harini. See how she was faring. The mayakari didn't know about the Collective or her ability to invade dreams. It could take some time to convince her that she was real.

Closing her eyes, Shakti concentrated on her breath. The healing tonic had worked quite well. No longer did her body feel exhausted. She felt re-energized enough to enter the Collective, unlike her last disastrous attempt.

When the faint blue thread appeared in her mind's eye, Shakti followed it and entered the Collective. She thought of Adil.

She materialized somewhere she had never seen before. A

towering stone building loomed ahead of her, six spiral towers stretching to the sky, strands of climbing ivy curling around them like snakes. The front garden was lush and carefully maintained. Various flowers were arranged in square plots: red roses, oleander and anthuriums, among many others. The centrepiece was a marble fountain, on the plinth of which stood the statue of a leopard in a sitting position with a minor spirit atop its head. The spirit's mouth served as a spout, from which water streamed. She walked towards it, marvelling. *What was this place?*

Shakti glanced to her right. In the distance, she spotted a familiar mist-laden mountain. An unpleasant twinge formed in her chest.

'Was this . . .' she murmured to herself, recalling the map in Adil's study, piecing together the location in her head. 'The Great Library?'

'You'd be correct.'

Startled, she looked up. Materializing in front of her was Emperor Adil. He wore clothing Shakti hadn't seen on him in some time: his funeral attire. White tunic and trousers, feet bare. No royal circlet adorned his head.

'Adil.'

'Mayakari.'

For a moment, they stared at each other, until Shakti broke the silence. 'I wouldn't have associated the library with you,' she remarked. 'It was a beautiful place.'

Adil glanced around. Shakti was caught by surprise when his harsh features softened before deciding it must've been a trick of the eye. 'Beautiful, but ultimately useless,' he replied. 'This institution failed to serve me.'

Spoken so dispassionately, Shakti wanted to curse him all over again, but she tamped down her irritation. 'I tried to appease the Great Spirit,' she remarked instead. 'It wouldn't accept it.' She didn't bother telling him how she'd lied to Aarya's face.

Adil seemed unaffected. 'Aarya still tried, then,' he remarked. 'I thought she might, though I'm not surprised by the result. Subha said as much.'

'Is she why you didn't continue mining?'

Jaw clenched tight, Adil turned away from her. 'She was the one who convinced the other mayakari to mine the mountain in the first place,' he said. 'She was also the one that convinced them to stop. *Witches.*' He spat the word out with vitriol.

'You told me that you'd lost to pacifism once,' Shakti said, recalling their first few conversations. 'Did you mean her?'

When Emperor Adil reared back like he'd been stung, Shakti knew she'd guessed correctly. 'Watch your tongue, witch,' he warned, hands clenched by his side.

She latched onto his response, wanting to draw blood. So much fury for one mayakari. It didn't make sense. 'I'm right, aren't I?'

He didn't respond at first. It looked like the emperor was battling within himself whether to answer her, until he let out a frustrated sigh. Perhaps he knew that there was no point in hiding. Not when she had access to his memories.

'Adherence to pacifism makes your kind weak,' he snapped, and made a shooing gesture. 'Leave. You aren't here for me this time. I sensed that much.'

More questions lay in wait at the tip of her tongue, but Shakti made no move to argue with him. She'd entered the Collective to speak to Harini and allowed herself to become distracted. Still, she was curious about what it was that Adil seemed to be burdened by. But that was a tale she needed to force out another time.

Stepping away from him, Shakti gave Adil a mock bow. 'Till we meet again, Emperor Adil.'

She thought of Harini and watched as Adil and the library faded away, until she was transported to the barrier that separated her from the mayakari's dream.

Harini's dream was in soft, muted colours. Eyes closed, she lay on a field of grass as the clouds passed above her. At least her dreams were peaceful, even if her reality wasn't. Steeling herself, Shakti passed through the smog barrier, feeling resistance with every step. The mayakari's mind was strong.

When Shakti finally pushed through and entered Harini's dream, she appeared behind the sleeping witch, an explanation of her abilities ready on her tongue. Somehow, Harini must have sensed her presence, for her eyes shot open and she sat up, turning around in a daze. Upon noticing her, the mayakari's eyes widened.

'*Shakti?*' her pitch rose, and with it, her brows. When she nodded,

Harini's expression morphed into one of understanding. 'The empress speaks the truth, then. You can enter dreams.'

Startled by her utter lack of surprise, Shakti found that she couldn't sputter out a confirmation. 'I . . . she told you?'

'While I was being interrogated, yes,' Harini replied. 'She assumed that I'd assisted you in some way. I didn't believe her at first, but now . . .' she trailed off, seemingly lost in thought.

'How'd you know I wasn't part of your dream?' Shakti asked her.

Harini shrugged. 'The moment you appeared, something felt strange. Natural and unnatural,' she explained. 'It's like I've cast a curse and summoned a Great Spirit in the same breath.'

Could mayakari sense her in their dreams much quicker than non-witches? How interesting.

'How are they treating you?' she asked Harini.

The mayakari smiled ruefully. 'Like an insect,' she replied. 'Food and water are scarce. They've hit me so much that my bruises have yet to heal. But they won't kill me. Not yet at least.'

'Aarya's holding your life as a bargaining tool.' Shakti pursed her lips. 'So I have no choice but to obey her commands.'

'I'm sorry,' Harini whispered. 'What has she made you do?'

Around them, the grass was preternaturally still. 'She made me curse someone,' Shakti admitted. 'I don't know who, and I don't remember what.'

Harini's expression was a mixture of pity and horror. 'Oh, Shakti,' she whispered. 'I'm sorry. Have you felt it enact?'

Shakti frowned. 'What?'

'The curse.' Now, it was Harini's turn to look confused. 'We feel and see death when we cast a curse, but you also sense it just before it enacts. Didn't – *ah*. Your aunt really didn't tell you much, did she?'

Not when it came to cursing the living and raising the dead. Shakti understood that her lack of knowledge hindered her more than she knew. Part of her was irritated by Jaya, but the other, logical part understood why she'd never taught it.

'But when I cast the curse on Adil, I didn't feel . . .' Shakti began, then paused to think. 'I suppose it worked immediately, so that imagery of death overlapped. I haven't felt death. Not that I remember. Maybe there's a chance it hasn't worked yet.'

'Perhaps,' Harini agreed, a pitying smile on her lips that Shakti disliked. She hated pity. 'That should give you some consolation, yes? Even time to recall what you've forgotten. What else has the new empress made you do?'

'It's nothing horrible,' Shakti replied, trying to sound upbeat. 'I had to visit the Collective and speak to Emperor Adil on her behalf. Appease the Great Spirit of the Mountain of Rebirth just this morning.'

At the mention of the Great Spirit, Harini turned her head sharply. 'A child of Adil Maurya asked you to perform an *appeasement rite?*' she exclaimed. 'On that spirit, of all creatures? I think she's just waiting until you disobey her.'

I already have. Quickly, Shakti informed Harini of the explosive mineral that Aarya was attempting to mine. The more she spoke, the darker Harini's face became.

'Shakti, that was a bad idea,' she said afterward, worrying her lower lip. 'On any other Great Spirit, there would be no problem. But this one is . . . even with my life at stake, I'd rather you didn't disturb it.'

A very Jaya-like answer. A very elder-mayakari answer, really, but an understandable one. Shakti just didn't know if she could say the same. 'I thought as much.'

'Did you . . . manage to appease it?' Harini inquired, raising her eyebrows.

'No,' Shakti said. 'I couldn't.'

The mayakari stayed quiet for a while before she finally asked, 'Couldn't or wouldn't?'

Sighing, Shakti lay down next to her. Above them, the false sky was an unusual blue. A white winged serpent darted in between the clouds. 'Both,' she admitted. 'I began the appeasement rite, but I didn't want to go through with it. Neither did the Great Spirit. In fact, it refused, and I won't force a Great Spirit's hand.'

She couldn't see Harini's expression. Didn't want to see it, in case she saw disappointment. 'You didn't perform the appeasement rite and yet you're still alive,' said the mayakari. 'Let me guess – you lied to the empress.'

'She wouldn't know a thing,' Shakti defended herself. 'Besides,

I warned her multiple times. "The Great Spirit is unpredictable". It's her fault for proceeding to mine the area anyway.'

'You want to hurt her.'

Uttered as a truth. Not even a question. Shakti shrugged. 'I do. So what?'

'She'll find out what you did,' Harini promised, her expression defeated. 'One way or another, and then . . . at least I've been lucky to be alive this long.'

Shakti knew from the mayakari's dejected tone that she expected death at any moment. 'Have you made peace with death?'

'No,' Harini replied. 'I should, because I'll be reborn as something better, but I fear death. Despite this life being a nightmare, I'm attached to it. I don't want to die, Shakti. Does that make me a bad witch?'

The last words were uttered with a slight catch, as if Harini truly believed it. Shakti's heart broke.

'*No*. No, it doesn't,' she said, reaching out to grasp Harini's hand. She wished fervently that the mayakari could somehow feel her squeezing but knew she wouldn't. The absence of physical sensation in dreams was maddening. 'I think the code we learn restricts us. Other than magic, we're no different from non-mayakari. We feel and think the same, and in that way we're just as human. I fear death, too.'

The more she spoke, the more Shakti's mind turned. They couldn't stay down in the cells for much longer. Harini was right. Who knew how long Aarya would plan to keep her for. They needed to escape but had no way of doing it. No plan. No outside help.

But I do.

Shakti sat up. She *did* have outside help.

'Shakti?' Harini sounded confused. 'What's wrong?'

'Nothing.' There was one person, far away in Taksila, who would return to the Golden City if he knew of their predicament. One person who could outmanoeuvre Aarya.

'I'll get us both out,' she promised, 'and I'll get Prince Ashoka's help to do it.'

CHAPTER SIXTEEN
Ashoka

Unable to get a proper sleep and needing to clear his mind, Ashoka visited the palace's serpent pens for an early morning flight. Rahil came with him.

Kalingan winged serpents were much larger than those in the Maurya palace. In comparison to the giant beasts here, Sahry was a runt. He regretted not bringing her. His serpent would've enjoyed the freedom Trikalinga afforded. Instead, he was advised by one of the handlers to fly on Mir. She was a beautiful, green-scaled winged serpent with pale silver wings and eyes and considered one of the most amenable of the lot.

He was able to saddle the serpent on his own without fuss. The handler had offered, but Ashoka waved him away. There was something calming about going through the motions of pacifying a serpent and saddling it. Mir, for her part, was calm and receptive.

'Want to join me?' he asked Rahil, once he'd finished tying the last strap.

Rahil hesitated and glanced at the handler. 'If there's a calmer serpent available,' he replied.

Ashoka knew what he was thinking. 'Don't worry. You won't break a leg. These winged serpents seem more welcoming than Sahry.'

'Any winged serpent is more welcoming than Sahry,' Rahil

muttered. When Ashoka glared, he smirked. 'Like owner, like pet, I see.'

'Oh, be quiet,' Ashoka retorted, but he was smiling. 'Go on, I'll wait.'

Rahil was directed towards a reddish-brown serpent the same size as Mir, and soon they were flying past the palace and circling the cliffs. The wind whipped his hair relentlessly as they flew, admiring the vast stretch of ocean in front of them. Below, Trikalinga looked like a maze. Ships entering through The Sea Dragon's Wall looked like a child's playthings.

In the dawn light, Mir's scales flashed silver, bringing Ashoka's thoughts back to the cursed hairpin. The drop of blood. Skin crystalized as if the young man had travelled to the Frozen Lands and died there. Each time the righteous part of his mind castigated him for murder, there always came a quick defence.

He was already marked for death. You just hastened the process.

It was, he finally decided, a regrettable truth.

Eventually, he lost himself to the sensation of flying. Rahil invited him to a race, which was a terrible idea on his part. It was one of the few things Ashoka could best him at and, sure enough, he did. Rahil failed to use the wind to his advantage and unintentionally kept his serpent lower to the ground, while Ashoka flew higher, increasing his speed.

When they finally landed on solid ground back at the serpent pens, he was in a much lighter mood. As they wandered back to his guest quarters, Rahil bumped shoulders with him.

'Done with your agonizing?' he asked, still sounding breathless from the flight.

'I wasn't agonizing,' Ashoka refuted him lamely, turning a corner into an open-air corridor. He'd been fixating on the blue and white tiled floors, sand-coloured pillars, and the view of the Odhi Ocean beyond, but Rahil's question made him break concentration.

Rahil's flat stare made him cringe. 'You were,' he said, before coming to a halt. 'Piece of advice, if you'll take it?'

It wasn't too long ago that Rahil's 'advice' had left them in silence, and Rahil seemed to recognize this, too. He held both hands up in a placating manner. 'I'm not trying to force you, Ashoka. I'm just telling you what I see.'

Eyeing him warily, Ashoka nodded. 'All right.'

'You keep wavering,' Rahil said, arms crossing over his chest. 'I can see it. Sometimes, you're all for revolution and violence. Other times, like with the prisoner, you get into your own head trying to justify a death. Don't.'

'Don't?'

'Having multiple moral quandaries when you're planning to take over the throne isn't advisable, and I think Sau will agree with me there,' replied Rahil. 'Innocent people will die, and though you can try to limit it, it'll happen anyway. Fully commit to your cause. Make decisiveness your strength, and not have indecisiveness become your weakness. Trust me. The latter is a death sentence in combat, and just as much so outside of it.'

Rahil was right. Deep down, Ashoka knew that every justification he'd made for violence was to subdue his inner idealism.

'You're right,' he said, watching Rahil's brows lift in surprise, as if he had expected a rebuttal. 'I already knew that, deep down. It's just hard to fully let go of my old self.'

Attachment to self. *Upādāna*. Did he still crave who he was before Taksila? In some way, Ashoka supposed, he did. That version of himself held an attractive, but ignorant idealism. This unintentional craving caused him needless suffering.

He didn't want to suffer.

Ashoka glanced at the sea. Was that who Queen Kalyani saw, too – an indecisive child? She wanted something of greater monetary value, and he had an inkling of what it was. It would be a blow for the Ran Empire to lose.

'Let's go,' he said, nudging Rahil gently. 'I need to find Sau.'

When they entered his quarters, Ashoka found Sau and Naila lounging on a settee and gulping down a pastel-yellow drink.

'Prince Ashoka, Rahil – the queen wishes to speak to you in her private gardens,' Naila said when they entered. The mayakari appeared a little tired. She'd visited Aarvi and Raya the night before to view the exact steps of creating a cursed weapon. As she explained it, the process was like casting spoken curses, but more taxing. Meanwhile, Sau had gone to speak with Queen Kalyani's advisors to glean a sense of their priorities when it came to the kingdom. Often, advisors made for better informants. They heard what was usually sanitized for royals.

Finally. Ashoka knew he had to offer her the Saankru Islands. There was nothing more appealing to the queen and the Kalingan Kingdom. Sau didn't like the idea. She continued to push against it, even now. 'What about giving her a majority of control, but not total?' she asked as he motioned for her to get up.

'No, that'll come across as disingenuous,' he said. 'It'll be as if I said "here, have most of your own land back, but still give me some control so I can make sure it's being used correctly". I want her help, not to make her dislike me. We'll offer its complete return.'

Bringing both hands to her face, Sau let out a frustrated groan. 'All right,' she said. 'Let's try and negotiate for an army.'

Queen Kalyani's private gardens were more beautiful than the atrium.

They faced the sea. Green vines twined around white marble pillars. Sea lavender and maple-leaved mallow grew in large, carefully cultivated clumps. Three circular blue pools in the middle of the garden bled into each other, each made to mimic the ocean floor. Clumps of red coral and anemone were scattered across the white sands, and seaweed drifted lazily in the still water.

The queen observed one of the pools in silence with four guards behind her. When Ashoka and his companions' arrival was announced, she glanced up and smiled.

'Ah, good, you're here,' she welcomed them. 'I heard you were absent for some time, Prince Ashoka. Riding our serpents?'

He nodded. 'Flying helps me think,' he said.

'And what is it you have to think about?' When he didn't answer immediately, she did it for him. 'Taking a life is difficult, but in your circumstance, necessary.'

Ashoka shook his head. 'I've done it before,' he replied, watching her eyebrows rise. 'As you say, a necessary death.'

'Hm.'

'I have another proposal for you,' he said. 'One I think you might be swayed by.'

For a long moment, Queen Kalyani said nothing else, only turning to watch as a breeze caused small waves to form. 'Prince Ashoka, you're young. Newborn. Idealistic, and in being so, foolish. If you wish to help every oppressed person you see, be my guest. But you will not truly understand the consequences till much later. Stepping into another state's affairs will sever ties and break bonds that have been forged since before you were born. There is a reason I err on the side of caution when it comes to you.'

Her words were in stark opposition to what his mother used to tell him: that the young and foolish could change the world. But he realized now she'd never suggested it would be for the better. After all, those changes Aarya was making certainly weren't.

'However,' she added, 'old age blinds in places youth does not. Tell me of your new proposal.'

'If you negotiate a security guarantee with Queen Malika,' he replied, 'and help me take control of the border – and the Satva state when my sister eventually attacks – and I win, I will return the Saankru Islands to the rule of the Kalingan Kingdom.'

The queen's red lips parted in surprise. Even her soldiers became slack-jawed. The queen composed herself quickly, a dint in her forehead appearing. 'You will return the islands to the Kalingan Kingdom?' she echoed in disbelief. 'In their *entirety*?'

'Yes,' he promised. 'Ran soldiers and their weapons will be removed, I guarantee it.'

'That is a mighty price,' mused the queen. 'Your family wouldn't dare give it up.'

'The Mauryas took control of it because it was a strategically advantageous location,' he said. 'But it was your land in the first place. I will return it to you. On my life, I promise.'

For a long while, the queen was silent, likely weighing up the benefits. The land and people would return to its rightful territory. The advisors would no longer press upon the queen, releasing her from such headaches. It would be a monetary gain for the Kalingan Kingdom. They could gain a profit from merchant ships as the

Ran Empire currently did. All in exchange for bodies and weapons that he could use against his sister.

'Specify your exact demands with Queen Malika,' Queen Kalyani ordered.

She was considering it. Good. 'Mahvo is a southern kingdom; spirits know how many natural resources they can provide you with in exchange for aid against a potential Ran assault,' he said. 'Once the deal is signed, your soldiers can arrive from the South Odhi Ocean – it's not controlled by us. Make the treaty known too; it'll infuriate Aarya, that I can guarantee. She's the worst parts of my father, Queen Kalyani, so I know her bruised ego won't sit idle while Ran weapons continue to be transported to the south. She will retaliate. She will trespass into Mahvo, and it will become the catalyst to begin my quest to occupy the throne.'

His Kalingan here was not advanced enough to explain himself, so he had Sau translate it directly, watching the queen narrow her eyes in consideration.

'I can only send so many of my soldiers to Mahvo's borders. Numbers will still be a problem, Prince Ashoka. If this is the path you choose to take, you must be able to stand your ground, and for that, I suggest you try and permanently secure that deal you made with Prince Ryu. I heard it got you Ridi soldiers in Taksila when Emperor Arush sent Ran soldiers up north, and I assume your sister won't keep those.'

'She's already removing them from the northern posts,' Ashoka replied. Aarya had been against sending soldiers to the Frozen Lands from the very beginning. 'But Crown Prince Ryu isn't a threat to us.'

'Oh certainly, he is not a threat to *me*,' the queen remarked. 'The Crown Prince and I have some vested interests, but his late mother and Emperor Adil have old agreements between them. The Ridi Empire has always been an ally of the Mauryas. When pressure reaches a tipping point, they will not be so beholden to you.'

'I disagree, Your Highness,' said Sau. 'The prince is still green. He's not his mother.' She defended Prince Ryu with such confidence that Ashoka wondered what made her so sure of him.

'*Green*,' Queen Kalyani repeated. 'Easily swayed, you mean?'

'If that is the connotation Your Highness chooses it to be.'

The queen chuckled, but it was humourless. Worried that she would soon turn down any further propositions, Ashoka played his last hand. 'There is no easy way to win a war, Your Highness,' he said. 'But I'm offering you the islands. Not guaranteed, but if you help me take the throne, they're yours.'

His proposition truly seemed to have stumped the queen. 'This is a gamble,' she murmured. 'It could very well end in disaster.'

'It could,' he agreed, 'but such is the nature of a gamble. What will it be, Your Highness?'

A long silence descended between them. The queen turned her attention back to the sea, appearing to be in deep contemplation.

'You have a deal,' she said.

CHAPTER SEVENTEEN
Ashoka

In his dreams, Ashoka saw his father sitting beneath the shade of a na tree.

Anxiety surfaced on instinct and turned his mind into a blank. Ruby circlet. Gold armbands. Trimmed black beard. A hard face made harsh by nature like granite worn and grooved over time. He had not changed. *Would not* change, not since he died so young. His father would never grow old because he remained immortalized in bitter memories.

The last dream Ashoka had of his father, he remembered plunging a sword through his heart. Dream Adil sat cross-legged; eyes closed. Despite the surrounds resembling a forest, the telltale shimmers of nature spirits were absent. When he cracked one eye open, Ashoka let out an unsteady breath.

'Ashoka,' his father called out. 'Why have you come to disturb me?'

'I haven't,' he replied, surprised to hear his own voice sound so steady.

'Useless boy,' his father muttered, closing his eyes again. 'Go hunt the deer and then return.'

His temper flared. Recollections of the deer he and Rahil buried resurfaced: the glassy eyes, the soft fur, the wet nose. The world turned grey before he pushed the memory away and the colours returned.

'No,' he remarked. 'I won't.'

'Weakling,' his father responded. 'Those who are weak cannot lead. Those who cannot lead will never become emperor. The Obsidian Throne is not yours, boy.'

Bastard, he thought viciously.

It was as if Adil had heard his thoughts, for he laughed. 'As are you,' his father said. The smile he shot was cruel. Spiteful.

Part of Ashoka wanted to force himself awake while the other half wanted to stay and spit fire against his father in retaliation. He wanted to say a thousand things he never had the courage to say when Adil was alive.

Young Ashoka had once dreamed of a more tolerant father. A father who didn't seem to critique and harangue his every decision, his very existence. A father who hadn't burned his ear. But when reality continued to fail him time and time again, his dreams eventually gave up on him, too. After all, there had been no strong foundation to begin with, only a shoddy mud castle built by an ignorant child.

Suddenly, a sharp flash of pain ricocheted through his head. It felt as if something had smacked right through his skin. His father's body went rigid; eyes turning vacant. When his gaze refocused on Ashoka, a desperate, triumphant gleam overtook what had once been derisive.

'The Obsidian Throne can be yours,' his father said. 'Others may doubt you, but I don't.'

His father was smiling. At *him*. The expression stopped Ashoka dead in his tracks. 'I – what?'

Praise? Something was amiss.

'You want the throne?' Emperor Adil asked. 'Take it, my son.'

This was not his father.

'Who are you?' Ashoka asked, eyes narrowing. 'Tell me.'

'Interesting.' His father's features vanished, leaving behind skin as smooth as a forearm. For a moment, Ashoka stood rooted to the spot, staring at a faceless horror until his father's figure shifted. It shrank and morphed into one that was slender, bonier. The royal regalia disappeared. The hair lengthened. A face began to sketch itself anew; hollowed cheeks, two-toned lips, a strong nose and a pair of eyes burdened by despair.

He knew this face. All those eyes were missing was that gratuitous shadow of kohl. He hadn't seen this face in what seemed like years.

'Shakti,' he said.

'Prince Ashoka,' she greeted him. Her voice sounded strained. 'It's been quite some time.'

What a strange dream. 'Are you a manifestation of my guilt?' he asked her.

The mayakari frowned. 'This is no dream, Prince Ashoka,' she began, before pausing. 'No, I misspoke – this *is* your dream, but I'm no manifestation. I'm real.'

He cracked a smile. 'Dreams aren't real.'

'Spirits,' he heard her mutter. 'I have no time for this. Listen to me, Prince Ashoka: *I am real*. I have the power to invade dreams, and I've entered yours.'

Rationality cautioned him, but intuition advised him to believe her. 'Then prove you are.'

'In a dream?' She sounded incredulous. 'I just morphed from your father to myself. What else do you want – to reveal an unsaid secret of yours?'

Shrugging, he motioned for her to go ahead.

'Perhaps a reminder of one of your dreams that I observed,' she said finally. Wariness tinged her voice. 'One where you and Rahil sat together and observed the hills. One where your father materialized, goaded you, and you tried to dagger him through the heart.'

That dream remained as clear and sharp as a lived memory. It had given him a wild rush of emotion, of vindication.

His thoughts went into disarray. *Impossible.* Mayakari couldn't invade dreams. *How had she been there?*

'How are you able to do this?' he responded, thunderstruck. 'A witch's powers are limited to three. I do not know a single mayakari who can invade dreams.'

Each question was fired like an arrow: precise, direct. He watched Shakti train her gaze upward for a moment like she was sifting through them. A groan escaped her lips as she stood, the motion forcing the spring-green tree above her to shift into one that was dead and withered.

'Of course, you're right – mayakari powers are only limited to three. But not me,' she confessed. 'I attained this power because I cursed your father and suffered an unexpected consequence. Now, I can invade dreams – and speak to him.' With each answer, she took a step forward until they were face to face. Bruises and lacerations appeared and disappeared on her skin.

Ashoka froze. '*You* were the witch that cursed my father?' he asked, astonished. The knowledge didn't hurt him. It only bothered him that she hadn't trusted him enough to say it while she was in the palace. Each new sentence was more unbelievable than the last. 'And what do you mean you can speak to him? He's dead, Shakti.'

The mayakari's entire body twitched. 'I'll tell you everything I know, Prince Ashoka,' she said, wincing, 'but I need your help first. Please.'

She uttered every word with an air of fatigue, as if it cost her energy to remain here. Concerned, Ashoka started towards her. 'What happened? Are you safe?'

'No. Your sister discovered that I'm a mayakari and she's been keeping me trapped in the palace cells. There's no way for us to escape.'

Ashoka blanched. That explained the cuts. Trust Aarya to hurt innocents and keep them in cages. 'What do you mean by "*us*"?'

Shakti hung her head. 'She has Harini, too,' she whispered.

Ashoka's stomach lurched.

'No,' he said woodenly, stepping back. She'd been safe all this time. *How* . . .

'It was my fault,' Shakti said. She appeared wracked with guilt. 'I used my new abilities too recklessly and . . . I told her to run, and she did. But – but Aarya caught her.'

Ashoka found himself unable to string a coherent thought together. He'd wanted to take them both to Taksila, but his sister intervened, keeping Shakti chained to her. And then Harini – selfless or stupid, or both – elected to return to the capital after she'd helped him in Taksila. She was one mayakari he had protected for years. To have her be discovered, facing certain death . . .

But something was amiss. 'Aarya is keeping you both prisoner?'

When it came to mayakari, he couldn't believe that she would simply let one rot away in a prison. They were burned immediately. 'She doesn't keep witches alive. Unless . . .'

'She knows what I can do,' Shakti confirmed. 'Not only can I invade dreams, but once in them, I can force others to follow commands when they wake. She's forcing me to carry out her orders by keeping Harini alive as leverage.'

Ashoka could barely tamp down his myriad thoughts. Curses. Dream invasions. Shakti and Harini, imprisoned. Begrudgingly, he had to appreciate Aarya's methods. How else could she control a witch who flouted their codes?

He wracked his brains to recall any strange dreams as of late. 'Have you been entering my dreams? You said you saw one.'

'Not under her command, and not since the one I told you about,' Shakti said. Behind her, the tree revived itself once more. 'She's scared because – because I've used it against her before. A few times. I can't remember anything that happened after I was captured. They drugged me for most of it.'

A chill ran down his spine. They would've used a concoction with milk of poppy on her. 'What has she made you do?' he asked quietly.

'Speak to your father, for one. He's a very unpleasant person,' Shakti said. It seemed to be an attempt at humour, but Ashoka found himself rooted to the spot, unable to smile. 'Your sister wants to excavate a mineral she's found near the Mountain of Rebirth, and I was asked to appease the Great Spirit.'

As she launched into a lengthy explanation about his *father* existing in her consciousness, the strange mineral deposits and the Great Spirit of the mountain, he couldn't help pitying the complicated web Shakti had found herself trapped in. When she admitted to not following through on Aarya's orders and appeasing the Great Spirit, he found himself shaking his head in disbelief and grudging respect.

'Can you help us escape?' Shakti asked at the end. She sounded defeated. 'You're the only chance I have left. If it had just been me, I would've tried anything. But Harini is here, and I can't risk her life.'

He needed to leave Trikalinga as soon as he could. From the sounds of Shakti's story, there didn't seem to be a lot of time left for the two mayakari. It would satiate Aarya for the time being, too, having him return to the capital. Going to see the mayakari, however, posed a problem. Aarya wouldn't trust him around witches at all, now.

'For you to have a chance of escape, I need to twist her arm.' Ashoka didn't realize that he'd said it out loud until Shakti let out a malicious laugh. 'What?'

'You can threaten her with a secret, Prince Ashoka,' Shakti said. 'She was the one who poisoned your brother.'

'*She* did?' he exclaimed. He *knew* there had been something odd involved with his brother's condition. 'Are you certain?'

Shakti nodded. 'The empress said it to my face, Prince Ashoka,' she said. 'Crushed sea mango in his drink. The plant is effective at affecting the heart. She's made people believe that I had something to do with it. Gives her an excuse to keep me locked up and not burned immediately for prolonged "questioning".'

Blaming a witch for her mistakes – Ashoka expected it. That kind of behaviour was exactly like their father's. But for Aarya to even *think* of poisoning her own blood. He knew she was ruthless, but this was a new level of cruelty. Between the three of them, Arush was more Aarya's ally than he was.

'Who knows the truth?' he asked.

'No one,' Shakti replied, laughing sadly. 'She said so herself: who'd believe the word of a witch over the word of an empress?'

A viper, that sister of mine. Eager to protract her fangs. Eager to bite and kill. She was correct. No one would believe a witch.

But it would do him good to control a venomous snake. To make sure those fangs weren't bared at him. People might not believe a witch, but they might believe a prince.

Aarya was human. She could be threatened. Except, there was a small problem.

'If I confront her about this, won't she know who would've told me?' Ashoka asked. 'She'll hurt you more. Or worse, kill you.'

Shakti shot him a wan smile. 'Oh yes, Aarya will hurt me,' she replied. 'I can manage that. She won't kill me, though. I once asked her outright and she refused.'

'That's . . . unexpected.'

Shakti tapped the side of her head. 'Adil's consciousness and my powers are what's keeping her from killing me,' she said bitterly. 'I'm *useful*.'

You're a weapon, he thought, but didn't say it out loud. Shakti's dejected expression made his heart clench. 'I'll come for you both,' he promised. 'I'm in Trikalinga, but I'll return to the capital as soon as possible.'

Surprise flashed across Shakti's face like she had expected to have to put up a fight. 'Thank you,' she whispered. 'And I – I must tell you something else. I've done something, I think. Something terrible. I . . .' She seemed to consider what she was saying before she shook her head. 'Something for later.'

Ashoka grasped her hand. Scabs and indents lined the thin skin, but he could not feel them. 'I can't help every mayakari,' he said quietly, 'but I can help you. And don't thank me – I should be thanking you instead.'

'For what?'

'For cursing him,' Ashoka replied simply, 'you did me a favour that I didn't realize was needed.'

His companions took some time to get over the shock of Shakti and her ability to invade dreams when he informed them the following morning. They were more uncertain during his proposed idea to help Shakti escape and return to Taksila. Funnily enough, they took little time accepting the fact that it was Aarya who had poisoned Arush.

Out of all of them, Sau took the longest to convince. It wasn't that she rejected his claims, but more that she questioned his plan to free Shakti.

'What is it you think you can do?' she'd asked brusquely. 'Waltz into the prison cells, flash a pretty smile at the guards and hope they look the other way? There's a *mayakari* in the palace, one who has powers other witches do not. Best believe your sister will have her under lock and key. Can you—'

'—I won't be the one—'

'—and not to mention that every person in the palace, including the leopards, know that you're a mayakari sympathizer after Taksila. They won't let you within a thousand paces of the cell. Threaten Aarya all you want, but she'll find a way to keep you out.'

'Sau,' Rahil had placed a gentle hand on her head, one which she brushed off in irritation, 'perhaps let Ashoka get a word in before you berate him?'

'Don't patronize me, idiot,' she'd grumbled. 'I know what Ashoka's thinking. Instead of him helping Shakti escape, he'll have one of us attempt it instead and my bets are on you – *am I wrong?*'

She wasn't. In his defence, crafting an escape plan for what could be a heavily fortified area while fighting sleep had been difficult. For Sau, who appreciated proper planning, it read like a disorganized mess.

When he'd hung in head in deference, she scoffed. 'I knew it. Discard your plans. We can only make one when we return to the capital and assess the situation there.'

They set sail for Luth the following day.

Queen Kalyani had been more than willing to provide an unassuming charter ship for their journey back to Luth. From Luth, they would return to Taksila. Suspicion would be raised if they returned to the Golden City by sea. Returning by riverboat down south was the obvious option.

Surrounded by watchful soldiers, Queen Kalyani stood outside on the steps of the palace, waiting graciously with them as the carriage that would take them to the port arrived. Sau and Rahil were whispering between themselves while Naila stood silently next to him. She looked perturbed.

Glancing around them to make sure no one was listening, Ashoka leaned down to whisper into the shell of her ear. 'Are you all right?'

Wincing, Naila wrung her hands together behind her back. 'I still can't wrap my head around it,' she whispered back. 'She cursed the emperor but obtained an ability where she could speak to him *and* invade dreams? That doesn't make sense.' It seemed that Shakti's powers were still gnawing away at her.

'It doesn't,' he agreed, 'but I'm sure there's a reasonable explanation.'

'Well, once you bring her to Taksila, I'll be sure to ask her,' Naila replied. Unlike Ashoka, Sau, and Rahil, the mayakari wouldn't journey with them to the Golden City but rather stay in Taksila and instruct the resistance on how to construct cursed weapons. It would've been laughably stupid to risk her life in the capital.

He was about to say more but stopped when a shadow fell across them. Amid their hushed conversation, Queen Kalyani had approached them, observing with a polite smile. Under the sun, her sari glimmered a deep blue, reminding him of the ocean here glowing at night. 'Prince Ashoka,' she said. 'Am I interrupting?'

'Not at all, Queen Kalyani,' he replied.

'I wanted to thank you again,' she remarked. 'For offering to return the Saankru Islands. Your father would never have done so.'

'Its people are Kalingan,' said Ashoka, 'and I'm willing to make such sacrifices to keep innocent mayakari alive.'

'You have the makings of a just *chakravartin*,' the queen remarked, before her attention was momentarily taken away. 'Ah – your carriage is here.'

Pulled by horses, an inconspicuous carriage stopped at the base of the palace steps. Compared to the Ran Empire's giant leopards the horses appeared diminutive.

'How unfortunate that you had to cut your visit short, Prince Ashoka,' the queen remarked. 'Perhaps next time you can bring your winged serpent and enjoy Trikalinga's sights for longer.'

Next time. She said it with such assuredness. Ashoka, however, was more wary of keeping such a promise. Who knew what awaited him in the Golden City?

'While you travel back home, I shall meet with Queen Malika,' the queen continued. 'If negotiations prove successful, soldiers will be sent to the borders. The generals I send will be instructed to follow your orders. All correspondence will be sent to Taksila – I assume you have no qualms with that?'

'None.'

'Good,' she said. 'May fortune favour you, Prince Ashoka.'

Ashoka bowed. 'Queen Kalyani,' he replied. 'I cannot thank you and your generosity enough.'

'War is never generous,' Queen Kalyani said before motioning a curious Naila closer to them. 'Before you go, Prince Ashoka – a small gift for you and the young mayakari.'

Gesturing for two attendants to come forward, she placed one hand lightly over what the men held in their hands: a wooden tray covered by a blue cloth. With a practised flourish, she swept it away to reveal two pairs of slim daggers and a set of the same pins he'd used two nights ago nestled within soft-looking cushions. Beside each dagger pair was a customized sheath.

The back of his throat dried up. Though the daggers appeared innocuous, he could hazard a guess as to what they were, as did Naila.

'I would hardly call cursed weapons a *small gift*, Queen Kalyani,' she said, gaze fixated on the daggers. 'Why would you—'

'You have been taught the method of construction,' the queen interrupted in a gentle but firm manner. 'It seems rather imprudent to send you back to Taksila to rebuild a cursed weapon from memory alone. Aarvi insisted you have them, so please – the daggers are yours. As are the pins – a reminder that any object can be turned into a weapon. Customarily, the mayakari don't carry swords. Hairpins are inconspicuous enough. Easy to hide and easy to use if you're ever in trouble.'

The attendant closest to Naila presented the first pair of daggers and the set of hairpins to her. Ashoka expected her to protest, but she accepted them without question.

'Aarvi cursed them with something simple,' the queen continued. '"Quick death" for the pearl-encrusted hilt, "unforgiving illness" for the plain one. "Return to the earth" for the pin on the left, and "stripped bare" for the one on the right. She's quite straightforward in her application.'

'Thank you, Queen Kalyani.' Naila bowed. 'And please thank Aarvi for me.'

Nayani would salivate over the cursed weapons. He could picture her animated face assessing them already.

'As for you, Prince Ashoka,' Queen Kalyani continued, gesturing to the remaining pair, 'These daggers are yours. Raya named them Dukkha and Sukha. She is more . . . flamboyant with her creations than Aarvi.'

Suffering and *happiness*. Raya had an interesting sense of humour. 'Thank you,' Ashoka said with a bow. Gingerly, he took the box from the attendant and held it as if he were holding a fragile baby bird. Daggers weren't his favoured weapon, but it would be bad manners to reject them – especially since they were cursed. 'Although, I can't leave without knowing what the curses are.'

The queen smiled, squinting against the sun. 'She informed me that Sukha's curse was "sudden peace". Dukkha's was "to spread and drown in good spirits".'

The second curse sounded as ambiguous as Usra's – the mayakari who had cast a curse against the Great Spirit in Taksila. He could not make head or tail of their intended meaning, only that these weapons could not be used without premeditation. The curses worked once and once only; he needed to be careful with them.

'Safe travels, Prince Ashoka.' Queen Kalyani reached out to touch his shoulder in parting. 'Be young, but do not be foolish.'

CHAPTER EIGHTEEN
Shakti

A WEEK PASSED WITH NO INCIDENT.

Shakti was surprised, wondering what was happening in the Mountain of Rebirth. Why the Great Spirit had yet to retaliate. It was likely due to miners and surveyors still finalizing their plans with the empress, and the work needed to clear the rubble obstructing the entrance of the abandoned mine. Each new day only heightened her anticipation. Her fear. She was waiting for the consequences of her actions.

While both her and Harini's lives continued to be spared, it meant that she was subject to follow Aarya's every little whim. In the latest instance, Shakti was shepherded to the throne room, where the empress was to have an audience with a consul who had recently returned from Taksila. Shunted to the dark corners of the room, Shakti was instructed by the soldiers to keep quiet and listen, wondering what she was needed for. The content did pique her interest. The consul, a short greying man by the name of Daman, sputtered out apology after apology as he explained how his entry into Taksila had been denied. A lockdown to ensure the safety of Taksilans and visitors, the latter of whom were turned away. Some sort of minor spirit disturbance, though Shakti now understood otherwise. That was likely a ploy, since Prince Ashoka was in Trikalinga, of all places. She hadn't pressed him in his dream as to why he was there but knew that there was a reasonable explanation.

After the empress' audience concluded, Shakti had been moved again, this time to Adil's study. She was a game piece being moved about a board. It was in the privacy of the room that Aarya ordered her to invade Consul Daman's dreams. The empress knew the specifics of her dream-invasion abilities after she'd threatened the answers out of her. She knew that for Shakti to invade another's dream, she needed to recognize their face and name. It dawned on her why she'd been taken to the throne room.

'Daman can be easily manipulated,' was Aarya's reasoning. 'He was extremely loyal to my father because, like everyone, he feared and respected him. But above all else, Daman cares about money, and I don't trust Ashoka's decision to fortify Taksila. You will invade the consul's dreams and force him to tell me the truth. I want to know if he was paid off.'

Distrusting her own consuls. That didn't bode well, but Shakti agreed. The same night, she entered the consul's dreams to interrogate him. Luckily for him, no bribes had been paid, but it didn't dissuade Aarya from suspecting otherwise the following day.

Tasks like these were starting to fray Shakti's sanity. Now that she had been given tonics to allow her body to heal, she was growing restless. She wanted out of this damp, dark box.

As usual, karma granted her wish in its own twisted way.

That afternoon, sleeping off her tiredness in the cell, Shakti was startled awake when the ground began to shake.

This was no light rumble; it was strong enough to make her whole body shake. Her chains rattled, eyesight unsteady. Layers of dust fell from the roof. Shakti held on to her own shackles that were nailed into the wall to keep herself steady. Panicked and bleary, she wondered what was happening until she heard a loud, bone-chilling wail. In here, the sound was muffled. She could only begin to imagine how painful it would be to hear outside. The wails turned into screams, ancient and furious, followed by a single voice so loud that she had to cover her ears:

'*Chakravartin.*'

She froze. That voice. *The Great Spirit*. Its wailing was loud enough to be heard from the palace. She could hear it so clearly.

'Chakravartin.'

This was the second time she'd heard it reference a chakravartin. Why was it calling for Aarya?

'You've awoken me.'

Shakti gasped, clutching her chest. Strange sensations began to take over her body. It felt strung tight, as if she had slipped into a river of cold water on a humid day, hairs standing on end. It was the same sensation she had at the base of the mountain. Anger threatened to pull her beneath deep water, a raw, unrestrained ferocity that she could not quite place. *Spirits*. It was talking to her.

The noise outside her cell was raucous: the pounding of feet, the sharp, raised voices. Soldiers were likely being dispatched to the site of the commotion. Shakti almost expected them to barge inside and beat her, but no one did.

With each passing second, the pounding in her head worsened. Her bones, too. It was as if both brain and bones were attempting to jump out of the skin. A surge of energy passed through her body from head to toes. Familiar and unfamiliar, bringing with it the phantom scent of soil after rain, pinwheel flowers and the image of a broken tusk.

What's happening to me? she thought in a panic. There was an overflow of energy within her body. It was too powerful to contain.

'Return.'

It couldn't just be her who heard this voice. Any mayakari within the city would hear it. Ordinary citizens would only hear a terrifying cry. 'Return to me.'

The energy pulsing through her body became too much. Shakti wanted to tear through skin and wrench out her heart. Pressure continued to build in her head, filling up a space that had no space left. Clutching her head, Shakti screamed loud enough that she was sure any soldier remaining outside would've heard, and her vision turned black.

She awoke, groggy and confused.

It took a moment for Shakti to orient herself. She'd woken lying on her side. Groaning, she sat up and tenderly rubbed the back of her head. That strange energy was gone. The quakes too, had ceased. How long had she collapsed for?

Just as she thought it, her cell door suddenly opened with a loud bang, taking her by surprise. Three soldiers barged inside, their expressions grim.

'On your feet, mayakari,' one barked, moving behind to detach her shackles from the wall while the other two frogmarched her out. They handled her worse than one would a sack of unbrushed potatoes, elbows digging into her ribs, her feet catching on stone steps.

'I can walk!' she exclaimed, attempting to twist herself out of their ironclad grasp. 'Where are you taking me?'

'Quiet, witch,' one snapped, 'you're being taken to see the empress.'

The moment he said it, Shakti knew what she was being summoned for.

Dread settled in the pit of her stomach when they eventually arrived in front of the throne room. Another guard opened the doors, revealing that all too familiar midnight landscape.

The giant leopard statues and their ruby eyes stood watch beside the Obsidian Throne which shone like paddy water beneath a full moon. Seated upon it was Aarya, dressed in glimmering black. Advisors flocked beneath her on the steps with their heads bowed low. Shakti could hear their frenzied conversation as she was brought in:

'—seven dead, nine injured—'

'—managed to excavate a dozen cartloads, but this is dangerous, Your Highness—'

'—the body was enormous. What kind of creature—'

'—I *understand*, Rangana. Have the roads into the mountain blocked to civilians for now—'

Ah.

No guesses were needed; she knew what they were discussing with absolute certainty.

When the soldier behind Shakti cleared his throat, announcing their presence, Aarya and her advisors fell silent. All wore that usual mask of antipathy when they saw her. The empress beckoned her forward, but Shakti kept herself rooted to the spot, unwilling to approach an incensed viper. Huffing impatiently, the soldier behind her gave her back a cursory push, causing Shakti to stumble forward.

'There was an incident this morning,' Aarya began, 'at the excavation site.'

'I see.'

'Our miners excavated a large deposit of the unnatural metal, and the Great Spirit . . . retaliated,' the empress continued. Shakti was aware that she was being watched like a leopard eyeing its prey. 'It appeared in its angered form.'

Shakti gasped. 'You saw it appear?' Stuck in the dingy cell, she couldn't witness a thing, was only subject to hearing its wails. 'What did it look like?'

'Even those coming into the city's seaport could see it,' Aarya remarked. 'A giant, beastly yellow creature with no proper form. Humanlike arms but an amorphous body. White eyes.'

Shakti's mind was swirling with a hundred thoughts until she fully digested Aarya's remark. It made her pause. 'Wait – its *angered* form?'

'Yes,' Aarya snapped. 'Are you deaf, witch? The sheer power of . . .'

She continued her tirade, but Shakti stopped listening. Something wasn't right. Angered Great Spirits were difficult to understand. According to Jaya, their words tended to be unintelligible. And yet, she'd heard this one so clearly. It had thundered the word 'chakravartin', asked for a return. A return of what? Of whom? Was it speaking to her, or the chakravartin – Aarya? *What was happening here?*

'The earth shook,' Aarya continued, dragging Shakti out of her reverie. Her voice getting louder with each new word. 'Some of the mineral exploded and killed and injured several people within its vicinity. The rumbling spread to the city, and to the palace. Rice fields, polluted. A mudslide on the eastern outskirts. I'm sure you had a sense of what was happening.'

Shakti kept her face impassive. If Aarya was waiting for a slip up, she wouldn't give her one. 'An unfortunate accident,' she replied, shrugging. 'I wish the dead a pleasant rebirth, but such are the consequences of these endeavours.'

Aarya's left eye twitched. 'Except, there were to be *no* consequences, mayakari,' she said irritably. 'The appeasement rite of yours – did it not work?'

'It did,' she lied. 'But you said it yourself, Your Highness, the Great Spirit of the Mountain of Rebirth is . . . unnatural. It's not whole, but rather a splinter of itself.'

It was not Aarya who next spoke, but rather Consul Rangana, who had been listening with rapt attention. 'Are you saying that the Great Spirit reneged on its promise?'

The consul was trying to catch her out. 'No,' Shakti said. *It never accepted appeasement in the first place.* 'I'm saying you should've listened to me. That Great Spirit is angry. Taking more from it is like sawing one finger after another. Innocent people are now dead.'

The truth was that they were dead because of *her* but this was blame that required redirection. The Great Spirit would never agree to an appeasement; there had to be consequences to learn a hard lesson.

She hated that a part of herself found it exhilarating, using a Great Spirit against the people. Jaya wouldn't recognize that part of her at all.

Shakti knew her accusation struck when Aarya snapped out a grating 'Shut your mouth, mayakari.'

'The Great Spirit is unpredictable,' Shakti continued, ignoring the tug of her shackles. 'Don't keep looking for trouble, Your Highness. Nothing found in the mountain is typical. All you're doing is repeating history.'

The empress and Consul Rangana shared a brief, indecipherable look. 'Did you appease the Great Spirit?' Aarya repeated.

'I performed the appeasement rite as you asked, yes,' Shakti replied, keeping her gaze firmly on the royal circlet. 'But I told you the risks—'

'Oh, I'm aware,' the empress interrupted, leaning forward on the throne, chin propped up by a fist. 'The Great Spirit is unpredictable. I heard you the first time.'

For a long while, she stared at Shakti, expression inscrutable. One could only wonder what thoughts were running through her head. She knew she hadn't answered Aarya's question properly but hoped that it was vague enough to appease her.

Straightening back up, Aarya waved her hand in dismissal. 'All right,' she said. 'I've heard enough. Take the mayakari back to her cell.'

Shakti couldn't mask her surprise. *That was it?* No order for punishment. No open mockery. Had Aarya truly believed her?

'I suggest that you rest, witch,' Aarya told her as she was shepherded towards the doors. 'Gather your strength. I'll need you for an important task tomorrow.'

Never had such words sounded so ominous.

CHAPTER NINETEEN
Shakti

Trouble was coming.

Shakti could sense it in the pit of her stomach. Aarya's words stayed with her all throughout the night and weaselled their way into her dreams.

The quake hadn't been the empress' desired outcome. Her command to begin mining was what caused the Great Spirit to retaliate and subsequently take the lives of those in the vicinity. It made her look foolish.

Gather your strength. What did she want Shakti to do, this time? Perform another appeasement? Surely not. The Great Spirit was an anomaly. It wouldn't accept an appeasement, anyway.

The unease made her feel nauseous. It almost felt like she was an animal being fattened up for slaughter.

In fact, she was almost relieved to have her suspicions proven correct when she was escorted to the throne room once again around midday, the following day. Aarya sat upon the throne in full regalia. Green sari with intricate stitching. *Birds*, Shakti realized, in mid-flight. Gold throatlet. Cuffs. Earrings. She was dressed for an occasion. Briefly, she wondered if they were to return to the Mountain of Rebirth.

The empress was in the midst of listening to a consul from her seat, expression placid. It brightened when she noticed Shakti being brought in.

The hairs on the back of her neck prickled.

'Mayakari,' Aarya greeted. It was deeply unpleasant, her smile. Shakti couldn't decipher what awaited her. It felt eerily like realizing Kolakola was about to be burned to ashes. 'Perfect timing.'

She waved her hand dismissively. A soldier approached with a red cloth around his hands that he tied around Shakti's mouth. She didn't struggle. She could not hear neither an inhale nor exhale from him, as if he was utterly fearful of taking even a breath around her for fear of misfortune. As if *breath* would prevent it.

'Good,' Aarya remarked once the soldier finished his work. 'We'll depart for the palace gates. There's something you should see.'

Shakti said nothing, couldn't say anything. What sort of twisted machination did Aarya want her to see now? Or perhaps it was something intended to humiliate her. Embarrass her. If they were heading to the palace entrance, there would no doubt be a crowd.

Does she intend to humiliate me publicly? Shakti wondered. If the empress didn't intend to burn her alive, there was nothing she could possibly do to make her feel more degraded.

With Aarya striding ahead, Shakti was roughly led from the winding passageways of the underground cells and into the outdoor jade pools of the Golden Palace. The courtyard was the same stark white that she remembered, devoid of anything natural, anything green. Palace staff who passed by eyed her with mixtures of surprise and fear. Some would recognize her, but she refused to meet their gazes.

She was taken far outside the palace walls to an open space where the Mountain of Rebirth was in full view. Trees sparsely scattered the area, a welcome relief from the palace. Beneath her feet, the grass was dry and green. Her body relaxed for a brief, blissful moment.

Her relief soon shattered once she became aware of the large crowd gathered beyond the palace walls. At first, she couldn't discern who or what they surrounded from the sheer number of heads. Only when she glimpsed the wooden pole that jutted from the centre did her blood run cold. Memories came plummeting like birds shot from the sky and threatened to turn her muscles to lead: Kolakola, Emperor Adil, Master Hasith, smoke and flames.

Jaya.

Shakti had seen enough of those wooden poles now to know what they signified. She knew all too well just who would be bound to it, surrounded by kindling.

People parted as Aarya walked past, heads bowed in reverence and eyes to the ground. They only dared to look up once she passed, whereupon Shakti became the object of assessment. Perhaps seeing her hands tied and mouth gagged gave them an indication of who – or rather, *what* – she was, for their expressions turned vehement. Nasty.

The object of the crowd's fascination soon became clear as the last of the crowd split. Surrounded by straw, paper scraps and wood chips, a young woman knelt on the ground. Her head was drooped, her long black hair matted and singed, skin bruised and still in a maidservant's uniform. Oil glistened against every inch of exposed skin and cloth.

The young woman raised her head. Her wide brown eyes shone with tears.

No.

Shakti's gag stifled her gasp as she made to run towards her but was violently jerked back by the neck of her tunic.

Harini.

She tried to scream, but the cloth muffled any sound. Bile rose to the back of her throat, her stomach bloated and churned without mercy. If she retched now, she would be forced to swallow her own vomit.

There was no time to consolidate her skittish thoughts. Like a leashed dog, she was dragged towards the centre, where Harini was tied to the post. Under Aarya's unfeeling tone, the royal guards formed a barricade around her and, as a result, Shakti, forcing the throng of people to scatter back.

Shakti couldn't care less about the dozens upon dozens of eyes on her as she twisted her head. Her vision narrowed and focused on Harini behind her. The mayakari stared back, the whites of her eyes now tinged red. A streak of dried blood ran from her forehead to the side of her temple. Her chest rose and fell rapidly but her posture was slumped. Frightened and defeated.

Save me, her eyes seemed to say.

The gag around Shakti's mouth threatened to suffocate her. *Save. How?* How could she save her? She glanced around, surveying the area for something, *anything* of consequence, but—

What is it you think you're looking for, little bird?

As Shakti's panic rose, Aarya stepped forward. Murmurs died once again.

'Seven dead, nine injured,' the empress began, her tone sympathetic. 'That was the distressing outcome for my people who were ordered to excavate a newly found mineral in the Mountain of Rebirth. The mountain is unnatural, yes, and that's why I had a mayakari perform an appeasement rite in the hopes that all will go well for the sake of prosperity. Unfortunately, that was not how it ended.'

Shakti's blood ran cold. No, she couldn't be . . .

Gesturing to Harini, Aarya raised her voice. 'The mayakari you see here before you – she did not complete the appeasement rite properly. Or perhaps, did not perform it on purpose.'

That should've been her up on the pole. That should have been her, begging for her life. Not Harini. Why was she—

Briefly, the empress' gaze caught her own. Shakti was reminded of Emperor Adil, then. Aarya was her father's daughter, right down to the maniacal gleam in her eyes.

Her life hangs in the balance. Disobey me and I will harm her.

Aarya knew.

'The Great Spirit, angered. Nine dead because of this witch,' Aarya proclaimed to the crowd. 'Seven of my people gone. Their last few moments must have been awful. It took tremendous effort to find their bodies and return them to their families. Some were pulverized.'

This was her punishment. Being forced to watch Harini die. Because of her.

How did she know I lied?

'So many dead because of one mayakari's wretched anger,' Aarya continued. 'The dead need justice. We need justice. Her life for theirs. The witch will burn.'

Raucous applause followed. Jeers, too, aimed at Harini. Shakti could almost taste the unrestrained fury amongst the crowd.

My fault.

Shakti thrashed about in her shackles. She cursed Aarya aloud, promising retribution. No one understood her, but it seemed that the acting empress recognized her intent, for she gestured to her right. Moments later, a soldier came darting forward, holding a flaming torch in his hand. Shakti flinched at the sight of fire, as did Harini in her peripheral vision. The mayakari squeezed her eyes shut, forcing more tears to streak down her cheeks, and Shakti felt her throat constrict.

'Oh, you will not watch me burn her, mayakari,' Aarya remarked, her voice stone cold. 'Rather, *I* will watch *you* burn her.'

The words didn't register, at first; Shakti's ability to process anything became largely impaired. *You, me, her. I, you, her.* It took several repetitions for the meaning to settle like mud in a lakebed.

Burn her. *Burn* her?

Shakti couldn't have lashed out hard enough. She launched herself at Aarya like an untrained leopard. Almost immediately, she was jerked back. The rough bands of her shackles dug in and grated her neck and wrists, but she didn't register the pain.

'Go on.' Aarya didn't bat an eye as she motioned the soldier behind Shakti, who proceeded to push her forward. Shakti tried to dig her heels into the ground to halt her movements, but it was useless. Once she was steered in front of the pile of kindling, the soldier swept his legs underneath her, forcing Shakti to lose her balance. Caught off guard, she landed on her knees. This time, the sharp sting of pain was palpable.

'Give her the torch,' ordered the empress. She sounded impatient.

No. Shakti curled her hands into tight fists and refused to relax them. She would not be given the torch. She would *not* be forced to burn her own.

'Stop making things so difficult, mayakari,' the guard behind her snapped as he leaned over to force her hands open.

Gritting her teeth, Shakti held firm, but his hold was ultimately stronger. Her fingers relented, the muscles sore and tense as the guard forced a flaming torch against her grip and held it there. Heat fanned her face, an unwelcome guest that she couldn't force away.

Salt stung her dry skin. A familiar wetness tracked down her face. Her shoulders trembled; it took all her effort to prevent herself from collapsing.

You're not attached to your own life. Why not let go of it?

It was her own inner voice again. Distorted, higher pitched and pleading, but hers. What if she aimed the fire towards herself? What if she jumped in with Harini, and lit them both aflame? Or inhaled a lungful of smoke so that she fell unconscious and wouldn't have to feel the pain of death.

Shakti didn't realize that she was drawing the torch closer to herself until she was halted by a pair of rough hands. The soldier had stopped her. Aarya, too, was in her line of sight within moments, incensed and somewhat rattled.

'No, Shakti,' the empress hissed. 'You will not burn.'

You will help me. What had Shakti expected other than this? Fear had forced her hand then; she had chosen to save herself before thinking of the consequences she would bear. Karma was cruel, but the cost was self-inflicted. She had no one to blame but herself.

'Your first mistake was in thinking you could bargain with a royal,' Aarya whispered. 'I told you that your friend's life lay in your hands, and you flouted my rules anyway.'

Me. All her attempts to shield Harini lay shattered on the ground. *This is all my fault.*

If she'd only listened. Harini's life could've been spared, and maybe Ashoka would have arrived in time to rescue them both, but Shakti *had* to let her need for vengeance get in the way.

'You can't save her,' Aarya continued. 'Monsters don't save. Monsters destroy and eat their own. Now, burn her.'

Without warning, the soldier pushed Shakti forward. The moment before the flames touched kindling, Shakti met Harini's eye. She couldn't imagine what her own face looked like, but a portrait of abject fear stared back.

You can't save me.

Her hand was roughly forced towards the kindling. Fire met tinder.

The pyre lit up in flames.

An awed gasp erupted from the crowd just as yellow-orange flames met Harini's body and blossomed into a bright, horrific blue.

Shakti didn't hear the scream, but she saw the moment Harini died. She forced herself to watch the horror. This was her doing. Harini's death was on her conscience. It felt like betrayal to look away. She saw the moment the pain became too much for Harini to bear, the moment that her eyes rolled back and her eyelids shuttered. Fire several shades darker than the sky burned brown skin black, caused fluid-filled vesicles to form and pop like the body on the pyre was being fried in hot oil.

Then came the smell.

Burned meat.

Unable to bear it any longer, Shakti turned away as she was dragged to the side. Her whole body was shaking now, a natural tremor made worse by distress. The smell was excruciating. Her mind flashed back to Kolakola, to the three witches burning in the night. Reactionary bile rose in the back of her throat. It pooled in her mouth, acidic and rancid, and with the gag firmly over her mouth she had no choice but to swallow it back down again.

That night, Adil had been the one to kill her aunt. Today, the harbinger of death was her. Her own recklessness had cost Harini her life.

Murderer, the voice in her head sang. *Murderer, murderer, murderer.*

A shadow fell over her. Blinking away her tears, Shakti looked up to see Aarya watching her.

'The witch cared about you,' she said in a low voice. 'That was a mistake.'

Shakti's heart stopped.

'Intuition told me you lied yesterday, mayakari,' Aarya continued. 'So, I went in search of answers. Though I can't understand a Great Spirit's lamentations, I knew there was another mayakari who could. She put up a fight, I'll give her that. Interrogation didn't work well. She said she heard the angered Great Spirit but couldn't understand it. How convenient. Then, I threatened your life. It seems that she had more integrity than you. The thought of you dying made her frenzied, and she told me the truth. That you never appeased the Great Spirit in the first place. For her honesty, I told her I would keep you alive. I never promised the same for her.'

The candid confession stunned Shakti into silence. There was no guilt in the empress' eyes. None whatsoever. In fact, she sounded *proud*.

I hate you.

Anger swelled anew in her chest.

I will curse you into the next life, Aarya Maurya, you wretched tyrant.

She wanted Aarya dead in every way possible. Slitting her throat. Smashing in the back of her skull. Tearing each limb separately while she lay awake. Severing neck from body and then gouging out her eyes.

But none of it can bring Harini back.

Shakti's thoughts – impossibly – stilled. A preternatural calm took over, likely momentary. She closed her eyes for a moment, willing the tears collecting behind her lids to vanish. For now, she needed to let this anger go.

'Please,' she whispered, keeping her head bowed. 'Let me cremate Harini properly.'

The silence that followed was excruciating, broken by one resounding response:

'No.'

A soft shudder escaped Shakti's lips as she lifted her head. 'No?' she echoed. She wondered what her expression looked like at that moment: surprised, scared, furious. Perhaps a mix of all three.

'No,' Aarya repeated. 'I have something better in mind.'

Something better was something infinitely worse. After all, it was Aarya – what else could she have expected? After Shakti was marched back to her cell, she collapsed from the aftereffects of shock and stress. There was no time to crawl onto her mattress; Shakti slept on the cold, hard floor without a second thought. When she awoke, having dreamt of being swallowed into a pillar of fire, a soft scream escaped her mouth.

Bones. She was surrounded by them.

Rib bones fractured into sharp shards. Leg bones still intact, coloured blackish grey. Small bones from the hands dislocated and scattered like pebbles. They were everywhere. A skull stared back at her. Dark lines demarcated the sutures of the head, to which straggles of singed hair were still attached.

Warm droplets of water hit the back of her hands as Shakti struggled to right herself into a kneeling position.

'Harini.' Her friend's name came out as a guttural sob. How cruel. How unbelievably, terrifyingly *cruel*. 'I'm sorry. I'm *sorry*.'

The skull said nothing, but her own inner voice did:

I should have died instead of her.

My audacity doomed her.

At the same time, Jaya's reassuring words followed: *you will not let this break you, little bird.*

The four walls around her seemed to shrink, causing the tremor in her hands to intensify. An acute sensation of who she was pressed like a heated iron brand into her skin: a wild animal ensnared in a savage hunter's trap.

She could taste blood on her tongue. Shakti's throat seized, mind going blank. She saw her memories as an immaculate oil painting of a forest untouched before the figure of Aarya took a dagger and slashed away at the canvas and left behind gaping holes.

The pressure in her throat built up until she vomited the meagre amount of food she had last night.

This is all my fault. This is all my fault.

She'd been the catalyst for Harini's death. She'd cast a curse that she couldn't remember. She was forced to follow Aarya's command. If Jaya were here, she'd watch her with disappointment. Fear.

Curling into herself, Shakti pressed her nose into the fabric of her trousers. Her whole body shook. Harini's burning body was imprinted in her mind's eye in vivid detail. The scent of smoke still lingered, and she retched up nothing but bile. The phantom voice of Aarya Maurya echoed in the cell:

Her death is on you, mayakari.

Shakti let out a desperate wail.

CHAPTER TWENTY
Ashoka

The Samnal River shone a lacklustre blue-grey as their riverboat docked on the outskirts of the Golden City. It had been a never-ending journey to the capital. A few days had passed since their return to Taksila, where Ashoka had ordered the city gates to be reopened. Before he left with Sau and Rahil, Ashoka had made sure that Naila showcased the cursed weapons she'd received to the resistance and reiterated the exact process on how to create them. The cursed pins, too, were kept under her watch. He knew the weapons intimidated her; she handled them delicately, as if they could burst into flame at any moment.

Nayani, however, had been excited over the prospect of creating cursed weapons, though she'd understood the need to make them in limited amounts. There was too high a risk in mass manufacture and having them fall into unsuspecting or wrong hands.

For the time being, he elected to keep production controlled. He ordered Taksilan blacksmiths to manufacture swords and daggers made of solid silver without metal-mixing. It was an odd request, but one that was accepted without pushback. Ever since the mines were opened in the northern forests, the blacksmiths had been satisfied with being provided increased resources to work with. The specially made silver weapons were to be transported by Ridi soldiers to the base of operations of the resistance, from where they would begin to imbue them with curses.

As for his own pair of daggers, Ashoka elected to take them with him to the Golden City. He didn't want to risk them being used by accident. In addition, any correspondence he would receive from either Queen Malika or Kalyani had to be directed to Sau. While in the capital, he never received correspondence, and him suddenly doing so would rouse Aarya's suspicions.

He'd taken Sahry with him, this time. The winged serpent had followed their boat from the skies, stopping whenever they docked. She'd sped ahead of them half an hour ago. Ashoka hazarded that she would have landed at the palace by now.

Despite the early morning arrival, there was a lot of activity. Large amounts of wood and stone were being carted off ships. Soldiers with royal leopards watched the area. The arrival of their boat, emblazoned with the royal symbol upon its hull, seemed to baffle them, and for good reason. His arrival was completely unannounced. Meant to surprise.

'Prince Ashoka?' A female soldier bowed, expression flummoxed, once he disembarked. 'I – I *thought* I saw your winged serpent … Forgive me – your arrival is unexpected. Does Empress Aarya know?'

'My dear sister did invite me back on multiple occasions, soldier,' Ashoka responded. *Ordered, more like.* 'I am simply taking up her offer. Now, I must commandeer two leopards. Since my presence here is unannounced, I assume there are no carriages waiting for me.'

'Right away, Prince Ashoka.'

The three of them were given two of the loitering soldiers' own leopards. Ashoka rode his alone, while Sau and Rahil took the other. He was aware of the curious stares he was getting. The youngest prince, the mayakari sympathizer, returning to the city with no warning. It would be an odd sight.

Except, there was something else. Something he'd missed. At first, Ashoka hadn't questioned it until they were travelling past the city entrance. He dimly registered incidental cracks on buildings here and there, but frowned at the exorbitant price of one rice sack being sold at a vendor's stall. Sudden price increases like that were highly unusual. Only once the crowds parted in deference at the sight of the youngest Maurya riding atop his giant leopard did he manage to catch slivers of conversation about an earthquake, and the destruction of nearby paddy fields and homes. *What happened here?*

When they finally arrived at the palace, he was greeted with similar dumbfounded expressions. Ashoka waited on the front steps as Rahil ordered the leopards to be taken back to their stables and observed the gleaming white outer walls of the palace. Sau left them early, wanting to announce her return to the head advisor and to get an understanding of the supposed quake and Great Spirit awakening that had occurred during their absence. In her travelling sack were the cursed daggers. He'd given them to her for safekeeping. No one would look in her quarters for weapons, after all. Sau was inept with them.

'Best to steel yourself, Prince Ashoka,' Sau had advised before leaving. 'I fear you'll be walking into a leopard's den.'

He'd snorted. 'A leopard's den will be more inviting than subjecting myself to whatever Aarya has done.'

The palace walls loomed over him imposingly, as they had always done. Shakti and Harini were inside, sequestered in the palace dungeons. Home held a new, eerie quality. Ashoka couldn't put his finger on it. *Home* felt different; or perhaps it was him who had changed.

He inhaled deeply. That familiar sense of sterility and coldness greeted him like a long-lost lover. He fervently wished to sink like a stone into his bed; seasickness didn't act kindly on him. But he still needed to meet Aarya to ascertain what she was planning to do with Harini and Shakti. He needed to see his mother and Arush, and feed Sahry, who would be hungry after her flight from Taksila.

'Good to be home?' Rahil asked. He was so close that Ashoka could still smell the soap that he'd used on his skin. Comforting, but not enough.

Ashoka couldn't answer with a definitive *yes* or *no*. Oddly enough, he was already missing the royal estate in Taksila and its refusal to shun the natural world, unlike the palace. Instead, he answered with a noncommittal shrug.

He reminded himself repeatedly to maintain his composure as they were escorted inside by soldiers. According to them, his sister wasn't in the throne room. She was reportedly in their father's study, reading through reports – a task that Arush would've found tedious. Their older brother didn't care much for reading.

The tiles beneath his feet were freshly polished as they wandered down the open-air corridors, the white pillars engraved with patterned art. To his right were the jade pools, winking in the afternoon light. Their father's study was on the second floor. The room held no good memories for him. It was where his father had burned his ear. The memory was always so visceral. Ashoka had to stop himself from tugging at the scarred bit of skin.

When they finally arrived in front of the study, where two more soldiers stood outside, their escort attempted to knock on his behalf, but Ashoka stopped them.

'Thank you, but it's all right,' he said, and stepped forward to twist open the knob. 'You may leave us. Rahil – with me.'

The door opened with a slight groan, and the smell of old books and wood hit him immediately. The room was large and airy. Behind what used to be his father's desk was Aarya. Her head was bent in concentration as she swiftly signed a parchment letter, oblivious to his presence. Ashoka stepped forward as Rahil closed the door behind them.

'Knock, soldier.' Her head was still down, but she sounded irritated. 'Don't just come barging in here like—'

Finally, she glanced up and her eyes widened in shock. '*Mūsī?*' She stood up abruptly. 'Rahil. What are you doing here?'

It was the first time he had seen her in months. Nothing about Aarya had changed, except that she wore the royal circlet. Though he was loathe to admit it, his sister wore the circlet with much more grace than Arush had.

Ashoka wondered if he would look the same.

Irked by the nickname, he gritted his teeth and kept his expression neutral. Even now, it sounded demeaning. From the corner of his eye, he saw Rahil bow. 'Heard there was an earthquake,' he said, not bothering with a greeting, knowing it would annoy her. 'How terrible.'

'Yes,' Aarya replied curtly. 'The Great Spirit of the Mountain of Rebirth was awakened. An . . . oversight on my part.'

'What happened to wake it?' he asked, surprised. Of all the responses she could've given him, he hadn't expected that.

'Later,' his sister said dismissively. 'Answer my question first: why are you here?'

'You asked me to return, didn't you?'

'At least have the decency to write to me beforehand,' Aarya replied, frowning. 'Finally solved that issue with the minor spirits, did you? Consul Daman was awfully annoyed that he couldn't enter the city.'

From her wry tone, Ashoka knew that she hadn't believed his lies. Still, he kept his expression blank. 'A bit of trouble around the forestland,' he said, shrugging, 'and yes, it was resolved. Thanks to the mayakari.'

Aarya scowled at the word 'mayakari' as if he'd slapped her. 'Good,' she gritted out. 'How was the journey back home? I must admit, I expected your stubborn self to hold out in Taksila a little longer.'

'This isn't me giving up control of Taksila,' he said lightly.

Lips curling in distaste, she shook her head vehemently. 'I thought I made myself clear,' she said. 'Don't play the fool; reverse the ban.'

'I won't.'

'Idiot,' his sister snapped. 'Then why. Are. You. Here?'

'I'm simply here for a . . . familial visit,' he said idly. 'To offer you congratulations on becoming *acting* regent. I hope you carry out the vision Arush had for the empire when he was first coronated. Which reminds me, I must see him. See how he's faring.'

Aarya gave him a sickly-sweet smile. 'As well as one can, under the circumstances,' she replied. 'Poor Arush. That mayakari you employed turned out to be quite the terror. Mother has been by his bedside all this time. She's very distraught.'

It struck him how easily she could lie to his face. How there wasn't a shred of guilt visible for having poisoned her own blood. 'And you're not?' he asked innocently.

'I am, but I've been burdened with Arush's title,' Aarya replied, not sounding the least bit upset. 'There are tasks to attend to, *mūsī*. I can't wallow in my feelings all the time. Nothing would get done. I'm more dedicated to this position than you think.'

He didn't doubt it. Aarya was very good at this game. 'I wonder why she didn't kill him outright,' Ashoka said, adding, 'Shakti,' to see if it would induce a reaction.

Sure enough, he caught the slight tensing of Aarya's shoulders. 'Perhaps she wasn't that much of a monster,' she replied. 'Some have a conscience too, you know.'

'A monster with a conscience is weak,' he ventured, wanting to see if he could pull any more from her.

'I disagree,' his sister replied stiffly. 'It's . . . compassionate.'

'Is compassion why you've kept Shakti imprisoned and not burning on a pyre?' Ashoka said. 'It's unlike you to worry about one mayakari, let alone two.'

His sister stilled, eyeing him with suspicion. 'Who told you there were two?'

Ashoka cursed inwardly. He wasn't supposed to know about Harini. 'Gossip reached my ears the moment I returned.' He tried to sound unaffected. 'You imprisoned another one of my staff?'

'Hm. Harini. Yes, I did,' Aarya replied, the ghost of a vindictive glimmer behind her eyes. 'Did you know she was a mayakari, too? Did *you*' – here, she tilted to observe the man behind Ashoka – 'know this, Rahil? That's grounds for punishment.'

Scowling, Ashoka stepped closer until it was only the desk that separated them. 'Don't you dare threaten Rahil,' he snapped. 'Why are you keeping two witches alive?'

Aarya mock-clucked sympathetically at him. 'Oh, little brother,' she said softly, watching him with an expectant gleam. 'There's only one left.'

Ashoka's breath left his lungs. Behind him, he heard Rahil draw in a sharp breath.

No. No.

Out of the two mayakari in the palace prison, he knew for certain which one Aarya would kill and which one she would leave alive. 'You didn't.'

For a moment, he fervently hoped Aarya was joking. That she was only doing this to taunt him, to catch him out.

'Of course, I did,' she said. 'Your Harini burned a beautiful blue, little brother.'

Harini would've been so scared in those final moments. Remorse pounded into him like a mallet. This was his fault. He should've been quicker to get here, and now another blameless witch – a *friend* – had died.

Under Aarya's hand, this nightmare would never stop.

'You – you—' Without thinking, he moved around the table quickly. He didn't miss the transient but real worry flash in his sister's eyes. One moment, his hands were so close to her throat. The next minute, he was being held back by a pair of strong arms.

'Let me go,' he hissed at Rahil, trying to twist free but to no avail.

'Ashoka,' Rahil whispered, low enough that only he could hear. 'Stop.'

'She *murdered*—'

'I know.' Rahil's voice turned softer. 'Play the prince.'

He stopped struggling. That was a command he hadn't heard in some time. Rahil loosened his hold. Meanwhile, Aarya watched him with a newfound wariness. Her hand was clutching a sharp quill in a death grip. He could tell that she hadn't expected him to pounce.

'You'll regret that,' he ground out.

'Oh, you won't hurt me, *mūsī*,' Aarya remarked assuredly. 'For all your bravado, you won't. I'm no unimportant governor. I am your *sister*.'

Ashoka couldn't believe what he was hearing. *Blood* was her reasoning against violence. It hadn't been when she poisoned Arush.

Grasping Rahil's arm gently, Ashoka squeezed. Rahil let him go, and he composed himself.

'But I can't have a mayakari sympathizer be involved in the empire's most intricate affairs,' his sister said. Unadulterated glee radiated from her features. 'That deal you and Arush made, little brother? Consider it void. I'll respect Father's wishes and allow you to govern Taksila until your term ends, only if you reverse the ban on mayakari killings. And you won't be leading the war council, either.'

Fine. He'd stopped caring about the war council and the legalities of succession, anyway. He wanted the throne by any means necessary. Still, he needed to act as if that initial promise mattered. 'You can't dissolve an already brokered deal. You're only the acting regent.'

His sister's nostrils flared. 'I have the same power Arush has.'

'But not his vision,' Ashoka fired back. He wanted to rip the royal circlet straight off his sister's head. *Underserved.* Its home was on his head, not hers. At least then he could prevent senseless deaths like Harini's. 'You know the unspoken rule as an acting regent: carry out the true monarch's duties in the manner befitting your superior until their return.'

'The good thing about an unspoken social contract, *mūsī*, is that you can break it,' Aarya said, her voice low and deadly. 'Don't push me. You must obey my command.'

Ashoka almost laughed out loud. 'No,' he replied, smoothing back his hair, feigning nonchalance. There was one more hand he had to play. 'I will continue to govern Taksila, and I *will* uphold the ban. Otherwise, everyone from the capital to the far west will know you poisoned Arush.'

Aarya froze. Her mouth dropped open before she seemed to collect herself. With stiff movements, she crossed her arms over her chest. 'I beg your pardon?' she scoffed, but there was an undercurrent of worry in her voice. 'Are you addled in the head?'

'Oh, spare me the lies.' Ashoka rolled his eyes. 'I know it was you, sister, because it was Shakti who told me. You falsely accused her.'

The mayakari's name made a muscle in his sister's jaw pop. He kept going. 'The mayakari who cursed our father can also invade *dreams*. Command people. No wonder you've been keeping her alive.'

'She told you,' Aarya remarked flatly.

'I can't believe you poisoned Arush.'

'Our brother was going to run this empire into the ground!' Aarya exclaimed. *Finally*. Some emotion. His sister had been sufficiently rattled. 'Soldiers sent to the *north*. That was a fool's errand. Because of his blind desire for a legacy, he missed catching our military weapons being illegally sold down south. He's an idiot.'

'And you thought killing him would solve the issue?'

'I wasn't going to kill him,' Aarya said, looking offended, of all things. 'Only incapacitate him enough to step down. I'm no monster.'

'No,' he replied woodenly. 'You're just a monster with a conscience.'

Aarya frowned. 'I would *never* kill family. Trample, yes, but never kill. Blood is blood. The concentration of poison was low for a reason. He's simply asleep.'

Aarya was delusional. 'He can't swallow. His body will deteriorate,' he replied. 'You'll kill him anyway.'

'He won't,' his sister shot back. 'I had Shakti use her dream-invasion powers on him. Magic keeps him from withering away, but he's trapped in sleep. I doubt the witch will remember she did any of that.'

Shakti hadn't mentioned it, so he guessed the same. 'Still, treason is treason,' he said.

Exhaling loudly, Aarya tipped her head back for a moment, as if considering her next words carefully. When she looked at him again, there was a steely determination in her eyes. 'No one will believe you.'

'If I get Mother on my side,' he sneered, 'she will act immediately. Who is more likely to be believed? The mad princess or the wise dowager empress? It's not a hard decision. You won't be wearing that circlet for long if I do, sister.'

Visibly bristling, Aarya's hands curled into loose fists. 'Don't you *dare* tell her.'

Ashoka grinned victoriously. She was cornered. 'Then I have some demands. Agree to keep my original deal with Arush. Taksila's burning ban will continue to be upheld. If you agree, I'll keep my mouth shut.'

The glare she sent him could've fried his skin. 'Fine,' she said.

That one word promised a lifetime of retribution, 'but you'll deeply regret this, *mūsī*.'

Before Ashoka could respond, there came a sudden knock at the door. He eyed Aarya and found her to be doing the same. A silent understanding passed between them. His sister returned to her seat and he to his original position in front of the desk.

'Come in,' Aarya called out. Her voice betrayed nothing.

An anxious-looking messenger hurried in, carrying several scrolls of parchment.

'Forgive the intrusion, Your Highness and – Prince Ashoka? – but I come bearing news,' he remarked hastily.

Beckoning the man forward, Aarya pointed towards his papers. 'Go on.'

'Another wagonload of Ran military swords were found being sold in Mahvo,' the man replied. 'Their supplier is unknown.'

Supplier. *Hah*. Ashoka hoped to see the look on Aarya's face when she discovered it was him. When it was too late.

His sister seemed vexed. 'What is this nonsense?' she glowered. 'The merchant couldn't be interrogated?'

'Reports state that when the merchant was questioned, he was unsure,' the messenger replied, appearing nervous even to speak. 'Said the weapons were handed to him by a tertiary supplier.'

The so-called tertiary suppliers were Taksilan merchants who he'd paid handsomely for their silence. The weapons were taken as part of a mixed array of goods as merchants often did when they crossed territories, wagons which contained teas and silks, as well as their military weapons.

Bristling like a wildcat being approached by humans, his sister sent the messenger away with a curt dismissal. When he left, she let out a series of expletives. Keeping his expression neutral, Ashoka clucked his tongue in sympathy. 'You seem overwhelmed.'

'Not overwhelmed,' Aarya replied. 'This is just a headache. Mahvo's queen must be aware of this. We've seized some weapons now, but who knows how many have made their way into her kingdom. She knows it's a violation. If this continues, I'll be forced to act. Ran weapons must be kept within Ran borders. Our arms must be safeguarded.'

'Take action?' he asked innocently.

Aarya pinched the bridge of her nose. Even the way she lounged back on the chair was like their father. 'I'll issue correspondence first, little brother. A warning. Then, if she doesn't respond to my orders to have our weapons returned, I'll consider harsher action. Father would approve.'

It was the most diplomatic course of action, but Ashoka knew for certain that it wasn't their father's way. He knew that Aarya thought the same. While the old Ashoka would've respected her decision to correspond with Malika first, he needed Aarya ready to incite violence. Much like their father – both his sister's strength and weakness.

'Would he?' Ashoka replied. When Aarya shot him an incredulous look, he shrugged. 'I thought you of all people would want to follow Father's example perfectly.'

'I would,' she snapped. 'I *have*. I've kept up the hunt for Ghost Queens. I've returned our soldiers from the Frozen Lands. I'm trying to reverse your fucking burning ban. I've kept to his vision more than Arush.'

'Father wouldn't have bothered with pleasantries,' Ashoka remarked. He was keenly aware of Rahil's gaze burning a hole into the back of his neck, likely wondering what on earth he was doing. 'He would make the first move. Invade sovereign territory.'

His sister eyed him strangely. 'He would,' she said. It was rare for them to agree about their father.

'Which is why I'm surprised you won't. Though, Mahvo will only attack us,' he added to soften what Aarya would deem to be a suspicious for-violence remark coming out of his mouth.

Aarya snorted. 'Queen Malika won't be able to defend her kingdom against me,' she said. 'They're too weak.'

'Then why bother with a courtesy letter?'

Her resulting silence let him know that she was mulling over his words. *Good.* Trying to manipulate Aarya and succeeding was an uncommon feat, which made this moment a personal victory.

His sister let out a frustrated groan. 'Weapons,' she huffed. 'A Great Spirit. A murdered aunt, and now *you*. Keep well out of my way, *mūsī*. You can only threaten me so—'

Ashoka had stopped listening to her at the mention of a murdered aunt. 'What did you say about an aunt?' he asked.

'Oh.' Aarya's uninterested tone was aggravating. 'Another of Shakti's reveals. Our aunt didn't die from an illness, little brother. She was burned by Father, because she was a witch.'

Stunned, Ashoka turned to Rahil, who wore an equal expression of surprise, before turning back to Aarya. 'Our aunt was a *mayakari?*' he asked. His father's choice to burn them was more insidious. How had Shakti . . . ah, *of course*. Adil's consciousness. 'Does that mean Mother . . . ?'

'No. I'd have died of shame had we been blood-related, but thankfully not,' Aarya replied, shrugging. So that was why she appeared so unaffected. 'But it wouldn't do well for the public to know, so don't speak so candidly about this. Pester Mother about it if you must, not me. She'll want to see you.'

CHAPTER TWENTY-ONE
Ashoka

Arush looked as if he were dead.

Ashoka's older brother lay sleeping in his room, surrounded by silk pillows and cotton sheets. Every few hours, a physician checked on him. The firstborn son of Adil, now confined to a bed, his potential to reawaken uncertain. *When would he wake*, Ashoka wondered. *Would he ever wake?*

As Aarya had said, his body didn't seem to have deteriorated. It looked much the same. *Crushed sea mango.* Despite her actions, Ashoka couldn't help but appreciate Aarya's plan. If Shakti didn't have the power that she had, his sister would be sitting smug on the throne, hands washed free of blood. It bothered him, how Aarya outwardly despised mayakari and their magic, but used it to benefit herself anyway.

Not long after his conversation with Aarya, she'd sent him away. The presence of Kalingan soldiers in Mahvo seemed to have disconcerted her, and she called an urgent meeting with the consuls. Since Ashoka wasn't privy to the goings-on within the meeting, he went to see his brother.

There, Ashoka also found his mother, silently watching the view outside his brother's window. When he first rushed towards her, she'd been elated, smothering him in an embrace so tight that he could hardly breathe.

'Oh, thank the spirits, you're finally home,' she'd whispered.

After chiding him over not letting her know he was arriving, she inquired about Taksila. No mention of him killing the governor, Ashoka noted, wondering if his mother was purposefully avoiding the topic.

Sitting beside his mother now, Ashoka felt safer than he had in a long time. She radiated comfort. The coconut oil in her hair was familiar, her jasmine perfume soothing as she absently rubbed circles on the crown of his head. 'You look different, my dear,' she remarked gently, 'and it's not just your hair. Something is altogether new. Perhaps . . . assuredness. Yes, that'd be it. There is a newfound confidence about you.'

'There is?' Ashoka asked. He didn't feel any more confident. Humming in agreement, his mother briefly turned away to adjust a pillow beneath Arush's head.

'Well, you did resolve Taksila's spirit rampages,' she said. 'They won't tell you to your face, but the advisors and consuls are quite impressed. Though I did fail to see how killing the governor helped.'

There it was. That admonishing, half-disappointed tone he hated hearing from her. It only ever produced guilt in the past, but now, Ashoka could brush it aside without worry. He'd done what was needed.

'Are you upset because a man died,' he asked, 'or because it was me who killed him?'

'The latter,' she answered.

Ashoka sighed. 'I did what I had to do, Mother,' he said. 'Kosala was a nightmare for the mayakari.'

His mother sighed. 'I know, my dear.'

Part of him wanted to tell her all of it. His deal with Queen Kalyani. The cursed weapons. His plan to take the Obsidian Throne from his siblings. Yet, he held himself back. She'd conditioned him to follow the path of nonviolence, and here he was rejecting it. Telling her would make him feel guilty. Rethink his decisions. She wouldn't agree that violence was needed to achieve better means.

So he tamped it down, creating a hairline fracture between them that only he could see.

'I heard you ordered for ... whatever was left of Harini's body to be ground,' he changed subjects hastily, staring intensely at the window to avoid tears from welling up. After the messenger had left his father's old study, Ashoka had demanded to know what had happened to Harini's remains. 'Thank you.'

'That should not require a thank you, my dear,' his mother replied, squeezing his arm. 'She was a sweet young woman. You were friends. Aarya initially left her bones scattered around the other witch – Shakti's – cell.'

Ashoka winced. 'That was needlessly brutal,' he whispered.

'I know,' his mother replied, looking disgusted. 'A cruel and shameful act. Aarya is like Adil. Your father was her guiding star. Even as a child, when I tried to change her behaviour, she resisted. And as your children get older, they become harder to change.'

Ashoka's attention flicked back to Arush. 'Aarya is all the worst parts of Father. What was the point? Why keep hurting mayakari?'

His mother sighed. The last few months seemed to have taken a toll on her; there was a distinct tiredness to her features now. 'Aarya was ashamed. Caught off-guard,' she replied. 'Imagine being your sister and hating the witches, only to have one work under her. The same one who cursed Adil, at that. And she was the one who forced her away from you. She won't say it, but your sister is licking her wounds, my dear.'

His mother uttered the fact that Shakti had cursed his father with such nonchalance. Ashoka frowned. 'Don't you hate her?' he asked. 'For cursing and killing Father?'

Curious brown eyes stared back knowingly. 'Do you?'

No.

It was pointless to say out loud when they both knew the answer.

Manali reached out and rubbed his burnt ear. His mother's fingers were usually cold, but sensation was absent there. It felt like gentle pressure. 'She's caused me pain, too. Aarya told me that it was the mayakari who poisoned Arush. When I first heard that ... I was so angry. She hurt my *child*. But despite what she did to Arush and Adil, I cannot bring myself to truly hate her, my dear, because she has been hurt beyond comprehension. She's lost her loved ones, too. The mayakari suffer so much. At least Arush is still alive. He can still wake.'

How would his mother feel if she knew her own daughter had poisoned him? Ashoka so badly wanted to expose his sister but he remained silent. It would break their uneasy deal.

'I was going to offer Shakti the chance to scatter her friend's ashes,' his mother added, ruffling his hair. 'Would you like to come with me?'

Ashoka jumped at the chance. Here was the perfect opportunity to see Shakti. Speak to her, perhaps. 'Aarya won't bar us?'

Manali shook her head. 'The most she'll do is have soldiers stationed around us for protection,' she said. 'She's keeping the girl in chains. Poor thing – she's treated worse than a muzzled leopard.'

They met Shakti at the top of one of the palace turrets. A strong gust of wind whipped Ashoka's face as he stayed close to his mother, who held a velvet purple sack that held Harini's ashes. Ashoka hadn't wanted to hold it. Knowing that the contents used to be his friend made him miserable and ill.

Shakti had been hauled there before them, several soldiers keeping a watchful eye on her. She seemed confused. Upon noticing his mother, and then him, she visibly startled. A brief look of relief flashed across her face before she wiped her expression clean and gave him a minute nod.

You're here, her expression seemed to say.

Beyond the northern turret was forestland, shining green, a woodland sea. He saw her observe it longingly. Ashoka took in Shakti's bedraggled state. There were chains around her hands and neck. Soot stained her skin. The bandages around her arms were dirty.

His blood simmered in anger.

'Dowager Empress. Prince Ashoka? I – what are you doing here?' she asked them.

His mother spoke first. 'We've come to offer you the opportunity to scatter Harini's ashes,' she replied, gesturing at the pouch.

Ashoka saw Shakti's face go slack before it contorted into one of myriad emotions. Shock. Sadness. Vehemence. Shame. He understood her more than she knew.

'Why?' she asked.

His mother frowned. 'Why?'

'I hurt your family,' Shakti replied. 'Why give me this?'

Stepping forward, his mother presented her Harini's ashes. 'Because I understand where your anger came from,' she replied, 'and it is fruitless to solve violence with more violence.'

He saw Shakti glance at him. 'That sounds like something Prince Ashoka would say.'

Despite himself, he let out a weak smile. If only she knew he ventured further towards the opposite these days. The remark seemed to have amused his mother too, for she let out a soft chuckle. 'Where do you think he learnt it from?' she asked before her expression sobered. 'What do you say? The wind is strong. The ashes will scatter far.'

Shakti agreed without much hesitation, taking the pouch.

'May I have a flask?' she requested. His mother seemed to understand what she was asking for and murmured for a soldier to step forward. Eyeing Shakti with about as much disgust as one would a pile of cow dung, the woman handed her an opened heavy flask of water.

Ashoka watched as Shakti wet her index finger, opened the string pouch, and dipped it inside. When she retracted her hand, grains of grey stuck to the fingertip like pollen. Muttering a stanza for a good rebirth, she painted a circle on her forehead. Then she turned to him.

'Come, Prince Ashoka,' she invited him, voice barely intelligible in the wind. 'Harini would want you to be a part of this. She cared about you.'

Feet walking of their own accord, Ashoka approached Shakti. She performed the same ministrations on his forehead, and he was transported back to the Mountain of Rebirth. His father. The circle, symbolizing samsara. All he could think in this moment was that Harini's death had been so unjust. When he locked eyes with Shakti, he knew she felt the same.

His father tied them together in anger, but Harini now tied them together in grief.

Once she finished painting his forehead, Shakti opened the pouch wider and scattered Harini's ashes, murmuring to herself.

The wind rushed against them and took with it the fine grey particles. There was no fanfare, but the knot that had formed in his throat seemed to ease. Like dust from a sandstorm, Ashoka watched the ashes spread out and descend.

'May your next rebirth be plentiful,' he said. For good measure, he repeated the same phrase, this time in a whisper as if that would bolster his plea. Harini deserved more than what she got.

Noticing Shakti's hunched shoulders and trembling hands, he stepped forward, irritably waving away the immediate responses of the soldiers, and placed a hand on her shoulder. 'I'm sorry,' he murmured. 'For her death, and for you being forced to burn her.'

For a moment, Shakti didn't respond to him. 'My recklessness killed her,' she whispered, before muttering a slew of phrases he couldn't hear.

'What?' he prompted.

'I said,' Shakti's voice was so low, so soft, that he had to strain to hear it, 'my recklessness killed her. I made a dangerous play.'

He didn't know how to respond because she'd spoken the truth. There was no softening it, and Shakti seemed to understand that. Sighing, she observed the forestland in silence before shaking her head in frustration.

'That Great Spirit,' she began. 'According to your father, your aunt summoned it successfully. Other mayakari have tried and failed, including me. It never appeared in front of me after I tried to summon it. I only heard its voice.'

'But it appeared,' he said. 'The quake . . .?'

She shook her head. 'That wasn't my doing. The Mountain of Rebirth has remained untouched for so long. Mining it caused the spirit to react and appear in its angered form. A Great Spirit's animal form and angered form are separate things.'

This he knew from Taksila. Meanwhile, Shakti appeared stumped. 'I don't understand – what did Subha do that was different?'

'I don't know,' Ashoka told her sheepishly, 'and I can't say there's much information on that Great Spirit.'

'Nothing at all?' Shakti's pitch rose with each word. She sounded frustrated, and for good reason. 'Not even a scrap of paper left behind after your father burned the mayakari's library?'

'Not that I know of,' he admitted. There were the notebooks his father had in his study, the ones he'd read when he was young. The ones he'd been punished for reading. Ashoka hated reliving that memory, but those notebooks outlined terms and theories on karma. Nothing conclusive about the Great Spirit. 'Why the vested interest in the Great Spirit?'

Shakti opened her mouth but seemed to think better of it and shook her head. 'Everyone knows that the mountain is an oddity,' she said. 'But after seeing it for myself . . . I want to understand why. Call it curiosity.'

'Even before the library was burned, the mayakari were no closer to understanding what was wrong with the Great Spirit.' His mother's voice startled them both. She'd been listening to their conversation in silence. 'Not even my sister, though I can't say she shared much about it with me.'

An unreadable expression passed across Shakti's features. 'It seems to be an unusual creature,' she said solemnly. 'It sounded angry. Hurt. I wish I could help.'

This time, his mother didn't answer. Instead, she signalled to the soldiers that they were done. As they moved to grab Shakti, Ashoka made a move. Leaning in, he made to grasp the pouch from her hands. Seemingly startled by his proximity, Shakti stilled. 'Visit my dreams again tonight,' he murmured softly enough that no one could hear. 'I have questions. A potential plan.'

Shakti's expression turned hard and determined. She let him take the pouch.

'I'll find you,' she promised, before she was hauled away.

CHAPTER TWENTY-TWO
Shakti

THAT NIGHT, SHAKTI ENTERED THE COLLECTIVE TO enter Prince Ashoka's dream.

The barrier that separated her from his consciousness was foggy. She could just make out the scene: it looked like a destroyed building. She entered with great difficulty. His mind seemed to unconsciously push against her with each step.

It took her a moment to place her environment. She stood in a room that had been utterly razed. Stone walls were crumbled, tapestries shredded. Bodies littered the floor, heads decapitated, abdomens sliced open to reveal lacerated pink intestine. In front of her was a mangled seat, the back twisted and reaching as high as a na tree, the armrests shattered, and the black colour bleaching into grey. Part of the leg had been blown off, and it wobbled every now and then.

Attempting to rebuild that wreck of a chair was Prince Ashoka, his back to her. He was free of all royal regalia and appeared more like a common citizen.

'I've never seen the Obsidian Throne in such a sorry state,' she called out as she approached closer.

Prince Ashoka stilled, then turned. Upon spotting her, he dropped a stray piece of debris he held. 'Shakti?'

'The one and only,' she replied.

He watched her, those large brown eyes drowning in sorrow.

'I'm sorry. About Harini,' he began. The name caught on his lips, voice cracking between syllables.

Shakti flinched. Recently, whenever she descended into a spiral about her lost memories, she imagined the torch in her hands. Harini's body burning blue. The Great Spirit awakening in a rage. Adil's warning.

'I'm sorry you lost someone you tried to shelter,' she said.

The smile he sent her was tired. Guilty. 'She didn't deserve such an ending. Every time I think I've successfully managed to protect a mayakari, misfortune turns around and slaps me,' he said, fists clenching. 'I can't imagine how you feel.'

'I want to kill your sister and drag her body through the streets,' Shakti said without so much as a speck of remorse.

Prince Ashoka's eyes widened. For a moment, she thought he would chastise her. For a moment, she thought he would somehow pivot and defend the very family he rebelled against. Then, 'I would think you'd want to burn her yourself, but each to their own ideals of punishment, I suppose.'

'Aarya deserves more than death for what she's done to me,' Shakti spat out, her fury rising. She kicked at the rubble, accidentally sending a severed ear flying in the process. 'She *drugged* me. I have gaping holes in my memory, Prince Ashoka. I can't *remember*. Do you know how frightening that is? Especially because I've cursed someone. Or something, and the only person who knows is Aarya. I want to *kill* her but she knows. She knows—'

'Shakti, stop. *Stop.*' Within moments his hands were cupping her shoulders. 'What did you just say?'

She told him. Of her gaps in memory. The *feeling* of having cursed, scraps of recollections. Realizing that Aarya had asked her to enact a curse. Or curses – how would she know? Her invading Aarya's dream to learn whom she cursed and failing miserably.

When she finished, Ashoka's face was ashen. 'Aarya,' he murmured, stepping away from her. 'That – no memories of it at all? No idea of whom she asked you to curse?'

'I . . . no,' she admitted. 'My mind recalled a fragment of it, I think. Her voice. *Hurt* and *pride*. Not much else.'

The prince's expression was troubled. 'Do you have an inkling of who she would curse?'

'I don't think Aarya would waste an opportunity on someone inconsequential,' Shakti admitted. She'd been thinking this for some time now. 'Knowing your sister, she could've asked me to curse Arush. Get rid of him for good.'

Ashoka shook his head. 'I don't think she would kill him outright,' he said. 'She made you keep him alive.'

She paused, not sure if she'd heard him right. 'Excuse me?'

Ashoka shot her a sympathetic grimace. 'She had you invade his dreams, keep him alive without deteriorating somehow. You said you can command people in them. Maybe that's what you did. You don't remember, do you?'

Shakti shook her head, feeling hollow. 'I hate this,' she muttered. Hated being told of something she'd done but couldn't remember. The only comfort she had was that she didn't care enough about Arush to feel guilty. 'I only remember wanting to be free from the pain. That's probably why I obeyed her.'

'Don't wake him up,' Ashoka said. When she raised an eyebrow, he added, 'If my brother won't wake, so be it. It's one less obstacle for me to take the throne.'

'Not like I can remember what I said,' she replied, before letting out a harsh chuckle. 'Your sister is a monster. She might've lied to you. Maybe she asked me to curse Arush instead. Who knows, Prince Ashoka, maybe she asked me to curse *you*.'

To her surprise, the prince laughed. *Was he mad? Why wasn't he more troubled by the thought.* Eventually, she concluded that each Maurya was mad in their own way.

'Possibly,' he shrugged, but looked sceptical. 'But I'm still alive. Besides, she has no motive to curse me other than for being an irritating pest who won't listen to her. One could call that a perfectly normal relationship between siblings. She wouldn't kill family.'

He sounded so sure, but Shakti didn't believe him. Despite not having siblings of her own, the way the Maurya brood acted was far from normal.

'Curses can take years to act,' she reminded him, wondering if the prince was trying to convince himself otherwise, 'and I fear I won't be able to remember it, and one day, it'll suddenly manifest. Not knowing is the worst part. There's this empty space in my head, and it's frustrating. The guilt is even worse. The only solace I have is knowing that the curse hasn't worked yet. That much I know.'

Ashoka pinched his burned ear. 'I'm sorry,' he said, moving back to sit on the Obsidian Throne. It didn't collapse under his weight. 'I can't bring back your memories, but I think I can help you escape.'

Escape. She'd never heard a sweeter-sounding word. Shakti eyed him inquisitively. 'How so?'

Ashoka sent her a grim smile. 'I'm going to persuade Aarya to send you back to the Mountain of Rebirth.'

Shakti was sure she heard him wrong. 'Impossible. She'll never agree.'

'Oh, she will,' Ashoka told her. The assuredness in his voice was rather admirable. Less prince, more emperor. 'Apparently, the quake caused a mudslide and polluted the nearby crop fields. Homes closer to the area have been damaged. People are rightfully scared. They'll be wondering if it'll happen again. Who else can re-attempt to speak to the spirit other than a mayakari?'

'People already think it retaliated *because* I lied about appeasing it.'

'No,' Prince Ashoka said, his face hardening. 'They think *Harini* lied. Aarya just used her to calm their fears down.'

Used. She hated that word.

Though Shakti understood his logic, she doubted its application. 'Aarya won't trust me,' she stressed. 'Not after I lied to her.'

'You said it would only retaliate if we continued to mine that mineral, correct? What if I convince her to halt the operations. Stopping them means that the spirit won't be angered. To communicate this properly, she'll be forced to send you as an envoy to speak on our behalf.'

She pondered this. It wasn't a bad idea. 'They won't send me to the mountain alone.'

The prince's eyes were lit up in determination. 'I expect guards. I won't be allowed to travel with you, that much I know,' Ashoka continued. 'If you're able to speak to the Great Spirit and let it help you, I can have someone wait at the base of the mountain. Help you escape and hide in the city.'

She considered it. Asking this capricious Great Spirit for help was a risk, but one she was willing to take. Shakti couldn't explain it, but there was a greater sense of familiarity to this spirit that she'd never felt before. It had whispered strange words to her. Suggested they were the same.

That bottomless cavern. A maw that threatened to swallow her whole. Normally, a mayakari could sense a nature spirit's emotions just as she viewed others' dreams before entering them. They registered, empathized, and understood. This spirit, however . . . its emotions felt like they were her own.

'You should speak to my father,' Ashoka remarked, then paused and shook his head, looking dazed. 'I still can't believe that's real. Or that my aunt was a mayakari, either, but him burning her is more in line with his character.'

Shakti winced. 'I'm sorry I didn't tell you about your aunt. It slipped my mind.'

Shaking his head, Ashoka waved his hands in a dismissive manner. 'Understandable,' he said. 'You should try to understand how you both were able to summon it. I can't offer an explanation there, unfortunately.'

Ashoka was right. To escape, she'd need the Great Spirit's help, but wasn't sure if it would appear *or* assist her. According to Adil, Subha had tried multiple times and succeeded once. She'd attempted a summoning once and half-succeeded on the first try. There had to be an explanation locked away in Adil's memories. 'I'll wrangle an explanation out of him,' she said.

'Good,' Ashoka smiled, before his expression settled back into a pensive one. 'So, what do you say? Is my plan of escape worth a try?'

It was a risk, but Ashoka was right; there were worse things to try.

'All right,' she said finally. 'Who will help me escape?'

Prince Ashoka's eyes gleamed. 'Rahil,' he said.

CHAPTER TWENTY-THREE
Ashoka

'Your idea is harebrained,' Rahil told him, tone dry, as they hurried to his father's – now Aarya's – study the next day, just before she was set to depart for a meeting with the consuls. They were running behind – Ashoka had given in to entertain Rahil's sweet tooth by diverting from their path to procure some sweets from one of the cooks, Ruchira, down in the palace kitchens.

'Hares are quite intelligent; I don't know who you think you're insulting,' Ashoka replied, grinning. 'My plan requires my strongest, most trusted soldier, and that's you.'

The rejoinder that had clearly begun to form on Rahil's lips died without being spoken. Ashoka convinced himself that it was because Rahil was so easily worn down by his sparkling personality. 'Spirits help me,' he sighed, flicking the bridge of Ashoka's nose in half-hearted resignation. 'You'd better hope Shakti can stand her ground.'

'She can,' Ashoka said firmly. Shakti was worn down, but she was strong. In her eyes was the desperate gleam of one who wanted to live at all costs. The gleam of a witch who didn't question having to be violent to free herself. When he'd told her about the cursed weapons, her eyes had nearly bugged out of her head. Her surprise had quickly been replaced by a deep hunger. A cursed weapon in her hands would be a terrible threat to anyone. 'You'll have to stand yours, too.'

'Doubting me already?'

'Never,' Ashoka replied. 'But I worry about you, too.'

When they finally arrived at the study, Ashoka was relieved to find that there were guards present. Aarya was still inside.

Knocking this time, Ashoka announced himself before entering.

From her seat, Aarya glanced up at the sound of his voice. Her expression turned frosty. 'What, *musī?*' she greeted him offhandedly. 'I have a meeting with the consuls soon.'

There was an undercurrent of irritation in her voice. Sau had informed him from the correspondence being redirected from Taksila, that the defence agreement between Queens Kalyani and Malika had been made public. Perhaps Aarya had heard of it now, too.

'This will be quick,' he said, coming to stand in front of her desk, arms clasped behind his back. 'I hope. I have a proposition for you.'

That seemed to spark her interest, but not in a good way. Ashoka sensed that his sister's hackles were already raised. 'A proposition?' she intoned. Her tone held all the contempt in the world, as if he was nothing but a nuisance of a child. 'Or another threat?'

'Both,' he said coolly. 'Admittedly, I wasn't here to witness the quake that occurred, but I have heard from Sau the general mood amongst our people. Having to clean or rebuild fallen homes, the nearby paddy fields completely sullied – there are fears that the Great Spirit will reawaken. Don't you feel the same?'

'Only a fool wouldn't,' his sister replied, tone stiff and suspicious.

'We're in agreement, then,' he said. 'Wouldn't the logical course of action be to halt mining and pacify the spirit?'

The snort that she let out was like their father's. 'That mineral holds the power to create advanced weaponry, and you want me to *give it up?*' she exclaimed. 'That mayakari didn't appease the Great Spirit in the first place, little brother. There is still the possibility that it could be pacified.'

'You're risking people's lives based on a possibility,' he argued. 'That Great Spirit isn't an ordinary one, and you know it. Continue to mine, and it'll cost you. If you want to keep power, sister, concentrate on placating the people instead. I've seen what angered spirits will do in Taksila and trust me when I say you want nothing of that here. Having these disasters continue is a sure way to lose a race you've only just begun. You don't want to be known as a poisoner *and* an incompetent.'

When she didn't respond, he added, 'You want to lead, don't you?'

Aarya's eyes narrowed to slits. His threat had landed. 'Look at you,' she said, raw fury evident in her tone. 'Commanding me. Threatening *me*. Never thought I'd see the day the little mouse grew its claws. Father would be impressed.'

Curling his lips in distaste, Ashoka ignored her remark. Aarya knew he hated being compared to their father. 'It's neither a threat nor a command,' he replied. 'Merely a suggestion.'

'What a suggestion,' his sister muttered. 'Halting an endeavour I've been aggressively pushing for. I'll look like a fool.'

Ashoka braced himself for the subsequent onslaught when he added, 'Have Shakti taken to the mountain and have her speak to it.'

The way she reacted, he might've taken a match and burned Aarya's ear. She reared back in abject horror and thumped a fist on the table so hard that it rattled. Every little mannerism was so much like Adil that Ashoka felt a singular prickle of unease before it disappeared.

'Little brother, I'm no idiot,' she sneered. 'What game are you playing? Has she been in your head, too? I assume you want to follow along on this expedition with her.'

'She hasn't been in my head since T— Taksila,' Ashoka caught himself just in time, 'Trikalinga' ready to leave his lips. 'And I'm not offering myself on this little expedition, sister. Send as many soldiers as you want, that isn't my choice to make. I only want to be assured that the Great Spirit won't be awakened again, and I don't see any other mayakari willing to work for you to make that happen. You murdered the last one who could've easily agreed.'

Aarya watched him with a flinty expression. She was searching for a trick, he could tell. Luckily for him, years of touting pacifist ideals would provide him a reasonable cover. The subsequent, lengthy silence told Ashoka that Aarya was weighing her options.

Not that she had many. His threat of revealing her as Arush's poisoner was what she cared about the most.

When she next spoke, Aarya's voice was deathly cold. 'The consuls have become invested in the mines as well. Such a turn-around from me would reflect poorly,' she said.

'I will publicly show my support for you,' he offered, 'if you allow me into the meeting. Spin the story in your favour.'

Aarya considered his proposal, albeit grudgingly. 'Speak one word against me and I will break your neck,' she warned.

Behind him, Ashoka heard Rahil shift. Aarya, too, had noticed, and she let out an aggrieved sigh. 'Does it look like I'm going to snap his neck?'

'Probably not, Your Highness,' came Rahil's cold voice.

'Then stand down.'

'You won't, anyway,' Ashoka parroted Aarya's own words back to her. 'I'm your *brother*.'

Rolling her eyes, Aarya stood up and stalked towards the door. Before she opened it, she shot him a look of utter contempt. 'Come on, then,' she said. 'Act with grace.'

With a mock bow, Ashoka followed. His threat had worked. Aarya must really fear being found out for her to concede. Silently, he walked a few paces behind his sister as they descended to the first floor of the palace where the council room was.

His presence was met with looks of surprise.

The seven consuls were already sitting around the large na wood table, clad in formal robes of deep red. Upon Aarya's arrival, they stood and bowed. Murmurs of 'Empress', and 'Prince Ashoka' followed.

'My brother will be observing today,' Aarya told them, smile stiff and wooden as she took the seat at the head of the table. Meanwhile, he sat on a spare chair at the opposite end. 'He has some thoughts to share on his governorship thus far.'

Caught off-guard, Ashoka could only smile politely and nod. Though, he guessed that Aarya had offered him a chance at transitioning into the topic of mining.

'We'll begin,' his sister declared briskly as she turned to Consul Hiranya. 'We have news from the governor of Mathura?'

Ashoka sat back and observed as the consul launched into a detailed statement on an issue regarding rice crops in flatland areas of the northern state. He learned that there had been a low crop yield, causing prices to rise. Rising prices meant disgruntled citizens complaining to the governor. Apparently, continued clearing of trees to make way for more agricultural crops caused the soil to be eroded. Without any plant cover, the eroded soil had affected crop growth. This issue was another leftover from their father, who tended to blame the mayakari for human-made problems.

He knew the answer: to balance both crop farming and preserving natural habitats. Perhaps even shrink the area of land to allow for any disgruntled spirits to be appeased and allow for the soil to return to its usual state. Even easier – have a mayakari perform an appeasement rite. But his siblings were too blinded by inherited hate to acknowledge the truth. When it came to the mayakari, he would tell them the sky was blue, only for them to call him a fool and say that it was red, as their father believed.

Eventually, after multiple proposals were discussed and settled on, Aarya redirected conversation, this time to Mahvo. As he thought, she'd received news of the negotiations, too. Feigning confusion, Ashoka waited patiently for Aarya to explain the situation.

'After hearing of our weapons being taken down south without consequence, I thought to enter Mahvo's territory. Begin what Father hadn't started,' Aarya began, expression growing flinty as her gaze cut to him for a moment. 'Unfortunately, the situation down south has become rather complicated. Queen Malika has reached a defence agreement with Queen Kalyani. Any act of trespassing on our part will now be considered an act of war. Kalinga will retaliate.'

'Crafty woman, that Queen Malika,' Consul Rangana added, nose wrinkling in distaste. 'Why agree to such an arrangement unless she's aware of the illegal transport of our weapons?'

They were ruffled. Irritated that the Ran Empire now looked foolish. Though they ended the topic by agreeing to remaining still for now, Ashoka knew his sister. The more of their military weapons were found, the more agitated Aarya would get. She would succumb to their father's sense of violence soon enough. It was just a matter of when.

Eventually, it came time for him to speak.

Clearing his throat, Ashoka waited till all the consuls' attentions were on him, before launching into a rather hastily thought-out speech about his governorship in Taksila. The consuls wore expressions with different degrees of respect. Some hadn't liked that he employed the resistance. Others had felt it was the only course of action but had never said it aloud in front of his father.

'A Great Spirit is now awakened in the capital, where it wasn't before,' he said. 'If we want to avoid more damage to the city and the flatlands around it, we need to stop mining the explosive mineral my sister rediscovered.'

From the apprehension visible on their faces, his suggestion wasn't being met well.

'We've already begun preparations, Prince Ashoka,' one remarked.

'After being privy to this meeting, it seems that we have bigger problems to direct our attention to,' he said. 'Mahvo, for one. Illegal exports are a violation. This mineral can wait.'

Looking like she'd chewed a raw bitter gourd, Aarya said, 'And the mining will be halted for an indefinite period until we find a way to procure it safely. I don't want more people dying from something preventable.'

'But, Your Highness, preparations are already underway,' Consul Daman piped up. 'The monetary gain you can receive from leveraging—'

'Would you want the Golden City to become what Taksila's north was, consul?' Ashoka interrupted firmly. 'There will be no monetary gain if the Great Spirit becomes enraged. This is why I'm proposing that you send a mayakari to communicate with it. Guarantee we will leave the creature alone for now. And who better to send than the one currently sitting in the palace prison?'

A dangerous hush settled like phlegm after a series of unsettling wet coughs before chatter arose.

'—let the mayakari loose, Prince Ashoka? How—'

'—*murdered* Emperor Adil. We can't trust her to—'

'—she could very well curse us into our next rebirth—'

All except Aarya were in a fit. Unlike the consuls, his sister leaned back against her seat and watched him with guarded eyes. A silent agreement seemed to pass between them. At least it was he, the prince, and not the acting empress who had touted the idea.

'I agree with Ashoka,' she said finally, causing the consuls to fall silent. 'The Great Spirit is unpredictable. For now, I agree to halt mining. My people need assurance, and I cannot have the Ridi prince question the empire's state of affairs when he visits.'

Ashoka stilled, unable to hide his surprise at the unexpected declaration. *Crown Prince Ryu?*

His sister watched him from the head of the table, lips tipped into a small, victorious smile.

'Ah, you arrived home so soon that it slipped my mind, little brother,' she said. 'Prince Ryu has agreed to pay me a visit. I'll be hosting my first state dinner in a week's time as acting regent.'

'For what purpose?' he managed to say, keeping his tone as unaffected as possible.

'Your job as Taksila's governor has gone splendidly,' Aarya smiled. On the surface, a compliment. Beneath, an insult. 'How you and Arush came to an agreement with the prince was admirable. However, since I've recalled our soldiers from the Frozen Lands, and there are no more spirit rampages, I think it's high time that the Ridi soldiers in Taksila return home.'

No. She was going to replace the Ridi soldiers with their own again. They answered to her, not him.

A cobra, his sister.

Surely, the Ridi prince wouldn't dissolve their arrangement. Not with Aarya as acting regent. Ashoka briefly considered pulling her aside and threatening her to stop this visit, but gathered that it had been planned well before he arrived home. Abandoning the dinner now would reflect poorly on the Maurya family.

His mind was racing. He needed to make sure that Prince Ryu would keep to their original deal, and not cower to Aarya's demands. It meant that he would need to stay in the capital a little longer. He couldn't risk leaving now. Losing the Ridi soldiers in Taksila would be a big blow.

Aarya was watching him. He forced a pleasant smile.

'I look forward to meeting Prince Ryu, sister,' he said and dipped his head in false acknowledgement. 'Perhaps this will give you all better incentive to have this matter sorted, what with the prince's impending arrival. I hope the Great Spirit can be placated soon.'

As he expected, Aarya imposed harsh restrictions on when and who Shakti would travel with.

The plan was to have Shakti travel to the mountain tomorrow morning in the early hours of the dawn. Ashoka had locked eyes with Rahil when Aarya finalized the time, and an implicit understanding passed between them. It meant that Rahil would have to leave the palace unidentified before dawn.

The rest of the day was spent with a certain degree of restlessness. Impatient, Ashoka paid a visit to his mother and Arush, took Sahry for a late morning flight, and sparred with Rahil in the training yard. He spoke to Sau, inquiring after any further correspondence from Taksila. According to her, the resistance had managed to create around two dozen cursed weapons so far. Most were everyday objects that could be used to defend themselves, while others were standard daggers. It was a taxing endeavour for those involved, and mass production was inefficient. The process would be slow, but as long as they had cursed weapons to use, that didn't matter.

Night fell when he returned to his chambers after dinner with Rahil close behind. Where Rahil would normally be stationed outside his doors for the night, Ashoka asked him to come inside.

He sensed Rahil track his movements, from the displacement of his daggers on the large desk, to the absentminded removal of his travelling cloak, and then to his unceremonious thump upon the bed.

Inside, Ashoka was descending into a slow panic. He was now worrying for two, and second-guessing himself and his entire plan.

What if Shakti was unable to be rescued? What if Rahil was found? Aarya would never trust him afterward. It seemed so obvious just to take one of his cursed daggers and nick his sister's skin. In mock combat, in the training yard, in her sleep. See the curse enact in moments. She would be dead, and the throne would be his.

Ashoka frowned, perturbed by the thought. That was certainly one way to depose of a ruler, but imprisonment was kinder. Using a cursed dagger against his own blood... he couldn't quite imagine it. What a horrible end that would be. While he didn't see eye-to-eye with Aarya, he could understand her twisted argument of hurting but never killing family. Blood was blood. Besides—

... I cursed someone. Or something...

... the only person who knows is Aarya. I want to kill her, but she knows...

Hurt Aarya and Shakti would likely never find out the true nature of her curse. What a bind.

'Stop thinking.' Rahil's gentle command drew Ashoka from his rumination. He'd never speak that thought aloud to him.

'Now that's a deceptively difficult task,' Ashoka told him. Slowly, he shifted himself towards the pillows and lay stomach up, observing the candlelight dance upon the ceiling. 'I don't think I can.'

'I can ask the physician to make you a tonic?'

Ashoka shook his head. He doubted that would work; neither did he want to rouse the poor woman from her sleep. Instead, he ignored the restless side of his brain and patted the empty space beside him in an invitation. Briefly, he wondered if the inability to sleep was wreaking havoc on his rationality, but all thoughts vanished when Rahil set down his own weapons and joined him.

Sandalwood, he thought as Rahil sat down. Unlike him, however, Rahil didn't make to lie down. Rather, he leaned against the headboard and brought his knees closer to his chest. Ashoka turned to face Rahil, curling into himself like a cat. For a moment, they stared at each other, words unsaid.

'What's bothering you?' Rahil asked softly.

Casting his eyes skyward, Ashoka sighed irritably. 'There's a chance my plan might fail, and Shakti remains imprisoned. You could be discovered. Hurt.'

A low chuckle escaped Rahil's lips. 'Back to doubting me, I see. Think I can't fend off a few soldiers?'

He could never doubt Rahil, but part of him was already regretting this. However, he knew that even if he voiced his concerns, Rahil would do it anyway. Shakti was important to him, which meant she was important to Rahil. Blind loyalty. Sometimes, Ashoka foolishly misconstrued it to be something more.

'Rahil.' Ashoka huffed. 'I'm serious.'

He felt a gentle pressure on his arm as Rahil grasped it. 'So am I,' he said. 'Trust me.'

'That's hardly difficult. I trust you more than anyone.'

Rahil smiled. His eyelashes cast long shadows to the curve of his cheekbones. At that moment, he was too close. It was exhilarating and terrifying at the same time. And it was not as if Rahil was never close – by nature he was. He had to be. But this felt different; intensified.

Cross the line.

Cross the line, Ashoka. What do you have to lose?

Loud and insistent, his fanciful emotions waged a silent war against him. He didn't realize that he was angling his head up, higher and higher till he was close to Rahil's face, and he heard him take a sharp breath.

Stop.

Ashoka paused and looked away, mortified.

'Do it.'

The litany of excuses he had at the ready died on his lips as he refocused his gaze on Rahil. His heartbeat tripled when Rahil leaned down to match him.

'Do what?' he whispered.

Rahil shifted closer. *Close.* He was too close, but it wasn't unwanted. Hair falling into his eyes, eyes challenging and mischievous, he was a dream turned real. 'What you didn't do in Taksila,' he replied.

Cross the line.

Shock kept him rooted to the spot. *Rahil . . . he felt the same?* No, this couldn't be. Was he hallucinating?

'And what is it,' Ashoka murmured, suddenly emboldened. Their noses were almost touching now, 'that you think I didn't do?'

'You tell me,' Rahil replied.

Ashoka's mind descended into a frenzy. Firecrackers exploded in his head. Wild forests regrew where humans had burned them down. He could only stare at Rahil's lips, dumbfounded. *Kiss me.* Was that what he'd meant?

I could do it so easily, too.

But what if that *wasn't* what he meant? Stubborn royal pride kept him from asking. The fear of rejection kept him at bay. 'I don't know,' he whispered instead, feeling like a fool.

For a moment, his gaze drifted down, watching the slow rise and fall of Rahil's chest. When he glanced back up, Rahil was still watching him, a knowing glint in his eye. 'I hope you figure it out,' he said.

Weakness would be to say the truth out loud: that he knew. This pride was a leftover vice from his father, one that he'd unfortunately inherited.

Groaning, Ashoka bumped his forehead against Rahil's, a light touch. 'Return in one piece,' he said gruffly. 'I command it.'

Rahil's answering laugh was soft. 'As you wish,' he replied, before sighing. 'You really should sleep. Are you sure you don't want a tonic?'

'No, but you can sing to me,' Ashoka joked, and was rewarded for it by a pointed flick to his forehead. The fragile moment between them vanished.

'I hope you're reborn as a worm,' Rahil replied, adding, 'and Sau, too,' after a brief pause.

'Pettiness is unattractive, you know,' Ashoka murmured, smiling. 'Why don't you tell me something about your time in the Ridi Kingdom with Sau? Maybe that will help me sleep.'

It took Rahil little convincing. He launched into a story about how Sau, after feeling embarrassed by making a small error in translation in front of the crown prince, proceeded to drown her sorrows in bitter plum wine. Thoroughly inebriated, she'd then attempted to abduct someone's cat and take it back to the palace with her.

At first, Ashoka laughed. After a while, Rahil's voice turned into a dull hum; he caught a few words here and there but not enough to comprehend the sentences fully. The gaps in understanding became more frequent, and before he knew it, he drifted off to sleep.

CHAPTER TWENTY-FOUR
Shakti

AFTER SPEAKING TO PRINCE ASHOKA, AND UNABLE TO keep her curiosity at bay any longer, Shakti returned to the Collective, thinking of Emperor Adil. He appeared seated upon the Obsidian Throne, and she standing a few paces in front of him.

'Me again?' he asked wryly. 'Grown tired of Emperor Ashoka, have you?'

The emperor. He hadn't been on her mind for the past few weeks. Every other problem had pushed him to the side. 'No,' she said, 'but I need you, Adil. I need to see your memories. You said that you visited the Mountain of Rebirth a few times with Subha after the landslide. I want to see the memory of her trying to summon it and hearing its voice.'

The emperor eyed her with suspicion. 'Why?'

'I want to find out what's wrong with it,' she said.

'Stupid girl. Don't disturb the creature,' he began, but Shakti cut him off.

'You can't refuse my order,' she commanded. 'Show me.'

Given the return of his usual scowl, Adil was still unused to having a mayakari give him orders. 'As you wish,' he said, and the throne room faded into darkness. Shakti closed her eyes.

When she opened them, the first thing she saw was Subha's back. She was viewing the memory as Adil again. Ahead of him, the mayakari hurried upward. She seemed intent on getting to their destination, likely the peak of the mountain.

They passed by a puddle of water and Adil happened to glance down. Shakti saw his face reflected for a brief moment. A young man still, perhaps a couple of years older than the last memory of him she'd seen. It was hard to tell.

The scene faded, and the memory shifted forward in time. Now, they were at the peak of the Mountain of Rebirth. Shakti-as-Adil stood behind Subha while she knelt, palms touching the ground.

'How many times will you try this?' he told her. 'Even if the spirit is dormant, it won't wake. This is futile.'

'You didn't need to follow me all the way here to say that,' Subha retorted, clearly irritated as she dipped her head. 'Besides, Great Spirits can be summoned one way or another. I believe this one will, too.'

Adil didn't offer a biting remark. Instead, he watched as Subha slipped into spirit-speak. He wouldn't have understood a word of what she said, but, observing his memory, Shakti did.

'*Great Spirit of the mountain. Surveyor of this vast domain, I call upon you.*'

The summoning was no different from hers. In fact, it was the same; a standard phrase used by mayakari. It didn't seem to work here, either, for the first invocation yielded no result. No Great Spirit materialized.

'Perhaps, I shouldn't have come,' Adil muttered to himself. He was still watching Subha, who kept her head down. 'Let's go, Subha.'

Suddenly, a soft whisper echoed around the peak, dazed and distorted. Shakti startled, as did Subha. The voice was groggy and irritated, as if waking up from sleep:

'*Mayakari. False chakravartin. Wheel turner. The false chakravartin is here. King of the golden wheel.*'

The Great Spirit's voice. She could recognize it immediately.

The voice continued to echo: '*mayakari, false chakravartin. Golden-wheeled king.*' Subha craned her neck in every direction, likely watching for the arrival of the Great Spirit. The mayakari's gaze was frantic. Expectant. Unfortunately, it didn't appear.

'Subha?' Adil asked again. He didn't seem to have heard anything, not even a wail. He sounded slightly concerned. It was a foreign emotion to witness. 'What is it?'

The mayakari turned her head. They locked eyes. A frown came and disappeared in a blink.

'Nothing,' she told him, worrying her bottom lip. 'You're right. We should go back.'

Once more, the memory dissolved. Once more, Shakti was thrust into darkness, and she closed her eyes. When she reopened them, she was Adil again. This time, the memory took place in his study. He was poring over some documents. Shakti caught a glimpse of one: a letter with several signatories, stating they refused to perform appeasements until money was reapportioned to the Great Library. As Adil read the letter he swore softly under his breath.

'Damn mayakari,' he muttered, flipping to the next page. 'Who are they to decide—'

His lone tirade was interrupted when there came a knocking at his door. Just as he opened his mouth, the door swung open and in came Subhadrangi. Her figure came into sharp focus. She was in disarray, although by some miracle the singular saraca flower in her hair remained undisturbed. Unlike the last time Shakti saw her, the mayakari was in a simple tight-fitting black tunic and trousers. Her breathing was laboured. Had she run here?

'Subha!' Adil set down his papers. 'What are you—'

'Come back,' she interrupted, panting.

Shakti-as-Adil's vision turned sharper. No, that wasn't it. Only Subha turned sharper, while the rest of the study had a blurriness to it. 'Back where?' he asked. Shakti was surprised that he hadn't castigated her for interrupting him. 'I need to see Manali. She's having trouble with Arush. The physician says its teething pain.'

Manali had given birth. Much time had passed then, since in the last memory the empress hadn't shown any signs that she was with child. Teething pain – the baby could be anywhere from four to twelve months old.

At his response, Subha's urgency deflated. 'Oh,' she said. 'Yes, of course. See to Manali and the baby first. This can wait.'

'Can it?' Adil asked dryly. 'It seems urgent.'

Subha laughed, the sound still strained from exertion – *why was it suddenly so loud?* – and shook her head. 'I have a working theory that I wanted to test,' she said. 'I . . . I lied to you last time. At the mountain. I did hear a voice when I tried to summon it. When I went back the day after, I tried again – nothing. I've been trying since, but I can't hear its voice.'

'What?' Adil's voice was lacking its usual austerity. 'Why did you lie?'

For a moment, they stared at each other in silence, until Subha broke it by looking away. 'I don't know,' she said, frustration evident by her rising pitch. 'Never mind. I'll come back another time.'

Shakti-as-Adil stood up, the chair screeching loudly as the mayakari turned to leave. 'Wait, Subha. What did it say?'

Subha tensed, eyes on, but not completely focusing on, Adil. '"The false chakravartin is here",' she said. 'At least we've confirmed that the spirit is alive. Somewhat.'

The phrase was like what the Great Spirit had told her at the mountain: *you and I are the same, little witch. You, me and the false chakravartin.*

That title again. *Chakravartin.* She wracked her brains for a possible connection. Taken literally, it meant 'wheel-turning king'. The title referred to a universal, ideal ruler. A righteous one. She'd hardly ever heard of the term being used nowadays. Neither had she heard the phrase 'golden-wheeled king' before. That was new. But the Great Spirit also suggested that said king wasn't noble. At first, she'd thought the Great Spirit was talking about Aarya, given that she wasn't the true monarch. Arush was. But now, given this memory, the creature was most likely talking about Adil. How strange.

The man in question wasn't taking to the description well. 'Does it think that I'm some sort of – of false monarch?' he thundered. 'I am no mere king. I am an emperor.'

The mayakari sighed. 'I knew you'd react like this,' she said. 'Go. See to my sister. Find me once you're clear-headed.'

Shakti couldn't see Adil's expression, but assumed it would have echoed hers: dumbfounded that a mayakari could speak to an emperor so casually. And without rebuke. The memory faded, and she was returned to the Obsidian Throne room. Adil had reappeared and was watching her intensely.

'You're a false chakravartin,' she told him.

Adil's lips curled in distaste. 'I am no false king, witch,' he thundered, expression as angry as it had been when Subha had said it. 'I am an *emperor*.'

Two days later, in the early morning when not even the birds had woken, Shakti was taken to the throne room.

Bleary-eyed and fighting away sleep, she was brought to a halt beneath a decidedly more awake Aarya. Even at this hour, she appeared put-together in a lilac antariya and uttariya pair. Presentable. Then again, Shakti hadn't been afforded the luxury of a bed, or half-dozen staff to do the most basic jobs for her. Soldiers stood alert on either side, situated on every third step from the base of the steps to the throne, right to the top. They watched Shakti like starving jackals.

'Mayakari,' the empress proclaimed, waving the advisors off to the side.

'Empress,' Shakti began. 'What am I here for this time?'

She was mostly certain what Aarya had summoned her for. Prince Ashoka must've convinced the empress to send her back to the Mountain of Rebirth.

Slowly, she became aware that Aarya was watching for any signs of deception. 'Against my better judgement, I've decided to entertain my little brother's request,' Aarya continued with a ferocious scowl that recalled an aggravated tiger. 'Dubious, but worth trying. You will travel to the Mountain of Rebirth today to speak to the Great Spirit.'

Shakti feigned surprise.

'Let the Great Spirit know that we will halt mining for the time being,' Aarya continued, before frowning, 'and beg it to return to dormancy. All this trouble for a creature that doesn't seem to care for others. How pitiful.'

Shakti jerked back. *Pitiful*. As if Great Spirits existed to protect witches from harm. As if they had a mutual give-and-take relationship.

The corner of Empress Aarya's lips drew upward in amusement. 'Why care so deeply for beings that do not seem to care for you?' she asked innocently.

She could almost *hear* Adil gloat: *My daughter asks a fair question, witch.*

Shakti glowered. 'Why pose questions you have no understanding of, *Your Highness?*'

Raw vehemence blanketed Aarya like morning mist as she mirrored Shakti's expression. 'Careful, Shakti,' she replied. 'I have no qualms about taking a match to your fingers.'

Oh, what a *wretched* woman. Shakti wished for nothing but a miserable rebirth for the young empress. May she be born into suffering. May she have everyone and everything she loved taken away from her. May she die just when it seemed like her life was about to gain good tidings.

Gritting her teeth, Shakti bowed her head. 'Of course, Your Highness,' she said. Even enunciating one word was painful.

The smile that Aarya sent her was plagued. 'Good,' she said. 'Go on then, witch. Have this issue settled before nightfall. Don't you dare try any of your tricks – have no doubt that my soldiers will bleed you dry.'

Shakti had only ever seen the peak of the Mountain of Rebirth through Emperor Ashoka's memories. As she observed it now, it appeared much the same.

They'd travelled by carriage from the palace, down to the city, and from there to the infamous mountain. Despite knowing she could never spot him, Shakti couldn't help glancing out the window in her shackles as they continued from the base, watching for Rahil.

This part is dependent on you alone, Shakti.

The trek up to the peak was tiresome on her legs. She hadn't walked this far in a long while. At least the air was cleaner the higher they ascended, delightfully sharp when she took a deep inhale at the peak.

The mist was beautiful and smothered everything. Fallen, rotten logs suffocated under a layer of moss, crawling with insects. From healthy na trees hung vine trails and birds' nests huddled into the crooks of trunks. There was something delightfully beautiful and eerie about it. A welcome and a warning, an admission and a secret.

She knew they would release her gag. That was already more than enough of an advantage. And yet, Shakti had the suspicion they wouldn't release her bonds. That posed too much risk.

'No funny business, mayakari,' the soldier behind her warned. 'Speak to the Great Spirit and be done with it.'

Shakti waved her bound hands in front of him. 'Let me out of my chains, then,' she requested. Might as well try.

'Absolutely not,' he replied. 'Empress' orders.'

Spirits. 'If you want to risk your lives, be my guest,' Shakti cautioned them. 'I don't know what state this Great Spirit is in, and I don't think it will react well to seeing a mayakari in chains.'

As expected, the soldiers' faces turned circumspect. The leader of the group let out a tired sigh and gestured to another woman who, at first, didn't seem to be listening and instead observing the area from which they had come.

'Kuvi,' he repeated. 'Didn't you hear me? Undo the witch's shackles.'

The soldier started, looking sheepish. 'Sorry, sir,' she apologized. 'I thought I heard something.'

She came forward and unlocked Shakti's chains. 'Don't try anything,' she said somewhat fearfully.

Silver shackles hit the ground will a dull *thud*. Freedom. Shakti had half a mind to tackle the closest soldier to the ground, steal their weapon and use it to fight her way out immediately to find Rahil. Logic would have cautioned against such an audacious idea by citing her health, but oddly enough, she felt stronger. Never mind the cuts and bruises on her body – she felt invincible enough to escape the Golden City and never return.

What was in this mountain air?

And yet, she wouldn't. Not when she knew that a Great Spirit was troubled. Help it first, then escape.

'Stay back,' she advised the soldiers. 'I need to summon the Great Spirit, so don't interrupt me.'

They obeyed without question.

Getting down on one knee, Shakti placed both hands on the ground where red flowers blossomed and withered. This place was so peculiar; she couldn't quite put her finger on it. The last time she had summoned the Great Spirit at Kolakola, she had sensed the natural cycle of life and rot. Here, something felt *unnatural*. The simultaneous existence of two opposites was far more acute. Land reflected a Great Spirit, so what did this phenomenon say about it?

'*Great Spirit of the mountain*,' she called out, '*surveyor of this vast dominion, answer my call.*'

At first, there was no response. The air was still like it was holding its breath. A lone squirrel scampered up a tree. A bird dropped from the sky in front of her without even a cry, startling Shakti. Horrified, she watched as it decomposed within seconds, flesh and bone melting into the ground, from which sprouted a small green sapling. Chills wracked her body.

This was nothing like the summoning in Kolakola. It was as if she was noticing everything wrong. The wind picked up, bringing with it speckles of ash. The mist pooling around her legs turned greyer.

Like the last time, she felt a pleasant surge of power. She chased it.

Behind her, the soldiers gasped. When Shakti turned her gaze away from the mist swirling upon the ground, she saw the air shimmer. Sounds of wind chimes and flutes played a soothing lullaby in her head as an enormous ghostly elephant materialized before her, nearly ten times her height.

Its body was a greyish yellow. The colour reminded Shakti of the filmy layer that usually formed over a wound. Still healing, not yet recovered. Where two long ivory tusks should have been was only one, the second cracked and splintered like the trunk of a fallen tree. Bamboo leaves sprouted from within its ears, curving and reaching around to form a sort of crown above the head. A faulty crown, Shakti noted, for some leaves were a white-brown while others retained a vibrant green hue.

'Great Spirit,' she greeted it, bowing. When she looked up again, it still had not responded, gazing down at her like she was an ant. Extending its wraithlike trunk, it hovered over the crown of her head.

Shakti could sense the Great Spirit with more awareness. Its appearance, its manner – she understood it. The Great Spirit of Kolakola had exuded power. The Great Spirit of the Mountain of Rebirth was exhausted. Distrusting. Worn down.

Like her.

'*Little witch,*' it replied.

Creaking wood. That was what its voice reminded her of. A loud groan, an animal awoken after months of hibernation. Around them, the air turned crisper. Each inhale stung her nose.

'*I apologize for calling on you again,*' she said, '*but I come bearing good news.*'

Eyes of muslin white stared back, unfocused. The pupil and iris were difficult to see; only a pale green ring was visible. Shakti frowned; its eyes had the appearance of a creature who was half-blind.

'*You have not greeted me,*' the Great Spirit replied. '*Greet me.*'

Wary, Shakti assessed its demeanour. The elephant spirit didn't seem angered. Not yet, at least. How had it not heard her greeting? Was it hard of hearing? Surely not.

'Greetings,' she repeated.

'Good,' the Great Spirit replied. Maybe it *was* hard of hearing, or confused. '*I see the burdens you bear, little witch. Minds other than your own. Minds that corrupt, fused to its mayakari host. What is it you have called me for?*'

Shakti stilled. No doubt, a Great Spirit could sense the Collective. After all, the tiger spirit in Kolakola had. But this felt odd, as if her eyes had been covered by a blindfold, left only to the graces of her remaining senses to survive. Its description bothered her. *Host.* That sounded entirely unpleasant.

'I come bearing news from the empress,' Shakti began hesitantly. 'She has agreed not to plunder the mountain. She asks that you not rage against her people for now.'

Cloudy eyes narrowed in confusion. '*I raged?*'

'You did, Great Spirit,' Shakti said, frowning. Was its memory addled? It certainly seemed that way. *'Do you not remember?'*

'Sometimes, memories elude me, little witch,' it said. *'They are fragments. Broken shards of glass. Tarnished paintings.'*

They were kindred in that way, then. 'You were angered, Great Spirit,' she remarked. *'I heard your voice. It was so clear. I don't understand how.'*

The elephant's body wavered. *'You and I are much the same, little witch. We are both broken,'* it said, and let out a scornful laugh so loud that it caused her ears to ring. A hint of green revived in its irises. *'Ah, I do remember. After angering me, the young empress now wishes to concede? These Mauryas are no better than the last. The oldest, trapped in snow. The daughter, muzzled by pride. The youngest, iron in quartz.'*

The creature sounded angry. Shakti tried to placate it. 'Great Spirit, the empress asks for peace.'

She wasn't hallucinating, its irises were becoming greener. *'Do I not deserve to wake upon my own domain? I have slept, and now I refuse to sleep again. But you lied, didn't you, little witch? Fooled them into thinking they could take from me. You hurt me, and you killed others. Why?'*

'They needed to be taught a lesson,' Shakti said. 'Why did you not accept the appeasement, Great Spirit? Most do.'

'My brethren hold a fondness for humans that I do not understand,' the elephant replied. *'All they do is take and lie and destroy. Why should I bow to humans? I was turned this way by one of them.'*

Shakti frowned. 'Turned this way?'

Its skin turned a hue that was a sicklier yellow than before. Above its head, the leaf crown stirred in the breeze. *'Do you not understand? Can you not see my condition, little witch?'*

'You're ill,' Shakti said. Tentatively, she reached out a hand to run over its serrated tusk. Nothing but a tepid warmth met her. 'Or weak.'

'Both.'

'How?'

'Attachment.'

On instinct, frustration welled, but Shakti violently pushed it aside. Who was she to become vexed by a Great Spirit? It was fruitless to needle too much.

The elephant let out a horrible trumpet. It caused the soldiers behind her to startle and cautiously step forward, but Shakti waved them back. Her mind was still latched on to the spirit's earlier remark.

'A human made you this way?' she pressed.

'Human greed,' the elephant wailed. Beneath her, the ground cracked and formed a perfect spiderweb. Its eyes paled. 'And a mayakari's anger. The false chakravartin must give me peace.'

Suddenly, the pale-yellow glow around the elephant's body started to dim. Its body seemed to shrink in size.

'Great Spirit,' Shakti said, panicking, 'Are you all right?'

'You and I are the same, little witch,' it told her. What was left of its broken trunk began to crumble away. 'Help me. Release me. Your awakening is mine, and my awakening is yours'

'Tell me what you need, Great Spirit,' Shakti urged it. 'I don't understand.'

The elephant let out another loud groan. It sounded like a child being tired after hours of crying. 'Rest. I must rest. Farewell, little witch.'

'Wait!' she cried out in a blind panic. 'Great Spirit, I'm bound. I'm trapped. Please, help me escape.'

'What do you seek?' it asked with what sounded like sympathy.

'A diversion big enough to halt a dozen soldiers,' she pleaded.

'I will grant it.' Just before it vanished completely, Shakti saw the elephant's iris change into a vibrant moss-green.

CHAPTER TWENTY-FIVE
Shakti

An emptiness settled in the pit of Shakti's stomach after the Great Spirit's departure.

'It's gone,' the soldier called out, sounding relieved. 'Re-shackle her.'

For a beat, Shakti felt her heart stop. For a singular, unbearable moment, she thought the Great Spirit had lied, and she was being forced to return without a chance of escape. But then, several things happened at once.

Suddenly, the mist turned dense. Thick. More like a fog born of perpetual storm. It began to obscure the air around her, as opaque as smoke from a wildfire.

Beyond the clearing, Shakti saw a flash of movement. From the shadows emerged a tall, muscular figure clothed all in black, everything except their eyes hidden from view. A blink of her eyes, and they disappeared. She wondered if it had been a hallucination.

A lone *caw* sounded from above them. Downy black speckles fell from the sky. They looked like – no, they *were* – feathers. Then, something wet and solid hit her right shoulder with a resounding *squelch*. Initially, Shakti hazarded it might have been a stray water droplet, but it was too heavy. And then, that same unsettling sound repeated, again and again.

She touched her right shoulder. Her little finger came away with something soft stuck to it. Something pulverized. Pink.

Two of the soldiers screamed. Others pointed in terror at the sky.

It was difficult to see, what with the fog turning heavier, but Shakti could make out dozens upon dozens of winged creatures, their wings flapping in unison. *Crows*, she realized with fresh horror as she observed what she'd seen here before. The birds remained in the air, stalling, until all at once their bodies began to decompose. Their feathers fell first before their bodies separated; muscles separating from bone, decaying as flesh hit the ground and them.

A horrific distraction, but a perfect escape.

With the fog as her cover, Shakti sprinted left, intending to track a wide arc around the soldiers, pushing past fog and attempting to scurry back into forestland. But first—

She spotted a soldier who, in his disconcertion, had wandered away from the main group, attempting to rub off bits of crow flesh from his uniform. His sword was sheathed but open for borrowing. Keeping her footsteps light, Shakti made her way towards him.

When his back was to her, she took a running leap and tackled him to the ground. The man let out a horrified yell as he landed face first. Before he had any time to react, Shakti kept him down using her legs to force a lock and grasped his neck in a chokehold.

She didn't know him, but she wanted to kill him.

You killed an emperor, little bird. You burned a fellow witch. Is that not enough?

As the soldier sputtered beneath her ever-tightening grasp, a furious roar sounded:

'Fucking witch – find her, *now!*'

Spirits. There was no time. Shakti counted for eight, nine heartbeats until the soldier's eyes rolled back in his head, driven unconscious. Quickly, she released her grasp and removed his sword from the scabbard. A typical longsword, slightly unbalanced, but it'd have to do.

It was hard to see now; the fog had shrouded everything. She couldn't see more than two paces ahead of her. *Damn it.*

Nevertheless, she needed to move as far away from the unconscious soldier as possible. That unusual surge of energy was fuelling her forward; Shakti found that she hadn't yet succumbed to the usual dizziness and fatigue of the last few weeks. Managing to orient herself, she ran towards the edge of the clearing where open space met the downward slope of forestland, sword ready by her side.

Far behind her, she heard several exclamations. A name being repeated – the unconscious soldier had been discovered.

'Be careful – the witch has his sword.' She heard the order clearly. 'Move in pairs. Listen for movement.'

Pairs were good. Fewer people to set upon her at once. Shakti fervently hoped she could enter the sanctuary of the forest before then. She moved slowly, careful not to make a sound.

I can make it, she thought, triumphant. *I need to keep myself hidden for some time before I find Rahil, but I'm* free.

Karma seemed to tell her, rudely, *not yet*.

Shakti heard an audible crack. Her heart dropped.

From her left, two figures emerged from the fog. Soldiers. They held their swords in front of them in a defensive position as they eyed her with a mixture of surprise and fear. One of them, a woman with narrow eyes, smirked.

'Here!' she yelled. 'She's—'

Shakti ran into the fog, away from the pair. They would follow, but she was betting on them splitting up to cover more ground. As she suspected, she heard the heavy thud of footsteps right behind her. It sounded like one person, not two. Turning, she raised her sword just in time to meet that of the rampaging soldier, metal connecting in a loud *clang*.

Master Hasith's training came to her like breathing. When the soldier moved their sword in a horizontal arc, aiming for her chest, Shakti dropped to the ground and rolled, coming up to slice the side of their thigh. Metal carved into flesh like meat, the resounding yell of agony like music to her ears.

Kill. Kill. Kill.

The soldier was open, distracted.

Do not kill. Do not harm. The mayakari do not—

The mayakari side of her still refused to entertain a proper kill. It still refused to give up total control, kept one finger on the leash.

It took only a split second of inattentiveness on her part for the soldier to regain his bearings and strike at her heart. Shakti leapt back, but not fast enough. The tip of the sword made contact just above her left breast. A sharp flash of pain shot through her chest. The cool sting of fog made it worse.

'The empress surely won't mind if you return dead,' the soldier hissed. Raising his sword, he charged like a leopard at full speed. Gritting her teeth, Shakti tensed. Waited. Waited until the last moment, and right before his sword tore through her ribcage, she whirled right and ducked, coming up behind him.

Do not harm. Do not k—

Shakti drove the sword through the back of the soldier's chest, straight through where his heart would be.

He fell to the ground, muscles convulsing before he became still.

Little bird.

No. There was no time to lament. There was no time to consider the repercussions of her first combative kill. She needed to run.

Except that a beat later, another soldier came. His pair, she guessed. The soldier took one look at her fallen comrade, then at Shakti, before she charged.

I'm going to die here, Shakti thought.

Just as their swords clashed, and Shakti aimed to kick out at the soldier's knee, another figure materialized behind the soldier. Fear spiked, hot and fast. Thinking that this would become a two-to-one fight, Shakti gripped the sword hilt tighter.

Their shape became clearer — it was the same form that she thought she'd seen at the edge of the clearing. This wasn't one of Aarya's soldiers; they were unidentifiable with the face covering on.

The figure flipped their sword in the opposite direction and aimed the hilt at the back of the soldier's head. The resultant *crack* was loud enough for Shakti to wince. The woman crumpled to the ground, motionless.

Were they going to kill her, too?

'Shakti.'

Their voice was deep. Recognizable. Shakti watched as they moved to lower their mask, and a familiar face with umber eyes stared back.

'What are you—'

'No time,' Rahil said hurriedly, and grabbed her arm. 'We need to go. *Now*.'

She let him drag her towards the forestland, chest still aching from the slash. Rahil was here – she'd expected him at the base of the mountain, but this was a far better outcome. For whatever reason he'd chosen to ascend to the peak; she was grateful. Spirits knew she would be dead, or even worse, recaptured.

Leaves rustled in sharp whispers as they tore through the forest. Birdsong was absent, with only a gentle hush and the sound of their hurried footsteps crunching and snapping on twigs present.

Rahil, for his part, seemed to know where to go. He was likely taking the same route he'd taken up. Nearly slipping during their downward trajectory, Shakti grabbed his arm with her free hand. There was no dense fog now, but breathing was becoming difficult. Invisible chains seemed to compress her upper chest, forcing her to take deep, unsteady inhalations.

'Breathe,' she managed to huff. 'Stop. Let me . . . breathe . . .'

Rahil eventually had them stop and take cover behind a decaying fallen trunk, further obscured by a thick grove of foliage. Shakti plopped herself down and leaned back against the rotting wood to catch her breath.

Crouching next to her, Rahil eyed her injury with mild concern. 'Looks nasty. Do you think you can make the rest of the journey down?'

She nodded, brushing off his concern with a wave of her hand. 'Yes, but give me a moment,' she said, purposefully taking slow breaths. Rahil waited in silence, observing both her and their surroundings. He was still, listening for movement.

When Shakti calmed herself down, she turned to look at him. 'I was told to find you at the base of the mountain,' she whispered.

Rahil grimaced. 'I'm aware,' he said.

She didn't press him any further on that, except to ask, 'Why did you follow us?'

A soft *snap* caused Rahil to whip his head around, peeking over the log ever so slightly to spot the cause. Shakti let him survey the area before he returned his attention to her. 'Because Ashoka's plan to leave arguably the most crucial aspect of this operation on you was too risky,' he said. 'I know you can fight, Shakti, but trying to escape a dozen soldiers after being imprisoned... I thought you'd be too fatigued and need more help. Before the Great Spirit intervened, I was planning to fight them all.'

'But realistically, could you have? Fought them all, I mean?'

He shot her a flat look. 'Didn't register that not many soldiers found you except that pair, did you?'

Shakti considered it. 'I thought the fog was a great ally.'

'For you and me both,' he said. 'Luckily, they split into pairs. They were easier to find and disarm. There are some left up there – I found you before I got to the rest.'

'Thank you,' she muttered.

Rahil let out a small smile before sighing. 'Sometimes, I think Ashoka forgets that mayakari powers don't make you invincible,' he remarked. 'He places too much of his hopes on you.'

'In his defence, I also placed too much hope on myself,' Shakti said. 'Or rather – I took a risk I shouldn't have, and tried to steal a sword when I could have run.'

Shakti couldn't help but think of the irony. After Kolakola had burned, she'd fled and decided against picking up a weapon. Here, she'd done the opposite, arguably with direr consequences had Rahil not intervened.

'Sometimes it can be difficult to decide when to wield a weapon and when to let it lie,' he replied. 'Are you feeling somewhat better?'

The cut continued to sting, but her breaths had begun to steady. 'A little more time,' she requested. 'Do you frequently go against Prince Ashoka's orders?'

Rahil snorted. 'Not often,' he replied. 'But I didn't want to leave anything to chance. Though I suspect his orders were, in part, to keep *me* from harm as well. Which is stupid. It's as if he thinks I can't fight multiple combatants myself.'

Despite the gravity of the situation, Shakti let out a weak chuckle. 'I think that's his way of protecting you,' she said. 'He cares.'

'It's my duty to protect him,' Rahil said, 'not the other way round.' He sounded both agitated, baffled, and enamoured at the same time, as if the very idea were as complicated as sums.

'When two people care so deeply about each other, is that not expected?' Shakti reached an arm out, pressing it against a spread of moss that grew along the trunk. Dew still clung to it, not yet evaporated beneath the morning sun. The cool press of water on her hot skin provided a modicum of relief. 'Do you not love him enough to understand that such acts of service are mutual?'

Rahil seemed lost in thought when he said, 'Of course, I do.' Then, 'A specialist at giving advice on matters of the heart, are you?'

'The heart?' she intoned, bemused by his sudden flush. It made him look more endearing. 'Not my area of expertise. It actually took me a while to see it, but you two are obvious.' Romantic love had always been something of a nebulous entity. A priceless jewel put on display; one that she could visibly see but never wanted to steal.

'You sound like Sau,' Rahil replied.

'Why don't you two act on your feelings, then?' Shakti asked in honest confusion. 'Or is this a matter of station? Prince and guard – that sort of thing.'

'Hardly. It's more because Ashoka has built up walls higher than the palace,' Rahil said with a shrug, but he didn't sound frustrated. 'He fears rejection; tries to avoid hurting himself. People have that instinct naturally, but his is extreme.'

'Doesn't it hurt you?'

Rahil appeared to consider it. 'No,' he said eventually. 'I know him. He just needs time.'

'If I were you, that would hurt me,' Shakti remarked, more to herself than him. 'What if he never acts on his feelings?'

A bemused smile graced Rahil's lips. 'I suppose I have more faith in him than you do.'

Shakti hummed, and for a while, they sat together in silence until she felt her breaths steady.

'I think I'm ready to leave.' She stood up, brushing away bark from the backs of her thighs. 'Best go before the remainder of the soldiers find us. Which reminds me – where are we going?'

Assessing her once more, Rahil stood up with her. 'We'll take a crosscut to the city,' he said. 'Ashoka and Sau managed to find someone willing to let you hide in their home. You know her – Ruchira.'

CHAPTER TWENTY-SIX
Ashoka

'Care to place a gamble, Ashoka?'

'Your addiction to gambling becomes more concerning with each passing day,' Ashoka replied. The dawn sky cast a bluish-purple glow, tinged with streaks of orange. Leaning against opposite ends of the stone rails of his balcony, he and Sau observed the dark green of the wild forests north of the palace. Every so often, he could spot unearthly glows moving in that wild darkness; minor spirits drifting like ships along gentle waves. Still, he did not make to deny Sau. 'What is it?'

'The chances of Rahil and Shakti escaping in one piece,' Sau replied. 'Two silver coins on them making it out but bruised and nicked in some places.' She picked at the inner corner of her eyes every so often to remove rheum, tired. The fault was his; she'd kept him company the night before while he descended into worry after Rahil departed. Some three hours had passed now, a little less since Shakti was taken to the Mountain of Rebirth.

'Then we would both be placing bets on the same side,' he remarked. 'Do you think my plan was wise?'

'Do you want an honest answer?' Sau asked. When he motioned for her to proceed, she shook her head. 'Wise is not the word I'd use. Risky is a better one. You're placing too much hope on Shakti.'

His muscles were strung tight. *Did she not trust him or Shakti?*

'She's a fighter. She's powerful. She's a mayakari that doesn't seem to care for following their code,' Ashoka snapped.

'Why're you being so irritable?' Sau retorted, frowning. 'You wanted an honest answer, and I gave you one.'

Palming his face, Ashoka dipped his head. Pressed it against his kneecaps. He would have rather her agree with his plans than not. Criticizing them felt like she was indirectly calling him a failure.

Stifling a curse under his breath, Ashoka breathed a soft 'Sorry' into the skin of his knees. There was little point in lashing out at Sau. In truth, he was worried for Rahil. His inner voice kept screaming at him that he shouldn't have sent him out by himself. Entertaining any thoughts of misfortune falling upon Rahil made his skin itch.

'Apology accepted,' Sau replied, smoothing the crown of her head in an absentminded fashion. It did nothing for her hair; the ringlets remained crimped. 'Listen – about Prince Ryu. When he arrives, we need to find a way to get him alone.'

Ashoka knew what Sau was about to suggest before she said it. The arrival of the Ridi prince seemed to weigh more on Sau's mind than it did his. He was more confident that he could convince Ryu to keep his soldiers where they were. Sau, however, wasn't completely sure. The number of times she'd brought it up with him in private was indication enough. 'You really think he'd remove his soldiers from Taksila?'

'He agreed to my proposition under Arush's rule,' Sau sighed, 'but you heard Queen Kalyani. With Aarya on the throne, he'll be pressured to remove them.'

'Aarya won't risk damaging the relationship between our empires,' Ashoka said. His sister was no fool. At least, not enough to destroy relations with the second-largest empire in the known world. They were too much of an asset.

'A foreign monarch keeping his soldiers on Ran soil when it's in direct opposition to the empress' demands?' Sau remarked. 'He's already going against the policies of his mother. He's risking a total severance in good relations.'

'*Acting* empress,' Ashoka reminded her. The title rang hollow as he thought back to his conversation with Aarya. *The good thing about an unspoken social contract, mūsī, is that you can break it.* Convention wouldn't matter to her. 'Sounds as if you know his character well.'

At that, Sau looked away. '*Know* is too strong a word,' she said. 'I understand him, to an extent. I had to. Otherwise, Taksila would still be plagued by Ran soldiers. If he's considering removing his soldiers from Taksila during this visit, you should—'

'—tell him about Queen Kalyani informing us about the cursed weapons?' he finished for her. 'I thought the same.'

The assured tilt of Sau's lips was the only indication that she was pleased with his answer. A comfortable silence passed before she gestured beyond the balcony door, towards his bed where he kept the cursed weapons hidden beneath the mattress. She'd expressed so much unease about keeping the daggers that he'd asked for them back. 'I didn't like keeping these,' she remarked conversationally. 'Felt like they would hurt me in my sleep, for some inexplicable reason.'

Strange. Unlike her, Ashoka felt comforted by their presence.

Suddenly, he heard a sharp rapping coming from his chambers. Someone was knocking on the door.

'Prince Ashoka.' The rapping became louder. 'Prince Ashoka, are you awake?'

He and Sau exchanged a look. *Spirits.* Who could be knocking on his door this early in the morning? Not his personal staff; he was by nature an absurdly early riser, and they only woke him if he hadn't already stirred awake himself. News of Shakti, then? Surely not. A daring escape required more time.

'Wonder what it could be about,' he whispered to Sau as they both rose hurriedly.

'Guards,' Sau remarked, a knowing glint in her eye as they hurried from the balcony. She grasped his arm and gave him a quick once over. 'Answer the door, but before that – make yourself look . . . dishevelled. And don't let them in.'

'Why?' he enquired, confused.

'Pretend you're with someone.'

He flushed as Rahil came to mind almost immediately.

'Oh, good – keep that look,' said Sau. 'Open that robe of yours some more and answer that door. I'll be here.' Without a moment's hesitation, she lifted the covers of his bed and hid herself under them, so that only an amorphous lump could be seen.

Ashoka obeyed her orders before moving quickly to open his chamber door partway. Outside, four soldiers greeted him, one with her clenched fist raised halfway, preparing for a third knock. When he appeared, they bowed immediately.

'Sorry to disturb you, Prince Ashoka,' she began. 'We were looking for . . . Rahil. He's not outside your doors.'

What did they need Rahil for at this time? They weren't part of his personal guard, either.

The answer came immediately: Aarya.

'He's asleep,' Ashoka answered, keeping his voice low. 'Whatever you need him for, request it later.'

'He's *asleep*?' the soldier repeated, astonished, brows furrowing. In response, Ashoka opened the door just wide enough so that they could see the body-shaped lump covered by his sheets before closing it again. Realization dawned on the soldier's features, a pale red flush creeping onto her high cheekbones. 'I . . . all right, Prince Ashoka. I'm sorry to trouble you.'

Bowing, the four turned and left.

Once he was sure their footsteps could no longer be heard, Ashoka closed the door. Not a breath later, Sau sat up. 'I didn't think Aarya would watch you this closely.'

She'd surmised the same as him, then. 'She's probably under the assumption that I'll be conducting some kind of trick,' he guessed, 'I was the one that convinced her to send Shakti away.'

For the first time, Sau appeared more worried than him. 'I hope she can – *was* able to escape.'

Spirits knew he did, too. Only time would tell.

Ashoka's fervent hopes were answered a few hours later as he stood next to his sister upon the steps of the Obsidian Throne.

'The mayakari escaped, Your Highness.'

Not even a Great Spirit could match Aarya's tempest in the throne room. She paced and raged expletives that promised death in a variety of forms It was not so much an explosion, but rather an insidious disease that threatened to infect any who dared come into contact. Ashoka surmised with some chagrin that, in some sense, she was less like their father that way.

'How?' his sister roared. 'How could she escape a *dozen* soldiers?'

The unfortunate soldier who had returned to relay the news winced. 'She . . . she must have asked the Great Spirit to help her, Your Highness,' he said. 'The mist on the peak turned into a fog. *Crows* started dropping dead from the sky. We were blindsided. She killed one of our men and – and it appeared that she had help.'

Before he could stop himself, Ashoka tensed. *Help?*

What did you do, Rahil, he thought, watching his sister carefully, as her lips pinched together in visible fury.

'*What help?*' her voice was lethal. If tone was poison, they would all be dead.

Hesitant, the soldier shook his head. 'Forgive me, Your Highness,' he admitted. 'It was extremely difficult to discern who the second assailant was; only that they were highly skilled in combat. Disarmed and incapacitated nearly every soldier. A male, based on figure alone.'

Spirits. He'd *told* Rahil to remain at the base of the mountain, undetected. Incredulous laughter threatened to bubble from his lips; of course Rahil had gone against his command. It was almost unsurprising. As long as there was someone in danger, Rahil's sense of duty overrode any semblance of needing to keep himself safe.

He could've died, and I would have never . . .

Thank goodness he had somehow gone unnoticed. He would've covered himself up, somehow. But, Ashoka realized with dawning dread, a facial covering was useless if he'd used his broadswords against the other soldiers. Not when they were easily recognizable.

It seemed that Aarya was following a similar train of thought when she asked, 'What weapon did the attacker wield?'

'From my squadron's accounts, a single longsword, Your Highness,' was the swift reply. 'Not one commissioned for the army.'

Ashoka relaxed, but it didn't last long. Quickly, he became aware of Aarya's vindictive gaze being trained on him. Instead of ignoring her, he addressed her outright.

'You seem intent on burning me alive with your eyes alone, sister,' he drawled. 'Is something the matter?'

'Where's Rahil, little brother?' she asked. In her words, a cobra lay waiting to strike. 'Where's the man that follows you like a ghost?'

'I've asked him to accompany Sau,' came his immediate lie. 'She wanted to travel to the city to purchase a new set of quills.'

Snorting in disbelief, his sister clenched the fabric of her sari. The fine silk came away creased when she released her hand. 'Of course,' she said. 'Where was he this morning?'

Not more than two drops of blood in the water, and Aarya had already smelled it.

'It sounds as if you're accusing me of something,' Ashoka replied calmly. 'He was with me.'

'He's *always* with you,' Aarya snapped, 'except this instance, I hear. He wasn't outside your door.'

Ashoka fought back a frustrated groan. Those guards hadn't told her the full story, then. It was likely a kindness on their part, letting Rahil have his privacy. It did, however, leave him with the uncomfortable task of having to explain himself.

Ashoka gritted his teeth. 'I wouldn't be surprised if they were unable to see him,' he replied. Anxiety threatened to claw away the confidence he meant to muster when he went to explain himself further, but he reined it back like it was a disobedient dog. 'Since he was *with* me. In my bed. Are you quite satisfied, sister?'

His confession seemed to render her into silence. Belatedly, Ashoka wondered how he was going to explain this to Rahil. With a great deal of embarrassment, he construed.

'Well,' Aarya said after a while. She appeared somewhat nauseated, in the same way he was whenever he heard palace staff gossip about her romantic encounters. 'How dreadfully unsurprising. A hearty congratulations to you, I suppose, but that means nothing to me. You *say* Rahil was in your bed, but can anyone confirm it?'

'Did you want them to come in and observe?' he responded dryly.

'I do believe that everyone involved would have found that rather uncomfortable.'

If possible, Aarya appeared even more nauseous. 'All right,' she said hastily, 'no more of this. What a fucking hassle.'

'A hassle indeed,' Ashoka replied smoothly. 'Shakti could be anywhere, sister. I suppose the worst she could do is curse you for keeping her imprisoned.'

He spotted the exact moment Aarya's face blanched. That should keep her sufficiently rattled. Distracted.

She's your nightmare now, he thought happily.

'She won't get far,' Aarya thundered. The muscles in her neck tensed. 'I'll impose a citywide lockdown. Soldiers will be sent to canvass the outskirts, the docks. The witch cursed the emperor. She has now killed an innocent soldier – her story was written before she escaped. It won't be long before our people will give her up.'

Ashoka didn't doubt her. Hopefully Shakti only needed to lay low at Ruchira's home for the next few days while he met with the Ridi prince to confirm their agreement.

'The witch will be found,' Aarya remarked. It sounded as if she were making a last-ditch plea. 'And when I do, I'll burn her fighting hand like Father burned your ear, little brother.'

CHAPTER TWENTY-SEVEN
Ashoka

After feeding and taking Sahry out on a short flight, Ashoka returned to his quarters. Performing death-defying tricks in the air had temporarily soothed his worry, but it had now returned. Rahil was still absent after he left Aarya some time ago. If he and Shakti had run into trouble . . .

Just as he was about to descend into a spiral of unease, he opened the door to his chambers, coming face to face with a weary-looking Rahil.

'You're here!' he exclaimed. The words felt empty, especially when he'd been worrying for the entire period Rahil was absent. *You're here* didn't sound like enough. *I won't make you do this again* did.

Relief quickly replaced his melancholy, rendering any other thought null and void as he pulled Rahil into a bone-crushing embrace. He was warmer than usual. 'Is Shakti . . . ?'

'Safe,' Rahil muttered, his voice muffled, cheek pressed against the side of Ashoka's head. The long, weary breath he exhaled seemed to burn Ashoka's skin. 'She got a nasty cut, but I took her to Ruchira's home and bandaged it. I gave her strict orders to stay inconspicuous.'

'Good,' Ashoka murmured, before releasing his hold and levelling Rahil with a glare. 'I thought I told you to wait at the base of the mountain, not launch into an offensive.'

'If I'd done that, Shakti would be dead,' Rahil remarked, not looking the least bit ashamed. 'She spoke to the Great Spirit – it was a terrifying creature, Ashoka. I think she tried to negotiate with it, though with what level of success I don't know.'

'Aarya is placing the city under a lockdown,' Ashoka added, 'and Prince Ryu is due in a week. I've never seen her so flustered.'

In response, Rahil reached out to grab the sides of Ashoka's arms. Smoky quartz eyes observed him with the curiousness of a young pup. If he was tired from the morning's events, he didn't show it. In fact, he appeared exhilarated. Energized, as if the Mountain of Rebirth had provided him with a renewed vitality.

'Speaking of confused,' he said quietly, softly, 'tell me why, Ashoka, when I returned from the city, that Dara asked me how long I've been visiting your bed?'

Suddenly, Ashoka felt acutely aware of how close they were. The nervousness only multiplied sevenfold when Rahil stepped even closer so that their noses just brushed.

'I needed a convincing lie to tell Aarya,' he answered, ducking his head to avoid meeting Rahil's gaze, 'when she asked me why you weren't guarding me outside my chambers.'

He heard Rahil's breath hitch quietly enough that he almost thought he imagined it. 'And . . . you and I,' he began, 'that is convincing?'

Still, Ashoka refused to look up. Embarrassment was starting to replace the nervousness, and he wondered if telling the absolute truth had been a good idea. 'It's apparently unsurprising,' he whispered. 'Aarya offered me her congratulations, though she seemed nauseated by the thought.'

'No sibling wants to hear such stories,' Rahil supplied, shrugging. 'It's an affront to their ears. Would you want to hear about hers?'

Shuddering at the thought, Ashoka pulled away, while Rahil chuckled and summarized what he'd seen at the mountain. The Great Spirit. Crows dropping dead from the sky. Shakti killing a soldier. While the description of the elusive elephant spirit was certainly interesting, Ashoka found himself feeling restless. They were back to their usual chatter, but something was missing.

Ashoka came to the sudden realization that he hadn't got the reaction from Rahil he imagined. Or wanted.

'Are you opposed to it?' he asked Rahil pointedly.

Rahil, who had been in the process of stretching his arms, paused. 'Opposed to what?'

'My story,' Ashoka said, before gesturing uselessly around his room. 'Being . . . here.'

'I'm always here,' Rahil replied smoothly. When Ashoka made to complain that he wasn't understanding, he saw the ghost of a smirk appear and disappear on Rahil's lips.

Ah. A game.

'I meant my story of you visiting . . . my bed. You aren't upset by it?' Ashoka inquired, cautious. 'It was the only thing I could think of at that moment.'

'Why would I be upset?'

'Rahil.'

For an agonizingly long time, Rahil stayed silent. It was enough for Ashoka to tense, cast his eyes to the ground and begin to mutter his apologies before Rahil snatched his wrist, quick as a viper, to hold him still.

'I'm not upset,' he said, hand squeezing tighter on his wrist.

Ashoka met his eyes. They were honest. Not a lie to be found. 'Good,' he said. Only a single word, but it came out stilted. *Pathetic.*

'According to the guards, I must've wooed you well enough for that invisible wall of yours to break,' Rahil continued, smiling softly.

'Oh, please,' he said without thinking. 'If anything, *I* would have wooed *you*.'

Cross the line.

'Really?' He'd never heard this kind of tone from Rahil; an indulgent, dangerous thing laced with expectation. 'Show me, then.'

Every last shred of self-preservation vanished into thin air. Rahil knew. Just as in combat, he had just been pushing and prodding, waiting for Ashoka to respond.

Stop playing the prince. Cross the line.

'I will,' Ashoka murmured, stepping closer until he was a hair's breadth away.

He didn't have to think too hard. In fact, his thoughts were eerily still when he leaned up and kissed Rahil.

CHAPTER TWENTY-EIGHT
Shakti

A LARGE, PLAITED CLUMP OF HAIR DROPPED TO THE ground with a soft *thump*.

Dispirited, Shakti stared down at the pathetic mass. She sat in Ruchira's small bedroom, away from the windows and clutching a knife in her hands. The cut hadn't been clean; she would look like a child raised by leopards. Setting the knife down on the bed, Shakti caught a peek of herself in the small, dusty mirror hung on the opposite side of the room.

The reflection that stared back was unrecognizable. Gaunt, hollow cheeks looked as sickly as a jaundiced child. Serrated, uneven hair fell just above her shoulders. Her collarbones were more pronounced. A dark purple colour stained the thin skin of her under-eyes. And without her usual dark smudge of kohl, Shakti felt more exposed. Naked. Young.

She'd finally seen what Aarya had carved into her back. *Mayakari*. Written in ugly handwriting and scoured deep enough for the skin not to heal over the indentations. This was a permanent scar that left no room to guess who she was. The empress might just as well have branded her forehead.

Her arms bore signs of violence. Dark red impressions of chains and scarred tissue from whips trailed from her shoulder to her wrist like vines. Slowly, she dragged down the top of her shift, completely exposing the upper torso. The injury she'd been dealt on the mountain was angry and red, the skin stitched together like a torn rag doll's arm. Rahil's suturing skills had been impressive, his hands deathly still during the entire procedure. Without a numbing agent, she'd gritted her teeth and borne through it, biting back a scream.

'I need to leave, otherwise I suspect people will wonder why Ashoka's by himself,' Rahil had remarked after he was done. 'Ruchira will be back by nightfall. This goes without saying, but *do not* leave this house. Understood?'

It seemed like she was moving from one prison into another, but at least this one was safer. After the morning's events, she had no desire to expose herself. She'd been sapped of energy. She wanted a bath. She wanted to rid herself of her foul, stained clothes. 'I won't be so stupid,' she promised Rahil. He'd informed her of the slight change in Ashoka's plan when they got to Ruchira's home. He needed to delay their journey to Taksila to speak with the Ridi prince, who was due in a week. Shakti hadn't minded too much. It would, at least, give her more time to recuperate.

Looking pleased by her answer, Rahil had left, leaving Shakti alone. She'd bathed in Ruchira's outhouse, the cold water an uncomfortable but much-needed shock. From the older woman's small clothing shelf she'd procured a long-sleeved blue tunic to cover her scars, and long trousers, before thinking to cut her hair.

The scars weren't something she was ashamed of, but they would raise too much suspicion if seen. The back of her neck felt colder. Sifting through the dry strands of hair, Shakti lay back on the bed.

She was free, but not really.

She was still in the Golden City. The Great Spirit's connection to her remained an unknown. Her missing memories still bound her to Aarya.

Spirits, she wanted to wrap her hands around Aarya's neck. Watch it turn purple, distend under pressure, and stop her from breathing. Burn her and watch pathetic orange flames engulf her body. An ugly feeling settled in the pit of Shakti's belly; she felt violated. Taken advantage of. But now, at least she had a safe space from which to try to regain her memories.

THE WITCH WITHOUT MEMORY

. . . I curse you . . .

She forced herself to assign her problems in order of importance. As much as she wanted to find out what or whom she cursed, it wasn't the most pressing concern. The Great Spirit was. She re-ran her conversation with it.

Its energy had been so potent. Its words echoed, loud and insistent: *my awakening is your own, your awakening is my own.* They were connected somehow. Perhaps because both were addled in memory. Poor, sickly creature.

An overwhelming sense of lethargy washed over her body as she made her way to the spare bed. Feeling clean after so long made her relaxed. Drowsy. It quickly lulled her into a deep, unbroken sleep. Broken words and phantom pain infested her dreams. Strange whispers echoed in her mind: unintelligible spirit-speak and cursed language, followed by Aarya's voice.

—*curse – pride*—

Mayakari – obey me—

Shakti was woken by the sound of Ruchira's voice. The cook had found her seemingly in a state of deep sleep in the dead of the night but proceeded to wake her for a late dinner. Her head was pounding from crying herself to sleep, but her stomach was ready to eat itself.

Brinjal, spiced gourd, steaming hot brown rice – she'd entered her next rebirth a queen.

'Don't eat too fast,' Ruchira scolded as they sat on the floor, the food laid out over a low table.

'Aarya starved me to the point that I thought sweat tasted good,' Shakti retorted. 'Please don't judge me.'

Ruchira winced. 'Thank goodness you escaped,' she said. 'That Prince Ashoka was able to even convince Empress Aarya to send you away was a feat.'

Humming her agreement, Shakti said nothing and continued to shovel more rice into her mouth.

'Saudamini has asked me to pass on a message to you,' Ruchira said. 'Stay hidden.'

'Rahil said the same,' she replied. 'Don't worry, I'll be as quiet as a mouse.'

At that, Ruchira smiled. 'Good. Apparently, after the Ridi prince's visit, they'll arrange for you to travel with them to Taksila,' she said and paused. 'You're going to leave?'

The cook sounded sad. Guilt twisted into Shakti's stomach like a knife.

'Taksila is safer for me,' she said. 'Burnings are banned.'

'You know, I passed through an abnormal number of soldiers on my way back home,' Ruchira said. She hadn't touched her food much. 'The empress has already sent them searching for you. Come the morning and the city will be under heavy lockdown. I can't imagine how Prince Ashoka will get you out without his sister realizing.'

'They'll find a way. I can't stay here forever, Ruchira.'

'I know that, my dear, but for now you need to be careful,' Ruchira admonished before her small smile slipped. 'One small slip and you'll be dead. Harini took one risk and . . .' She said no more, choking on her last few words as fresh tears fell.

Shakti's heart missed a beat. 'I know,' she said, chastened. 'Thank you. For helping me hide.'

'No need to thank me,' Ruchira sniffed. 'Saudamini expected a bargain when she came to me, I think. Political advisors tend to be jaded that way. But after Harini, I didn't want to watch you be found and killed as well.'

Touched, Shakti briefly stretched out her free hand to grasp Ruchira's, squeezing tight. For a while, she was silent as the older woman told her about the impending arrival of Prince Ryu in less than a week's time. He was supposedly very handsome and still unwed. Shakti found the tension in her body relax over the mundane topic. There was a sense of normalcy that she hadn't felt in a long while. For a moment, she revelled in the brief tranquillity. Imagined an existence where she made a different choice that night in Kolakola. Where, instead of cursing the emperor, she escaped and lived the rest of her life hidden and not bound to the Collective.

A fantasy, that's what it was. Even if she had the opportunity to go back to the past and change her actions, she wouldn't. Killing Adil was justice served. She would rather live as she was now than regret not taking action.

The hollow in her mind still nagged at her, the unknown curse. But for now, no shackles bound her. There was no fear of being force-fed milk of poppy. Safe for now, while a forgotten curse lingered, its enactment unknown. The relief should've made her feel guilty, but for the moment, Shakti pushed it aside and enjoyed the quiet.

CHAPTER TWENTY-NINE
Ashoka

A FULL WEEK PASSED WITHOUT FANFARE, UNTIL IT CAME time for the arrival of the Ridi prince.

All throughout the palace, staff were preparing for Crown Prince Ryu's arrival that night. The already spotless floors were being polished to a near offensive sheen, the palace ponds being filtered of debris, the leopards' coats brushed to a high shine. If one wandered down to the kitchens, one could easily smell the enticing roast of banana flower, fowl, and imported fishes, along with the familiar spices of long-pepper, ginger and clove.

Ashoka spent the week in relative quiet. He knew Aarya was watching him. Shakti's escape had sent his sister into a mild panic. In front of consuls she put up a composed front, ordering tighter control of entry and exit through the city gates. Behind closed doors, she was flustered. Having a mayakari loose in the city – one who could invade dreams, at that – kept his sister in a state of paranoia. The first few days following Shakti's escape, Aarya slept at irregular hours of the night to avoid having her mind invaded.

Ashoka had doubted Shakti's immediate concern was to hurt Aarya, a hunch that was proven correct when the mayakari came to his dreams the night after her escape. The Great Spirit had been placated for now and, at present, her plan was to lie low, heal, and regain her strength. The Great Spirit's condition also bothered her; she wanted to find out what was wrong with it. Thankfully, it sounded as though she could try to piece its history together by using the Collective and not having to leave Ruchira's house, so he left her to pursue that avenue without protest. After speaking to Prince Ryu, they would return to Taksila as planned. For her to escape without notice, he would need Rahil's help again.

Rahil.

The air had shifted between them. Every glance, every single accidental brush against skin felt charged. Laced with newfound giddiness. Much to Ashoka's chagrin, however, he couldn't dwell on it. He had other matters to attend to, and Rahil knew it, too. Namely, seeing what Aarya was proposing to Crown Prince Ryu tonight.

Extravagant song and dance took place at the banquet hall to welcome the prince. Aarya had ordered several opulent gifts, ranging from animal figurines carved from lapis to diamond-encrusted brooches, to be presented. Prince Ryu had accepted them graciously and was now drinking a liquor whose bitterness was offset by a mango and condensed milk combination. He was seated next to Aarya, who made pleasant conversation about the food, the dancers, and sights the Golden City had to offer. Her command of the Ridi tongue was not as polished as Ashoka's; and so, to her side sat a translator.

Their mother sat on the opposite side of the prince, and Ashoka right next to her. Likely his sister's design. He'd have to lean over to speak to him.

As Prince Ryu continued to speak to his sister, Ashoka observed him in silence. The man held himself with a sense of confidence that recalled Queen Kalyani. It wasn't the arrogant sense of entitlement that his father and siblings had, but rather a humble and almost resigned one. Handsome, too, as Sau once mentioned. Cold and beautiful, with pale skin, eyelashes that almost rivalled Rahil's, a sharp jaw, and hair so black it looked almost blue under the lanternlight.

Yet he looked tired underneath the pristine front, as if he were already exhausted after assuming his mother's position as regent. Ashoka hoped his youth wouldn't fail him.

Spearing his okra, he strained to hear the conversation between Prince Ryu and his sister.

'Is there usually such a large military presence in the city?' he heard the prince ask. 'I noticed a great number of soldiers on my way to the palace.'

As if by chance, he and Aarya locked eyes. Irritation flashed across his sister's face for a moment before she quickly smoothed it away. 'Searching for an escaped prisoner,' she answered. 'She caused some chaos, but not to worry, Prince Ryu. You are perfectly safe. My soldiers will find her soon enough.'

'What kind of chaos?' Prince Ryu asked.

'This is the witch who poisoned my older brother,' Aarya replied, sounding wracked with grief in a way she hadn't sounded before. They locked eyes briefly before she turned away, a glass to her lips.

Hah, thought Ashoka, *still sticking to that poison story like her life depended on it.*

'A witch?' the prince sounded dubious.

'You sound disbelieving, but it's true,' Aarya confirmed. 'My father knew how dangerous those monsters are, and they continue to prove him right.'

For the first time since he arrived, Prince Ryu's gaze flitted towards Ashoka for a beat, a thousand questions in his eyes, before refocusing on Aarya's tirade. Beside him, his mother tensed. Frowning, Ashoka laid a gentle hand on her arm. At his touch, she sent him a placid smile. 'Yes, my dear?'

'Are you all right, Mother?'

Patting his hand in a reassuring manner, his mother nodded. 'Yes,' she said. 'I thought I felt a slight chill, that's all.'

There was no chill, but sensing that his mother didn't wish to discuss any further, Ashoka left it alone.

The remainder of the welcome dinner passed without fanfare. Somewhere in the back of his mind, Ashoka half expected another earthquake, but it never came. He sat through a beautiful song played on a sitar, sung in a delicate tenor by the vocalist. It was one he had heard countless times before; a folk song from Mathura of a sea voyager who had lost her love to the waves and mourned his death beneath the stars.

Once the guests began to mingle, Ashoka excused himself and motioned for Rahil to follow him to where the banquet tables were set up for both Ridi and Ran officials, in search of Sau. Ashoka couldn't help but notice the knowing glances that were sent his and Rahil's way. Gossip was truly a quick beast in the palace.

It was hard to spot Sau at first; she had dressed plainly for the occasion, conversing with a Ridi official in an unembellished blue sari. When he called out her name, she started and waved them towards her. Shaking his head, Ashoka gestured for her to meet them closer to the corner of the hall where no one could overhear them.

'Aarya's making a big fuss over Arush being poisoned by a witch,' he remarked bitterly once she approached them.

'As expected,' Sau said with a grimace. 'At least Shakti's safe.'

'For now,' Ashoka whispered. 'There'll be soldiers at Ruchira's door soon. Aarya has ordered a large dispatch over the next few days.'

'Prince Ashoka.'

The three of them quieted at the sound of his name. Belatedly, Ashoka realized how suspicious they must look in their huddle. But it wasn't a consul or soldier. Instead, Prince Ryu approached their group, two guards stoic by his side. Midnight blue robes hung off his figure gracefully. Unlike the Ran monarchs and their rather simple royal circlet, his was a larger, more ostentatious one. The diamonds on his silver crown sparkled like fresh dewdrops not yet evaporated under the midday sun.

He held out a pale hand that Ashoka shook. 'Good to finally meet in person, Prince Ryu,' he said, speaking in Ridi. 'Welcome to the Golden City.'

'Your sister has provided me with a grand welcome,' Prince Ryu replied, moving to stand with his arms clasped behind his back. 'But likewise – I've heard nothing but favourable things about you.'

Ashoka didn't miss the sidelong glance the Ridi prince threw in Sau's direction. Oddly enough, Sau was no longer listening. Instead, she was pointedly watching the sitar player strum a joyful melody to his contented audience.

'I'm glad,' he responded, bewildered. 'Thank you for agreeing to keep your soldiers in Taksila. They've been a useful presence.'

'Thank your advisor,' Prince Ryu said, this time switching to accented Ran. 'Hello, Sau.'

The sudden switch in language must have startled her, for she shot him a tentative smile and bowed. 'Prince Ryu,' she greeted him.

It was only then that Ashoka registered that the Ridi prince had referred to her not as Saudamini, but Sau. Interesting. She sounded strange, too. Almost breathless, almost restrained.

'Ah, yes,' Ashoka said carefully. 'Sau told me that she helped you with some business of your own. I hope the matter was resolved.'

'Indeed.' Prince Ryu smiled. 'Sau was of great help. When you have the time, I'd like to discuss the placement of my soldiers in Taksila, Prince Ashoka. I'm sure it's no secret that your sister now wishes to reverse the deal your brother made with me. Is your family usually this inconsistent?'

There was no malice to be found in the prince's tone; he sounded curious as to the state of the Maurya family.

'Not inconsistent, but different,' Ashoka said, shrugging.

It looked like Prince Ryu was about to say more, but his name was called out somewhere in the din. Aarya stood with Consul Rangana, watching them suspiciously. They couldn't talk so openly here.

'Prince Ryu, I would like to invite you to ride with me and my winged serpent tomorrow afternoon,' Ashoka offered.

A polite smirk graced the other man's fine-boned features. 'Offering me a ride on a Kalingan native animal in the Ran Empire? How amusing. But I accept.'

Before he returned to an expectant Aarya, Prince Ryu dropped his voice low. 'I have now sat through three Maurya monarchs, Prince Ashoka,' he said. 'I wonder if I will see the ascension of one more.'

CHAPTER THIRTY
Ashoka

PRINCE RYU COULD HOLD HIS OWN ON A WINGED SERPENT.

He'd joined Ashoka for an afternoon flight the next day. The prince had marvelled at Sahry, though he had to step away due to her nonstop hissing. In Makon, Ashoka learned, there were giant white foxes. Apparently their near-human laughter was more shiver-inducing than a winged serpent's hiss.

Ashoka found that he and the prince held similar ideas. Like him, Ryu was more interested in keeping the mayakari alive instead of hunted. He found the Ran Empire's continued expansion and murder of mayakari needless. And when Ashoka tried subtly to bring up his secret visit to Kalinga, Prince Ryu acknowledged them outright.

'I gather Queen Kalyani has shown you the cursed weapons?' Prince Ryu asked with a dry smile. At his stunned expression, the prince laughed. 'I was made aware of your visit. The queen and I have vested interests.'

'Such as?' Ashoka inquired, leading Sahry back to the serpent pens.

'Such as making sure our nations are well equipped for any future disturbances with yours.'

When they exited the pens, Ashoka found Rahil and Sau waiting for them. Ashoka shot Rahil a soft smile that he returned, which Sau caught and feigned annoyance.

Prince Ryu raised an eyebrow at the three of them. 'Is this an ambush, Prince Ashoka?' he asked.

'Hardly,' he replied. 'Sau is here to translate if I can't find the right words.'

'Your advisor called me a worm on her first day in Makon,' Prince Ryu remarked, a gleam in his eye.

'*Worm* and *mighty* have similar sounds,' Sau retorted, her tone unapologetic. In apparent distraction, she drifted to Ashoka's side, and he observed the single jasmine nestled behind her ear.

The prince laughed. 'You know, when Sau first negotiated moving soldiers to Taksila on your behalf, I thought you two were . . . involved. After all, what kind of advisor would make informal requests in favour of their prince and not their emperor.'

Sputtering, Ashoka felt the back of his neck prickle. 'She's not — we are not — Sau is one of my dearest friends,' he said.

'I realized when my soldiers heard the gossip about you and your guard.' Prince Ryu held up his hands in peace. Behind them, Rahil let out an endearing chuckle before attempting to cover it up as an awkward cough.

Sau prodded him. 'Ashoka, your propositions, please.'

Flushing, he turned back to Prince Ryu.

'When I had Sau ask you to send some of your soldiers into Taksila, it was to protect the mayakari,' Ashoka began. 'But since then, I've had a . . . change of heart, so to speak. It's no secret that the moment I leave Taksila, the burning ban I placed will be lifted. They'll be persecuted again. They need someone who can guarantee their protection not just in Taksila, but throughout the empire.'

'And you think this protector to be you?'

Ashoka couldn't dance around it any longer. 'When I went to Queen Kalyani, it was to ask her for a favour,' he said. 'I want to seize the Obsidian Throne from Aarya, and I have a plan to do it. Kalyani agreed to forming defence negotiations with the queen of Mahvo. When my sister trespasses into their border, Kalingan soldiers will attack.'

Here, Ashoka needed Sau. His command of the Ridi language

wasn't as proficient as his Kalingan. When Sau finished translating, Ryu appeared disturbed.

'You want to start a war?' This he asked in the Ran language.

'Not a war,' Ashoka replied. 'A revolution. I simply want your support, Prince Ryu. I want assurance that if Aarya tries to annex Mahvo, that you'll be on Kalinga's side. My side.'

Ryu sighed. 'You're putting me in a bind, Prince Ashoka. Your sister is requesting that the agreement I made with Arush be voided. You know what that means.'

Disconcertion gone, Ashoka thinned his lips, frustrated.

'She's threatening – albeit politely – the restriction of Ran exports,' Ryu continued, 'your iron ore, in particular, which will be a blow.'

The Ridi Empire wasn't known for its abundance of iron ore like the Ran Empire was. It, like Kalinga, relied on imports. Delicate trade agreements. Losing iron ore supply would dramatically reduce their weapons production. Though it was unfortunate that weapons were all they seemed to be concerned by.

'You place your hopes on being able to manufacture weapons, Prince Ryu,' he pointed out. 'Should you?'

The Ridi prince huffed. 'Forgive my directness, but the empire your family built is itself a threat. There's a delicate balance that smaller empires must deal with, and if I am offered materials by the most threatening power to defend my empire with, I'll take them, if only to defend against the very people that offered me such gifts.'

Sau translated half of it, her expression perturbed. Unsettled. It mirrored Ashoka's own feelings.

'Aarya would never declare war on your empire,' he said. This was taking an unexpected turn. 'That's a tactical mistake. She expects you to agree with her like your mother did with our father.'

'I'm not my mother.'

'Then, will you keep your soldiers in Taksila?' he inquired.

'Like you, I don't want the mayakari here to die,' Prince Ryu remarked. 'I accepted Sau's initial proposition in part because Arush was unlikely to press, what with his fixation on the Frozen Lands.'

'You know, the mayakari in Taksila and its surrounds have agreed to fight with me,' Ashoka added. 'Against my sister. My family.'

Only the barest hint of shock graced Prince Ryu's features. 'Fight with their bodies?' he inquired. 'Or fight with their cursed weapons?'

'Both,' he replied. 'My problem are numbers. Ideally—'

'Pay attention to your own words, Prince Ashoka,' Ryu interrupted, adjusting his silver crown absentmindedly as they arrived at the jade pools, the water eerily still, reflecting the pale blue of the sky. '*Ideally*. Nothing ever is ideal.'

Before Ashoka could comment on that oddly pessimistic train of thought, Sau, who seemed to be holding back a few choice words, finally burst. 'There's nothing about a planned uprising that's *ideal*, Prince Ryu,' she remarked heatedly. 'Toss idealism aside – think realistically. Whom among the Maurya family would be a better trade partner, a better ruler, because I can assure that if Ashoka takes the throne, you won't need to waste money on keeping your soldiers here to prevent targeted murder.'

Stunned by her outburst, Ashoka managed to grasp Sau's wrist to get her to stop. Enraging the Ridi prince was not a particularly intelligent plan. But, to his surprise, Prince Ryu didn't react with anger. Instead, it seemed to reduce him to a state of pensiveness before focusing on her with eagle-eyed precision.

'Do you serve the emperor or the empire?' he asked her.

An interesting question. Emperor and empire were usually treated as one and the same, but based on Ryu's tone, it suggested a greater degree of separation between the two.

'My answer remains the same as it was back then,' was Sau's only response.

'I see.' Entire rebirths seemed to pass before the Ridi prince spoke again, this time with greater conviction. 'All right. I will keep my soldiers in Taksila for now. But you'd best win this gamble you've placed on yourself, Prince Ashoka.'

CHAPTER THIRTY-ONE
Shakti

Almost two weeks of blissful quiet passed, and in that time Shakti slowly recuperated.

She hadn't once left Ruchira's house, choosing to stay out of sight as much as possible. Ruchira had returned from the palace one day, face grim and holding up a piece of paper with Shakti's face painted on it. The notice was plastered throughout the Golden City. The artist's portrait of her was extraordinarily accurate.

Mayakari. Wanted alive. Five thousand gold coins.

That was an unbelievable amount of money for one witch. Part of her was almost offended. Though five thousand was a considerable sum, *that* was how much she was worth? Then again, make the bounty higher, and it could rouse suspicion. Yes, this mayakari killed Emperor Adil, but what *about* her was worth this much? Could she be used as a leverage against the empress?

In her newfound freedom, Shakti also visited the Collective to view more of Adil's memories regarding the Great Spirit. It was too risky for her to return to the Mountain of Rebirth for now. According to Ruchira, Aarya had ordered soldiers to patrol the mountain. Covering all areas – she had some begrudging respect for the young empress.

Most of Adil's memories recalling the Great Spirit involved Subha in some way. In the memory she'd seen the night before, Adil and Subha were trekking down the Mountain of Rebirth, escorted by soldiers who trailed ahead and behind them. They were speaking in low voices. This had been the third instance of Subha trying to summon the Great Spirit only to hear its voice. The period between this attempt and the last one was much bigger. From what Shakti had understood, the mayakari had spent a long time trying to understand the mountain's history. Adil continued to entertain her, possibly because he held on to the foolish hope that an appeasement could be done.

'What a pitiful-sounding creature,' Adil said, grimacing. 'That wailing reminds me of a child.'

'It sounds ill,' Subha replied, huffing. She rubbed her upper lip and ran her tongue along her gums. 'It still won't materialize. I just don't understand how it responds only when you're present.'

'I don't think we'll ever understand,' he grumbled, 'but we've confirmed its existence three times. Not once have you tried to appease it. Why not attempt it now? Then, I can reconsider mining—'

'I'll speak to the elders,' Subha said, but there was no conviction to her tone. 'But there's something strange about that creature. I wouldn't disturb it.'

When they eventually reached the base of the mountain, Subha lifted her hand up in farewell. 'Wish Manali well for me.'

Adil stopped in his tracks, looking conflicted. 'You're not staying?'

'No. I'll be with a friend in the city tonight,' Subha replied. 'How's Aarya?'

Adil's tone softened. 'Still a quiet baby. Much quieter than Arush, which is a relief. She likes me. Doesn't cry when I hold her, but fusses when Manali does.'

At that, Subha cracked a mirthless grin. 'Already chosen a favourite?'

'It appears so,' Adil replied. 'Manali wants another one.'

Subha hummed. 'I know,' she said. 'She's always wanted three.'

Grunting in acknowledgement, Adil manoeuvred Subha around a mud puddle. 'Two more than I did,' he replied. Observing the memory, Shakti couldn't even imagine the emperor using his hands on a mayakari for anything other than violence. For a while, the party continued downward in silence. Subha, for the majority of the journey, appeared fidgety.

'Adil,' she remarked, a note of hesitancy creeping into her voice. 'About—'

'Ask them,' Adil interrupted hastily. 'I expect total agreement. They cannot refuse their emperor.'

Inscrutable brown eyes watch Adil. 'Of course, Emperor,' Subha said with a practised bow, and the memory faded.

Shakti knew the rest of the story. No witch would agree to appease the Great Spirit, and this would stoke Adil's anger. It led to the beginnings of his relentless tirade against the mayakari.

The Great Spirit's calls for a false chakravartin continued to confound Shakti, and she turned to Emperor Ashoka for advice. For once, the emperor was less helpful than Emperor Adil when she asked him about it.

'Perhaps it means "of false blood",' he'd suggested. 'A tainted Maurya, though I would argue against it. No Maurya would be called a false monarch.'

'I agree,' she'd told him. 'Then, it just speaks of a king who pronounces themselves righteous and is anything but. Like Adil.'

The emperor had sighed. 'Is this worth your time, Shakti? You've cast a curse that you can't remember. Isn't that more pressing?'

Shakti had disagreed. The Great Spirit's condition continued to haunt her. She was waiting for the chance to speak to it again.

The following night, she continued rifling through Adil's memories once more. She knew the late emperor despised it but couldn't decline her. Despite herself, she understood his irritation. No one would wish for their closest memories to be picked apart.

The memory she was viewing tonight was dimmer. Greyer. She-as-Adil sat not upon the Obsidian Throne, but rather on the steps. He fiddled with an elaborate gold necklace in his hands. The piece was intricately made but without any inlaid jewels. Simple by royal standards.

Suddenly, his head snapped up to watch as Subha hobbled into the throne room. Dressed in a loose shift and trousers, she seemed tired. Dark shadows had formed under her eyes since the last memory Shakti had seen her in.

Hands still clutching the necklace, Adil stood and approached her.

'You disobeyed me, witch,' he called out, the beginnings of a thunderstorm clear in his voice. His tone startled Shakti. No longer did it hold the same polite timbre that she had come to expect. This voice was closer to the Adil she knew. The Adil who hated her kind. 'You sided with them. How dare you decline an appeasement?'

'People died in that landslide, Adil,' Subha replied, wearily. She tucked a loose strand of hair behind her ear, careful not to displace the saraca nestled in between. She took another step forward, and Shakti saw that her ankles were swollen. No wonder she walked so awkwardly. 'And I haven't been able to summon it fully. That creature is ill, and you still cling to the hope of mining its domain?'

'Yes.'

'I will not help you.'

Looking down, Shakti saw Adil's hand had started to bleed where he'd clutched the sharp point of the necklace too tight, a thin stream running down the necklace before splattering on the floor. The emperor didn't seem to notice or care.

'That is not for you to decide,' Adil snapped. 'I'm your emperor. You answer to *me*.'

The glare she shot back at him was ferocious. 'The mayakari listen to the land, not you,' she snapped. 'We keep the land and its spirit at peace. Continuing to mine will enrage it.'

'*Peace?* Your kind act as if you hold a moral high ground with that pacifistic nonsense,' Adil retorted. From Subha's lack of response, it seemed as if she'd heard this before.

'*My kind*,' she laughed without humour. 'Listen to yourself.'

'Going against me is treason,' Adil threatened in a low voice. 'Treason demands punishment. Manali's position won't help you.'

The sentiment felt half lie, half truth. Subha seemed taken aback before she schooled her expression into a determined one. 'You won't hurt me,' she remarked. 'There's something I need to tell you, Adil. Something important.'

'*Shakti!*'

Someone was shaking her. The movement disrupted her concentration, and Shakti was pulled out of Adil's memories and the Collective, only to blink groggily up at Ruchira. The cook was in her room, having returned from another late night's work at the palace.

'Come.' She motioned towards the kitchen. 'Dinner. You haven't eaten.'

On command, her stomach rumbled. Laughing, the cook gently pushed Shakti towards the door. Knowing that she wouldn't be able to return to the Collective unless she ate, Shakti followed.

As they shovelled down their dinner, there came a loud rapping at the door.

Both startled. Confused, Shakti eyed Ruchira, who shook her head. 'I'm not expecting company,' she said, before her shoulders tensed. '*Soldiers* – quick, into my room. Now.'

Quick as a hare, Shakti moved, slipped into the bedroom, and shut the door softly. In the semi-darkness, she heard Ruchira's footsteps before the front door creaked open. There was a shuffling of footfalls further into the house. Muffled voices floated through, and Shakti turned rigid.

'. . . dismissed from work . . . late dinner . . .' Ruchira's voice came, pleasant and unhurried. Spirits, Shakti hoped that the cook wouldn't suffer through any trouble.

'. . . thank you for your . . .' an unknown voice this time. Another creak, then the soft sound of a goodbye; it sounded like the door was being closed.

Shakti breathed a sigh of relief, but it didn't last long. She heard Ruchira yelp and whispered an expletive under her breath. Why had—

'. . . eating for two?'

Spirits. There were two bowls on the dinner table.

She could hear Ruchira begin to stutter and acted fast. No doubt the soldiers would ask to look around her house, and there was no way out.

The knife she'd used to cut her hair was still lying on the floor of the bedroom. Tucking it into her sleeve, Shakti opened the door and stumbled out.

Letting out a soft, disgruntled yawn, she entered the kitchen area. Ruchira stood stock still. To her credit, she kept her face impassive. With her were two Ran soldiers, swords sheathed by their sides, fully armoured. Shakti stole a quick glance outside – the street appeared to be empty.

Time to put on the act of her life.

'Aunty?' she called out, making herself appear as confused and sleepy as possible. 'What's all this – oh. Is something the matter?'

The soldiers looked surprised, but not distrustful. 'You are?' one asked. A man, burlier than his partner.

'Her niece,' Shakti said, 'Jaya.'

One of them seemingly relaxed, but their partner – the man – said nothing and continued to eye her and Ruchira. 'You look rather tense, girl,' he pointed out. 'Are you feeling all right?'

Her tongue went dry. Sallow skin. Lifeless features. She knew she looked like a walking corpse, but at least her strength had returned. 'Recovering from a fever,' she explained.

The female soldier took a cautious step back. 'All right,' she said hurriedly. 'Let's go, Var.'

But the soldier didn't budge. 'No, Sav, not so fast,' he said, and reached into the pocket of his trousers. 'The Empress impressed on us that the escaped witch was a young woman.' Shakti couldn't help but flinch as he fished out a matchstick.

'A burn test, if you don't mind, miss,' he said. It was said so calmly, so clinically, that Shakti wanted to scream. Run for the mountains. He would never have to experience burning in his life. That tiny matchstick was routine for the soldier, but for her, it was no better than a freshly sharpened axe. Both promised death.

She couldn't talk her way out of this. And when communication wasn't possible, only one way remained.

Shakti stepped forward, appearing as if willing. Stupefied by her readiness, the soldier looked around for something to strike it with. His partner stood behind, close to the door and watching the process with sympathy, arms crossed.

She was no better than him.

The knife was ready and waiting. Shakti thought she could act with grace, a modicum of measured control. But when she heard the soft swoosh, the small flame that was birthed into life, part of her ground to a halt. Harini's fearful face flashed across her mind, the horrible blue flame that engulfed her body. Jaya, charred beyond recognition. Adil. Aarya.

I will not be burned.

Just as the soldier brought the match towards her hand, just as he was distracted, Shakti slipped the knife out. In the low light, the steel glinted dull and menacing. The soldier noticed it too late, eyes widening.

With the handle held tight against her hand, she pulled back, swung in an arc, and lodged it firmly in the side of his neck.

Gargled noises of surprise came out of the soldier's throat as he fought to grasp at her and his sword. Blood gushed out upon impact; she'd aimed at the great artery. Dimly, Shakti heard the clap of skin hitting skin, a muffled scream as Ruchira covered her mouth with her hands to avoid screaming loud enough to attract attention.

'One of us was going to die,' she told the man now choking on his own blood. 'Better you than me.' She dislodged the knife. The soldier dropped to the ground, twitching uncontrollably. Death would come for him soon enough.

In the commotion, his partner let out an alarmed yell. Shakti turned her sights on the second soldier. Her hands were slick, a hideous wetness present while she held the knife.

'You fucking *witch*,' the soldier growled, all previous sympathy gone, and leaped forward, sword drawn before Shakti could even blink. She managed to duck and come up right behind her just in time. A quick glance to her left, and Ruchira threw an empty clay pot her way. Shakti struggled to catch it with her free hand that was soaked with blood and nearly dropped it but managed to grasp it tight. Just as the soldier began to turn, she smashed it directly across the side of her face.

The soldier crumpled to the floor, the sword dropping with a *clang*.

Bending down, Shakti swept the woman's hair back. Her bloody hands left red marks on the skin. There was no blood, no open wound. Next, she felt her pulse; it still beat. She'd given her a concussion. But it wouldn't last long. She would wake up.

'*Spirits*,' she heard Ruchira exhale.

Shakti looked up. The kitchen was a disaster. One Ran soldier lay dead, blood pooling from the open wound on his neck. The other lay concussed but alive.

She'd killed. *Again*. Her hands were trembling badly enough that Shakti dropped the knife. Palms slick with red, she felt like a monster. The exact kind of terrifying beast that Adil had painted mayakari to be.

Regret came soon after.

If I feel regret with every kill, am I made for violence? she wondered. Adil had cared very little for the deaths he'd caused, but Shakti felt twinges of remorse every single time.

Because mayakari do not kill, little bird. Should not, and yet you do. Wretched girl. Pathetic mayakari.

Brushing away the voices, Shakti sighed. 'Get some rags, Ruchira,' she told her gently, eyeing the blood. 'The blood needs to be mopped up. You might need to wrap a thick cloth around his neck – otherwise, it'll continue to pool.'

When the older woman said nothing, Shakti refocused her attention on her. Ruchira watched her with a half-shocked, half-horrified expression.

'You killed someone,' she said, looking dazed, as if speaking the words aloud would somehow make the situation clearer.

'Soldiers burn us all the time,' Shakti replied. 'The only difference is that a mayakari has committed murder. But at least I know what to call it. All that the monarchy calls it is a removal.'

Ruchira continued to stay silent. Her chest heaved up and down.

'Are you going to tell me to leave?' Shakti asked.

'No. *No*, dear. Just . . .' Ruchira's breaths were coming in short, staggered bursts now. 'I promised to help you, and I will. But, Shakti – there's a *dead* soldier in my house, and one alive but unconscious. What're we going to do?'

With each uttered word, she appeared to become more distressed. Sinking onto the ground, on her knees, Ruchira covered her face with both hands. Soon after, Shakti heard soft sniffling.

'Breathe,' Shakti ordered. How she herself was able to remain so calm in this situation was beyond her. But one of them had to be. Her mind flitted from one thought to the next, rifling through solutions hummingbird-quick. 'Prince Ashoka – I'll ask him to help dispose of the dead. He'll need to be kept here, but the body won't begin to smell just yet. It'll take a few days, but I won't keep it here for that long.'

Ruchira appeared decidedly ill. Shakti couldn't fault her. Their night had been horridly disrupted. Additional problems kept piling up like bodies at a crematorium; cremate one, only to be given another to burn. She still needed to speak to Adil, but that had to come later. First—

'What will you do with this one?' Ruchira nodded towards the unconscious soldier. Savi.

The knife was right beside her, a dangerous temptation. It would be so easy to pick it up and carve a thin line along the jugular. At least the soldier wouldn't be conscious to register her death.

But Shakti wavered. She didn't want to kill. There was another way, one less violent but more potent. She knew her name. She knew her face.

'I'll take care of it,' Shakti assured her. 'Come, we'll need to hide them for now.'

While Ruchira scrambled to find an adequate number of rags to mop up the blood, Shakti closed her eyes and concentrated.

There was a dream she needed to enter.

CHAPTER THIRTY-TWO
Ashoka

NOT EVEN THE BIRDS WERE CHIRPING THIS EARLY IN THE small hours. The palace was asleep, resting, but Ashoka was wide awake.

Dressed in his dark travelling cloak and head free of the golden circlet, he all but ran from his bedchambers. His destination was the serpent pens where Rahil waited for him.

It hadn't been long since Shakti visited his dreams, hands bloodied. Calm and unhurried, she explained her situation. One dead soldier, one who was alive. Ruchira was safe. She simply required help disposing of the dead body but had already taken care of the other.

Of all the traitorous things he could be caught doing, this wouldn't be the highest on the list. Convincing Prince Ryu, who had departed a few days ago after his visit, to keep to their original deal under Aarya's nose would be, but not this. Still, it was risky. It didn't help that Ruchira's residence was in the tightly packed outskirts of the Golden City. There was a higher chance of being spotted, but it was also closer to forestland.

The serpent pens were deserted when he arrived, save for the lone figure of Rahil. The low light turned his face into a portrait of sharp lines and soft shadows. He was in full Ran armour; Ashoka hadn't seen him in such uniform in a while.

'You're taking Sahry?' Rahil asked as soon as he arrived. 'People will be wondering why a winged serpent is loitering around the outer residences.'

As messengers often elected to take the winged serpents for long distances, the city folk were accustomed to seeing them in the skies. However, due to their sheer size, they were rarely taken to busy areas. 'I won't fly her too close to the area,' he said. News would travel fast to Aarya, and it wouldn't take her long to suspect why he'd taken his winged serpent there. 'We'll stop near the southern forestland – she'll get us there quicker than the leopards.'

They needed to burn the body somewhere further away. The forestland south of the city outskirts was the better option, but every step needed to be completed quickly. In Ashoka's diminutive arsenal, Sahry was the best gamble when it came to speed. That, and she could unhinge her mandible wide enough to fit a human-sized body in her mouth.

Sensing his restlessness, Sahry hissed loud enough to stir the remaining winged serpents. Ashoka saddled her quickly. Once Rahil had seated himself – albeit reluctantly – they were up in the air.

Not even a quarter of an hour later, Sahry landed in forestland, leaves rustling violently to the flap of her wings. He had her land on a hilltop that looked out into the flats that compromised the outer residences. Most homes were squeezed together. Others were afforded more space; small gardens and plots of land that were used to grow vegetables or keep fowl roaming uncaged. Minor spirits were more noticeable here, too, since the area was greener, and closer to forests.

After ordering Sahry to stay put, he and Rahil wandered down to the street. According to Sau's description, Ruchira's home was easily distinguishable. It had an overabundance of miniature stone nature spirit statues. Hurrying past several homes, Ashoka made a note to harangue Sau about her use of geographical markers – every second home seemed to be littered with statues.

'This one?' Rahil gestured as they approached a small flat with significantly more minor spirit statues than the rest. Ashoka glanced at the window; he could see the faint glow of lanternlight inside. And then – slight movement.

Already ahead of him, Rahil rapped softly on the door. At first, there was an eerie quiet before the sound of soft shuffling was heard. The door creaked open slightly to reveal Ruchira's drawn, tense face. Her eyes widened as he stepped forward, closer to the light.

'Prince Ashoka,' she breathed out. She made to bow, but Ashoka stopped her hastily and moved inside.

'Ruchira,' he greeted her, eyeing the entrance. He could see right into the kitchen – nothing appeared to be upset. There were no signs of a scuffle. 'Where is she? Where are the soldiers?'

Silently, Ruchira led him and Rahil through the kitchen area and into a small entryway that he hazarded led to her garden. He stopped short of the back door. Sitting on the stone floor and leaning against the wall was Shakti, scratching her upper chest. A dim lantern sat on her right. To her left lay a body.

The soldier. His eyes were closed, neck wrapped with a thick cloth.

At the sound of their footsteps, Shakti scrambled to her feet.

She looked so different. The long hair he'd remembered was cut in such an irregular manner that he half-wondered if a child had taken to the job. A minuscule dark spot stained through her green blouse, just above her left breast. The neckline was low enough that he could just spot the telltale darkness of the stitches Rahil had sutured.

Rushing to her immediately, Ashoka assessed her for any more injuries. 'Did they hurt you?' he pressed.

'Not enough to kill. You came quicker than I thought, Prince Ashoka,' she said by way of greeting, a small smile on her lips at his apparent worry.

'Just Ashoka.'

'All right, Just Ashoka.' She let out a heavy cough. 'Rahil.'

Her acknowledgement seemed to fall on deaf ears as Rahil manoeuvred forward and knelt to observe the dead body. Ashoka watched his expression closely. Though Rahil supported his cause, Ashoka understood there was a sense of collegiality he felt towards fellow soldiers. They were alike in some way, bound to the Ran Empire and its monarch. A small part of him would feel odd at seeing one killed.

When Rahil looked up, his expression was calm. 'How did you kill him?' he asked. 'Slit the throat?'

'Blade to the jugular,' she replied, confused. 'I couldn't slit the throat from my angle.'

Rahil looked almost impressed. 'You covered the neck,' he commented. 'Good.'

Ashoka noted that Shakti kept scratching at her chest. 'Are your stitches irritating?'

She shook her head. 'The skin is scratchy,' she said. 'I applied aloe on it to help.' The easy tone with which she said it was almost comical when there was a dead soldier on the floor.

One body.

'What did you do with the second soldier?' Ashoka remarked. 'The one who was unconscious.'

Shakti didn't appear to be as worried as he was at the prospect of the missing soldier. 'I let her go,' she said.

Ashoka started. 'You *what?*' he gaped. 'Shakti, of all the decisions you could have made—'

'And what would you have done?' she interrupted, frowning.

'If I were you,' Ashoka said, 'I would've killed them.'

Ruchira shot him a horrified look. A bitter laugh escaped Shakti's lips. 'Spoken like a mercenary,' she replied. 'I didn't want to kill an unconscious person, so I acted with grace. I gave her a small mercy and made her forget.'

'What do you . . .' Ashoka began, and realized immediately what she inferred. '. . . You used your powers. Your *other* powers.'

She nodded. 'It was easy to invade her dream and command her to forget,' she affirmed. 'Some minds are more malleable than others. She's outside an eatery right now, probably confused about why she drank so much on patrol last night.'

With her power, it would be so easy to drive someone to madness, to force them to take their own life without a second thought. The notion terrified him. There was an intimacy in being made privy to the inner workings of someone's mind, that it felt like a more twisted violation. Shakti had suffered under the hands of his sister. If she ever decided to turn against him, too, there was no stopping her.

'We'll take him to the forest,' Ashoka said. 'Sahry's waiting there. Rahil – help me lift him up.'

It took three of them to lift the body, with him and Rahil grabbing beneath the armpits and Shakti holding the head gently as if afraid it could tear off. When they straightened, placing one arm around each of their shoulders, the head lolled forward. Advising a concerned Ruchira to remain at home, Ashoka and Rahil exited her residence with Shakti close behind them.

It was still silent outside. No soft lanternlight shone behind shut windows. A limited window of time remained before the world woke to the sound of birds.

Ashoka grunted. Let any wandering eyes think they were a band of drunkards taking an overly inebriated friend back home. The body was heavy, but they managed to drag it all the way back to where Sahry was waiting.

Ashoka could make out her large body shrouded behind the trees. When he called out her name, she slithered towards them. Milk white, she could have passed for a Great Spirit had her body been more translucent. Ever cautious, Rahil took a step back. Sahry's presence was one of the rare occasions that forced him behind Ashoka without consent. Meanwhile, Shakti stepped closer.

'We meet again,' he heard her say. Some of the tension had disappeared from the mayakari's frame as she reached a hand up. Sahry complied, bending her giant head down to accept Shakti's touch. It baffled him the second time.

'Sahry,' he repeated, watching her gaze shift to him, and pointed to the body, 'hold.'

She blinked, tongue forking out to brush against his face and then to the soldier's. Then, she opened her jaw, fangs extending out and glinting dangerously as she unhinged her mandible and picked up the body. Rahil openly winced.

'Good,' Ashoka patted her underbelly, 'follow.'

Motioning Shakti forward, he allowed her to lead them further into the forest. The trek was long but not taxing; the area they travelled along was mostly flat. Bark crunched and branches thwacked behind them as Sahry slithered behind, wings tucked by her side.

Shakti led them to an unassuming area where the foliage was so thick that light could barely shine through. The ground beneath them was soft. Perfect for excavating. Ashoka briefly wondered if she thought to dig a grave after he commanded Sahry to drop the body.

'We're burning him, yes?' Ashoka inquired, turning to her. 'Did you bring a match?'

To his chagrin, Shakti shook her head. 'No,' she said. 'No burning. The smoke will be seen.'

'Then, what?' he asked, confused. 'We dig a grave, bury him? They can still be found by accident.'

There was nothing to bury the body with, either. They'd have to return to Ruchira's house to find proper tools.

'*You* do nothing, Prince Ashoka,' Shakti said, her tone flat. 'The forest will bury him.'

Before he could ask how exactly she planned to achieve this, Shakti put up a hand to silence him. Rahil snorted at his abject surprise. Part of him was unused to being silenced by those that weren't immediate family.

Kneeling with one foot, Shakti placed one hand on the ground. Vexation gave way to curiosity as she opened her mouth and spoke a familiar, melodic language.

Fascinated, he watched as the air around them shifted and shimmered. From above a na tree, a pale-yellow minor spirit descended onto the ground like a feather. From an unruly shrub fixture, the rectangular grey head of a second spirit peered out. Both creatures had mismatched eyes. Star-shaped, cavernous black holes on one side, the other almond shaped, eerily humanoid.

They approached Shakti like old friends, mouths upturned and chattering unintelligibly in flute and birdsong. Every so often, the mayakari frowned as if not understanding what was being said before resuming conversation. She gestured towards the body multiple times, the tone of her voice sounding like a plea.

Time seemed to grind to a painful halt as the two minor spirits approached the soldier's body. Shakti waved him and Rahil back with a hurried order: 'Give the spirits some space.'

Nature spirits never failed to amaze Ashoka. He wasn't quite certain what they would do, and how they would bury him considering they weren't corporeal.

The yellow spirit chittered in a harmonious tune that recalled celebrations and dance. As it continued to speak, the ground beneath the na tree shook. In the blink of an eye, brownish-black roots emerged from the ground. With terrifying speed, they grew and stretched towards the body like tentacles, covering it enough that Ashoka could see that where it touched, skin decomposed.

Brown skin gave way to a white fat layer, then to red muscle that darkened and fell easily like slow-cooked meat from bone. Horrified, he realized that not only was the body decomposing, but it was also sinking into the ground.

The grey nature spirit acted next. Long, thin branches shrouded with leaves snaked towards the sinking body and entered through the ears and nose. Part of him watched without fear. After all, he'd seen Usra raised in Taksila. Another part found it to be grotesque and mesmerizing at the same time; he couldn't look away. Not when shrubs began to sprout from the nose, eyes, and heart, twigs glistening with bodily fluid. Not when a putrid smell came and went with a soft gust of wind. Not when the body continued to disintegrate and sink until all that was left was the faint scent of fertilizer and newly grown shoots scattered on the ground.

Ashoka dimly registered Rahil intertwining his hand with his sometime during the process. For a man who could harm another without a second thought, Rahil appeared shaken. 'I'm fine,' he said before Ashoka could even ask, in a tone that suggested he really wasn't. 'I just didn't . . . it's unexpected.'

Absentmindedly, Ashoka reached out to pat the side of Rahil's cheek. Still looking dumbfounded, Rahil leaned into his touch but used his free hand to keep Ashoka's in place. Meanwhile, Shakti watched them curiously, a small, knowing smile flitting across her face.

'The earth takes what comes from it,' she said.

Ashoka couldn't help but marvel at the power that the mayakari had. Powers that could topple a dynasty. An empire. Powers that could have him seated upon the Obsidian Throne, with women ten times mightier than an average soldier at his command.

He halted his train of thought when Shakti stood, wiping away soil that clung to her palms. She watched them warily, as if expecting an onslaught of brutal rhetoric. 'As I said,' she said, a slight tremor in her voice belying the assuredness, 'we didn't need to burn.'

'What did you ask the minor spirit?' Ashoka asked.

'"Take him to the earth",' she replied. 'No one will find him if he becomes part of it.'

A beautiful, if not sobering statement. Death and life were so inextricably linked.

They stared at the plot of ground where the soldier's body once was. All were silent, until Shakti broke it.

'The Great Spirit of the mountain,' she declared, 'appears in the form of an elephant.'

Ashoka nodded, mystified by the sudden remark. 'Rahil told me,' he said. 'He also said it appears sick?'

'Woefully ill, is the phrase I would use,' Shakti replied, her expression despondent. 'Its memory seems not quite there. At one point, it told me that we're the same. That human greed and a mayakari's anger made it this way. I suspect it's telling the truth, because a Great Spirit has no reason to lie. I think it might be cursed.'

Ashoka started as the realization hit him. 'Cursed?' he echoed, before pausing to contemplate. 'After what I've seen in Taksila, that's an entirely valid concern. Were you able to understand why?'

'Not really.' Tipping her head back, Shakti palmed her cheeks as if to soothe herself. 'I suspect it's connected to me. Or rather, the Collective — what allows me to speak to your father,' this last part she added on, likely due to his and Rahil's open confusion.

Ashoka's head spun. Shakti's very existence was breaking what he knew of the mayakari and the limits of their magic. Just as in Taksila, he needed to adapt to shifting circumstances, and quickly. It seemed like Shakti herself was struggling to understand it.

Perhaps she needed to confirm her own theories by voicing them out loud. 'I saw a memory of Adil's, where he spoke to your aunt. She tried to summon the Great Spirit on her own but couldn't. Apparently when Adil went with her to the mountain, she heard its voice. Supposedly saw its true form once. It kept asking for the "false chakravartin",' she said, and chuckled. 'I'm inclined to think it's your father.'

Frowning, Ashoka mulled over the phrase. Now there was a title he hadn't heard in some time. 'False chakravartin, you said?' he asked. When she nodded, he let out a small hum. 'If the Great Spirit is talking about legitimacy, or blood rule, no Maurya has been illegitimate. Unless it refers to the term in a metaphorical sense. Do you know what "chakravartin" means?'

'In literal terms, a wheel-turner,' Shakti answered, and paused. 'But it means ruler. Or rather, an *ideal* one. A perfect king. Turner of the wheel. Hence the reference to a golden wheel, yes?'

'Mostly correct,' he said, trying to recall his lessons on philosophy. The knowledge wasn't widely taught unless one had a vested interest in history. 'It's a very old term that once used to reference four types of kings. Gold, silver, bronze, and iron. It's not used any more, because emperors refused to entertain the idea of being called a king. It's lowly. The ideal was a golden-wheeled king, a *suvarna-chakravartin*. One whose enemies surrender without declaring war – but that's pure fantasy.'

Shakti snorted in disbelief. '*Adil* wouldn't consider himself a golden-wheeled king?' she asked.

Despite his father's vainglorious nature, Ashoka knew that even he had his limits. 'It's not a title that's taken lightly,' he said. 'All kings have naturally been bronze or iron. A bronze-wheeled king means they are "victorious after a quarrelsome confrontation". Iron-wheeled is what my father would be. A *balachakravartin*: "victorious by means of the sword".'

Going by Shakti's puzzled expression, Ashoka guessed that he might've confused her even more. 'No such thing as a golden-wheeled king, then,' she murmured.

Not quite. 'My namesake,' he told her. 'Emperor Ashoka. He was the first and last Maurya to receive the title of golden-wheeled king. He *was* the last Mauryan king, really. Before he became emperor. Before he created the Ran Empire.'

Shakti looked confused. 'What?'

'Golden-wheeled king,' Ashoka repeated. 'It was a self-appointed title. A bit presumptuous if you ask me.'

Beside him, Rahil nodded in agreement. 'Very,' he said. 'Conquering without bloodshed? That's a far reach.'

He saw Shakti freeze. 'Wouldn't that be an accurate title for him?' she asked cautiously. 'Maybe it was figurative. He was a good king, wasn't he? A good emperor.'

He shrugged. 'Emperor Ashoka was known as a great monarch,' he agreed, 'but he created the Ran Empire through annexation. Warfare. A true warrior king. While my family would be more than happy to tout him as a *suvarna-chakravartin*, he wasn't. He was the same as any Maurya before him, and all who came after.'

Shakti appeared ill. Ashoka stepped towards her in concern. 'Did I say something wrong?'

The colour had leeched from her face, but Shakti shook her head. 'Prince Ashoka,' she asked. 'Can you do me a favour?'

'What is it?'

A muscle in Shakti's jaw ticked. 'Take me to the Mountain of Rebirth,' she said. 'I think I know why the Great Spirit is sick.'

CHAPTER THIRTY-THREE
Shakti

F ALSE CHAKRAVARTIN. IT HADN'T BEEN AARYA. IT HADN'T been Adil, either.

Standing at the peak of the Mountain of Rebirth and looking out towards the Golden City below, the Great Spirit's voice rang in her head again.

Human greed. A mayakari's anger.

The false chakravartin must give me peace.

'Shakti?'

She turned around. Prince Ashoka stood next to Rahil. Both he and the guard were watching her with concern. Behind them, Sahry had curled into herself, dozing. At Shakti's request, the prince had flown them here, but she hadn't told them why other than she needed to speak to the Great Spirit.

'I won't take long,' she promised.

A centipede crawled along the ground, its legs in a ceaseless march. One by one, its legs dropped off. The brown body began to turn lighter, until the little creature sputtered to a halt and moved no more. It took Shakti a moment to realize that there was nothing left of it, no inner organs. What was left behind was the shell.

False chakravartin. Golden-wheeled king. She was trembling, both in anger and anticipation. She recalled fragments of the emperor's voice, whispering the story of how the Mountain of Rebirth came to be.

THE WITCH WITHOUT MEMORY

Let me tell you a story, Shakti. One of a warrior, a mayakari, and a Great Spirit.

... the mayakari taught the warrior ... the Great Spirit, angered by the warrior, destroyed its own domain ... sapped the warrior of strength ... slept while life and death flourished ...

Shakti shoved the memory of Emperor Ashoka's voice aside. Kneeling beside the dead centipede, she closed her eyes and summoned the Great Spirit.

It took much longer to appear, but when the greyish yellow elephant finally did, Shakti dipped her head into a bow.

'*Little witch,*' it greeted her as she stood up. Its filmy eyes shifted to Ashoka and Rahil behind her. '*You bring ... allies, this time.*'

'I do, Great Spirit.'

The elephant's eyes looked faraway, not fully focusing on her. '*The Maurya prince, blood of his blood, iron in quartz,*' it said. '*By his side, an afflicted warrior. The one who saved you.*'

Shakti frowned. The spirit had referred to Ashoka like that before. *Iron in quartz.* That was an amethyst. Odd, but she didn't have time to entertain its cryptic words. She needed to confirm her suspicions. 'You are correct, Great Spirit,' she said.

'*You have summoned me again,*' it said, form flickering in the light. '*What possesses you?*'

'"*The false chakravartin must give me peace*",' Shakti repeated the spirit's own words back to it. 'You told me this, Great Spirit.'

'*Did I?*' it asked her, sounding confused. Her heart ached. Poor creature, subjected to fractured memories, just like she was.

'You did,' Shakti confirmed. '*I think I understand you now. It's Emperor Ashoka, isn't it – he is the false chakravartin.*'

The moment she asked her question; Shakti's heart skipped a beat. Next, it sputtered out an irregular rhythm, one that caused her to feel dizzy. The world caved in around her, the sky descending, the earth rising. It threatened to crush her in the space between. Dimly, she heard Ashoka and Rahil calling out to her in concern, but she waved them away. It was disappearing as quickly as it came.

The tightness in her chest receded, replaced by a pleasant buoyancy. As if she were floating in the air. This was *relief*.

Shakti met the Great Spirit's white eyes. The green of its irises was clearer now. Its form pulsed, glowing faintly. A beacon that guided ships towards the docks while in the stranglehold of a thick fog.

'You see a sliver of truth, little witch,' it said. 'You are right. He is the false chakravartin.'

'It's the Collective, isn't it?' she asked, hoping she was wrong. 'Is it somehow connected to you and me and him? Is that why you said we are the same?'

The crown of leaves atop its head started to shimmer. 'Almost. The Collective is not simply tied to me, little witch,' it said. 'I am the Collective.'

Shakti's breath caught. Her entire body froze in shock.

The tiger spirit in Kolakola flashed in her mind's eye, and she remembered its words: *This is ancient magic.*

It couldn't be. If the Collective was born from the Great Spirit, its consciousness was bound to her. Within her was the energy of a creature older than her.

Suddenly, she understood why she had been able to understand the Great Spirit's angered voice. 'That's why I feel stronger when I'm here,' she murmured to herself. 'Why I feel your emotions so acutely.'

'Yes, little witch. You are me. I am you. Like will command like. Kin will command kin.'

'I don't understand,' she sputtered out. 'How could this happen? Was Emperor Ashoka . . . a witch?'

The Great Spirit's laugh was downright malicious. 'Don't be foolish. Magic is not born from a man,' it said. 'I tied my life to your precious emperor. I kept him alive when death chased him.'

'Then, can you not untie yourself from him? From me?'

'No.' A deep wail came from the elephant's mouth. 'Not when he refused to let me go. Not when a mayakari's curse prevents me.'

She'd assumed as much, but it still pained her to hear.

The Collective was never a gift. It had always been a curse. To create it, a Great Spirit had – and continued to – suffer. The truth was uglier than a half-rotting corpse. Uglier than Adil's hate, uglier than Aarya's belief in her vicious father.

'Ashoka, the first of his name. The first Maurya to claim the title of emperor,' the Great Spirit continued. 'He who named himself the suvarna-chakravartin. Because of him, I suffer. Selfishness infects him like a wound left untreated. He lies. He has shrouded the truth from you.'

Part of her didn't want to believe it. All this time, he had been like a guiding light. He was the first to explain the Collective, allow her the choice of keeping the newfound ability or letting it go. He was the one who gave her advice on how to coax answers out of Adil, kept her company while her body and mind suffered under Aarya's cruel punishment. She trusted him the way a student trusted their mentor.

The Great Spirit seemed to read her thoughts. 'Trusting non-witches is a grave folly,' it continued. Bitterness like she had never heard coloured its voice. 'They, by their very nature, are violent to the core. Violent in action. Violent in speech. Violent in thought. I learned this the hard way.'

Spirits. All this because she'd cursed a man, one who was *already* cursed. 'Rebirth was never meant for me,' she found herself muttering.

The Great Spirit let out a noise like rain in a heavy monsoon. *'Why do you think that, little witch? What has Ashoka told you?'*

Shakti grimaced. 'That once I am attached to the Collective, I'll be denied reincarnation. I might not be reborn. I knew the risk and accepted it.'

'Hah. A liar indeed,' said the Great Spirit. *'Despite what Emperor Ashoka has told you, the Collective is not like your own limb. It is someone else's. Mine. A limb that has been stitched together almost seamlessly, but still not yours. You can remove the stitches and free yourself from it, little witch. You will be alive, and rebirth will claim you still. Lift the mayakari's curse and then release me. This land has suffered enough. I am in a state of stasis, my presence weakened. Release me, so that the mountain and I become whole again.'*

A plea. She stood in front of a Great Spirit who was begging to be released from its shackles. 'How can I free you if I don't know the mayakari's curse?' she asked hesitantly.

'*Ashoka exists within you. He holds the memory,*' the spirit roared, its body glowing brighter. '*Find it. Undo the mayakari's curse. Free yourself from the Collective. Free me.*'

'I . . .' A terrible, twisted feeling crawled up her stomach. The request was simple, but—

'*You hesitate, little witch.*'

Without the Collective, she was just another mayakari. Without the Collective, she couldn't invade dreams. There was nothing stopping her from being burned. Her leverage was gone.

Free myself from the Collective. The Shakti who had cursed Adil would have rejoiced at this knowledge. There would have been no hesitation on her part to let go of the Collective. An easy confirmation was on the tip of Shakti's tongue. So close, so achingly close to an agreement, and yet she couldn't find it in herself to say it. Not yet.

The Shakti of now was too attached to the Collective, too attached to that glorious, vengeful vision she had dreamed of after Jaya's murder. She knew without any uncertainty that the right and selfless course of action was to give up her power and return it to its true owner. Any mayakari would know it was neither good nor wise to upset a Great Spirit, but for now, she had to defy virtuousness and cling to her own objectives.

'I will make you a promise, Great Spirit,' she said, steeling herself. '*I will willingly give up the Collective, but only after I set out to do what I intended to when I first accepted it; and that was to destroy Adil Maurya's legacy. Then, you will be whole again. These are my terms.*'

She felt the Great Spirit's disappointment course through her, as deep as a ravine. The ideal mayakari would have helped a Great Spirit, not prolonged its suffering. It would hate her, but she needed to do this. The power that she had was found nowhere else. She was a weapon, and weapons were meant to be wielded.

'*Humans gamble their lives on promises, and they break them again and again,*' the elephant remarked. '*Your jailer made such a promise to me, and I allowed myself to be bound to him – with disastrous consequences.*'

'I don't want immortality, Great Spirit,' Shakti said, '*I want a rebirth, as all mayakari do. I want to achieve nirvana in a future* lifetime on my own terms, not held down in chains to this one. Upon my life, I swear it.'

That aching disappointment she felt began to recede, replaced by a buoyancy, like she was floating in the clouds. Hopeful.

'Very well,' it replied, and Shakti sagged with relief. 'Keep to your promise, little witch. I trust the word of a mayakari over a Maurya.'

'Then, do you agree to my terms, Great Spirit?' she asked.

The elephant sighed. 'I do, little witch,' it said.

Immediately, the temperature changed into one that was pleasant and warm. Above the elephant's head, the crown of leaves sprouted more curlicued branches. 'A settled promise,' it declared. 'I accept. Carry out your quest. We will meet again, perhaps when your memories have all returned. When your own curse is revealed.'

Her tongue felt thick. Mouth, dry. *It knew?*

'You know what I've done?' she whispered.

'A muddied mayakari cursing a muddied Maurya born without sorrow,' it mused, sounding like it was holding in a laugh. 'How unfortunate.'

Without sorrow.

An old memory between her and Emperor Ashoka resurfaced. A memory with Adil's voice.

. . . for she bore him without sorrow. Would you have rather he died?

Without question.

Her blood chilled. *Did it just say—?*

'Farewell, mayakari. We will meet again.'

Before Shakti could say anything, the Great Spirit disappeared, leaving her alone with an earth-shattering revelation.

CHAPTER THIRTY-FOUR
Ashoka

When the Great Spirit disappeared, Shakti collapsed.

'Fuck,' he heard Rahil curse softly, and rush towards the witch. Ashoka followed, coming to kneel beside her. Around them lingered the smell of rotting wood and tree sap. Nesting on a half-dead pinwheel tree, a murder of crows watched them patiently. The mayakari was on her hands and knees. When Rahil directed her to sit back, Shakti didn't look at them. She was looking at the spot where the Great Spirit vanished.

'Oh no,' Shakti was muttering, hands coming up to tug at her short hair. 'No, no, no . . .'

Befuddled, Ashoka reached out an arm to steady her tremoring shoulders. 'Shakti?' When she didn't respond, he squeezed her shoulder harder. '*Shakti*. What's wrong?'

Suddenly, Shakti let out a gut-wrenching scream so loud that it disturbed the crows, and they startled, some flying away. Pure panic flashed across her face, and she grabbed his arm in return. 'She made me do it,' Shakti sputtered out, her breaths turning frantic. The grip she had on his arm tightened to a painful degree, but Ashoka made no move to extricate himself. 'I thought . . . I'm so sorry, my *memory*—'

Fear. That was the secondary emotion beneath that panic. She watched him with worry, as if expecting a harangue from him.

A sharp tingle ran down Ashoka's spine. He didn't like that look. 'What is it?' he urged.

Lower lip wobbling, Shakti openly winced. 'I cursed you,' she whispered.

At first, Ashoka thought he heard her incorrectly, thinking this must be some sort of delirious after-effect. Not long after, the words hit him like lightning.

'You *what?*'

'*A muddied mayakari cursing a muddied Maurya born without sorrow,*' she whispered. 'It was you. I cursed *you.*'

The confession shouldn't have been a surprise, but it was like a punch to his gut anyway. She'd told him of her suspicions, and he'd waved it away, unconcerned. In his mind, Aarya wouldn't ask a mayakari to curse him. Why should she? Even the reminder that she'd poisoned Arush hadn't been enough to make him doubt. After all, he thought she saw him as nothing but an irritating yet harmless pest. There was no *need* to curse him.

Apparently, he was wrong.

Ashoka knew his lack of a reaction wasn't one the other two were expecting.

'Undo it.' Rahil had grabbed both Shakti's shoulders and was forcing her to look at him. Shock was plastered across the mayakari's face, and for good reason – Rahil had never looked so terrified. Eyes wide, brows tense, radiating pure unadulterated fear. 'Do you hear me – *undo it!*'

Ashoka couldn't help but think, *that should've been my reaction.* It should be him raging like an angered Great Spirit, him violently shaking Shakti as if that could make her remember. Though his chest was feeling too tight, his mind descended into a dull hum. Rage collected into a pool, water turning into poison.

Aarya.

Him. She'd asked Shakti to curse *him*, her younger brother.

'I can't,' Shakti whispered, at the same time he said,

'Rahil, she doesn't remember. Aarya—'

'I know what Aarya did,' Rahil snapped, and when Ashoka flinched, he softened immediately. He seemed to understand what he was doing, and let his hands fall from Shakti's shoulders. 'I didn't mean – I'm sorry, I just . . .'

'I know,' Ashoka said gently, and took a breath to steady himself. 'Shakti isn't at fault. We all know who is.'

'That pit snake,' Rahil growled, eyes narrowed into slits. 'Fucking viper. We need to force it out of her.'

'I agree,' he replied. The calm tone he spoke with appeared to unnerve both Shakti and Rahil, the latter of whom remarked, 'Are you not . . . scared?'

'Considering I don't know what my precious sister forced Shakti to curse me with,' Ashoka said, 'of course, I am. But I'm looking at this rationally. Look – in all this time, I haven't been struck with an affliction. Or died. That means the curse has yet to work.'

Shakti nodded wearily. 'It can still be undone,' she said. 'I haven't felt . . . death.'

Well, that was a relief, as sad as it was. 'I can force it out of her,' he assured them. 'I still have leverage. If I ever reveal that Aarya was the one who poisoned Arush, she'll be ruined.'

The tension in Rahil's shoulders had vanished, though there was a grimness to his handsome features still. Ashoka knew what that meant: he didn't like it, but he understood.

Muddied Maurya. The phrase bothered him.

'It called me muddied,' he remarked. 'Why? Because I'm cursed?'

'I don't think so,' said Rahil. 'What did you say, Shakti, about *cursing a muddied Maurya? Born without . . . sorrow*, was it?'

'Yes,' she replied. 'Great Spirits can be vague, too.'

Ashoka frowned. Vague, but as he understood it, easier to understand than minor spirits. Naila once told him that the smaller creatures communicated in images, which were harder to decipher. The Great Spirit of the Mountain of Rebirth seemed to be more forgiving. '"Without sorrow",' he quoted Rahil. 'That's what my name means. It simply confirmed your suspicions.'

'No,' Shakti murmured. She stared at a fixed spot on the ground. 'That's not it. The Great Spirit described you in a few different ways. "Blood of his blood", "Maurya prince, iron in quartz". That last one is the strangest. It described you that way twice.'

Ashoka latched onto the last phrase. 'Well, what does it mean?'

Shakti offered him an equally confused shrug. 'The presence of iron in quartz makes it an amethyst,' she said. 'It's a pretty stone. Used in jewellery, but there's no specific significance to you—'

Suddenly, the mayakari's eyes widened to owlish proportions as she craned her neck to stare at him. Glazed and distant, it was as if she was looking beyond skin and bone to what was unseen: his consciousness.

'Iron in quartz. *Muddied*. I'm muddied. You're muddied,' she muttered. 'I'm muddied in memory. You're muddied in . . .' Her mouth dropped open.

Glancing at Rahil, Ashoka found him to be wearing an equal expression of concern as he helped her sit up. His guard then looked over Shakti's head to mouth '*muddied*' at him. In response, Ashoka gave a subtle shake of his head. He didn't quite understand what she meant.

'Shakti,' he began, 'are you all right?'

The mayakari instead answered with a giggle. It started small, girlish and contained, until it morphed into a loud, deranged cackle. Tears sprung in the corner of her eyes.

'It was never going to be easy with you,' she said in between fits of laughter. 'Muddied. The Great Spirit gave me two answers. I understand it now.'

'Understand what?' he asked, frustrated.

Beneath his palms, Shakti's skin was hot. He couldn't make head or tail of her babbling. He shot Rahil a bewildered look.

Rahil huffed. 'We need to get her back to Ruchira's,' he said. 'She must've overtaxed herself.'

Nodding in agreement, Ashoka stood, ready to lift Shakti's left arm while Rahil took her right. Before they could haul her up, Shakti twisted out of Rahil's grip and latched on to Ashoka's hand. Her eyes were impossibly bright.

'No, listen to me. I saw your father's memories, Prince Ashoka,' she said. The previous manic quality of her voice was gone. Instead, it was firm. 'He wanted this mountain mined, just like your sister.'

'I know,' he said.

'He had your aunt help. Subhadrangi.'

'I *know*,' he repeated, this time with more force. 'Come on, now. You need to—'

'She was pregnant!' Shakti burst out, frantic.

His grip on her arm loosened. 'What?'

'I should've put the signs together,' she replied, not quite listening to him. 'The last memory I viewed. Adil . . . Subha looked different. Looser clothes. Tired. Swollen ankles. Her *gait*. Oh, and the flowers in her hair. The memory Emperor Ashoka once showed . . . you must believe me, Ashoka. She was with child.'

A horrible, sick feeling clawed its way up his throat. 'And what? The child was my father's? Impossible. He'd never – she was a *witch*.'

'That man's hatred wasn't born. It was made,' Shakti told him, grimacing. 'It gives me no pleasure to admit it. But I think that at some point, he cared about her.'

'No!' he exclaimed, feeling ill. 'He was a violent-tempered man.'

Violent to whom? his mind whispered. *The mayakari and you.*

Shakti just looked at him sadly.

'Fine. Even if he did, he ended up burning a witch who was with child,' he said, ignoring the burn against the back of his throat. 'I can't say I'm surprised.'

Shakti shook her head furiously. 'Either he burned her alive while she was with child, or she gave birth first and he killed her after.'

His hands were shaking. The left side of his head was pounding. He could so acutely feel the presence of his burned ear.

'Amethysts are semiprecious stones, Ashoka,' she told him. 'They're also naturally impure.'

Maurya prince, iron in quartz. His intestines felt like they were pulverized.

'I think she gave birth,' Shakti continued, and fixed her cavernous brown eyes on him, awash with sympathy. 'And I think that baby was you.'

CHAPTER THIRTY-FIVE
Ashoka

WHO WOULD WANT A FALSE MAURYA UPON THE OBSIDIAN Throne?

No one, Ashoka decided, was the answer.

Muscle memory guided his steps as he and Rahil entered the palace, on their way to see his mother after taking Shakti back to Ruchira's home. The mayakari had been apologetic.

'That was what the Great Spirit meant by calling you iron in quartz, a muddied Maurya,' she'd said. 'You're an impurity in the royal line. Muddied in blood.'

He'd seen the pity in her eyes and wanted to crush it. How else would she expect him to react to the absurd notion that he was not his mother's son?

It's not true, he thought ferociously. *Ludicrous, that's what it is. I am no bastard child.*

Repeating it silently to himself hadn't helped. All it had done was to make him remember almost every interaction he had with his father. The dead Myna bird, the indifference, the burned ear. The *will*.

Perhaps, it wasn't just my pacifism that irked him.

The sunlight blinded his eyes. His footsteps sounded like the thumping of a giant leopard's. Every sense was heightened. Tall, thick columns cast soft shadows on the marble floors, with only the soft thudding of their footsteps to be heard. Ashoka could barely think.

'Ashoka.' Despite being just behind him, Rahil's voice sounded far away. Ashoka didn't have time to consider what Rahil was thinking. Was he looking at him differently? No point pondering. He needed his mother. According to one of the guards passing by, she'd taken her breakfast, had a stroll about the jade pools and was with the palace physician in Arush's room.

'*Ashoka.*' His furious pace was halted by Rahil grasping his wrist, tugging until Ashoka was forced to stop. Closer to Arush's quarters the hallways were quiet. 'Look at me.'

He couldn't, so Rahil did it for him. Free hand pinching the underside of his jaw, Ashoka let himself be guided to lock eyes with Rahil. Part of him felt exposed; an animal baring its underbelly, the most vulnerable part. It was too easy to pierce through. One deliberate slice and all manner of organs would spill out in a slick, bloody mess.

'Are you sure you're in the best state of mind to ask?' Rahil inquired, voice soft .

'No,' Ashoka replied coolly, extricating himself from Rahil's grip. 'But there'll never be a good time to ask.'

Soldiers stood guard outside Arush's room when they arrived. They bowed as he approached, opening the door for him. Expecting to hear footsteps behind him, Ashoka noted the silence and turned just before he entered his brother's chamber. Rahil stood where he was, unmoving.

'I'll be outside,' Rahil said softly. 'You don't need me, Ashoka.'

The usually unassuming door was suddenly imposing. Beyond it was his mother, clutching a terrible secret to her chest. He had never felt so distant from her.

'You're wrong,' Ashoka whispered. 'I do.'

'Not for this,' Rahil replied with a sad smile. 'This is between you and your mother.'

He was right. Nodding, Ashoka squeezed Rahil's hand, spotting the poorly concealed grins from the soldiers around them.

When he stepped inside, he saw his mother by Arush's side.

Upon a red settee, she sat with her legs tucked under her, the soft blue of her sari spilling over like water. Two layered gold necklaces adorned her neck; her thick black hair tied into a topknot. A book lay open on her lap.

'Reading to Arush, Mother?' he called out, closing the door behind him.

She didn't startle, instead turned to him with a welcoming smile. 'Yes, my dear – his favourite collection of folktales,' she replied. Ashoka noticed her take in his windswept appearance. 'Look – you can see him stirring.'

On the bed, Arush was entirely still, save for the slow rise and fall of his breath. Not even a single flutter of an eyelid.

'Perhaps not at the moment,' she told him, disappointed. 'He responded to touch, my dear. He's blinked a few times.'

'That's good news,' he said carefully, though it was anything but. He hoped that Arush would stay unconscious.

'You haven't visited him much since your return,' his mother noted. She sounded sad. There was a trap here, somehow. *Was* he supposed to be by Arush's side every day?

'Even I know when to temper expectations, Mother,' he said. Emotions were starting to rise like water in a dam during the monsoon season. He couldn't keep his composure for too much longer. 'I pity him, but what will my presence do? Arush and I weren't exactly affectionate siblings.'

He hadn't intended to sound so curt in front of her.

'All three of you butt heads more often than oxen,' his mother sighed, 'but I think you need to learn to be civil and respectful of each other. When the day comes that I am but ashes in the wind, you three will only have each other left.'

'I'll have Rahil,' Ashoka retorted, with some stubbornness. It was a childlike refute, but in front of his mother, he was nothing *but* a child. Her child. 'I'll have Sau.'

'*Family*, my dear,' she responded. 'Civility between siblings will keep this empire intact. Infighting will only cause trouble.'

'Siblings?' Like a leech on skin, Ashoka latched on to her words and drew blood. No point in stretching this conversation out any longer. 'Mother, I want you to tell me a truth.'

'A truth?' His mother repeated as she closed the book and observed him curiously. 'About what?'

'About *whom*,' he corrected. 'You said that our aunt was a mayakari. That is a truth, yes?'

In the quiet that followed, Ashoka heard his mother's breath hitch. 'Yes,' she said.

'Father killed her,' he continued. 'Is that a truth?'

'Yes.'

'When he killed her, she was with child. Is that a truth?'

'Ye—' his mother said instantly, before the weight of his question seemed to settle over her. A soft gasp escaped her lips as she drew a hand to her mouth in disbelief. '*How did you know that?*'

Whatever little resistance that was in his heart gave way, and it flattened completely. 'Answer the question, Mother.'

'I—' she began, 'Ashoka, who—'

'Mother,' he said, watching her intently. 'Please.'

She looked at him like he was a Great Spirit, moments away from becoming angered. Whatever she saw on his face caused her shoulders to slump.

'Yes,' she replied, as if the one word was torture to sound out. At his silence, she rose to her feet and hurried towards him. The book on her lap fell on the floor with a heavy thump, but she didn't seem to care. Taking a step backward, Ashoka raised his left hand up. Shooting him a look that was both hurt and panic, his mother stopped in her tracks.

'Was that child Father's?'

Pursing her lips, she nodded mutely.

'Final question,' he whispered. He so badly wanted Shakti to be wrong. 'Where is this child?'

'I . . .' Her hands fell to her sides. Her breathing became shallow. Laboured. He could see the divot at the base of her throat retract violently, as if she were struggling to breathe. 'I don't—'

'Mother!' he snapped, composure shattering at last. It was a struggle not to raise his voice lest the guards outside were to overhear it, but spirits, he wanted to yell. He'd never yelled at his mother. If her answer to the question was as he feared, he couldn't go back. 'I asked you a question. *Answer me.*'

Did he remind her of Adil, then? The raw anger. Or did she see him as someone entirely different?

When his mother next spoke, her voice was thick with emotion. 'You're right,' she said. 'Before Adil killed her, she gave birth to a child. That child is here. That child is you.'

The world around him fractured.

This was the answer he expected, and yet it was too difficult to accept. For as long as he could talk, he'd been likened to Empress Manali. He was the child that resembled her the most, but that was clearly a lie.

I'm not my mother's son. I'm my father's.

That last truth hurt the most.

Ashoka didn't realize he'd frozen in shock. Didn't realize his whole body was trembling until his mother's jasmine perfume overwhelmed his senses. Didn't sense the warmth of her arms as they wrapped around him and came to rest on his hair.

'Ashoka,' she whispered. 'I'm sorry.'

He couldn't think or do or say anything for a moment. Reality was cruel. It had hated him from the moment he was born.

'How could you keep this from me?' he asked hoarsely into the crook of her neck, hands hanging limp by his side.

'I did it for you.' She pulled him closer, tight enough that his chest constricted and left him wondering where she held the strength in such fragile arms. 'I – you are mine, Ashoka. Not by blood, but in every other way that matters, you are my child.'

'I'm not.'

His mother pulled away to look at him. Ashoka met her eyes; they were an atrocious red. Hurt flashed clear across them. 'He took Subha from me,' she said, expression far away. Haunted. 'I couldn't let him take you, too.'

'Why didn't you?' he asked. 'I'm another woman's son. A *witch's* son. He was your husband.'

'Our marriage was a duty,' was all his mother said, before wiping away the tear tracks on her cheeks. 'Adil, he – he loved her. At some point, he loved her, and he hated it. But I never hated her. She was my sister.'

Ashoka couldn't find it in himself to speak. Words failed him.

'You're of her blood, I know that. We share nothing, and yet you're mine,' she told him, eyes wide. 'For Subha's sake, you are mine. Mine, Ashoka. *My* son.'

Adil Maurya was a monster, that he knew. This was something else altogether. 'Why didn't he kill me?' He asked woodenly. All his life, he had been nothing but a nasty reminder to his father. 'He could've just killed me.'

His mother's delicate features twisted in disgust. 'If you were a daughter and not a son, he might have,' she replied. 'Men will never be witches. I think he found some comfort in that. And I – I managed to sway him. Even if I couldn't save her life, at least I could try to save yours.'

She was crying harder now. Like a chastened tiger cub approaching its exhausted mother, Ashoka placed a hand around her arm, he pressed a gentle kiss on her head.

'Your eyes are like hers, you know,' she sniffled. 'They're like a doe's. Adil's son, but you didn't get his eyes like your siblings did.'

Adil's son. The son of a man who persecuted the mayakari. The son of a woman he never knew, held no emotional connection to, and *was* a mayakari.

At that moment, as he soothed his tearful mother, Ashoka hated himself for thinking a horrible truth. He may have been a bastard child, but Adil Maurya's blood still ran in his veins. There was still Maurya blood in him.

The throne could still be his.

'She was stubborn, like you,' his mother murmured, drawing him out of his reverie. 'Even knowing she awaited burning she chose to name you Ashoka.'

There had been no Ashokas following the first. It was considered unsightly. Why name a child after the greatest chakravartin. The so-called golden-wheeled king. 'My name was an act of vengeance?'

'Of sorts,' his mother replied. 'Your name, my dear. What does it mean?'

'Without sorrow.'

'Yes, for she bore you without sorrow,' his mother smiled sadly.

A muddied Maurya born without sorrow. It hurt.

'I'm not your son,' Ashoka found himself saying again. 'I'm not yours.'

'My dear, you *are*,' she said, cupping his cheek just as the door opened behind them and Ashoka vaguely heard Rahil's voice raised in argument, 'I may not be your birth mother, but I love you just the same.'

'*What* did you say, Mother?'

Startled, Ashoka whirled around. Standing behind him, jaw hanging open, was Aarya.

Fuck.

Of all the people who could've walked into this room, it had to be her. Caught up in his emotions, Ashoka hadn't even heard her enter or the door close. Neither, it seemed, had their mother.

'Mother,' Aarya said. She wasn't looking at him. 'Repeat what you just said.'

Their mother winced, clearly not wanting to say those words again. *Ashoka is not my son.* There was no point trying to cover it up. From her shocked expression, Ashoka knew she'd heard them but was wanting confirmation anyway. A second confirmation made it true, so he did it in place of his mother.

'I am our father's child but not hers,' he said, extricating himself from his mother's grasp. 'Is that what you wanted to hear?'

Begrudgingly, he admired the almost detached way in which his sister spoke. 'Yes,' she replied. 'Whose child are you, then?'

His resulting silence must've been enough, for understanding dawned on his sister's face. 'Our aunt,' she said, voice quiet. Devoid of emotion. Then, 'You're a mayakari's spawn.'

The way she uttered *mayakari* made his skin crawl. 'I am.'

'Am I?' She turned on their mother in an instant. 'Is Arush? Tell me we're not, Mother! But I can't say I can trust anything coming out of your mouth right now.'

Their mother's tears had dried, and she was looking at Aarya with her usual exasperation. 'You and Arush are mine, Aarya,' she said. 'Do not speak to your brother that way.'

'Half-brother,' Aarya corrected. A sense of horrified wonder crept into her words. 'A *bastard* son: clearly a lapse of judgement on Father's part, I'm sure. But you . . . a *mayakari's* child – you're born from a parasite, *mūsī*.'

Ashoka didn't care about the disgusted tone with which Aarya uttered *half-brother*. He could only focus on one word: parasite. Only one of his parents was a parasite, and it was not the mother he had never known. But of course, Aarya would never see that. In her mind, he was now tainted.

'No wonder you were sympathetic to the mayakari plight,' Aarya continued. 'Did you know back then? Or is that because of your mother's blood?'

He clenched his hands. 'Stop it.'

As usual, his sister didn't listen. 'The people will never accept a royal who is half a monster.'

'*Shut your mouth*, Aarya.'

Shooting him a nasty sneer, Aarya shook her head. 'How dare you attempt to command me,' she said. 'You're not of pure royal blood.'

'*Aarya!*' their mother scolded.

Scoffing, Aarya shook her head. 'Oh please, Mother. You know I'm right,' she said, smiling hatefully. 'What a nasty little secret. What a scandal if it were ever to get out. Our father – the man who hated witches – having slept with one. Having sired a child.'

He didn't like that look, the wicked glee. 'What?'

'Nothing,' she laughed, 'because there is absolutely *nothing* you can lord over me, now.'

Viper. In an instant, Ashoka knew what his sister implied. 'You wouldn't,' he said, but that was a useless remark. Aarya would, so he jumped onto the one defence he had. 'Letting that secret out will hurt Father's name.'

'I can salvage his name while sullying yours,' she replied, before hesitating briefly. 'A lapse in judgement. Having no prior knowledge that the woman was a witch until much later. In the end, what our people will hear is that you are a mayakari's child.'

Ashoka stood immobilized in disbelief. She'd climbed over mountains to justify it. Her smug expression made him want to gouge her eyes out, and he stepped forward, hackles raised. 'No, you can't threaten me, Aarya. Otherwise, I'll make sure everyone knows about Arush—'

'Oh, little brother, I can live with that,' Aarya replied. 'Your secret, however, will cause absolute humiliation. I am of legitimate Maurya blood; the line of succession still falls to me. But you, with that dirty, polluted, mayakari blood? You are illegitimate. You have no right to the throne. You have no right to a *governorship*.'

Claws tore into his stomach and ripped his intestines into shreds. He knew where she was headed. In his mind's eye, Ashoka saw himself holding on to a rocky ledge. Rapids and sharp rocks waited for him with open arms below. There was no one to help him up, but he couldn't let go. Not yet.

'I'm still a *Maurya*.'

'One with polluted blood,' Aarya countered immediately. 'A bastard.'

Their mother, who had been listening in perturbed silence, finally spoke. '*Stop*. What is this about Arush?' she asked, glancing between them. 'What are you talking about?'

'Go on. Tell Mother, Ashoka,' Aarya said, looking at him in steely triumph. 'Tell the world. I don't care.'

Their mother turned to him. Ashoka could see her patience waning away. He gave Aarya one last warning glare, but she didn't break.

'A mayakari didn't poison Arush, Mother,' he said. 'Aarya did.'

Their mother's mouth dropped open. The way she looked at Aarya, it was as if she were desperately hoping he was lying. 'Is that true?'

For her part, Aarya remained stoic. 'Yes, Mother,' she said. 'Arush was going to run father's legacy into the ground. I had to do something. At least he's not dead. At least you can stay by his side.'

Their mother's eyes widened in disbelief, and she began to shake her head minutely. The shakes soon became more aggressive, and she muttered 'no' in a relentless repetition.

'That's your justification?' she asked, voice trembling with barely restrained fury. 'Poison your own brother but tell me I should be glad he's still breathing? You are no chakravartin, Aarya. You are a monster masquerading as my child.'

Ashoka swore he saw an imperceptible flinch cross his sister's face. 'I am more Father's child than yours,' she said, sneering. 'Curse my name. Curse my very existence, but Arush won't wake. He'll waste away.' Manali's eyes welled with tears, but Aarya was not done. She turned to Ashoka. 'And with your polluted blood, *mūsī*, no one will accept you as a legitimate heir. The Obsidian Throne is mine, and you have no claim to it.'

'Fuck you,' Ashoka snapped.

'Hate me all you like, but you *will* obey me,' his sister retorted. 'Rest assured, I will make the necessary repeals in Taksila. As for Shakti – I know you know where she is. That's why I came here in the first place. Early morning flights to the Mountain of Rebirth? You can't hide from me.'

'I don't know where she is,' he replied mutinously.

Aarya reminded him of a violent-tempered child having been given a mallet. No good would come from it. 'You do,' she said. 'If you don't want the knowledge that you're illegitimate exposed to the world, you will bring the witch to me. *Immediately.*'

CHAPTER THIRTY-SIX
Shakti

'You lied to me, false chakravartin.'

After Prince Ashoka and Rahil took her back to Ruchira's empty home, Shakti transported herself directly into the Collective, with only one man in mind. Emperor Ashoka now sat cross-legged beneath the shade of a na tree, beautiful face impassive, as she raged in front of him. He'd appeared within a memory of the Mountain of Rebirth before its affliction.

'The mental anguish over being denied a rebirth,' she continued, tone cold and clipped. 'What was the reason? Why didn't you tell me the Collective exists because of the Great Spirit?'

'Because it wasn't relevant to you at the time,' the emperor replied. His nonchalance made Shakti clench her jaw hard enough to hurt. 'Your only purpose was to hurt Adil and his children. There was no need to bother with extraneous details.'

'Extraneous? Knowing these details could've changed my mind,' Shakti hissed. 'I could've rejected the Collective instead. Severed the limb early on. You hid important details on purpose.'

A smug, knowing grin played across the emperor's lips. She didn't like the look on him. It was anathema to everything she thought she knew. '*Would* you have rejected it?' he asked softly. 'I think that's a lie, Shakti, because even when the Great Spirit asked you to give it up, you didn't.'

'My reasons are justified!' Shakti exclaimed. She almost added that she had no other choice, but she stopped herself. The emperor wasn't spouting a lie. He'd obfuscated the origins of the Collective on purpose, but it had ultimately been her desire to rid the world of two of Adil Maurya's three children that convinced her to accept it.

'Oh?' He sounded disbelieving. 'If you say so.'

'What were yours?' she demanded, not caring for his insinuation. 'You were the original keeper. Why didn't you let it go?'

Above him, the leaves of the na tree began to lose their green shimmer. 'The Great Spirit stopped me from dying,' Emperor Ashoka replied. An eerie quality tainted his words, now. Or had it always been there, as obvious as a cobra in dry grass, and Shakti had simply been too ignorant to notice? 'Kept me alive so that I could rule my kingdom. Great Spirits live for hundreds of years, Shakti. Why can't we be afforded the same; be able to oversee the way in which this world unfolds?'

Shakti suppressed a shiver at his words. He wanted ... what, immortality? Great Spirits could die, too, although it took far longer for them to pass. Despite being considered higher beings, they didn't escape death. No one did. Unlike every other creature, though, they were thought to attain nirvana upon their passing.

The detached tone in which the emperor spoke aggravated her. 'Great Spirits and humans – we will all die one way or another, and that's just how life is. Immortality isn't real. Surely you know that.' Realization surfaced quick. There was one thing she'd forgotten. 'The *curse*.'

Looking pleased, Emperor Ashoka spread his arms wide. 'A mayakari's curse bound my consciousness and the spirit's forever,' he said. 'My physical body is gone, but my consciousness remains the same. As long as every Maurya accepts me – and thus far, they have – I remain on this plane.'

'Is that how the curse works?' she asked. 'It passes down the Maurya line, somehow?'

'I don't understand the cursed tongue,' the emperor replied carelessly. 'I wouldn't know what she – what the mayakari – cursed me with. The pattern I saw, however, was that the Collective was transferred to every firstborn Maurya. Until you, that is.'

Who would be so willing to be bound like this? To her, this was torture. An inescapable prison. 'You're trying to achieve some kind of spiritual immortality by evading rebirth, aren't you?'

'An astute observation,' Emperor Ashoka replied, sounding amused. 'Why subject ourselves to the endless cycle? Think back to the mayakari philosophy, Shakti. Your aunt would surely have told you. Yes, rebirth is expected, as sure as the sky is blue, but what is it that witches try to attain? What they taught others to attain?'

There was no malice, no murderous intent of any kind to be heard. Instead, something akin to reverence coloured the emperor's voice. Shakti knew the answer immediately, and a horrible shiver ran down her spine.

'Nirvana,' she whispered. Becoming extinguished. *The extinction of rebirth*. The flame quenching permanently without the transfer to a new wick. But the concept was heralded as good and honourable, the result of having achieved pure mental cultivation, the complete detachment to the material world and its suffering. But this . . .

'This isn't nirvana, Emperor,' she protested. It was an ugly and warped version of it, one that required the suffering of others to prosper. To remain permanently alive in a consciousness without ever being reborn. 'You've manipulated it to fit your own argument. You say you aren't reborn physically – fine. But your consciousness remains, unextinguished. This is no noble way to achieve it, and I think you know that. You don't want nirvana – you want immortality. No need to make it sound poetic.'

'Isn't it, though?' he asked gently, the way she thought a lover would. 'Imagine it.'

'Unlike you, I don't wish to exist forever,' Shakti replied. 'I don't want to transfer this power to another but rather let it go. The Great Spirit deserves to feel whole again. The Collective must cease to exist.'

'*Shakti.*' She'd never heard him say her name in such a calm but lethal tone. 'It's not just my consciousness you will likely end. There are several Maurya monarchs, ones whom you do not know, whose minds exist within the Collective. By ridding yourself of this gift, you will destroy lives. You are a mayakari, child. You cannot harm, cannot kill.'

She wavered, then, despite knowing that there were no living bodies involved. Only a consciousness, something that was intangible, unable to be seen – but was he right? Would she still be killing *something*?

'No,' she said, shaking her head and taking a step back. 'It's not killing. It's me letting karma and the cycle take its course.'

Emperor Ashoka's face fell for a moment, before pursing his lips and coming to stand. With his shoulder-length black hair, bright brown eyes and delicate features, he didn't look frightening, but rather eerie and ethereal. A beautiful liar.

'You are a mayakari with part of a Great Spirit's life force within you,' Emperor Ashoka said with a sense of urgency. 'Does that not intrigue you?'

In truth, it did, but that was better left unsaid. It wouldn't do any good telling him that the feeling was addictive, that it intrigued her more than it should. The very thought was reprehensible. Unfortunately, the emperor seemed to know what she was thinking.

'There's so much that remains untested, Shakti,' he continued. 'What more can you do? Surely you've wondered. Can you wander into the dreams of a dying man in that period between life and death when the mind remains live? Can you command spirits in a way that mayakari can't? With the Collective in your head and your natural mayakari abilities – you are limitless.'

His words gave her pause. 'Command spirits?' she echoed.

The emperor smiled, triumphant. 'You can clearly understand an angered Great Spirit when no other mayakari can,' he said. 'That is a gift. A weapon to be wielded.'

You are me. I am you. Like will command like. Kin will command kin.

Pretty words. Beguiling words, but Shakti knew what he was doing.

'Don't you worry,' she told him, moving forward until they were face to face. 'I'll use the Collective to my full advantage to help Prince Ashoka. But rest assured, once he takes the throne, I will be rid of you.'

CHAPTER THIRTY-SEVEN
Ashoka

Over the next few days, Ashoka tried to avoid Aarya. It wasn't a particularly difficult feat, but it didn't escape his notice that more soldiers were stationed outside his quarters. They observed him like a hawk as he wandered the grounds. More scrutiny was placed when he stepped so much as a foot outside the palace. Leaving for Taksila seemed like a hopeless endeavour.

If Aarya was expecting him to be so foolish as to leave the palace and lead her right to Shakti, his sister was gravely mistaken. He continued to feign ignorance over her whereabouts whenever Aarya attempted to weasel it out of him. He wondered what her plans were to recapture the mayakari. Attempting to glean any information from the consuls hadn't worked. Sau hadn't fared much better, either.

'The presence of soldiers has increased,' she told him in his quarters one day after returning from the capital's markets. Rahil was outside, guarding his door. 'Especially around the mountain. Notices are still up with her picture, but nothing else. The rice fields are being irrigated, but people are grumbling about prices for sacks. There're whispers of a burning, too.'

At the mention of a burning, Ashoka snapped to attention. 'Do you mean they've burned a mayakari or are planning to?' he asked.

Sau shrugged, apologetic. 'I don't know, Ashoka,' she said. 'The witches are probably from farming villages outside the capital.

Maybe it's already happened. We haven't seen a public burning in a while.'

Frustrated, Ashoka rubbed his temples and wandered towards his balcony, Sau following just behind. Forestland stretched far beyond them, but he felt trapped.

'We could just escape,' he told her. 'I'm expecting Aarya to come for us, anyway.'

'Good luck,' Sau replied, scoffing. 'That would've been possible before your sister found out you were . . . a half sibling.'

'You can say bastard,' he replied dryly. The word didn't have the same sting when it came from Sau. He was still a Maurya. But she was right. Aarya seemed to be anticipating his every move. The only way to escape without exiting through the palace gates – which were heavily guarded now – was to fly out from the pens with Sahry. What once used to be a simple task was now difficult. Aarya had commanded that the serpent pens be guarded day and night, and the time he had to fly with Sahry was controlled, too. Not that Aarya needed to worry about him flying away – leaving Sau and Rahil to their own devices wasn't an option.

Aarya was the worst possible person to find out he was a half-sibling.

'I will *not* be calling you that.'

Letting out a gruff chuckle, Ashoka absentmindedly tugged at his burned ear. 'Aarya's getting impatient,' he said.

'So is Shakti,' Sau remarked.

He understood the mayakari's impatience. Shakti didn't seem like someone who enjoyed being forced to lie low. She was restless, much like Sahry. 'Of course she is,' he snorted. 'All that power and no outlet. She can invade dreams. Command people. My father's consciousness is in her head.'

He still couldn't quite understand it. The consciousness, much like the human body, was impermanent, and yet his father's was stuck in Shakti's head. Unable to undergo rebirth. Though, from the sounds of it, it didn't sound like a static consciousness – one frozen at the time of his death. Every time Shakti spoke to Adil, he learned something new. Adil existed, just not in a physical sense. Ashoka's head hurt from thinking about it; mayakari philosophy tended to do that, sometimes. But, he supposed, there was the added layer of magic and a curse being involved. That tended to complicate things. 'What an act of misfortune.'

'And she's cursed you,' Sau added unhelpfully. 'What an even greater act of misfortune. Frankly, I'm surprised you aren't going mad at the thought.'

'Of the various problems I have to think about, it's not the most concerning,' he replied. The knowledge that an unknown curse had been cast against him lay in the back of his mind, an ever-present reminder. It did terrify him that the witch who cast it couldn't remember – that he could be affected by it at any moment – but there was no point in worrying his friends any further. 'I'm still alive. We need to leave the capital, but I can't force Aarya's hand now. Any bargaining power I had is gone. The only one who overrules her is Arush.'

'Too bad he's asleep,' Sau sighed.

Ashoka paused. *Arush.* A sudden, almost laughable idea appeared in his head. If it worked, Aarya would no longer hold any power over him.

He turned to Sau. 'I want you to do something for me,' he remarked. When she acquiesced, he said, 'Good. I hate to make you take the journey again, but can you travel to Ruchira's and find Shakti. Tell her to invade my dreams tonight.'

Strangely enough, Ashoka wasn't subjected to a nightmare that night.

His dreams jumbled together, changing from seeing himself as a Great Spirit, to seeing a cursed weapon be used against his father, and finally to a peaceful fantasy of rolling hills and emerald meadows. Dozens of giant leopards lay in a pack in the distance, some asleep on their sides, others licking their paws in contentment. One of them looked like Rāga. Here, he sat atop a dusty rock, cross-legged and watched them in silence.

Suddenly, he felt a strange pressure, as if he were being pushed. Moments later, he heard a familiar voice call out, 'Ashoka.'

Craning his neck behind him, Ashoka spotted the mayakari observe him with a curious expression.

'Shakti,' he said, patting the empty space next to him in an invitation.

Watching him warily, she complied and for a while they sat and stared at the beautiful beasts and the endless expanse of grass plains. 'Are you . . . all right?' she ventured.

'Fine. Aside from confirming that I'm a bastard child,' he replied without malice, watching her wince. 'Can't say the fallout has been good.'

Shakti reached for his hand. He grasped hers. The absence of sensation made the moment bittersweet. 'I'm sorry.'

'My . . . mother told me why I was named Ashoka,' he replied. 'I always wondered. It was an act of rebellion.'

Shakti hummed. 'Whenever I saw your father's memories of Subha, she always had a saraca flower in her hair,' she told him.

The red-and-orange saraca species were also known as the *ashoka flower*. He stored this sad, strange new piece of knowledge away, feeling numb.

'I – I will never know my birth mother, and I'm sorry for it,' he said quietly. 'She didn't deserve to die but I have no connection to her. I'm still my father's child. You know, when you first told me, I half hoped I was my *mother's* illegitimate child. Even with this, I'm still tied to my father. He's inescapable.'

'I'm sorry,' she said again. A long silence stretched between them.

'What is he like?' he asked suddenly, voice tentative. Unsure. 'My father. In your head, I mean. Is he . . . different. Or much the same?'

'What would you call easily irritated, tempestuous and pathetic?'

He sighed. 'Much the same, then,' he said. 'I never asked – what else did you learn from the Great Spirit.'

Shakti launched into a near-fantastical explanation of the Collective, the Great Spirit, and Emperor Ashoka, one that he had to ask her several times to repeat. It sounded like a terrible burden for a mayakari to bear. His first response was to advise her to return the Great Spirit's consciousness, but Shakti hadn't. In fact, she'd refused. It sounded as if she were contemplating what else she could do with the Collective at her disposal.

Ashoka didn't try to be morally upstanding. Otherwise, he'd be nothing more than a hypocrite.

'Pri— Ashoka,' Shakti began cautiously. 'What is it that you've called me for?'

'Aarya knowing of my birth has lost me my one bargaining chip,' he said. 'It's impossible to leave the palace at all, so I want a favour. Something to topple Aarya off the throne.'

'What, enter her dreams and command her?' Shakti asked. 'I've tried over the last couple of days to try and force what sort of curse she made me speak from her but found that I couldn't. I don't understand why – she should be asleep.'

Ashoka grimaced. 'Should be but isn't. Aarya's still sleeping at abnormal hours these days,' he explained, 'which, I gather, is to stop you from entering her dreams. I think she barely sleeps at night.'

'Weakling,' she replied with a scowl. 'I hope her face looks like a palm civet's each and every morning.'

'Let's not insult the poor palm civet,' Ashoka joked, causing her to smile a fraction. 'It's not my sister's dreams I want you to enter.'

Shakti seemed to understand his intentions immediately, for she went slack jawed. 'Ashoka. Are you mad?'

'Possibly,' Ashoka said. He had no choice. He needed to bring back a game piece that he thought was no longer needed. It would disrupt the entire board. Cause more problems for him than not. 'You commanded him to sleep, but no longer. I want you to wake up my brother.'

CHAPTER THIRTY-EIGHT
Shakti

WAKE UP MY BROTHER.

Mad. Prince Ashoka was mad in asking to revert the scales. One less Maurya made her breathe a little easier. Reawakening a comatose young emperor was the equivalent of spitting in her face.

And yet, part of her understood his reasoning. Aarya had tasted power, lived for a short while in a world that prostrated itself at her feet. There was no chance she would give it up – unless Arush were to wake.

Prince Ashoka was placing a gamble on his older brother, too. They wouldn't know how he'd react to the changed circumstances.

'Please try,' he'd told her before she left his dream. His tone had been sombre, but Shakti had seen the gleam in his eye, hopeful and calculating. Briefly, she wondered where the prince she met on her first day in the royal palace had gone. A change had happened in Taksila; new soil placed around him, a struggling plant reviving itself.

It would test the extent of her power, but Shakti was willing to try. In fact, she'd acted on her promise immediately and entered Arush's dreamscape the moment she left Ashoka's.

Despite his comatose condition, his mind was still alive and flourishing, albeit in a hazy, sluggish manner. She found Arush slaying a Great Spirit with nothing but his bow and arrows and snorted at the conceit. Foolish humans, thinking themselves to be more powerful than the embodiment of nature itself.

To temper Arush's suspicions, she appeared as Adil once again. This dream-Arush seemed to be dazed. Confused. Straddling the dreamworld and strangely aware of his physical body lying in his bedchambers. He told her-as-Adil that he could hear Empress Manali's sobs like distorted echoes, her soft voice as she read from his favourite collection of folk tales. An argument. An inkling.

Shakti entertained his ramblings for as long as she could before her patience vanished. She uttered a single sentence, a solitary command:

'Arush Maurya, the dreamworld will not hold you any longer – I command you to wake.'

'Remain hidden.' Cleaning a dirty plate with a wet rag in the kitchen, Ruchira shot her a beseeching, almost fearful look. 'Weren't those Prince Ashoka's express orders?'

'Which I'll do,' Shakti assuaged her as she shrugged on a light travelling cloak.

'My mistake for informing you of these things,' Ruchira muttered.

These things consisted of a rumour the cook had heard being whispered throughout the city that week. A group of mayakari had reportedly been discovered outside the walls of the Golden City in a small rice farming village. Usual brutal Ran Empire tactics would have been to burn them where they stood, but these witches were reportedly being transported for a public burning at an open-air stage in the east. The empress was to attend.

Shakti's stomach twisted into knots when Ruchira first told her of the rumour.

'That's highly unusual,' she'd whispered, feeling sick. Public burnings of mayakari not discovered in the Golden City were rare. Trust Aarya to do it, anyway.

She had a few ideas as to why. Public tension was high, what with the quakes and her loose in the capital. By now, the news of Ran weapons being transported to Mahvo was public knowledge. Gossip in the Golden City flew like stray cloths in a thunderstorm.

That wretch probably thinks burning a few mayakari will renew morale and faith in the monarchy, Shakti thought venomously. This also seemed like a trap. It likely was, but she couldn't sit in Ruchira's home, twiddling her thumbs, knowing that three innocent mayakari were set to be burned. If there was a chance that she could help them escape, she would take it. Besides, Aarya would be there, and Shakti still didn't know what the empress had asked her to curse her own brother with. Since invading Aarya's dreams was proving difficult, she might as well threaten her face to face.

Ashoka would call her mad. Foolish. Reckless. She was all those things, but she was tired of the gaps in her memory. She wanted an answer.

So she'd looked at a map of the Golden City lying in Ruchira's home. The open-air stage where the burning was set to take place was in the grounds of a large public park to the east. The park area was semicircular in shape. Its circumference was bordered by two separate waterways that joined together behind the stage to form one large channel that travelled north towards residential buildings. Unless they were to jump into the canals, there was only one way in or out.

'One misstep and you'll be back in that horrible cell,' Ruchira warned as Shakti strapped two plain daggers by her side. 'And I'll be dead. Please, Shakti. Reconsider. What exactly is your plan to free them?'

'Have a minor spirit assist me,' she said. 'It's a public park. There'll be plenty of trees around. Besides, the little spirits will always help a witch in trouble. And you'd be surprised by how much destruction they can cause.'

Ruchira didn't look convinced. 'I know the risks and I'll be careful,' Shakti added, softening her tone. She didn't want to answer the cook's question. 'If I get caught, I won't ever give up your name, but Ruchira . . . they're innocents. I can't imagine what kind of story Aarya has spun to make them appear monstrous. If there's a chance that they can be saved, I'll do it.'

'Is there a chance I can stop you?'

'None.'

The older woman sighed. 'The choices we make are of our own free will. So be it. May fortune favour you, Shakti.'

Half an hour later, Shakti departed for the eastern theatre.

Roasting spices and heated sugar hit her nose the moment she entered the main market. Sacks of rice piled high threatened to topple from a vendor's stand. Curved bridges and waterways wound around like a snake in high grass. Notices with her face were still plastered on walls, and she instinctively tensed every time she passed by one, even though her hood hid most of her features. Fragrant ground tea leaves were sold in small glass jars by merchants, claiming to be sourced from Chalamba and – spirits, had she heard right? – a deadland.

Shakti stifled a snort. Tea plantations grown over a deadland? Such lies. But it didn't surprise her that the common people believed it.

Shakti wandered in further. As she skirted by, scraps of conversation between a couple and a merchant caught her attention just enough to slow down:

'—wife gone to help excavate a deadland—'

'—ah, the Ghost Queen, yes? I heard from my uncle that the empress—'

'—rare. You might as well try to talk to a Great Spirit—'

Not that damned Ghost Queen again. Aarya was still insistent on procuring the plant, but it was a fruitless quest; a gamble of ridiculous proportions. It was like betting one's life savings with only a slim chance of success.

The market stalls soon gave way to the large public park where the open-air theatre was built. The main footpath petered off at the park entrance. Children sat upon the grass and played games with dice.

A large crowd was gathering on the grassy commons. They were waiting some paces in front of the raised, circular stage. It seemed like there were hundreds of people already, and more were coming through the entrance.

Towering decorative hora trees paralleled the common. There were rows of six trees on each side. Many city folk sat beneath their shade.

She spotted soldiers scattered around the perimeter, and her hackles rose. Gooseflesh erupted like tiny domes across her skin. Their gazes were hawkish. Focused. On the lookout. She kept to the middle of the crowd, head lowered beneath her hood, not daring to look anyone in the eye.

Off to the right side of the stage were a dozen more soldiers. One group was clustered together. The others – about five or six of them – were guarding a leopard-drawn carriage. Though, as she came closer, Shakti realized with a lurch that it was more a cage than a carriage. It was bolted shut. Inside it, three women sat with their heads bent low, cowed. One had her hand loosely latching on to one of the bars. Even from this distance, Shakti could see the dark smears across her exposed skin, fingertips red and raw.

She heard scraps of conversation from the onlookers. They were anticipatory. Wanting to see justice enacted against the witches who'd caused havoc outside the city. Shakti wondered if they even held a shred of sympathy watching mayakari burned.

Animals, all of them.

She wandered towards the left side of the stage. Found space beneath the shade of a hora tree that hadn't been occupied by someone else. This was perfect. She hadn't expected so many trees here. The minor spirits could cause a perfect distraction. All she had to do was wait.

Suddenly, the sound of drums beating low and fast came as a shrill voice called out, 'Bow for the acting Empress!'

A shiver ricocheted down Shakti's spine as memories of blood, pain, and fervent wishes of self-annihilation compressed her thoughts, made her feel nauseous. She bowed with the crowd.

The group of soldiers who had clustered together stepped back, and Aarya sauntered past them like an unwelcome heat. She climbed up the steps to the stage – four steps, Shakti noted, not too much distance – trailed by three guards. Oddly enough, she was not in her usual elaborate dress. Instead, she had donned royal battle armour. Strapped to her side was an *urumi*, a whip sword.

An uncommon weapon for the empress to use; she had rarely deviated from a longsword back when Shakti had faced her in combat practice. Shakti could see the *urumi* being wielded in her mind's eye; shining silver, not dissimilar to the ones used against her in the cell.

Her body betrayed her by trembling of its own accord, an inbuilt response to Aarya's presence. It threatened to seize in pure terror, but Shakti pushed the feeling aside.

Aarya stopped at the centre of the stage. 'Rise, my good people,' Aarya called out and waited till they'd obeyed. She then gestured towards the three trapped, terrified mayakari. 'These witches have been accused of destroying rice crops in their village by flooding them. Using minor spirits to aid their defiance – those poor creatures – and in turn harming our production. It's as if they want us to starve.'

The crowd jeered. White-hot fury threatened to boil Shakti's intestines.

Shakti watched Aarya scan the curious faces that observed her like she was a rare jewel. For a moment, she swore the empress' gaze landed on her, but she refused to duck her head. That would only make her look suspicious in a crowd who were otherwise enraptured.

The three women in the cage didn't cry. Were they already prepared to face their deaths?

As Aarya continued her speech, Shakti saw the moment one of the soldiers unlocked the door to the cage and shepherded the three witches out one by one.

Now.

Placing her palm against the tree, Shakti whispered as quietly as she could, in spirit-speak.

'*Little spirit, please help me. Please stay quiet.*'

Her entire body was strung tight. Perhaps, this minor spirit sensed her anxiety, for a green, transparent glutinous ball-sized head poked through the trunk, and right through her palm.

Immediately, a single colour flashed in her mind's eye: grey.

'*You see the mayakari, don't you, little spirit?*' she murmured. '*Over there. Help me to help them escape. They don't deserve death.*'

The spirit cooed, softly. Another image came, of a vine strangling a rose. Its full body came through the tree trunk and it puffed out its round chest. As it did so, the row of trees around her began to tremble. Its lone chittering multiplied; the other spirits had heard it and were mimicking the same sound. The people sitting beneath the trees closer to hers started to stand in confusion. And then—

Screams erupted as the ground shook. The roots of the hora trees on either side of the grass common began to rise from the ground, in an undulating motion. Shakti watched in awe as the roots broke through the ground. It looked like they were stretching to an abnormal length. Travelling. *Spreading*. Slithering like a dozen snakes in the direction of the open-air stage. Footsteps thundered around her as people started running towards the egress, trying to find solid ground.

The leopard at the carriage startled and began to buck. Some of the soldiers rushed to try to calm it down. Others were starting to coordinate a controlled exodus under Aarya's orders. A few were quickly coming in her direction.

'She's here!' Shakti heard Aarya's harsh yell. 'Watch the exits.'

Damn it.

The minor spirits were still chattering in birdsong. The tree roots continued causing havoc. One ran right through the stage, splitting it in two. Aarya, who had been in the centre, yelled and jumped to her left, landing on her back. The root continued to undulate, separating the empress from her soldiers. Another drove straight through a group of soldiers, sending them tumbling. People tripped over them, were blocked by them, or were flung into the air by the roots that whipped around like a monkey's tail.

The three witches, hands still bound, had taken advantage of the commotion. While the soldiers were attempting to calm the agitated, roaring leopard, they'd run into the crowd. Shakti watched them meld in. Her relief only lasted for a moment. She hadn't got what she wanted yet.

Steeling herself, Shakti ran straight for the empress, daggers in hand.

CHAPTER THIRTY-NINE
Shakti

SHAKTI SPRINTED UP THE STEPS OF THE STAGE AT FULL speed.

Aarya was still walled off from her guards by the undulating hora root. They were shouting for her. It gave Shakti the perfect opportunity to tackle her.

Almost.

Shakti heard the birdsong of the minor spirits start to fade. The hora tree roots began to contract and pull back. It was as if they knew that the three mayakari had escaped. That their job was done.

'*Little spirits!*' she exclaimed. '*Please, I'm not—*'

Too late. Just as she stepped onto the stage, the root pulled back. In the blink of an eye, the partition fell away, and Shakti locked eyes with a soldier on the other side of the stage. His eyes widened. Shakti panicked.

She threw the dagger in her left hand, aimed at his throat. It didn't land accurately. Instead, the weapon lodged itself in the soldier's chest. The man screamed and tumbled to the ground.

Shakti dove straight towards Aarya. The empress reacted slower than she expected. It was only at the last moment that she turned, but it was too late.

Arms outstretched, Shakti latched her right arm around Aarya's neck while the other wrapped around her abdomen, using her entire weight to push them onto the ground. Aarya landed cheek-first with an ear-splitting yell; Shakti made sure to keep her dagger against the side of her face to avoid impaling her cheek with it.

They grappled, and Shakti used her foot to kick away Aarya's *urumi*. As far as she could tell, there were no other weapons on her. Shakti pulled herself up, dragging the other woman with her as a shield.

'Come any closer and I'll slit her throat,' Shakti called out to the soldiers who were gathering around them, holding their swords in anticipation.

'You fools!' Aarya shrieked out. '*Stop.*'

'Remove your hand from the empress' throat, witch,' a soldier ordered calmly, 'unless you want a painful death.'

'You'll kill me anyway,' Shakti retorted. 'All death is painful.'

Tightening her hold on an enraged Aarya's throat, Shakti kept her eyes firmly on the soldiers. They were all watching her carefully. Watching for an opening.

'I can shoot you where you stand,' the soldier said, bow drawn, expression twisting into an ugly sneer. 'Kill you before you can even harm the empress.'

'No,' Aarya bellowed, 'don't kill the witch.'

'But, Your Highness—'

'I said no, soldier,' Aarya bit back before she let out a hysterical laugh, 'because this snivelling rat will not kill me.'

They stilled. It turned so quiet that she could hear the faint burbling of the canal behind them. Shakti's breath hitched, and it seemed that Aarya noticed.

'I knew you would come,' Aarya murmured. A bold statement given her life was under threat. 'You can't sit idle when mayakari are brought here to be burned, not with that saviour's complex. And you want answers, don't you, about the curse? You're too predictable, Shakti.'

'Then, tell me,' Shakti hissed, clamping down on Aarya's wrists with a vengeance and repositioning the dagger in her right hand so that it rested against the delicate skin of her throat. 'What was it, you wretch? What did you ask me to curse Ashoka with? *Tell me!*'

Beneath her deadlock, Aarya stilled. 'You know it's Ashoka?'

Shakti tightened her hold on the empress' neck. 'I do. You want to kill your little brother that badly?' she hissed.

'Would never kill him . . .' Aarya choked out. '. . .won't tell you. . .'

Undeterred, Shakti pressed the dagger closer. A thin sliver of blood trickled where she had pierced the skin. The empress winced but Shakti could not find it in herself to feel guilt. Apathy drowned her in that moment. A small cut was nothing compared to what she had suffered through in the prison.

'Ashoka is still alive,' she said. 'A bastard son, but still Adil Maurya's child. If we both die here, he will be emperor. If you want to live, you will tell me what I asked.'

Shakti stumbled when Aarya kicked out forcefully with the back of her foot, but maintained her hold. No longer was her hair neatly tied. It fell in unruly clumps, sticking to her damp face. 'I'll take you back to the prison,' she muttered, each word more vengeful in tone than the last, 'and I will *break* you, mayakari. I will stand and watch you beg to die and then refuse to kill you just so that you suffer more.'

A promise spoken into existence. Shakti hoped that it would never come to fruition.

'The curse,' she repeated. 'Or did you want me to carve an ugly scar on your face to match the one on your arm?'

Vanity, of all things, seemed to frighten Aarya. 'You wouldn't dare.'

Shakti dug the tip of the blade in a little deeper. Aarya screamed. The Ran soldiers shouted and swore at her, but the upper hand was not theirs. They couldn't do anything.

'Stop – *stop* – I asked you to . . .' the empress wheezed out, 'Ashoka,' Aarya gasped as Shakti pressed tighter, trying in vain to find leverage, 'I asked you to hurt his pride . . . didn't want to kill him. . . I don't know what you said after that, mayakari – I don't – I don't understand your cursed speech . . .'

To hurt Ashoka's pride. That was the curse? No, that was what Aarya had *wanted*. It didn't mean that she'd repeated those words exactly. With cursed speech, hurting someone's pride could come in so many forms.

Aarya had given her an answer, but Shakti felt empty. She'd hoped it would jolt a long-suppressed memory, but it hadn't. The painting in her mind remained incomplete, and she was in danger. There was only one way to escape, and it was through the waterway behind her. Except, with this many soldiers, that would prove a difficult feat. She needed the nature spirits.

'*Spirits,*' she called out. '*Please help me! I need to escape.*'

She expected them to respond as they had before. Cause enough destruction that she could slip away in the chaos.

Instead, she was greeted with silence.

Shakti's stomach twisted itself into knots. *No. What's going on?*

'Whatever you're doing, witch, stop it,' Aarya remarked. 'Don't cause more destruction here. Let me go.'

Shakti wasn't listening to her. She was listening for birdsong. But there was still no answer. The little spirits weren't responding to her. Were they reluctant to? Why weren't they listening?

'Let *go*, mayakari,' Aarya snapped. 'I have had enough. End this quickly and submit to me, you stupid creature.'

Shakti's heart thundered. Escape now was difficult, if not impossible. Unless . . .

The soldier she'd killed. He was still there, face-down, blood staining his back dark.

Jaya would hate her for this, but she had no other choice.

'I'm sorry,' she whispered.

Aarya stilled. 'What?'

But Shakti paid no attention to her. Releasing a guttural breath, she cast her mind back to Harini. The day in the forest where she had raised a dead fawn, the exact words she had used. And then—

'*You who die and come alive again, halt,*' she called out. '*You who will become again, halt. Un-become.*'

Dimly, she heard Aarya's terrified gasp at her use of spirit-speak and cursed language.

Visions of death and rebirth flooded her mind. A human body burned; their bones crushed. A lotus blossoming, a foal delivered onto dry grass, covered in birthing fluid. Great Spirits forming with new land, Great Spirits dying with razed ones.

Let the dead rest, little bird.

But Shakti was too far gone, too concentrated on her task to consider respecting the newly dead.

She saw the moment it happened – when lifeless fingers twitched. When softened shoulders jerked. When the head snapped up.

The soldier rose, lifted himself up on restless fingers. Lifeless eyes and unsteady legs. A watercolour peony blossoming from his chest. The hilt of her dagger was still wedged into his chest. Unnatural, that was what he was. Freshly dead, not meant to be revived.

Shakti felt ill.

'Spirits help me,' she heard a soldier curse. Aarya quietly whispered a series of stunned expletives.

'Death magic. *Death magic!*' another one shrieked. 'Destroy the body!'

Before she could do anything, Shakti felt a gentle tremor. On instinct, she glanced towards the mountain, as did the soldiers, expecting a quake. No angry spirit could be seen or heard.

Suddenly, there came a soft, musical voice:

'Mayakari.'

There was a roaring in her ears. Startled, Shakti recognized the sound to be rushing water. Where was it—

'*The waterways.*'

A minor spirit. It had heard her pleas for help.

Shakti dragged herself and Aarya towards the back of the stage. The spirit had used words, hadn't communicated in images. It must be distressed.

In her distraction, Shakti made the mistake of loosening her grip on Aarya's hands. The empress reacted quickly, hands flying out to clamp around the arm that was still latched like a rope around her neck and dug her nails in deep. 'What are you doing, mayakari?' she asked. A twinge of fear was evident in her voice.

Shakti didn't answer. Instead, she glanced behind her quickly, towards the waterway. The sound of burbling water became louder and louder until a minor spirit appeared. It was a small creature with no eyes and an eerie human-shaped mouth.

The spirit floated up towards the stage. Fascinated, Shakti watched as it came towards her, flaccid arms touching the crown of her head.

Tidal waves. Relief. A rope frayed, broken in two.

Down below, what was once gently flowing water had turned into wild, rapid currents, foaming white. She knew what the minor spirit was about to do.

Shakti pushed Aarya away from her.

Lurching forward, the empress managed to right herself in time before turning around. Several soldiers rushed to her aid, but she halted them, instead plucking a longsword straight from one's hand. Blood stained her throat like a painted necklace.

'You'll never leave,' she snarled, raising the sword in an offensive position.

The sound of rushing water became louder and soothed Shakti's fears. She could feel it, too, cold and inviting. Glancing down at her hands, she saw that tendrils of water were winding around her legs and arms like vines around a tree.

With her use of spirit-speak and the cursed tongue abandoned, the dead soldier's body stilled, frozen in step, one arm stretched out, before thudding onto the ground. Shakti winced.

A shadow began to loom over them, that rushing sound reaching a crescendo as the minor spirit chittered happily. Horrified shouts erupted from the soldiers as they backed up a few steps, watching the wall of water rise behind her. Shakti smiled. The water coiled around her chest, kept her secured. She met Aarya's wide, horrified eyes.

'You will never find me,' she replied.

The tidal wave that loomed behind her slammed into Aarya and her soldiers just as it violently jerked Shakti into the waterway, and she was swept away from danger.

CHAPTER FORTY
Ashoka

IF WRATH HAD A HUMAN FORM, AARYA WAS IT.

She sat upon the Obsidian Throne, neck wrapped in white cloth, still in the same battle armour she'd left the palace in, speaking to Consul Rangana irritably. Ashoka eyed the dressings. He hadn't been there to see the depth of the wound Shakti had pierced his sister with, but from the lack of bleeding through the bandages, he suspected it hadn't been deep. He struggled to identify the resulting emotion as relieved or disheartened, before deciding on the latter. If only Shakti had pierced deeper with a sharper weapon, his sister would be prepared for cremation rather than still sitting on the throne.

A public burning. That was how she'd meant to draw Shakti out and recapture her. Sau's remark about mayakari being caught had been Aarya's doing.

He stood at the base of the steps, Rahil behind him. Aarya had called for an emergency meeting a few hours after the physicians finished attending to her wound.

'I can't believe she managed to escape me,' Aarya raged.

'Your Highness,' Consul Rangana beseeched, 'this must end. Find and kill the mayakari. The longer she stays alive, the more risk your people are put in. We were lucky there were only minor casualties.'

Palming her face, Aarya let out a low growl. Ashoka hadn't seen her this incensed in some time. 'I know that Rangana. The question is how I can contain her,' he heard her mutter.

'We can issue a stricter lockdown, Your Highness,' the consul suggested. 'It won't be met well, but if the mayakari is to be apprehended—'

'No,' his sister interrupted. 'I won't impose any more regulations. The mayakari has had ample opportunity to escape the city and she hasn't.'

'Why do you think so, Your Highness?' another consul inquired.

Because Shakti wanted answers.

He knew it. Aarya knew it, too, but Ashoka also knew she wouldn't admit to it.

'I'm not sure,' Aarya said, 'but I've hazarded a few guesses as to where she'd go. Double the bounty. Send patrols out to the southern forestlands and the Mountain of Rebirth by morning. She won't leave the city. I'm sure of it.'

The back of Ashoka's neck prickled. She'd narrowed down the forestlands. This wasn't good. The forests to the south were the closest to the homes in the city's outskirts. It left Shakti at higher risk of being discovered. When Aarya shot an infuriated look his way, Ashoka composed himself in a blink.

'Your initial plan to send Shakti to the Mountain of Rebirth has left us in a bind, little brother,' she said.

'Shakti was more cunning,' Ashoka shrugged. 'That's not my fault.'

Aarya narrowed her eyes and opened her mouth, likely to harangue him to no end, but seemed to think better of it. Instead, she turned on the physician and the consul.

'All those present – leave us,' she ordered, her voice creating echoes throughout the throne room. 'Thank you, Lata. Consul Rangana, I will heed your advice. Ashoka, stay where you are.'

The consul seemed taken aback but nodded and bowed alongside the physician before leaving. Once the throne room had emptied out, Aarya motioned for him to come up the steps to where she sat. 'Stay where you are, Rahil,' she ordered when Rahil made to follow behind him, 'be a good dog.'

Ashoka's body tensed. 'Speak to Rahil that way and I'll kill you.'

He said it without a stutter and without fear. Delivered in a cold, detached address, Ashoka knew whom he sounded like, and from the way Aarya reared back in surprise, it appeared that she did, too.

'Watch your tongue, *musī*,' she warned. 'Or else—'

'Or else what?' he challenged her. 'You'll kill me like you tried with Arush?'

You've already cursed me. Why don't you kill me, was what he left unsaid.

'I told you that I wasn't going to kill him,' Aarya seethed, 'and I won't kill you.'

'Why not?' he mocked. 'I'm a mayakari's son.'

'*Not even you*, though you are making an excellent case for it,' his sister snapped, clearly losing patience. 'Despite what you think of me, I won't kill family.'

'So unlike Father,' he replied nastily. 'Congratulations, sister.'

Muttering an unintelligible expletive under her breath, Aarya pointed to her throat. 'Give me one reason to think you value our family, then,' she said. 'Convince me that you have even one shred of loyalty. Tell me where Shakti is.'

'How many times do I have to tell you? *I don't know.*'

Letting out a low, frustrated scream, Aarya reached up, grabbed on to his burned ear and tugged down forcefully. He heard Rahil shout furiously behind him. Ashoka couldn't help the pitiful yelp that escaped his lips but reacted quickly. Clamping down on his sister's arm with both hands, he held it steady to keep her from moving.

'Liar,' Aarya whispered. 'I need her, so tell me *where*, Ashoka.'

Before he could respond the doors to the throne room opened behind them with a loud groan. Aarya sighed, letting go of his ear and craning her neck to the side.

'Did I not make it explicitly clear that no one—'

'Little sister, the throne does not suit you.'

Ashoka stilled. *Was that*—

'Arush?' Aarya's voice had turned wooden, viscerally stunned. 'You're – you're awake.'

Ashoka turned. His older brother stalked towards them, their mother following just behind. There was a stiffness to Arush's gait after being bed-bound for so long. Aarya remained unmoving as she watched him approach. Ashoka was briefly reminded of a raven perched atop a branch, observing the landscape around it as if it owned every inch of it.

It had worked. Shakti had woken him up. Thank the spirits.

'A miracle. I don't quite understand it myself, but I went from darkness, to drifting in and out of consciousness, to waking up and giving Mother a fright,' said Arush. 'But that doesn't matter, does it?'

'No,' Aarya replied stiffly. 'It doesn't. At least you're . . . alive.'

'I'm glad you're awake, brother,' Ashoka remarked.

Shooting him a funny look, Arush raised an eyebrow. 'I see,' he said, before turning to Aarya. 'Did you visit me at all, little sister? Or were you too preoccupied on that throne?'

'As you no doubt know, when one is given an empire to rule, time becomes sacred,' Aarya retorted.

'Given?' Arush echoed with false innocence. 'Do you mean when one has *taken*?'

A loud silence followed, his brother and sister eyeing each other cautiously. Rubbing his sore ear, Ashoka observed their struggle, thrilled. Arguments between his elder siblings weren't uncommon. When they did occur, it was delightful to watch their father's two favoured offspring puff up their chests and try to assert dominance.

Humming sympathetically, Arush took another step up. 'Mother told me quite a lot after I awoke,' he said, canines glinting like a leopard's when he smiled. 'Apparently, you've spent much of your energy on chasing a mayakari who has caused you a great deal of embarrassment. A *witch* of all people landing a blow on you. Are you weaker than a supposed pacifist, sister?'

'Hah,' Aarya laughed. 'Weren't you told the reason why I'm hunting her, brother? That witch put a curse on our father. *She* is the reason he is dead. She was the one that stole into the palace and attempted to harm us. Forgive me for not only putting our family's safety, but also the safety of our people, against a monster first. Unlike you.'

Ashoka fought a grin. If anyone could reprimand and humble Arush, it was Aarya. In fact, it was one of the few traits of hers he begrudgingly admired.

'Now she's on the loose,' Aarya continued. 'She was going to hurt our soldiers. Hurt me. She raised a *dead body* in front of us, one of our men she had killed in the fight. The corpse was left behind, but I had it burned immediately.'

'I don't understand,' Arush frowned. He looked unsettled by the notion of a dead man rising. 'How did she escape the first time?'

Aarya quickly summarized the ordeal. Ashoka noted with some annoyance that she painted it in a way that placed part of the blame on him. In this scenario, she was the benevolent empress allowing her inexperienced little brother some independence. However, he had to bear through it.

To his surprise, Arush didn't mock him for Shakti's escape. Instead, his older brother redirected blame.

'Let's not blame Ashoka for this, sister,' he said loudly, the beginnings of a smirk upon his lips. 'As empress, you must shoulder the responsibility of your people. That includes family.'

They were two leopards fighting for dominance, one gifted with agility, the other with sheer brute strength. Cunning was a given, though the one with the least amount of it attempted to maintain control.

'An earthquake, a dangerous mayakari on the loose, hopeless quests to explore deadlands . . . you have attempted much in my absence, sister,' Arush continued, 'but I worry about where this is leading us. Hence—'

In an instant, Aarya sat up straighter, a clear warning in her eyes. 'Now is not the time, Arush,' she said.

Ashoka stayed silent. There was no need for him to interfere. Let his siblings create chaos without his help.

'On the contrary, I think this is rather a perfect time,' Arush said. 'While you have performed . . . adequately during my illness, I'm here now. There's no need for you.'

Aarya's tone promised death. 'Excuse me?'

'You were nothing but a placeholder,' Arush retorted cruelly. 'You told me your time these days is limited, so let me take that burden from you. How unfortunate – there won't be a coronation for you after all, sister.'

CHAPTER FORTY-ONE
Ashoka

A THUNDEROUS, UNEASY SILENCE FOLLOWED ARUSH'S proclamation.

Glancing at Aarya, Ashoka noted that his sister held a white-knuckled grip on the armrest. *Good.* Now came the fight.

'No,' she told the silent room. Her voice wavered, but her eyes were hard and flinty.

Ashoka raised his brows. That wasn't Aarya's decision to make. An acting regent was not the true monarch. By law, she had to vacate the position since Arush was now awake and well.

Unlike him, Arush didn't seem surprised. It was almost as if he expected it. 'This isn't a choice, Aarya,' he replied. 'I am the firstborn.'

'No,' his sister stressed again, voice strung tight.

'Aarya,' their mother began, disapproval clear in her voice, 'your brother is awake. He is well. This isn't the time for you to be a child.'

'I'm not being a child,' his sister snapped. The comment seemed to have infuriated her. 'I won't have Arush return to his foolish plans again. We just had our soldiers returned from the Frozen Lands. Do you know how many weapons were lost to the snow? How many bodies because they were ill-prepared? He doesn't *care*, Mother. I do. I am the only one truly committed to Father's cause.'

Arush scoffed. 'And you're so for the people?' he shot back.

'The way towards expansion is south, not north,' Aarya replied. 'Besides, I've had enough reports coming back from Mahvo to justify us entering the state's borders.'

At this, Arush seemed to falter. 'What are you talking about?' he asked.

Aarya smiled, but it wasn't kind. 'You've missed quite a lot in your sleep, brother. Our military weapons are being illegally transported there. Possibly to be used against us. My guess is that this began under your watch. Given your preoccupation with the Frozen Lands, I can see how you could have missed such a glaring problem.'

Arush seemed to regain his composure and glared. 'Then I will familiarize myself with this new situation,' he said. 'It is as you say – I was asleep.'

'But, Aarya,' Ashoka jumped in, wanting to create more animosity, 'they've negotiated a defence treaty with Kalinga. The moment you step across the border they'll declare war. One kingdom and one state against you.'

Aarya scoffed. 'The Kalingan queen made a foolish choice,' she said. 'If this were a naval battle, I'd be more cautious, but they have no power over us on land, little brother. I can seize Mahvo by force, with or without Prince Ryu's help. It's what Father would've done.'

'*You?*' Arush asked. 'Sister, is that madness of yours still present? The throne is not yours. It's mine. Now stand up.'

The two glared at each other in a silent show of force, but the battle was useless. Aarya had no leg to stand on. As long as Arush remained alive, she had no authority.

'Wishing the dose of your poison had been higher?' Arush mocked, lips curling into a snarl. 'Get *up*.'

He, Arush, and their mother formed an imposing wall around Aarya. His sister was backed into a corner she had no way of fighting out of. The mention of poison caused her to visibly flinch, but there was no trace of regret to be seen. And, as always when trapped, Aarya attacked the one person in their family she thought was the easiest to hurt.

'Oh, don't look at me like that, Mother,' Aarya bit back. 'You've never been happy with anything I've done.'

'How would you like me to look after learning that my own daughter poisoned her brother?' their mother replied, tone deathly calm. She'd been watching Aarya with disappointment and revulsion; a rare combination. Ashoka had only seen disappointment once, and it was when she brought up Kosala's death. 'Not proud, I hope? Even Adil would be disgusted by your behaviour.'

Aarya's left eye twitched. Any mention of their father viewing her in a light other than positive was unfathomable, and it was evident in the way she ground out, 'How would you know? He never respected you. He didn't respect you enough to be *faithful* to you. He fucked a witch and fathered a half—'

A harsh slap rung in the festering quiet that followed.

Aarya clutched her left cheek in shock. Their mother had slapped her. Ashoka drew in a sharp breath, and by coincidence, he and Arush locked eyes. His older brother's mouth hung open.

Retracting her hand, their mother let out a harsh exhale. Her usually warm eyes were filled with fire.

'Do not disrespect your aunt or your brother,' she said. 'Do *not* continue to protest when your attempts are futile. An acting regent is a temporary position, Aarya. Remove yourself at once.'

For a moment, Ashoka thought his sister would refuse. Thought that she would raise her hand against their mother in retaliation. Upon closer inspection, her eyes had taken on a glazed appearance. Tears, but Aarya's pride would never allow them to fall. That was weakness. That was what their father had taught them.

Jaw set, Aarya stood and gave way for Arush to take his seat upon the throne.

'Good,' said his older brother, smiling. 'You know your place. Now, if you will – the circlet.'

Aarya didn't reply, instead removing the royal circlet from her head stiffly and presenting it to Arush. Looking pleased, their brother placed it atop his head, as Aarya moved to stand beside Ashoka, hands clenched into tight fists. He could almost feel her rage and humiliation as if it were his own.

Now who's the muzzled leopard, he wanted to say.

Larger and more muscular than their father, Arush cast a far more intimidating figure by size alone. Yet, there was something missing. Hairs didn't prickle at the back of Ashoka's neck like they did around Aarya, or their father. That was, he supposed, a good thing.

'Right,' Arush remarked, palming the armrest of the throne. 'I need to get some affairs in order.'

'Like what?' Aarya replied brusquely. 'Return our soldiers to the Frozen Lands?'

Arush snorted. 'After your meddling, it'd look disorganized on our part if I were to redirect. Besides, Mahvo won't get away with importing our weapons illegally. It makes us look weak,' he said. 'My affairs, sister, include your punishment for poisoning me.'

Good. Ashoka perked up with interest. Retaliation was what he expected from Arush, he just wasn't sure what form it would take. Something enough to keep Aarya at bay.

'Go on,' Aarya replied with no trace of emotion. Did she expect a slap on the wrist and nothing more?

'Your position in the war council will, at present, be revoked,' Arush replied instantly. Aarya made a sound of protest but was silenced. 'And you will be confined to your quarters for the immediate future. What – were you expecting me to burn a body part of yours, like Father did with Ashoka?'

Judging from Aarya's expression, she would've preferred it. Losing power was a far greater punishment for his sister than losing a body part, vanity be damned.

'The consuls will wonder why, brother,' Ashoka added, earning a suspicious look from Aarya.

'The consuls will wonder why I ordered the princess who carved the endless knot into her own arm to be confined? Unlikely,' Arush remarked, raising an eyebrow. 'Don't think you'll be getting away without a scratch, either, brother.'

'I beg your pardon?' Ashoka asked.

'You're a bastard child,' Arush continued. 'Of a *mayakari*, no less. Father's mistake. That promise we made so many moons ago? I cannot uphold it. A witch's son cannot govern Taksila. A witch's son cannot lead the war council. A witch's son will not be recognized by the rules of succession. You will be confined to the palace. Remain in the shadows, just like Aarya.'

CHAPTER FORTY-TWO
Ashoka

'Confining me to the palace? How dare he – ouch!'

'Oh, for spirits' sake, sit still will you?'

Sitting atop a wooden crate in the stuffy armoury adjacent to the training grounds, Ashoka winced as Rahil rubbed alcohol against his arm and shifted uncomfortably yet again. The midday sun streamed through the open window to his left, and he grimaced, shielding his eyes from the light. 'It stings.'

Rahil, who was dousing a clean cloth with more sterile solution, snorted. 'Stop fussing.'

Shooting him a doleful glare, Ashoka pointed to the underside of his forearm. Two deep lacerations marked the skin there. 'You cut me.'

'I had no idea this could happen while we were using weapons to spar,' Rahil replied in deadpan. 'Truly such an unexpected outcome.'

'Oh, be quiet.'

'You were distracted,' Rahil added, ignoring his petulance.

That Ashoka couldn't dispute. After Arush had commanded him and Aarya to be confined to the palace indefinitely, shock had kept him awake the entire day and into the night. The next morning, however, fury replaced it.

Part of him had expected it. There was no chance that Arush would let his illegitimacy go. The other, more idealistic part of himself – the part he was coming to hate – had hoped his own brother would provide him with some deference.

Needing to release the energy building up inside him, Ashoka asked Rahil to partake in mock combat. The last time they'd done so was painfully memorable, back in Taksila. At least, this time, Ashoka knew he wouldn't leave the fight broken-hearted.

As Rahil's hands carefully ghosted along his, Ashoka felt his own heart thumping in an erratic manner. A seasoned physician would check his pulse and deduce the cause to be anxiety.

Rahil was right: his response was disproportional to the extent of his injury. If Ashoka was being more honest with himself, he was playing it up. It made Rahil look at him with more concern. The rest of the world didn't matter. All that attention was on him. Pathetic, he knew. He was a lovesick young man struggling to find his words.

Quietly, he noted Rahil's dark, silky head bent in concentration as he covered the wound with a soft white cloth, strands of hair coming loose from his topknot. The distinct lack of jewellery because he considered it a distraction, a hindrance. The smooth brown skin, the handsome and sharp features so royal-like. His beauty was like that of a sunrise; it induced the observer into an appreciative silence.

'Ashoka.'

He startled. Rahil was staring at him now, finished with his treatment. Ashoka was quick to realize he'd been staring, albeit absentmindedly. 'Yes?'

'You're staring.'

'Am I not allowed to?'

Rahil cleared his throat, the beginnings of a pale flush creeping up his neck. 'Erm, I suppose not,' he muttered. 'No, I mean – you are.'

'Stuttering in my presence?' Ashoka smiled. 'How unlike you.'

Rolling his eyes, Rahil held out his hand, expression fond. 'Confident, are we?' he replied. 'I could very easily reject you. Hurt that princely pride.'

'But you didn't.'

For a brief moment, Rahil stilled. An inscrutable look crossed his face as his outstretched hand faltered a little. 'I didn't,' he agreed.

Ashoka took his hand, but the sudden shift in Rahil's posture made him frown. 'Did I say something wrong?'

'No,' said Rahil, running his free hand through his hair. His grip tightened, then relaxed. 'You didn't.'

Ashoka hummed noncommittally. Glancing at a pair of polished, gleaming longswords that hung on a wall mount, he imagined them pulsing blue. Cursed weapons to take into his hands and cause irreparable harm. Hopefully the resistance in Taksila had created a considerable stockpile in his absence.

'We can't stay here,' he told Rahil, using his hand to pull himself off the crate. 'Confinement. *Hah*. I need to return to Taksila immediately.'

From the continued correspondence Sau received from Sachith in Taksila, Queen Kalyani had a second contingent of soldiers sail to Mahvo's seaport that were slowly making their way to the border. The easiest way for them to travel inward was to use the Samnal River, which would take about four days.

Aarya had seemed more than ready to give the order to cross into Mahvo. Without her, the decision now rested on Arush. Like it or not, Arush's hand would be forced. He'd need to act on Mahvo. As such, it made little sense for Ashoka to remain here.

He needed to travel back to Taksila, and from there, the border between the Ran Empire and the Kingdom of Mahvo.

'All right,' Rahil said, nodding slowly. 'When?'

'Tonight.'

Perturbed, Rahil took a step back. 'Tonight?' he repeated. 'That's rather sudden. You can't just up and leave the palace. There'll be guards about.'

'Which is why I thought ahead,' Ashoka replied, tapping the side of his temple. 'Four of us need to leave the capital: you, me, Sau and Shakti. I've sent Sau to the city, and she'll be able to find Shakti and take her to the southern forestland. No one will suspect my advisor; she travels back and forth often. You and I will sneak out into the serpent pens and fly Sahry to the southern forests, and we'll make our way to Taksila from there.'

Biting his lip, Rahil pondered over his proposition for a long time. In fact, it was so long, and with no interruption, that Ashoka began to wonder if he'd made a mistake. However, his fears were soothed when Rahil let out an oddly placid, 'All right. Tonight.'

'Good,' Ashoka replied. 'Be ready.'

CHAPTER FORTY-THREE
Shakti

Misfortune was favouring her today.

After yesterday's debacle, the minor spirit washed her away to a secluded underground canal. If the creature had done it on purpose, she was thankful. However, Shakti had been forced to spend the night there, bleeding and exhausted for fear of being found. Getting to Ruchira's required cutting through a bustling marketplace, in which there was an increased presence of soldiers. She would've been too conspicuous if she'd left as she was, sopping wet from head to toe.

The following morning, after a sleepless night, but thankfully dry, Shakti made her way back to Ruchira's, keeping her head low.

Head down, she told herself as she made a hurried, wide berth around a pair of soldiers. *Head down. Don't interact. Don't interact.*

'You there – stop.'

Stiffening, Shakti continued to move forward. The crowd around her also responded to the loud call, some startling in confusion, some stopping in their tracks, but they were otherwise unruffled. Most of them didn't have anything to fear, after all.

Tightening the cloak around herself, Shakti quickened her pace.

'You! In the brown cloak – stop walking at once!'

Oh no.

Sparing a quick glance over her shoulder, Shakti spotted the familiar outline of red and black armour. *Soldiers.*

Attention was being drawn towards her now. If she didn't act soon, it would be harder to make an escape.

Run, little bird.

Shakti broke into a run.

Feet thumped furiously behind her. Calls for her to stop continued. The amount of people made it difficult for her to run straight, slowed her down. She was just running past a stall selling kitchen wares when suddenly someone grabbed her left arm from behind. Gasping, Shakti turned her head.

One of the soldiers had caught up. She gripped Shakti's left arm like a vice in one hand and held a dagger in the other. When they locked eyes, the soldier's eyes widened.

'It's you,' she said.

Shakti kicked out, catching the soldier by surprise, but not before she swung her dagger and sliced through Shakti's left arm. Acute pain blinded her vision.

'You won't get away, witch,' the soldier spat, twisting Shakti's injured arm. Shakti screamed, and pulled frantically, looking for something, anything to – *ah.*

With her free hand, she reached out towards the vendor's stand. She grabbed a clay pot and smashed it on the side of the soldier's head. Roaring, the soldier jumped back, clutching her head in pain. Shakti took the opportunity and bolted.

Bumping into shoulders and roughly pushing past bodies, she turned right towards the busier area of the market where stalls lined both sides of the street. Immediately, she noted that she was one of the few people that wore a cloak. Shrugging off her cloak, she discarded it by the side of a fruit vendor's stall. Ignoring the looks of surprise sent her way, she ducked past the stand and into the alleyway behind it.

She could still hear the soldiers' voices. Heart beating fast, she didn't stop to glance back. The laneway was narrow, with patches of green grass and earth, and dirty water puddling on the ground, thrown from the windows above her.

She didn't stop running, even when her legs began to tire, not until she reached the familiar streets that led to Ruchira's home.

No soldiers here. Good.

Stifling a groan, she hurried inside, clutching her injured arm. When the door slammed shut, she let out a deep sigh of relief and dropped to the floor, back against the wall. She chanced a look at her left arm, right palm smeared with blood when she moved it away. It looked like a nasty cut.

Just as she was about to wander into the kitchen, a sharp knock came from outside.

Shakti stopped breathing entirely. The knocks continued, more insistent this time.

'Hello?' It was a woman's voice, and a familiar one. She released a pent-up breath and stood up. Spirits, she was starting to feel woozy.

Shakti threw the door open to find Saudamini, her hand raised mid-knock.

'Oh. Shakti,' she greeted politely, 'good, you're still here, I came to get you—'

Her initial relieved expression gave way to one of horror as she saw Shakti's wounded arm. Before Shakti could say anything, the advisor was pushing her back inside the house and had closed the door behind them.

'Spirits, what *happened* to you?'

'Ran into some soldiers,' she summarized as Saudamini inspected the wound by lifting away the torn scrap of cotton over her arm.

'You just had to follow one rule,' the advisor replied, clucking at her wound in disapproval. 'This looks nasty.'

Shakti tried to bat her arm away, but Saudamini held on to her with a tight grip. 'Saudamini, why are you here?' she asked.

'Ashoka sent me to get you. Arush is awake and has ordered both Ashoka and Aarya to be confined to the palace. Ashoka wants to escape on Sahry to Taksila tonight. We need to get to the southern forestland and meet him and Rahil there,' Saudamini said, her tone reproachful. 'How could you be so foolish as to leave the house?'

Just then, she sounded like Jaya.

That irked Shakti more than she thought it would, possibly because it was true. 'My foolishness saved three mayakari,' she hissed. 'That worked out quite well in the end. Do you know why innocent witches die? Because even good people often don't make the hard decisions needed to try and save them.'

'A hard decision but not a *good* decision, Shakti.' The advisor's face was grim. 'The one you made was reckless. You could've been recaptured. Ruined our plan.'

Swearing under her breath, Shakti turned away. Saudamini followed her into the kitchen.

'Sit down,' she ordered, patting a chair near the small dining table as she made for the cupboards. 'Let's patch that wound up.'

Still smarting over her previous comment, Shakti sat herself down with a huff as Saudamini began to rummage through the contents. For a while, the silence was filled by the soft clinking of cups, the rattling of dinner plates and the soft scraping of clay pots.

'I didn't mean to berate you,' Saudamini remarked, her back to her. 'It's just that I don't think Ashoka wants to lose another friend.'

'You really do sound like my aunt.'

Saudamini turned to retort but stopped and instead squinted at her arm. 'Am I hallucinating or is your wound bleeding more than it did before?'

Shakti glanced down. Indeed, it was.

'Here.' Before she could blink, a clean rag was tossed in her direction. 'Use this.'

While Shakti kept pressure against her arm, Saudamini flitted around the kitchen anxiously. 'Suturing kit,' the advisor was saying to herself, 'suturing kit. Where is it? Doesn't Ruchira keep one around?'

Pressing the cloth tighter against her wound, Shakti asked, 'Can you suture?'

'I'm not a physician, but I can sew. I assume similar rules apply.'

If she wasn't in pain, Shakti would have laughed. She shifted, the movement causing the wound to be disturbed, and she let out a pained groan.

'Your wound needs to be tended to,' Saudamini said, a panicked dint appearing between her brows. 'Would her neighbours have anything of use?'

'I wouldn't know because I've never met them. But be my guest,' Shakti rasped, pointing to the advisor's blouse that was now stained red, 'ask them and watch soldiers eventually find their way here instead.'

'I'm sorry, would you rather I take you to a physician in the city?' Sau admonished. 'Code of no harm aside, they will report you immediately to the authorities, and I have no time to guess which of them are sympathetic to witches.'

Wincing, Shakti pointed Saudamini in the direction of Ruchira's room. 'None in the kitchen but there might be some spares in her room,' she said. 'There's a yellow salve on that shelf below. Helps ease the sting.'

Swearing in a language Shakti didn't recognize, the advisor raced towards the cook's room. For a moment, there was the soft sound of drawers being opened and slammed shut, sheets rustling and metal clinking, before she rushed back out, kit in hand, and a glass bottle of yellow salve.

Sitting down on one of the seat cushions around the low dining table, Shakti placed her arm out on the cool wooden surface. Saudamini hurried to kneel in front of her and began to rub alcohol over the skin. That stung horribly. Afterward, she lathered the yellow salve onto the wound. A pleasant tingling sensation followed.

'This might still hurt,' Saudamini warned.

Shakti nodded, and before long was gritting and whimpering her way through the process. It wasn't horrible, but whenever the advisor pierced too deep, a sharp pain followed. Saudamini's hands remained relatively stable, but Shakti could see a slight tremble here and there. When she was finally done, the advisor leaned back to observe her handiwork.

'Looks acceptable to me,' she said, tying a fresh bandage around the site.

Inspecting the area, Shakti found no fault, either. 'Thank you,' she said.

'You're welcome,' Saudamini replied, before hesitating. 'Listen.

You've got a hero's heart, which is admirable. I wish I had one. But you don't think before jumping into action. Like it or not, you've become valuable. Losing your life will be costly.'

'I can't change who I am,' Shakti returned stubbornly.

At that, the advisor cracked a smile. 'Is a mayakari telling me that she's unchanging?'

Shakti snorted. Saudamini had her there. 'My aunt really would've liked you,' she remarked. 'So, what do we do now?'

They both stood and glanced through the dusty window. Outside, it was getting to mid-afternoon. The sky was a bright blue, and people still wandered the streets. An elderly man across from Ruchira's home sat in front of his house and shelled king coconuts.

'We wait here till nightfall,' Saudamini said firmly. 'Little to no movements, if possible, inside the house. We make our way to the southern forestland then.'

Shakti was about to voice her assent when a sudden shiver ran down her spine. The hairs on her arms rose as if in anticipation of a chill, a sudden attack. She let out a deep, shuddering breath.

'Shakti?' Sau asked, appearing concerned. 'What's wrong.'

Images of death flooded her mind. A hunter being eaten alive by wild leopards, until there was nothing but thin strips of muscle hanging onto bone. Poison from a winged serpent's fangs travelling through the blood, paralysing and killing within minutes. A mayakari, burning blue in the pitch black.

Just as they came, the afterimages disappeared. They startled Shakti enough that it took her a moment to understand what happened.

'No,' she whispered, realization dawning. 'My curse.'

'What about it?' Saudamini inquired.

Closing her trembling fingers into a tight fist, Shakti caught the advisor's eye. 'I saw death,' she said, panicked. 'I think my curse on Ashoka has enacted.'

CHAPTER FORTY-FOUR
Ashoka

Night fell, and Ashoka sat on his bed, waiting for Rahil.

A gentle breeze blew in from his balcony, rustling the gossamer curtains as it did so. The smell of fragrant bath oils and incense still lingered in the air. On his deep red carpet remained a series of wet footprints after he'd left the bath. Lanternlights dotted the four walls and cast long shadows on the floor. Upon the balcony rails, flowering vines grew. They'd spread since he'd left for Taksila, and it seemed that no one had bothered to prune them.

Right foot jiggling restlessly, Ashoka absentmindedly patted the scabbard that housed his cursed dagger, Dukkha. Its pair, Sukha, lay in his travelling satchel underneath the bed.

He huffed impatiently. Where was Rahil? After their mock combat training, he'd come and gone intermittently. The last time he'd seen him was just past dinnertime, when Rahil had left to go to the armoury.

Sneaking out through his door wasn't a good option. There were other guards stationed outside. Ashoka had then decided to make use of his balcony. Jumping from it was a death sentence, since his quarters were three levels up. A thick rope would be more than sufficient to lower themselves down on, and he had one tied firmly to one of the posts, waiting to be used.

Where is he, Ashoka wondered, impatience growing.

Another half hour later, there was still no Rahil. Thinking that he might already be down in the serpent pens, Ashoka decided to act. There was no more time to waste; Sau and Shakti were waiting. Slinging his satchel across his shoulders, Ashoka made his way towards the open-air balcony. Crickets chirped loudly. The night brought out fireflies, their lights flickering in the vast stretch of forestland to the north.

Testing the rope's strength by tugging on it, Ashoka slung it over the balcony. Keeping a tight grip on the rope, he hoisted himself over the railing and climbed down. At some points, the rope burned his palms where he'd gripped too hard. He landed on the ground with a soft thud and straightened up. To get to the serpent pens, he'd have to take a crosscut through the courtyard that housed five of the palace's thirteen jade pools to the east.

'Where are you, Rahil?' he muttered to himself, and hurried in the direction of the jade pools. The stars were bright tonight. They reminded him of the sea glimmer in Kalinga, albeit dimmer and yellower. His footsteps were light as he darted down the high-ceilinged corridors and eventually arrived at the open courtyard with the five jade pools. Four circular pools were arranged in a diamond shape while the central pool was long and rectangular. On the far side, he could see the training grounds, armoury, and further in the distance – the serpent pens. There was a lanternlight visible there. *Rahil's?*

Ready to sprint across the courtyard, Ashoka paused when he heard footfalls behind him. For a moment, his mind went straight to Rahil, before realizing these steps were too heavy and too slow to be his.

'Going somewhere, little brother?'

Ashoka stopped in his tracks. Arush materialized like an apparition from behind a thick pillar, arms crossed. Alone.

What was he doing here?

'To check on Sahry,' he replied nonchalantly, walking out onto the courtyard.

'This late?' Arush commented, mimicking his tone and following him. 'What's in the satchel?'

'A salve. She's being temperamental.' Their repartee was too quick. The tension was too high. Instinct told him that Arush knew. Knew what he was doing and where he was going. He stopped next to one of the rectangular pools. 'You know how she gets.'

Halting as well, Arush hummed, but it didn't sound like he believed him. Here was a leopard approaching its prey, except it didn't feel like one who was tamed. This was a wild one, cursed by a witch's tongue. 'I'm afraid you won't find Sahry in her pen,' he said, in a manner that was far too casual.

'Right,' Ashoka scoffed. She was kept tied in her pen for much of the day. 'Where is she, then?'

'Out flying somewhere,' Arush shrugged, 'she's probably out in the northern forests. It's far easier to release an animal than shackle one, little brother.'

Arush was bluffing. He had to be. Who would dare . . .

'Fine. I'll wait for her to return,' Ashoka replied. 'She can sense me. I'll see to her then.'

Arush's pearly white teeth gleamed in the night. '*Mūsī* can lie, but not well enough,' he said.

Ashoka reared back. The pet name was foreign on his brother's tongue. 'You don't call me *mūsī*,' he said.

'I don't,' Arush agreed. '*Little mouse?* It's not appropriate. You're more like a rat scurrying in the sewage canals.'

A tame insult, even for Arush. 'Your words don't carry much weight,' he fired back. 'If I'm a rat, you're a pathetic worm with nothing to offer. But that's insulting to worms, isn't it? They're important. You're not.'

Arush could never hold his temper, and he unleashed it by ramming his fist against the pillar. When he retracted his hand, the stone was speckled with blood.

'Let's not play games, Ashoka,' Arush growled. 'I know where you were planning to escape to. Aarya told me.'

'*Aarya* did?' Ashoka echoed, stupefied. How would she know? Ever since she'd been placed under confinement, he hadn't seen or spoken to her. 'How?'

Sahry.

'You were going to Taksila?' Arush continued, clearly not having heard him. 'For what purpose? Govern, so you can taste power? You can't. Not when you're a bastard.'

'I am still our father's son,' Ashoka replied stiffly. He couldn't begin to understand why he was using their father's name to prove himself worthy. Perhaps because it was the only kind of power his siblings accepted and understood. 'He knew what I was and still ordered me there, I—'

'Forget the fucking will,' Arush snapped. 'You will stay here, Ashoka. I won't throw you out to the dogs, but you can't hold power. Accept that or suffer the consequences.'

'No.'

'This is my empire, little brother,' Arush warned him, 'as much as you'd like to hope otherwise. Return to your quarters or face my wrath.'

Ashoka laughed. It seemed to surprise Arush. 'What wrath?' he jeered.

His older brother's face schooled itself into a deathly mask. 'Aarya may poison,' he said, 'but I will fight. Break you, if I must. Last chance, *mūsī*.'

Spirits, he was tired. Tired of family politics. Tired of being strung about by his siblings.

Arush was observing him like he was nothing but a pest. An insect easily crushed beneath the heel of his foot. He was likely expecting Ashoka to grit his teeth but surrender anyway. He'd been so easy to read. That was the problem with pacifism: it came with a tendency to adopt diplomacy. And part of being diplomatic was to compromise. Those who went on the offensive tended not to do that, or if they did, it was a rare occurrence. There was no compromising to be made here. What else could he possibly do?

From the utter recesses of his mind, his inner voice answered. *Fight.*

Slowly, calmly, Ashoka shrugged off his satchel. Set it down on the ground and approached Arush languidly.

His older brother watched him curiously. 'What are you doing, Ashoka?' he asked.

At some point, when faced with an insistent sibling, it was natural to regress. To revert to a childish nature and settle arguments with fists instead of words. This was just about the most foolish act he could perform. 'What you wanted,' Ashoka replied. Before his brother could even move, Ashoka pounced and tackled him to the ground.

A surprised yell escaped Arush's lips before Ashoka sensed him adapt quickly to the situation. As his brother landed back first, his arms clamped around Ashoka's own back, squeezing with wheeze-inducing force.

Blood roared in Ashoka's ears as he wriggled his arm out of Arush's crushing hold, managing to hit his upper chest, elbow first. Momentarily winded, Arush loosened his grip, allowing Ashoka to scramble out of the hold, kicking at him along the way.

Just as he managed to stand himself up, Arush, still on the ground, lunged forward, latching onto his ankle, and tugging hard enough that he fell again. Ashoka landed on his side painfully before Arush clambered on top of him, the weight crushing, and aimed a punch directly at his abdomen.

'Think you can start a fight with me, little brother?' Arush growled. 'Think you can win? You pathetic little *runt*.'

Another vicious punch towards his gut. Ashoka let out a violent cough, sure his internal organs had been pulverized during that first blow. He twisted, an eel caught in a fisherman's net, using all his strength to jostle Arush off him and retreat backward.

From his scabbard, Arush drew out a weapon – his *kastane*. For a split second, Ashoka faltered. His brother had drawn a weapon. Against *him*. Words of assault, he expected. A threatening glare here and there, a tussle; that was unavoidable. But this was altogether unfamiliar and yet—

How had it taken them this long to fight with weapons?

His hands hovered over Dukkha, unsure. Who was he to harm his own kin, and with a cursed weapon, no less?

Why make a distinction when it comes to blood? the voice in his head inquired. There was genuine curiosity in that damned inner voice of his. *Look at Arush. When it comes to it, he will not hesitate, so why do you?*

Why indeed. What did he owe his brother? *Nothing*. Not loyalty, not understanding – nothing. Arush was simply an obstacle to the throne that required clearing.

He had two cursed weapons. Two siblings. Why not use one. Aarya might not want to kill family, but Ashoka had no misgivings about it. Dukkha called to him, pleading to be used.

Just as Ashoka began to pull out the cursed dagger, a frantic voice rang across the courtyard:

'*Children, stop this at once!*'

CHAPTER FORTY-FIVE
Ashoka

Both startled at the sound of their mother's yell. Ashoka glanced past Arush's shoulder, towards the palace, and spotted her running towards them, a group of soldiers close behind. Each wore looks of utter bafflement as they followed.

Onlookers. *Brilliant. Where on earth was Rahil?* This wasn't what he wanted. Neither, it seemed, did his brother.

'Mother, calm yourself, please,' Arush began. 'Ashoka and I were simply—'

'Do *not* tell me to calm down,' their mother replied, her voice deathly calm, 'when the both of you were just about to exercise a complete *lack* of emotional restraint and slice each other to pieces.'

His brother flinched at her admonition but didn't submit. 'This is not business for you to trifle in, Mother. We were discussing matters.'

'With swords, yes,' Ashoka jumped in, dryly. 'Mother—'

Arush scoffed. It was only a single sound. A sound so clearly filled with haughtiness and vitriol that Ashoka's last shred of patience snapped.

Violence to prevent more violence.

When he unsheathed his dagger, Arush laughed. 'A plain little dagger against a *kastane*?' he mocked. 'Ashoka, you're asking for a beating.'

'Continuing to underestimate me is fast becoming a flaw in this family,' Ashoka replied. Swinging his dagger out in a wide arc, he put himself in an offensive position.

'Ashoka – my dear – *stop*,' their mother cried out, 'I beg of you – please. Before someone gets hurt.'

Not Arush. Him. She expected *him* to lower his weapon. Even after Taksila, they continued to see him one way.

'Tell Arush to yield!' he shouted.

The order induced laughter in his brother. Flipping his *kastane* by the hilt over and over, Arush, too, took an offensive stance. 'Not a chance,' he replied, before sparing their mother a brief glance over his shoulder. 'You still call him your child?' he asked, each word laced with more criticism than the last. 'Ashoka isn't *yours*, Mother. He belongs to some whore witch—'

Their mother raised her hand, but Ashoka beat her to it.

Without a second thought, he charged towards Arush. Dukkha felt like a firecracker in his hands, waiting to explode.

Once he was close enough to Arush, he spotted an opening by the left side of his abdomen and jabbed. But his brother was a better fighter than him, had always been a better fighter than him. As if anticipating his move, Arush side-stepped out of the way and kicked out with his left foot. The blow hit cleanly against his chest and caused Ashoka to stumble back a few steps. Unfortunately, the back of his calf hit the edge of the central pool. Faltering, he managed to right himself and avoid falling into cool night water.

'Even your advisor would bet against you in this fight, little brother,' Arush goaded.

Ashoka said nothing, merely placed his weight against his right foot. He needed to gain momentum. Between the two of them, Arush had the advantage of strength. If he were to pounce on Ashoka and hold him down, it would be very difficult to escape without being bruised or lacerated significantly.

Unfortunately, Arush was not quite done with his provocation.

'Even Rahil would bet against you,' he continued, a wicked light in his eyes. 'Just because he loves you doesn't mean he can't see you for being the weak little—'

No doubt, Rahil would harangue him for losing his composure in this fight. It was the one cardinal rule he had taught Ashoka: to keep his emotions in check when weapons were drawn. A flood of emotions could distract, could blind, could result in a devastating loss.

Logic screamed at him to see sense, but it was locked away in a windowless room. All Ashoka heard then, was *weak*. That despite being loved, he was not seen as strong. Logic *knew* this was Arush saying just about anything to rile him up, but it was insecurity that made Ashoka believe it.

He charged again, tamping down the near-jubilant desire to ram the dagger into his brother's heart. Yet again, Arush dodged, the *kastane* meeting his cursed dagger briefly with a sharp *clang*. Before Ashoka could react, Arush struck out with his free hand and aimed a blow right above his collarbone.

His windpipe felt ready to collapse with the sudden force. Wheezing and unable to breathe, Ashoka clutched at his throat, springing back to give himself a moment, but Arush was relentless. He came charging, *kastane* aimed somewhere near his head. Despite the rush of panic, he managed to block the attack with his dagger. This did not seem to deter his brother, for he switched angles in a heartbeat, this time towards his lower torso.

Ashoka was too slow to react. The tip of Arush's blade sliced his right upper thigh. Letting out a strained grunt, Ashoka stumbled but ducked away from his brother's subsequent swipe. He heard his mother's panicked shouts.

'Father was right about you, little brother,' Arush called out, sneering. 'You're no warrior.'

Father.

Images resurfaced: a matchstick being lit, him being held down by his father, the flames reaching the lobule of his ear, and then – pain. Like he had never known. Like he should never have been subjected to as a child.

All those years attempting to prove him wrong by staunchly advocating for peace. All those years being degraded for it, only to choose violence himself. All those years in the shadow of his siblings.

I will destroy your empire, Father. I will destroy all of it – including them.

Ashoka's mind had never been so clear. Only a single thought remained, pulsing like a flame in the pitch black: *by any means necessary.*

Offense was Arush's speciality. He was usually the first to make a move. Defence was for the weak, for those who could not be brutal enough to attack first. But this way of thinking created flaws, especially if all one cared about was striking an opponent down without regard for their surroundings. And what better way to cause Arush to falter than to play his game of verbal assault.

'Father clearly saw Aarya as his worthy successor, brother,' Ashoka called out, walking slowly forward. His thigh burned; he could almost feel the skin moving, causing minuscule tears with every step. 'While you wasted our resources in the north, she put a stop to it. Her focus was the empire, not glory.'

Clear as day, he saw Arush's jaw clench, his posture stiffen.

'Out of the two of you, one is a failure,' he continued. 'I think *my advisor* could easily place a bet on who, and win.'

He could almost see the moment when Arush lost full control of his temper. How unsurprising. The three of them were their father's children, after all. Learned behaviours were sometimes hard to relieve. Predisposition to anger was the vice that threatened to choke their family whole.

The next few steps, Ashoka predicted like the forgotten clairvoyants of old. He knew that Arush would strike. He knew that he would attempt to tackle, and then to tear at the nearest muscle. He knew that his brother's attack would be driven by emotion, like his own had been. But this time, Ashoka had the upper hand. This time, he was observing.

Ashoka feigned offense and charged. As expected, when Arush got close enough, he lunged. For a moment, Ashoka feared he would be too slow, but he ducked, keeping Dukkha firmly against his side. Arush stumbled, having nothing to clutch on to.

He saw an opening when Arush lost his footing. Ashoka flipped the tip of his dagger to face his arm and swung in a wide arc, scoring Arush's chest.

Time paused. Ashoka felt as if he were watching the world go by while he was in a state of stasis. Arush managed to right himself in time. His brother paused, staring at his chest in disbelief. Dark spots were beginning to stain his tunic.

This dagger is called Dukkha.
The curse is simple – to spread and drown in good spirits.

'Pathetic,' Arush began, 'if you meant to hurt me, you should have—'

The ground shook.

A minor spirit emerged from the pool. Its body was pale blue like a summer sky. Unlike the other minor spirits he had seen, this one had no eyes. Only an eerie human nose and a mouth with pointed teeth.

Despite its rather horrific appearance, the spirit's voice was soothing. Melodious. An echo of an undisturbed forest no human feet had touched. Continuing to sing its delightful song, the spirit floated towards Ashoka.

Fascinated, he observed it glance fleetingly at his dagger before facing him once more. Then it began to chatter. Ashoka understood none of it. Smiling at him, the spirit then turned towards a dumbfounded Arush and spread its arms wide.

Beneath their feet, the tiles began to crack and splinter like rotten wood. Water from the central pool rose into a wave until it towered over their heads. The minor spirit cooed again, and the wave of water split into twelve different streams. They looked like tentacles.

The scene could've been purely majestic: a little blue spirit with a wave of water hovering in mid-air behind it. It stopped being so when the streams rushed towards Arush at full force. They reached his feet and slithered up his legs, covering his lower body. Arush dropped his sword and began to scream, struggling to break free, but the streams acted like vines, wrapping around him and kept him rooted to the spot.

'Help – help me!' he shouted, frantic. The muscles of his neck were visibly strained. '*Magic* – this – Ashoka, what did you do?'

Arush Maurya's pleas for help went unanswered for a moment. Everyone around him stood at a standstill, too shocked to move. Out of all of them, Ashoka was the one who willingly didn't. Clinical fascination clawed at him as he stared at Dukkha nestled in his hand.

'Arush!'

Their mother tried to rush towards him, but the soldiers held her back.

Arush's screams were terrible. A thick stream of water forcefully entered his mouth, stretching the brown skin taut and rendering him speechless. He started to wheeze and cough as he struggled, the base of his throat distending horribly. A slight blue hue began to show first on his swollen lower legs before spreading up to his neck. The gargling turned desperate, and Ashoka spotted the water in his mouth now tinged with faint pink. He was coughing up blood. All the while, the minor spirit continued to chitter happily, whizzing around in the air.

Arush was drowning. Dying in front of his eyes, and Ashoka's initial shock vanished, replaced by a deep hollowness. His brother had forced his hand, had *asked* for this fight. His brother had been the first one to introduce a weapon.

This emptiness that swallowed him: was this what their father felt when he looked upon a burning witch?

'Arush!'

Amid the noise, their mother had wrenched herself free from her hold and was rushing towards Arush, panicked, and topknot coming undone.

Arush's head was already lolled. He wasn't moving. The water would've long since filled up his lungs. An unsettling feeling tugged at Ashoka's stomach. He couldn't explain it, but he knew his brother was dead. There was nothing their mother could do. All he understood then was that danger would follow her if she touched him. Its wording nagged at him.

To spread and drown in good spirits.

'Mother,' he called out hastily, feet moving of their own accord. 'Stop, don't—'

But his warning came too late. The moment Empress Manali frantically pushed past the wall of water, now at the level of Arush's collarbones, to tug at his wrist, the clear tentacles slithered around her arms, spreading like an infection. Alarmed, his mother made to retract her arm but was unable to wrench free.

'Mother, no!' Ashoka shouted, running to her. His hands reached out towards her on instinct, but she let out a distressed yell, staggering away from him even as the water spread up her body.

'No, Ashoka – do not *touch* me,' her voice had taken on a commanding, fearful tone. The soldiers came stumbling forward, and she screamed at them, too. 'No, stay away. *No one touch me!*'

This wasn't what he had envisioned.

You weren't supposed to be here.

You weren't supposed to die.

You used the cursed weapon on your brother knowing it would result in the release of magic, said his father's voice, *and yet you cannot fathom it harming another. You cannot evade blame, boy.*

His right hand was empty. Unknowingly, he had dropped Dukkha.

Empress Manali was staring at the fallen dagger. Understanding was plastered across her already tear-splashed face.

'Mayakari magic,' was all she said.

'Why did you touch him, Mother,' Ashoka cried, tears streaming down his face. 'Why. *Why?*'

The wriggling mass of clear water was now at his mother's throat. Her eyes were blood red, cheeks glistening. 'I had to protect my child,' she replied. 'I . . . had to protect . . . both my children.'

Death didn't hold the scent of blood. In fact, there was no scent at all. Ashoka could no nothing but watch helplessly on, unable to help her.

'Mother,' he rasped, the word a plea for forgiveness. Despite her weak protestations, he stepped closer. The reckless side of himself wanted to join her in suffering, but self-preservation kept him from commitment. 'I . . . I didn't . . . Mother, I'm sorry. I'm so *sorry.*'

'She – birthed – without sorrow, and . . . you were . . . mine. Without.' His mother's rasp sounded painful. 'Still – my child – Ashoka.'

The stream of water forced its way into her mouth with a repulsive squelch. His mother sputtered and gagged, but she didn't struggle the way Arush had. His brother tried to fight his way out whereas she seemed to submit. The dowager empress knew she couldn't escape death.

Tears streamed down Ashoka's face as he watched her choke

out flecks of blood the same way Arush had. Her eyes widened and rolled to the back of her head. Her hands went limp.

Soft, melodious birdsong resumed, and Ashoka looked up, vision blurry with tears, to see the minor spirit smiling at him. Without a pair of eyes, it was unnerving.

Dukkha's curse. *To spread and drown in good spirits.* He understood it now.

The minor spirit vanished. The tentacles of water retreated into the jade pool, the last one leaving a single ripple to fan out before it stilled completely. No longer held up by its weight, his mother and Arush's unmoving bodies dropped to the ground, collapsing next to each other.

He ran towards them, dropping to his hands and knees, ignoring the protests of the soldiers behind him. Arush's skin was pale blue. When Ashoka placed a finger on his brother's damp throat, he felt no pulse. What a horrible end. Woken up having barely escaped death by poison, only to be killed by a nature spirit.

Breath trembling, Ashoka turned to his mother. Her eyes were closed, and she looked to be asleep. A trickle of blood ran down the corner of her mouth. Her skin, too, was a faint bluish-purple. Choking back his tears, Ashoka watched for the rise and fall of her chest, wanting her to breathe. Forced her mouth open to give her air, but there was no response. Nothing at all.

She was dead.

A horrible emptiness engulfed him. Becoming death's executioner had unintended consequences.

'Mother,' he cried out, grasping her cold, clammy hands and squeezing them tight. Wanting so desperately for her to shift, cough up the water that had no doubt filled her lungs, and say she was all right. Of the two dead, only one had deserved it.

Shock froze his limbs. He could dimly hear screaming around him. Someone was grabbing his shoulders, shaking them with the same ferociousness as a child with a rattle, but he hardly noticed. He could only stare at the bodies of Arush and their mother.

You killed her, came his father's voice. *Murderer. You proved yourself to be my son, but at what cost?*

Ashoka screamed.

CHAPTER FORTY-SIX
Ashoka

'What is the meaning of this?'

The voice came from behind him. Ashoka tore his gaze from his brother and mother's dead bodies to look upon Aarya's shocked face. Dressed in a long silk nightgown with a sheer shawl over her shoulders, she looked frazzled. It was one of the rare times he saw her that way.

His mouth didn't work. Only a soft, wet gasp escaped his lips. She'd arrived with her maidservants, and just behind them was—

Ashoka's throat constricted. *Rahil?*

'Brother,' Aarya's voice haunted his ears, horror-stricken. 'What happened? *What did you do?*'

Ashoka couldn't find the words. He kept staring at Rahil, who watched him with the same shock that everyone around him wore. Why was he here *now*? With Aarya.

'Rahil,' he called out, confused. 'What are you—'

'*Brother!*' Aarya roared.

Startled, his gaze returned to his sister's before landing on Dukkha, lying innocently on the ground. The tip was stained with blood. How could he begin to explain this without mentioning the cursed weapons? Not to mention that Sukha was still hidden in his satchel a few steps away.

He didn't need to speak. The soldiers who had been with his mother spoke for him.

'He – Your Highness,' came the sound of a man's voice, shattered beyond repair, 'Prince Ashoka – he fought . . . Emperor Arush. He fought – he *killed* him. He *murdered* the dowager empress.'

Silence stretched like glutinous rice being pulled by a confectioner before Aarya screeched out a disbelieving, '*What?*'

Another voice piped up, this time a female soldier. 'Your Highness – he – he tells the truth. Prince Ashoka killed them both with a magic. A *weapon*.'

Cold disgust graced Aarya's tone when she remarked, 'Magic? Mayakari magic, in a weapon? Don't you dare spin such fiction to me, woman.'

'She doesn't lie, Your Highness,' another defended her colleague. 'We all saw it. The emperor and the dowager empress – they were drowned. Engulfed by the water from this pool.'

'The *pool?*' Aarya's pitch rose.

The soldiers seemed flummoxed. Ashoka returned his gaze to his mother. 'A minor spirit appeared,' he said woodenly. 'When I used the weapon. Used the pool's water to drown them where they stood. Mother was – she wasn't supposed to . . .'

'You – you killed Arush?' Aarya said, her voice sounding oddly choked. '*Mother?*'

Murderer.

Killer.

'I didn't mean to kill her!' he roared, jumping up, breaths heavy. Around him, several of the soldiers had their hands to their waists, ready to draw out their weapons. Against him.

Me. Against me? I don't have the amount of blood on my hands that Aarya does.

'But you meant to kill Arush? You . . . Ashoka,' Aarya said again. 'This is – spirits help me, *how* did you manage to get your hands on a weapon that exudes mayakari magic?'

'It was a gift, sister. I can't refuse them, can I?'

'A gift from whom?'

He didn't answer.

'Ashoka,' his sister repeated, 'a gift from *whom?*'

He couldn't give Queen Kalyani away. Not yet. But Aarya seemed to have another culprit in mind.

'Was it her?' Aarya asked quietly. 'Was it Shakti?'

When he continued to maintain his reticence, his sister marched towards him and grabbed his chin with sharp fingernails, forcing him to look at her.

'That mayakari is a living abomination, *mūsī*,' she said. 'And using weapons cursed with magic – that's enough to make an empire fall. Drop your pretence. I know that you know where she is. Hand her over to me.'

'Forget Shakti. Shouldn't you be celebrating?' he asked cruelly. 'I killed Arush for you. Looks like you get to keep the throne after all.'

His acidic retort seemed to stun Aarya into silence, and she let her grip on his jaw go. She watched him carefully, as if he was a firecracker waiting to explode.

'Arush and Mother are dead because of you,' she said, pointing towards their bodies. Ashoka refused to look. 'No one can bring them back now. A Maurya has killed two of his own, but . . . you are not a Maurya. Not in the way it matters.'

She said this loudly enough that he saw the bewilderment from the onlookers turn into shock. He hated her with his very being.

'Don't you dare,' he began, but Aarya wasn't finished.

'You are lucky I'm letting you *live*,' she shouted. 'A mayakari sympathizer. A mayakari's *son*. A murderer. No one will want to see you in any position of power, brother. They'd rather you dead.'

'Liar,' Ashoka raised his voice to match hers. 'Not everyone sees the mayakari as monsters. Taksila—'

Aarya laughed. 'You truly believe your little stint in Taksila is a true indicator of the people's will? You've only continued to show me that all those wretches do is harm, *mūsī*. Father. Arush. Mother. *Me*. You used a weapon infused with mayakari magic – how did you come by it?'

Although Ashoka kept quiet, one person didn't.

'Queen Kalyani, Your Highness.'

Ashoka stiffened. His blood ran cold as Rahil stepped forward, expressionless, to stand beside Aarya. His mind couldn't make sense of the scene. Rahil had given him away. Rahil. *Rahil*. His secret-keeper. His guard. *His*.

I'm delirious, he decided. *This is delirium. This can't be happening.*

Even so, he couldn't help the choked gasp that escaped his lips. 'Rahil?' he whispered. 'What are you – I don't . . .'

'What's so difficult to understand?' Aarya retorted, her smile maniacal. 'Sweet Ashoka, your love sold you out.'

Not even a flicker of guilt crossed Rahil's stony features. *No. No, it couldn't be.* There was no rational explanation for this. Rahil would never betray him. Something was *wrong*.

'You told Aarya about tonight,' he said, the realization slow and painful. 'Rahil – what—?'

'*Mūsī*,' Aarya interrupted him, 'you will be punished for the murder of the emperor and the dowager empress. As the new empress, I command you come peacefully.'

Despite being surrounded by a dozen to one, Ashoka laughed. *Punished*, he thought. *I'm the saviour, not the villain.*

'You don't deserve the throne,' he snapped.

'*Hah!* And you believe that you do?'

In that moment of heated aggression, Ashoka lost his composure.

'I do,' he said. Speaking the truth out loud did little to lift the burden from his shoulders. 'You aren't worthy of it. Arush never was. Father all but disgraced the Mauryas of old. Out of our miserable family, *I'm* more suited to rule the empire than you.'

The proclamation appeared to stun his sister into silence, and for a moment Ashoka swore he saw fear flash in her eyes.

'Veering towards insubordination, little brother,' she replied. 'That mayakari blood of yours must be strong.'

She made it sound like an insult. As if he should be ashamed to have a mayakari for a mother. But it did not deter him. It would never deter him. 'I will wage war against you, sister.'

Aarya laughed. 'You and what army?'

He stepped closer. Immediately, Aarya's guards reciprocated.

'An army of mayakari,' he whispered. 'Mark my words, sister. You won't rule for long. The Obsidian Throne is *mine*.'

Twisting her lips into an ugly sneer, Aarya let out a low growl.

'Traitor,' she spat, and turned to the soldiers. 'Restrain him.'

Footsteps thundered, and the sound of metal clanging followed.

Soldiers approached him with weapons drawn. Instinctively, Ashoka backed away, gaze latching on to Rahil's once more. He still didn't understand what was happening. *What was wrong with him?*

'Come quietly,' Aarya called out to him. 'Or you will be hurt.'

Suddenly, a loud, terrifying hiss filled the air. A large shadow fell over them, backlit by the moon. He glanced up at the sky as the soldiers around him shouted to get into a defensive position.

Sahry flew towards him, fangs drawn. On her back were Shakti and Sau.

CHAPTER FORTY-SEVEN
Shakti

'Down there!' Saudamini yelled.

Glancing down to where the advisor was pointing, Shakti spotted a lone figure surrounded by a group, and directed Sahry into a steep, downward descent, wind whipping her hair. The winged serpent dived, hissing loud enough to startle the dead, agitated and furious.

After she'd informed Sau that her curse had enacted, the advisor was silent, rifling through several plans in her head. Eventually, she decided to take Shakti to the southern forestland to wait for Prince Ashoka and Rahil. 'We don't know what sort of curse this is,' she'd said. 'He might be fine.'

When hours passed while they hid, and neither Ashoka nor Rahil had arrived, Saudamini began to worry. She'd initially asked Shakti to stay where she was while she returned to the palace, and had been ready to leave, when a large shadow sped above them. Upon climbing a tree to see what it was, she'd been surprised to spot a winged serpent flying above without a rider. More concerning still was that the serpent was none other than Sahry.

According to Saudamini that was unusual. Sahry was kept chained at nighttime. She was not allowed to fly out on her own. Her being here alone was strange. Something had happened to Prince Ashoka and Rahil.

With the help of some nearby minor spirits, she'd called the winged serpent down. Strangely enough, she was saddled. Shakti had sensed her emotions; nervous and skittish. With Saudamini's reluctant approval, they hauled themselves on the serpent and took off, heading in the direction of the palace.

If Sahry was behaving so anxiously, Prince Ashoka must be in some sort of trouble. This serpent sensed her owner's emotions much better than others.

True enough, when the east courtyard of the palace became visible past its walls, she'd spotted the disturbance. One figure against a dozen. An unfair fight. It looked to be Prince Ashoka – not dead, thank the spirits.

But my curse worked, she thought frantically. *Has anything happened to him? Something I can't undo – no. No, not now. Help him first.*

It took her a moment to formulate a plan. They'd need to disarm what looked to be soldiers surrounding the prince, and Sahry was the best option they had.

The serpent, it seemed, had thought ahead of her. As they came closer to the ground, Sahry opened her mouth wide, protracted her fangs and sprayed a stream of thick, viscous yellow venom. Panicked shouts could be heard below, as people scrambled to escape the spray. It wasn't enough. They needed to cause enough damage to disorient. To give Ashoka time to jump onto the saddle.

'Hold on!' she yelled over her shoulder to Saudamini.

Shakti directed Sahry at breakneck speed towards the rectangular jade pool, Saudamini holding on to her waist for dear life. Just before Sahry would have landed headfirst, Shakti adjusted the reins, forcing the serpent to pull up and swerve hard left. Sahry's tail swung like an executioner's axe, shattering the stone walls of the pool, sending rubble scattering in every direction. Her tail was long enough to sweep several soldiers off their feet and send them flying.

Letting out a piercing hiss, Sahry's fangs continued to drip venom. Her head swung right and left, forked tongue slipping in and out. The serpent was looking for Ashoka, and so was she.

'I can't see him!' Behind her, Sau sounded frantic. Not even a moment later, the advisor let out a horrified gasp. 'Spirits – is that – is that Arush? The *empress dowager?*'

Shakti followed Sau's line of sight, recognizing the familiar shapes of Arush and Empress Dowager Manali lying deathly still on the ground. Her breath caught. *Were they dead? How? What had happened here?*

Shakti eventually spotted Ashoka, on his back, coughing and sopping wet. The rectangular jade pool was smashed to bits, the ground wet and slippery. Several soldiers were on the floor, coughing. Others were yelling for Aarya. One body with broadswords on its back was shielding another. *Was that—*

There was no time to think. Close to Prince Ashoka, she could see fallen soldiers stirring to life, hauling themselves up. No bows or arrows on them, which was lucky, but if he didn't get up quickly, they would overpower him. It looked like they would, soon. The prince was struggling to stand, and swaying horribly. She wouldn't let Ashoka Maurya be taken.

'Hold on to Sahry!' she yelled to Saudamini before sliding down the serpent's body and running to help him. On her way, she spotted a discarded longsword on the ground. One of the soldiers must've lost their hold on it when Sahry swept them away. Shakti picked it up.

'Prince Ashoka!' she called out. She couldn't see Rahil anywhere, which was worrying.

At the sound of his name, the prince looked up. The sheer relief on his face quickly turned to fear when Ashoka yelled, 'Behind you!'

Shakti turned just in time and narrowly avoided a knife slicing her throat. A soldier had sneaked behind her, waiting like a predator to pounce. He, too, held a longsword, but didn't appear as battered and bruised as she was.

'Die, witch!' he shouted, and brought his weapon down in a wide arc.

Shakti met his sword with a resounding, ear-piercing clang. Her muscles shook with the effort. Ducking out of the way when the soldier charged at her again, she dimly heard footsteps coming towards them. As she continued to defend, a muffled shout came from her left.

The soldier turned. A blade pierced his heart, but it wasn't hers.

Breathing heavily, Ashoka retracted his sword, expression inscrutable, the blade coming away smeared in red. With a pained groan, the soldier dropped to the ground. There were still ongoing shouts for Aarya, so where was she?

Shakti spotted her, lying on her stomach, nightclothes smeared grey, shawl torn. Bruises marred her bare arms. It appeared that she'd been knocked away by Sahry's tail, too. Shakti watched as Aarya stirred and lifted her head blearily towards them. For a moment, they locked eyes.

Pure terror left a shiver trailing down the points of her spine. Her body sensed that a predator was nearby. Faded scars across her skin seemed to redden, as if that look alone was enough to revitalize old wounds. Cause the scars on her back to bleed anew.

When I find you, you'll scream for death, Aarya's eyes seemed to say.

'Come on,' Shakti heard Prince Ashoka say urgently, snapping her out of the panic-induced stupor. 'Go, saddle yourself on Sahry and get her flying.'

'What about you?' Shakti asked, bewildered.

The prince's expression was grim. 'I dropped my satchel,' he huffed, breathing strained. 'It has my cursed dagger, and I need it. Just go, hurry – pull me up when I yell out.'

Unable to decline, Shakti obeyed. She ran towards the winged serpent. No one was coming near her. Saudamini was trying to control her, but was losing her grip, fast.

Sahry was still thrashing her tail about violently, opalescent wings lifted in a position that suggested she was ready to attack. As Shakti reached the serpent's body, she gave the rough scales a quick thump. 'Just me,' she said. 'Just me, Sahry. Calm down.'

Miraculously, the winged serpent stopped hissing. Just as Shakti was preparing herself to climb up onto the saddle, she spared a glance behind her. Amidst the carnage, Prince Ashoka had found the satchel he was looking for. Triumphantly, he turned to her and looked ready to sprint towards them when a familiar wraithlike figure arose from the group of soldiers protecting Aarya and came sprinting behind him.

She'd been wondering where he was.

Shakti watched in horror as Rahil grabbed Prince Ashoka's shoulders from behind and viciously tackled him to the ground.

CHAPTER FORTY-EIGHT
Ashoka

One moment, Ashoka had locked eyes with Shakti, ready to dash towards her and Sahry. The next moment, hands grasped his shoulders from behind and he was tackled to the ground. He lost his grip on the satchel as he went tumbling, and it fell to his left.

Landing on his chest with a painful thud, Ashoka just managed to turn himself over before his assailant clambered on top of him, grip tight. He smelled the sandalwood and myrrh before he saw Rahil looking down at him. He was breathing heavily, as though he had been running for several days without rest. All his weight bore down on Ashoka's stomach, making it difficult to breathe.

'Rahil,' he wheezed. 'Stop!'

As if by magic, Rahil stilled. Ashoka stopped struggling – was this fit of delirium over? Were Rahil's senses returned?

He was proven wrong when Rahil reached towards his waist and produced a knife.

Unadulterated fear shot through Ashoka's chest like lightning. *What's happening. He isn't – what is this?*

'Rahil,' he whispered, resuming his attempts to break free. '*Rahil. Drop the knife. You are not cruel.*'

A horrible, shiver-inducing smile split Rahil's lips. He looked both like a hero ripped from his dreams and a criminal destined for death. Both beautiful and terrifying.

'I've killed for you, Ashoka,' he replied. 'How am I not cruel?'

Taking the knife into his dominant hand, Rahil raised his weapon and brought it down. Ashoka flinched, and for a moment, closed his eyes, expecting the skin across his heart to be pierced, and for him to die sputtering Rahil's name with tortured breaths.

The pain came immediately. Swift. Brutal. *Agonizing*. But it was not his heart that Rahil had punctured.

It was his burned ear.

Ashoka screamed. The knife hadn't lodged into the lobe where sensation was absent, but somewhere higher, likely near the conch. Old memories resurfaced in distressing flashes of his father taking a match to his ear. Of the skin blistering. Burning. Him, unable to do anything but cry out for help that never came. He'd never thought such pain would be replicated again, but this infliction was far worse.

This was *Rahil*.

The knife was still in his ear, Rahil holding onto the handle with a death grip. Ashoka's screams did not even seem to affect him. In fact, there was no emotion on his face at all.

'What are you doing?' he cried out.

A wall of stone stared back, unmoved by his tears. 'You are a traitor to the throne, Ashoka,' Rahil replied. 'A traitor to the empire.'

This wasn't Rahil. Rahil wouldn't betray him like this.

'Rahil, whatever's affecting you – snap out of it,' he urged. 'Taksila. We have to get to Taksila.'

'No,' Rahil thundered. 'It is as Empress Aarya ordered – you are not to return to Taksila, Ashoka. You will remain here.'

A sudden, irrational fear followed. Had he nicked Rahil with a cursed weapon?

No, don't be stupid, Ashoka thought to himself. But magic had to be at play here. What else could be the cause for this response?

The rational side of himself chastised against emotion. This was no time to lament and ponder. Ashoka had a sinking feeling that he couldn't verbally beat sense into Rahil. He needed to make a decision.

What will you choose, son?

What will you choose, my dear?

Both his parents' voices intermingled, the only discord found in their address. *Son* was spat harshly, as if the very word was a curse. His mother's endearment contained only softness and regret. But it wasn't his parents' voices that pulled him out of his panic. It was Sau's.

Don't let love become your worst attachment.

Instinct told him he would only suffer if he tried to save Rahil. He had to make a decision he never thought he'd have to make.

Grunting, Ashoka twisted his head to glance at his mother's body. Bits of stone were scattered across it. The only member of his family who'd truly loved him was dead. He would never speak to her again, and it was his fault.

Rahil's gaze tracked his own, momentarily distracted. Despite the pain, a sudden burst of strength overcame Ashoka. Steeling himself, he strained his neck up, knocking Rahil's head with his own.

Half his ear tore off in the process.

The movement disoriented Rahil, and Ashoka buried his screams by biting into Rahil's arm like a starving leopard. The agony was too much. He tasted blood, unsure if it was his own dripping from his ear, or if it was Rahil's.

Roaring in pain, Rahil dropped his dagger, pushed him back with brutal force and levelled a glare filled with palpable disgust on him. It smashed Ashoka's heart beyond restoration. He had never seen such blatant hatred from Rahil. Impossibilities were turning into reality.

Impossibilities like Rahil raising his weapon against him. His hand against him. Wiping the blood from his mouth, Ashoka watched him reach for his sword. Watched him intensely to make sure that he didn't turn when a familiar figure silently picked up the fallen sword behind him. Watched him because Ashoka knew that Rahil wouldn't look away, not even when he had succumbed to some form of magic. For as long as they were alive, their eyes gravitated towards each other like the moon and the earth.

'Hurt me, then,' he called out, clutching his serrated ear. Half the world sounded submerged. There was a distant ringing that made it difficult to concentrate. '*Hurt me.*'

The subsequent reply was cold. Colder than his father's apathy. Colder than his own self-hatred:

'As you wish, Prince Ashoka.'

Ashoka watched Rahil stand. Watched him steady his broadsword. Not once did they break eye contact.

Suddenly—

Thunk.

The grip on Rahil's sword loosened, falling with a dull *clang*. Its owner dropped, too, a heavy weight thrown into ocean waters. In the blink of an eye, Rahil was unconscious, face down on the ground. Behind him stood Shakti, the hilt of the broadsword towards them. She had struck the back of his head.

Raw confusion marred her features as she ran towards Ashoka. He spotted remnants of tear stains that had tracked down her cheek.

'*Prince Ashoka!*' She helped him to stand. Every movement pained him. His feet were unsteady, but he managed to clutch the satchel containing Sukha again.

Rahil. Was he—

Shakti seemed to read his thoughts. 'He's breathing,' she placated him. 'I don't have enough brute force in me to kill Rahil of all people. Now hurry.'

Despite knowing she was right, Ashoka hesitated.

'Stay here and you will never leave,' she squeezed his arm hard enough for him to wince. 'We need to go.'

He didn't want to leave Rahil like this. It was as if he was severing a limb. Yet, Shakti was right. Foolishness was to stay. Intelligence was to escape.

Shakti tugged his arm, gesturing towards Sau and Sahry. '*Hurry.* Saudamini's struggling to control Sahry as it is,' she hissed, 'and I don't want to die.'

There was no need to remind him again. Ashoka let her lead him back to Sahry. The winged serpent had her wings spread, ready for flight. Attempting to keep her still was Sau. The advisor's face was drawn. Shock marred her face like a destroyed mural as she shifted backward so that she was at the end of the saddle before leaning over to help him clamber on. Shakti followed after, so that he was crammed between them and was holding Sahry's reins.

His head was pounding. He felt ready to faint.

Sahry began to hiss in concern.

'No, Sahry,' he murmured. 'Peace. I'm all right.'

Sau snorted. 'You most certainly are *not*. We need to tend to that wound immediately.'

'When we find a safe haven,' Shakti added. 'Not here. I know where we can go for now.'

Nodding blearily, Ashoka collapsed against Shakti's back. Both the young women swore in unison before Shakti directed Sahry up.

Chaos. This was what he had created. This was his future.

Ashoka turned his head towards the jade pools where he saw Aarya struggling to her feet. Dust and blood were splattered across his sister's sari. For once, she seemed stunned into silence. He saw her take in the sight of the three of them on Sahry's back, saw her register Rahil's unconscious figure, knew that she heard what had transpired between them, and welcomed the worst. Sahry let out a high-pitched hiss as she flapped her giant wings and got them off the ground, higher and higher until Aarya became little more than a speck.

As they flew away, his father's voice echoed in his head, unrelenting:

To destroy me, you must destroy my empire.

A destroyer he was. The notion pleased him more than he thought. As did his father's voice:

Violence suits you well, Ashoka.

CHAPTER FORTY-NINE
Shakti

THIS WAS MY FAULT.

Shakti couldn't stop berating herself as they flew away from the Maurya palace, eventually guiding Sahry into the hilly northern forests for a reprieve. Slotted between herself and Saudamini, Prince Ashoka was silent. Half his weight was against her back, and she couldn't turn to see if he had passed out. Judging by the lack of exclamations on Saudamini's part, she assumed that he hadn't.

Her curse had finally enacted, and it had somehow affected *Rahil* of all people. Aarya had asked for Ashoka's pride to be hurt, and though she couldn't remember the curse itself, Shakti had to admit that the now-empress had got what she wanted in a twisted way. She'd wanted to hurt her little brother, and she had.

This isn't your fault, little bird. Don't carry this burden – it is not yours to shoulder.

The logical part of her knew this, and yet guilt drowned her anyway. It clutched at her throat with talons sharp enough to puncture the delicate skin.

Sparing a glance over her shoulder, she saw Prince Ashoka's eyes flutter, his gaze unfocused. Blood was still flowing from his torn ear. If the bleeding became prolonged, it would be disastrous for him.

The moment they landed in the wild forests, Shakti went searching for yarrow. Jaya had used the plant enough for her to recognize it by sight. It hadn't taken long for her to find it and race back to an awaiting Ashoka and Saudamini.

Fortunately, Shakti still had the fallen longsword she'd picked up during the fight. Using the hilt of the weapon, Shakti ground the plant into a paste and spread it around Prince Ashoka's half-missing ear.

'The blood has already started to clot,' she told him, inspecting the wound with a grimace. How nasty. 'But this will make the process quicker.'

The prince nodded. She applied the yarrow poultice but soon noticed that his attentions seemed far away. Shakti's gaze found Sau's. They shared a brief look of concern before the advisor spoke.

'Ashoka,' Sau said. 'What happened at the jade pools? We saw your mother and Arush on the ground. They looked . . .'

'Dead?' the prince finished her sentence. He squeezed his eyes shut. 'That's because they are.'

Letting out a soft, startled gasp, Sau moved to clutch Ashoka's arm. Meanwhile, Shakti remained still. Emperor Arush, dead. The dowager empress, too. Only Aarya remained, the final barrier to peace for the mayakari. 'How did they die?' she asked him.

'My cursed weapon,' Ashoka replied, voice hollow. 'A gift from Queen Kalyani. I used it against Arush, knowing what might happen, but I didn't expect Mother to . . .'

The prince choked on his words. Paused before continuing. 'A minor spirit filled Arush's lungs with water,' he whispered. 'He drowned. It was only supposed to be him, but it happened to Mother, too. She touched him and . . .'

Spirits, Shakti thought. *That cursed dagger must've acted quick.*

She remained silent, letting Ashoka wallow. Sau was better at comforting him, rubbing his back, her own face pale and drawn. Eventually, with a frustrated groan, Ashoka wiped the tears from his eyes. They were pale red as he stared at her.

'Rahil.' The name sounded like diluted hope from his lips. 'That wasn't him.'

Shakti sighed. 'It was and it wasn't,' she began. 'It's a curse. *My* curse.'

An expression of bloodied shock met her. 'Your curse?' Ashoka asked before letting out a dead, empty laugh. 'Why am I surprised? I shouldn't be.'

Shakti winced. 'I felt it take effect when Sau came to get me,' she said. 'I didn't know how it would enact, but I'm glad it didn't kill you. To be honest, I don't think Aarya wanted you dead, either. It's a strange boundary that she's created for herself, willing to hurt family but not wanting to kill. She said she wanted to hurt your pride, and I suppose the way it worked was—'

She stopped short of saying Rahil's name.

'You can say it,' Prince Ashoka remarked. 'It possessed Rahil to hurt me.'

'Ashoka—'

'I don't blame you,' he said, though his eyes looked as angry as the Great Spirit's. 'I don't – it's not your fault. Aarya will pay for what she did.'

Saudamini, who had been listening quietly, jumped in. 'But you still can't undo the curse?'

That was the problem. 'I don't remember what I said exactly,' she told the advisor. 'I was drugged when I used cursed speech. All I remember are scraps. It's not enough.'

'What do you remember?' Ashoka asked her roughly.

'*Heart . . .*' Shakti began, then frowned. 'Something about *hate*. There's more to it, but I don't remember any more.'

A sombre disquiet followed her declaration. Saudamini's face was contemplative as she directed the prince to sit up before wiping away the paste with a clean cloth from her knapsack and wrapping gauze around his head. She then moved to wrap another bandage around the wound on his right upper thigh. 'Surely there's a way for you to remember?' she asked finally.

Shaking her head, Shakti shot them a sympathetic grimace. 'My aunt once said that our minds shield us from bad memories. Sometimes these memories can come back unexpectedly. Sometimes they don't return at all.'

Ashoka swore. 'So, Rahil could stay like this indefinitely?'

'If I remember the exact words, then I can undo the curse. Right now – I'm sorry. I can't. For now, he'll be on Aarya's side.'

The very thought was misery-inducing. Shakti sat down beside him. Watching Saudamini bandage his thigh, she was suddenly struck by a strange sense of jealousy. In this moment, they were one and the same. Children without their parents. But when she lost Jaya, she had felt – and to this day still felt – unbearably alone. She had nothing but the promise of vengeance on her lips. Ashoka still had people who cared about him. From where he stood, there was still hope.

Whether she liked it or not, all her hopes rested on him, and a small part of her hated that they did. That her dreams of peace for the mayakari rested in the shaking hands of a Maurya. He would feel powerless now, to be sure, but Ashoka still *had* a semblance of it. That name, that royal title, carried weight. Her name did not. Her lineage did not. All it carried was a death sentence.

She couldn't recall how long she sat there, hating their difference in power. Hating that a mayakari had more power than a non-mayakari and yet bound themselves to pacifism. Wasted potential, that was what they were. And Emperor Adil had exploited it.

Emperor Ashoka was right. She had so much untested potential. All she had to do was use it without guilt. At that moment, it wasn't a difficult feat to achieve.

'Troubled?' she heard Prince Ashoka ask her. When she turned to him, she found that he had been watching her.

'Angry,' she corrected. 'At myself, at your family, and, to be frank, at you.'

For a moment, she thought he looked offended before a weary expression settled across his face like silt in water.

'Why?' he asked.

'I don't know,' she replied, sighing.

He leaned back against the tree trunk, groaning in pain. 'It's fine. Be mad, even if you don't know why,' he said. 'Aarya's shocked. She'll need time to recuperate. By that time, I'll be waiting for her.'

'Hah,' Shakti scoffed. 'What, you'll kill her, too?'

'He will,' said Sau. There was no emotion behind it. 'Won't you?'

'To destroy a weed, you have to pull it out by its roots,' Ashoka confirmed, his face set hard. 'She's the last root. Dukkha's pair, Sukha, awaits her.'

It struck her how casually Ashoka said it. There was no resignation, no apparent anger. In that moment, he reminded her of Adil.

'Good,' she said. 'Your sister deserves to die.'

They sat silently for a minute, side by side, until—

'To spread and drown in good spirits.'

She started and glanced at Ashoka who was staring fixedly at the ground. 'Excuse me?'

'The cursed weapon,' he replied. 'Dukkha. The mayakari who made it — she told me that was the curse. It sounded so peaceful in my head, you know, but that was my fault to assume the true intention of a curse.'

Sau snorted. 'From what I've seen, curses rarely tend to be peaceful,' she said. 'Even Sukha's curse — what was it, something about "peace come too soon" — sounds innocuous enough, but I can't imagine how it'll enact.'

Shakti agreed. Curses were always cruel. It was foolish to assume otherwise. Dukkha's enactment *had* been rather brutal. It had acted quite literally; the emperor and his mother the dowager empress submerged in water by the actions of a minor spirit.

Shakti felt Ashoka's eyes on her, and before he could even open his mouth, she answered his question for him. 'I can't undo a curse that has taken lives. To ease your sorrow, I would've raised the dead so you could attempt to speak to her briefly, but you know we can't return to the palace now.'

Fresh guilt was an easy thing to spot on Ashoka. Every true feeling, every thought, was readable. The prince had lost one of the only people who truly loved him. Two, if she dared to include the still-alive but curse-influenced Rahil.

Tying a final knot around the prince's thigh, Sau stepped back and examined her handiwork before grasping his hand. 'She's gone, Ashoka, but you can't break,' the advisor told him, gentle but brusque. 'Not now.'

'I'm not broken. Bruised, perhaps, but not damaged beyond

repair,' he replied. Those doe eyes of his appeared a little dull despite the hardness in his tone. 'I need to travel to Mahvo, meet with the Kalingan generals before Aarya invades the southern border.'

'Won't she need to pass through Taksila to get there?' Shakti mused.

Ashoka's face was grim. 'It's the quickest route,' he confirmed, 'which means we need to fortify the city. Sau and I need to—'

'*We* won't be doing anything for the moment,' Saudamini remarked. Standing up, she wiped away a stray smear of yarrow poultice along her wrist. 'It's Taksila first. To that end – Ashoka, can Sahry fly us directly there? We'll have to avoid the Samnal River – there's too high a risk of being spotted. An alternative route needs to be taken.'

'She's not a machine,' Shakti replied, beleaguered. 'Sahry will need rest.'

'Shakti's right,' Ashoka confirmed. He too, struggled to his feet, waving away any attempts of help. 'We need to make camp for one night, at least.' In an absentminded fashion, he patted the side of his trousers, a look of panic immediately forming on his face. 'Where's my satchel?'

'Here,' Saudamini plucked the damp satchel from the ground to show him. She pulled out the remaining cursed dagger in what Shakti guessed was an attempt to appease the prince's sudden worry. The weapon wasn't properly encased. Shakti spotted a blue glow emitting from the dagger. Soft and beautiful, that was certain, but blue only ever reminded her of the way in which her kind burned.

'Thank you.' Prince Ashoka clung to the cursed weapon like it was a toy and he was the child who had lost it. 'Onward to Taksila, then.'

Despite the confidence with which he uttered the statement, his moroseness was palpable.

They slowly approached Sahry once more. Unlike the three of them, the winged serpent seemed bright and alert in the night. She'd calmed down considerably since leaving the palace and realizing that Ashoka was accounted for. Shakti was surprised she hadn't gone hunting for some other poor creature during their brief intermission.

After re-saddling themselves, Shakti guided Sahry into flight once again. Under the moonlight, she cast an imposing shadow above the treetops as she settled into a comfortable speed.

Behind Shakti, Saudamini and Prince Ashoka were quiet. She didn't mind the silence. It gave her time to gather her thoughts. Or rather, try to stop them from overwhelming her completely.

There were too many pressing concerns. Loath as she was to admit, there were only a few people who could provide guidance, or at least something resembling it. Two of them existed in her own head. It felt like betrayal of the worst kind, having to consider getting the advice of a tyrant and a liar. But if there was a chance that they could gain an advantage in this familial battle for power, this was it.

CHAPTER FIFTY
Ashoka

They arrived in Taksila two nights later.

Taking a longer route down had its downsides – mainly time. In between, he had Shakti give Sahry rest during the early hours of the day while the three of them, too, rested their eyes. Having Shakti with them was helpful. She had the ingenious idea to ask a minor spirit to watch over them and alert for trouble if needed.

Ashoka couldn't help but think how adept at guarding spirits could be.

The royal estate appeared unchanged when they arrived close to midnight. Sahry landed with less grace than she usually did. Poor thing – she had never taken such a long flight before. Rubbing the underside of her jaw and whispering encouragements, Ashoka led her to the pen that had been constructed for her. It took little time for the winged serpent to drift off into sleep. No hunting for her tonight, then.

The guards had immediately been alerted to their arrival. Sachith was one of the first to find them as they walked back, bedraggled, to the estate's entrance.

'Prince Ashoka!' he greeted them, visible relief on his face. That relief disappeared in a flash when he spotted the bandaging. 'Spirits – what has happened to your head? The physician – I'll call for one immediately.'

His torn ear pounded. 'Please do.'

Ashoka watched as Sachith next scanned the party, nodding at Sau, before his gaze landed on Shakti. Confusion gave way to recognition. 'I remember you,' he remarked, before frowning, 'but where's Rahil?'

His chest constricted painfully. The absence was palpable. 'Rahil's ... incapacitated, Sachith. I'll let you know what happened later, but first – I'd like to have my friends be shown to their sleeping quarters.'

After sleeping on the hard forest floor, he too craved the comfort of a soft bed. His back was decidedly sore.

'The staff can show the two to their sleeping quarters, Prince Ashoka,' Sachith remarked. 'Though, I should let you know – you have a visitor. Have had, in fact, for a few days.'

'A visitor?' For an agonizing moment, he imagined it was Aarya. Or Rahil, curse-bound and aching for his blood to be let.

Nodding, Sachith politely gestured for them to resume their course. He sensed Shakti's shifting mood, likely at the soldier's uniform, for her gait had turned stiff. Absentmindedly, he reached his left arm behind him to fumble around and eventually grasp her wrist before giving it a gentle squeeze.

'An advisor,' Sachith informed him, 'sent by Queen Kalyani. She arrived some days ago. Admittedly, she was rather surprised that Taksila was still without its governor but has been patiently waiting for your return.'

'What for?' he asked. 'Am I going to hear some unfortunate news?'

'I don't believe so. From what I understand, she's here for advisory purposes. Much like Sau, I suppose. She's asleep now, but I can let her know to meet you in the morning,' Sachith remarked, glancing at his head in worry. 'Or not. A full day of rest may be suitable for you, Prince Ashoka. I can't imagine that this injury of yours is bearable.'

'Yes, I'll see her in the morning,' Ashoka said. 'It's bad manners to keep a guest waiting for this long.'

Guards bowed as Ashoka passed by them and up the stairs. He didn't miss their inquisitive but perturbed glances when they saw his bandaged head. Once inside, he ventured directly towards the greeting room with its plush settees and large family portrait hanging like a curse on the wall. Sachith ordered for one of the waiting staff members to wake the physician.

Sau and Shakti lingered until the physician came, medicaments in hand. The woman's initial drowsiness was replaced by shock when she laid eyes upon him and rushed to manage the wound.

'Prince Ashoka!' She touched the side of his head. 'What happened?'

A few curious staff and some guards were watching on as he explained how he ended up with a lopped ear. How he'd killed his brother, mother, and escaping the palace as a traitor to the throne – that could wait till morning. He didn't want to be looked at with more horror just yet. When he uttered Rahil's name, shocked murmurs travelled like a strong wind. He could hear the disbelief, and did not fault them for it. That Rahil, Prince Ashoka's personal guard, would hurt him in such a way seemed like a fantasy.

The process was akin to having a new portrait unveiled. Ashoka could feel eyes upon him as the physician unwrapped the bandages. The gasps that erupted once the damage to his ear was revealed were almost humiliating. They all knew whom he had been burned by in his youth. Now, that same ear had suffered a worse injury, and from someone who was closer to him than anyone else.

I will not break, he told himself when his wound was re-medicated. *Rahil won't be the reason I'll break. He'd tell me the same.*

I will take Sukha to Aarya's throat, he told himself when the physician warned that he might suffer mild hearing impairment. *I will watch her die and enjoy it.*

I will take that fucking throne with bodies and weapons, he told himself when he was escorted up to his room with a healing tonic he was to take before going to sleep. *Or I will die trying.*

Pressing his shoulder gently, Sau let him stew and returned to her own quarters. Only Shakti remained at the end, standing like a statue in the corner of his room. At first he didn't say anything, partly because he didn't know *what* to say.

Unable to quiet his mind, Ashoka sat on the floor, leaning against the wooden frame of his bed, staring blankly at the floor and then at his hands. Wood dug into his back. His hands were clean, but he felt his mother's blood was on them. Imaginary streams of water snaked towards him.

'Prince Ashoka.'

He heard Shakti's voice. Heard the concern. However, there were far too many thoughts fighting for dominance in his head to consider it.

Murderer.

No, he told himself. *It was an accident. I didn't know Mother would – I didn't expect—*

An imaginary jury had materialized in his head now, seated at a long table. Rahil. His mother. Arush. His *father*. They all glared at him balefully. He was the convicted criminal, awaiting his sentence.

Your own family, Rahil's voice echoed first. It was strange – consonants harsh when they usually weren't. *The Mauryas' own butcher.*

Butcher. The word recalled bloodstained knives, crudely cut slabs of meat, fingers permanently imbued with the metallic scent of blood.

Not even Father would have dared, Ashoka. Arush spoke this time. *You have become something far beyond him.*

My dear, I had so much faith in you. His mother now, except this image of her wasn't the one he knew, poised and graceful. Her eyes were red, blood dripping down her cheeks instead of tears. *I loved you and you hurt me.*

Before Ashoka could plead otherwise, his mother's image shifted. Thick green vines tore through her eyes and mouth, spraying bits of flesh across the table's surface.

Dead. Bile threatened to spill.

A Maurya indeed, son. I am proud.

No. Ashoka chose to ignore his father's praise. He didn't want it, didn't *need* it. Even hearing a fictitious version of Adil in his mind was enough to make him feel ill. He had killed *family*. His brother. His mother.

Dimly, he heard Shakti calling out his name again. She was in front of him now, but her figure was blurry. It was as if he wasn't in his own body.

'Ashoka.'

Suddenly, he was pulled up roughly before warmth surrounded him. Heat. Skin. The unfamiliar scent of smoke. One hand around his back, the other cupping the back of his neck. Ashoka found himself being pushed gently into the crook of Shakti's shoulder.

I killed my mother.

Before he knew it, Ashoka was crying. Fat, salty tears clung to his eyelashes, unable to hold on for long, and they fell onto the thin material of Shakti's blouse.

He felt Shakti move, her hands leaving his back and coming to slide around the sides of his arms to push Ashoka back. The mucus that dripped from his nose collected in a trail. Mortifying, but the sight didn't seem to deter Shakti. Instead, she let out a weary chuckle, inspecting Ashoka like he was a newly polished weapon. 'Your eyes look like an angry spirit's.'

'I . . . I killed my mother,' Ashoka whispered. 'And Rahil is cursed.'

There was no mistaking Shakti's grimace out of the corner of his eye. 'Prince Ashoka,' she whispered. 'Do you want to hear a truth?'

For a moment, Ashoka was glad that they weren't eye to eye. 'Just Ashoka,' he reminded her. 'What truth?'

'One death – expected. One death – unexpected,' she said. 'Such is the nature of violence. As for Rahil – I will try my best to recall that curse. It can still be undone. Do you see what you've done? You only have Aarya remaining.'

Aarya. The final barrier to the Obsidian Throne. He was back to the start, back in Taksila when Arush was rendered comatose and only his sister remained. Except, the first time had been Aarya's secret. This time, Arush's death was on his hands. As was his mother's.

'You want the throne – there is a price,' Shakti continued, her voice taking on a grim tone. 'That price is violence. Bloodshed. It was never going to involve just soldiers and your siblings, and I think you always knew that. Innocents will die and that is unavoidable.'

'I know this,' he gritted out. 'I *understand*. I just need time to grieve.'

It was a fanciful wish. A laughable one.

'Time?' Shakti echoed. 'We don't have it. We lost it the moment you became a traitor to the throne. Emotional attachments cause us suffering, Ashoka. I understand this more than you know. My advice? We can't avoid suffering, but we can choose our attachments. Learn which ones to keep and which ones to let go. You will suffer less for it.'

Ashoka met the Kalingan advisor with Sau in his study early in the morning, ignoring Sachith's well-intentioned protests that he rest some more.

By the time he arrived, the advisor was waiting in the room, already seated upon a chair. As he entered, she rose to her feet and bowed.

An air of gravitas, just like the queen, he noted. The Kalingan advisor was a tall, middle-aged woman with dark brown skin, her neck adorned with a layered grey pearl necklace. 'Prince Ashoka Maurya,' she greeted him with a short bow. 'My name is Kaali.' She spoke in the Ran language, but the accent was Kalingan.

Ashoka reciprocated with a bow of his own and wandered towards his desk. 'A pleasure to meet you,' he replied.

'You as well,' she said. 'I've travelled here under the order of Queen Kalyani, though I have been waiting here for some days now.'

'My apologies,' he said, wincing. 'I returned to the Golden City to, erm, take care of some matters.'

'Have these matters resulted in a severe injury?' she asked, nodding towards his dressings. The question was not asked with cruel intention, but rather with interest and concern. Yet, an errant spark in his chest turned into a full-blown flame. He couldn't justify why.

'Someone I love hurt me,' he replied shortly. Rahil's expressionless face had left him waking up in a cold sweat the previous night. 'That's all.'

Despite his tone, the advisor did not let up. Instead, her gaze flickered straight to his burned – now mutilated – ear. 'Your brother?' she mused. 'Or sister? I understand that they share your father's penchant for—'

'My brother is dead,' he replied shortly. 'As is my mother. Only my sister remains – the empress.'

'I—' The messenger's mouth fell open in shock before attempting to compose herself. 'The *dowager empress*? Emperor Arush? This is – this is rather unexpected news. How . . .'

'A cursed weapon. Intended for my brother, but also hurt my mother. Only my sister remains,' Ashoka repeated the last sentence, this time more forcefully. 'Advisor, what news do you bring me?'

Despite her overt shock, a wry smile appeared on the corners of Kaali's lips. 'I've been sent by Queen Kalyani,' she said. 'To collaborate on an attack at the border. The queen is also suggesting sending some of her smaller war boats up between Mahvo and Devram,' she said. 'To create a blockade from the Samnal River. Soldiers on the ground in Mahvo's borders is all well and good, but this is an added advantage your way.'

Using Kalingan vessels to block any Ran boats from travelling south would certainly prevent the movement of iron ore from small mining towns. The less that Aarya could get her hands on, the better.

'I'll be sure to thank the queen,' he told Kaali.

'Of course,' the advisor replied before cocking her head to the side. She paused for a moment, as if contemplating her next words. 'Forgive me if this seems uncouth, but I can see him in you, Prince Ashoka. Your father.'

No doubt, his reaction must have been visceral, for she laughed. 'Not in the way you think, Your Highness,' she clarified. 'I met with Emperor Adil, and you have the same gleam in your eyes. A desire for glory.'

'His desire for glory led to murder driven by hate,' Ashoka replied somewhat heatedly, as ever wanting to place as much distance between himself and his father as possible. However, now, the endeavour seemed fruitless. 'Mine isn't the same. To help the mayakari, I need to seize the throne. The only way to do it is through war. I'm going to revert the Ran Empire to what it once was. To the time before my father's reign of persecution. The mayakari won't be hunted any more. There will be collateral damage, but what else do you expect?'

'*Collateral damage*,' Kaali repeated. 'Spoken from the mouth of the prince said to abhor violence. What a surprising change, indeed. I gather that you have finally learned the truth of the world, Prince Ashoka.'

Finally? No, he'd learned it the moment he took Governor Kosala's life.

'Death is death, advisor,' he replied. 'As long as I emerge the victor, nothing else matters.'

CHAPTER FIFTY-ONE
Shakti

'Spirits – Shakti!'

Shakti had never been so glad to see Nayani in her life. The older mayakari engulfed her in a bone-crushing embrace. Comforted by her presence, Shakti hugged her tighter.

She'd woken up in the comfort of a warm bed in the Maurya royal estate, feeling well rested. But it irked her to be there. The place was a reminder of Adil, and parts of him were still present. Portraits, busts, weapons – while his consciousness was still attached to hers, she didn't wish to be reminded of him even more.

Ashoka was already busy with Saudamini and the Kalingan advisor. Shakti had half a mind to join them, but she wanted to see Nayani first and so had asked if Sahry was available to take to the skies. The prince had barely raised concerns about her saddling the winged serpent despite his guard going pale in the face.

'Please tell Nayani that I'll meet with her by the day's end,' was all he'd said before resuming his conversation with Saudamini. With his head still bandaged, he appeared very odd indeed.

And so Shakti had taken a still-drowsy but not uncooperative Sahry towards the base of the mayakari resistance, following Ashoka's exact directions. It hadn't been difficult to find it, thereafter, having asked a minor spirit for vague directions. Leaving Sahry to her own devices outside the mouth of the cave, Shakti had entered to a wary group of women. When she used spirit-speak to prove her mayakari blood, she had been welcomed in. After asking for Nayani, she had finally found her.

'I almost thought you weren't – that you –' Nayani didn't finish her sentence, moving away to appraise her.

'I'm alive,' Shakti said, smiling.

'You look gaunt. What exactly happened to you?' Nayani demanded. 'I sensed that the prince was obfuscating somewhat when he told us of his plans to help you escape.'

Hesitantly, she began her story. There was no point in hiding the truth from Nayani. Shakti told her about the Collective, her attempts at dream-invasion, her period as Aarya's guard, her failures. Throughout it all, the mayakari's face was grim. Though she remained silent, Shakti could sense her shock. When she explained the origin of the Collective, however, her composure vanished.

'Part of a Great Spirit is *bound* to you?' she gasped.

'It sounds bad, I know. But I promised the Great Spirit that I would eventually let the Collective go,' Shakti said, fisting her hands into her trousers. 'Just not yet. I'm going to use the powers it provides me to help Ashoka take the Obsidian Throne to ensure peace for the mayakari. And until his sister is gone, I can't let go of it.'

'Sounds like a necessary burden.' There was something akin to sympathetic understanding in the way Nayani responded. 'You must make the Great Spirit suffer a little longer.'

The statement gave Shakti pause. 'Do you think I am – *we* are – viewing the spirits with more callousness than before?' she asked.

'Not really,' Nayani replied. 'I think we still see them as benevolent, powerful creatures. We don't disrespect them.'

'Causing suffering to a benevolent creature,' Shakti began cautiously, 'that would be a severe transgression, wouldn't it?'

'You can't hurt a nature spirit without facing some sort of consequence,' Nayani agreed, 'but you see it happen anyway. I saw it here.'

I'm actively harming a Great Spirit by keeping it bound to me, Shakti thought. *I'll suffer anyway, and if that's the case, maybe I could . . .*

No. That was an outlandish thought. It sounded like a deranged idea straight from Emperor Ashoka's mouth.

'Come,' said the mayakari. 'Let me show you how we make a cursed weapon. We'll need them soon enough.'

She took her further into the mouth of the cave where the sounds of metal scraping could be heard. It sounded like weapons were being handled and moved.

Sure enough, Nayani led her into what was a large, makeshift armoury. Weapons of all kinds were stockpiled, gleaming faintly in the lantern light. Most were swords and daggers, but she spotted a few bows and arrows, even an *urumi* like Aarya's added to the mix.

'Prince Ashoka had some of the blacksmiths smelt weapons to be used for cursed weapons,' Nayani explained. 'The blades are made with silver, no mixed metals. Naila – you'll meet her soon – was given some hairpins by the Kalingan queen. Also cursed weapons.'

'Hairpins?' Shakti echoed, flabbergasted.

'I had the same reaction at first,' Nayani replied, 'but all we need is a weapon sharp enough to puncture flesh. A simple hairpin can do that easily enough. For us, it's more inconspicuous to carry around than a sword.'

Shakti observed quietly as Nayani wandered over to a cartload of daggers and plucked one out before passing it to her. She weighed it against her palm. 'It's unbalanced,' she noted.

'It might be, but the point isn't to create a weapon to suit its user,' Nayani said. 'The point is to create an instrument that's sharp enough to pierce flesh. Cursed weapons can only be used once, so you must not miss.'

'Is the process much different to how we normally curse?' she asked.

'Somewhat. Ashoka's advisor had to translate it from Kalingan for Naila to try it,' Nayani explained. 'There's a specific phrase they used: "carry this curse unto the living, I curse this weapon to . . ." and then speak out a curse of your own choosing. We can be more specific with our wording with these curses. No vague mentions of suffering or death.'

As Nayani continued to explain the process and gave a quick demonstration. Shakti watched intently. It seemed straightforward enough, so when Nayani finally allowed her to try on her own, she jumped at the chance.

'Think of a curse before you use the cursed tongue,' Nayani encouraged her as Shakti balanced the dagger on her upturned palms.

Shakti closed her eyes and concentrated on the feel of the dagger in her hand. Its weight. The coldness of the metal. Everything around her descended into a dull hum as she slipped into the cursed tongue.

'*Carry this curse unto the living,*' she repeated Nayani's words. '*I curse this weapon to bleed blue fire.*'

The instant she uttered her curse; it was as if the energy within her body condensed. It travelled from her chest to the extremities, and she could physically feel a crackle of energy pass from the pads of her thumb to the cold metal.

When she opened her eyes, the dagger emitted a soft blue glow. Shakti's breath caught. It was beautiful.

Moments later, her entire body felt heavy, and she staggered on her feet.

'Easy enough, isn't it?' Nayani asked, chuckling when she let out a weary exhale. Cursing a weapon had taken more energy than expected. When Shakti made to return it, the mayakari shook her head. 'Keep it.'

Shakti clutched the dagger with her right hand. It felt natural in her hand, as if it were an extension of it. She hadn't yet seen a cursed weapon in action but had seen the result. Arush. The dowager empress. She knew what they were capable of. And yet . . .

'If these take an enormous amount of energy to create, production is limited,' she told Nayani.

'It is,' Nayani replied. 'The Kalingan mayakari haven't found a way around it. We haven't, either.'

'Have you used any so far?' she asked.

Nayani shook her head. 'No. Haven't needed to, yet. Naila's the only one who's seen them work in Trikalinga so far, but I gather we'll be using them soon enough now that Prince Ashoka is back. I can't imagine the destruction they'd cause.'

Glancing at the groups of mayakari whispering around a heap

of procured weapons, Shakti sighed. 'I've seen the aftermath of it,' she replied quietly. 'Ashoka killed his brother with one.'

'He *what?*'

When Shakti explained both Arush and Manali's deaths, Nayani winced. 'He's left perhaps the most conniving of his siblings behind,' she said. 'Killed his mother, too. He's a traitor to the throne now, a man who used mayakari magic to kill his own *family*. Empress Aarya will use this knowledge to destroy him. Destroy us.'

The statement was said without emotion, as if it were pure and simple fact.

Shakti observed the weapon in silence. A dangerous idea had taken root in her head. One she was ashamed to consider voicing. She could be mad. Unless she said it aloud to collective disgust, she might not know.

'Would you consider Great Spirits to be weapons?' she asked. It felt dirty to refer to them that way, and Nayani's resulting grimace was proof.

'To call them a weapon assumes that they can be wielded. Great Spirits can't be controlled, Shakti,' she said. 'They are neither sword nor shield.'

'That's not an answer.'

Nayani sighed. 'Yes,' she replied. 'One can consider them to be, but they're unpredictable when angered. What's your point?'

Collapsed homes. Polluted river-ways. Destroyed rice fields. The Great Spirit of the Mountain of Rebirth had created such destruction in the Golden City, and it had only been at half capacity. When they eventually marched further into Ran territory, there needed to be a force so brutal that it could bring whole battalions of soldiers to their deaths. Soldiers and innocents both, but—

What is the price you are willing to pay for peace?

That voice was not Jaya's. That voice was hers. It was the same one that had wanted nothing but death during her imprisonment that now whispered sweet songs of vengeance.

'There might be a better way to both remove Empress Aarya from her throne and destroy her armies,' Shakti said slowly, 'but it will go against everything we stand for. *Everything.*'

For a moment, she was sure that Nayani would dismiss her.

Tell her that there were only so many of the precepts they could break. But the mayakari said nothing. Instead, her eyes were ablaze with curiosity.

'Tell me,' she said.

'The Great Spirits,' Shakti said. 'I want to anger them on purpose.'

She expected Nayani's reaction. The mayakari's mouth dropped open in shock. 'You *what?*' she exclaimed. 'Do you not realize how difficult they are to speak to in that form? How difficult it is to pacify them?'

Shakti thought of the Great Spirit of the Mountain of Rebirth. How she had heard it clearly in its anger. How it had told her they were connected. That like commanded like. That kin commanded kin.

'I think I can pacify them,' she said. 'Let me do it, Nayani. I want this world reborn.'

ACKNOWLEDGEMENTS

I was told that writing the second book would be harder than the first. Like an overconfident fool, I thought *no, surely not. It can't be that hard.*

Dear Reader, it was indeed more difficult than I anticipated. Turning what I affectionately (and sometimes disparagingly) called the Primordial Soup Draft into its final version took time, effort, and periods of severe self-doubt. We got there in the end, though, and I'd like to thank the people who've helped me along the way.

Thank you to my agent, Maddy Belton. I'm forever grateful to have you in my corner. Thank you to the wider team at the Madeleine Milburn Literary Agency. A massive, heartfelt thank you to the Harper Voyager team: Natasha Bardon, Kate Fogg, Charlotte Trumble, David Pomerico, Catherine Perks, Isabella Ogbolumani, among many. To the wider Harper Voyager UK, US and Australia teams – I appreciate you all. Thank you to Ed Wall for your insightful copyedits. Thank you to the UK and North American cover illustrators: Julian De Narvaez and Tasia M.S. Your artwork blows me away every time.

My lovely Writer's Block group: I'm so glad to finally have met you all in person. That one week in Vaughn surrounded by so much creative energy allowed me to fly through my second-round edits. Thank you to my fellow author friends. It's nice to talk about this strange, wonderful job and be understood. I adore you all. To Soph, Scar, and Katie – thank you for your aggressive love and support. I may have spoiled the entire series for you guys at this point. Please read the last two books anyway. To my wider friends and family, thank you, thank you, *thank you*. This is a real job, I promise. To ආච්චි: you appear in my earliest memory of holding a chapter book in my hands. You will not remember that memory – or me – now, but I will remember it, and you.

I didn't dedicate book two to my dog again. Instead, I went with the second-best option: my parents and siblings. To my little brothers (what am I thanking you for, honestly), your encouragement and constant humbling has been much appreciated. One day, I will write a story with more wholesome sibling dynamics where no one is trying to kill each other. To my parents, thank you for nodding along like you understand whenever I speak at length about the publishing process. It might not be your area of expertise, but your support goes a long way.

Thank you to the booksellers and librarians – your hard work is what gets books into readers' hands. To the readers – thank you for choosing to continue with Ashoka and Shakti's story. I can't guarantee that things get better for them.